Birchfall *looked frozen with fear, his* eyes staring vacantly, but as Brambleclaw let go of his scruff, he clutched wildly at the branch and dragged himself along it until he could scramble onto the rocks at the bottom of the gully. Lionblaze let go of his end of the branch to haul Birchfall's limp body up higher; water streamed from his pelt and he vomited up a huge mouthful of liquid.

Brackenfur clawed his way along the branch to safety, and stood shaking the water out of his ginger fur. "Brambleclaw!" he yowled. "Brambleclaw, where are you?"

Cold horror flooded over Lionblaze as he realized that the deputy had disappeared. *He can't have drowned. What will we do without him?*

WARRIORS

THE PROPHECIES BEGIN

Book One: *Into the Wild*

Book Two: *Fire and Ice*

Book Three: *Forest of Secrets*

Book Four: *Rising Storm*

Book Five: *A Dangerous Path*

Book Six: *The Darkest Hour*

THE NEW PROPHECY

Book One: *Midnight*

Book Two: *Moonrise*

Book Three: *Dawn*

Book Four: *Starlight*

Book Five: *Twilight*

Book Six: *Sunset*

POWER OF THREE

Book One: *The Sight*

Book Two: *Dark River*

Book Three: *Outcast*

Book Four: *Eclipse*

Book Five: *Long Shadows*

Book Six: *Sunrise*

OMEN OF THE STARS

Book One: *The Fourth Apprentice*

Book Two: *Fading Echoes*

Book Three: *Night Whispers*

Book Four: *Sign of the Moon*

Book Five: *The Forgotten Warrior*

Book Six: *The Last Hope*

POWER OF THREE

WARRIORS

SUNRISE

ERIN
HUNTER

HARPER

An Imprint of HarperCollinsPublishers

To Lynn and Steve Wiman, with heartfelt thanks

Special thanks to Cherith Baldry

Sunrise

Copyright © 2009 by Working Partners Limited

Series created by Working Partners Limited

Map art © 2015 by Dave Stevenson

Interior art © 2015 by Owen Richardson

All rights reserved. Printed in the United States of America. No part of this book may be used or reproduced in any manner whatsoever without written permission except in the case of brief quotations embodied in critical articles and reviews. For information address HarperCollins Children's Books, a division of HarperCollins Publishers, 195 Broadway, New York, NY 10007.

www.harpercollinschildrens.com

Library of Congress Cataloging-in-Publication Data

Hunter, Erin.

Sunrise / Erin Hunter. — 1st ed.

p.   cm. — (Warriors, power of three ; bk. 6)

Summary: When Firestar's grandchildren, Hollyleaf, Lionblaze, and Jayfeather, finally discover who their true parents are, there are dire consequences for ThunderClan and the warrior code.

ISBN 978-0-06-236713-6

[1. Cats—Fiction.   2. Brothers and sisters—Fiction.   3. Identity—Fiction.   4. Adventure and adventurers—Fiction.   5. Fantasy.]   I. Title.

PZ7.H916625Sul   2009   2008051777

[Fic]—dc22   CIP

                                                              AC

Typography by Ellice M. Lee

20   21   CG/BRR   20

❖

Revised paperback edition, 2015

ALLEGIANCES

THUNDERCLAN

LEADER   **FIRESTAR**—ginger tom with a flame-colored pelt

DEPUTY   **BRAMBLECLAW**—dark brown tabby tom with amber eyes

MEDICINE CAT   **LEAFPOOL**—light brown tabby she-cat with amber eyes
   APPRENTICE, JAYFEATHER (gray tabby tom)

WARRIORS   (toms and she-cats without kits)

   SQUIRRELFLIGHT—dark ginger she-cat with green eyes
   APPRENTICE, FOXPAW

   DUSTPELT—dark brown tabby tom

   SANDSTORM—pale ginger she-cat with green eyes

   CLOUDTAIL—long-haired white tom with blue eyes

   BRACKENFUR—golden brown tabby tom

   SORRELTAIL—tortoiseshell-and-white she-cat with amber eyes

   THORNCLAW—golden brown tabby tom

   BRIGHTHEART—white she-cat with ginger patches

   SPIDERLEG—long-limbed black tom with brown underbelly and amber eyes

   WHITEWING—white she-cat with green eyes
   APPRENTICE, ICEPAW

BIRCHFALL—light brown tabby tom

GRAYSTRIPE—long-haired gray tom

BERRYNOSE—cream-colored tom

HAZELTAIL—small gray-and-white she-cat

MOUSEWHISKER—gray-and-white tom

CINDERHEART—gray tabby she-cat

HONEYFERN—light brown tabby she-cat

POPPYFROST—tortoiseshell she-cat

LIONBLAZE—golden tabby tom with amber eyes

HOLLYLEAF—black she-cat with green eyes

APPRENTICES

(more than six moons old, in training to become warriors)

FOXPAW—reddish tabby tom

ICEPAW—white she-cat

QUEENS

(she-cats expecting or nursing kits)

FERNCLOUD—pale gray (with darker flecks) she-cat with green eyes

DAISY—cream long-furred cat from the horseplace, mother of Spiderleg's kits: Rosekit (dark cream she-cat) and Toadkit (black-and-white tom)

MILLIE—striped gray tabby she-cat, former kittypet, mother of Graystripe's kits: Briarkit (dark brown she-cat), Bumblekit (very pale gray tom with black stripes), and Blossomkit (tortoiseshell she-cat with petal-shaped white patches)

ELDERS (former warriors and queens, now retired)

LONGTAIL—pale tabby tom with dark black stripes, retired early due to failing sight

MOUSEFUR—small dusky brown she-cat

SHADOWCLAN

LEADER **BLACKSTAR**—large white tom with huge jet-black paws

DEPUTY **RUSSETFUR**—dark ginger she-cat

MEDICINE CAT **LITTLECLOUD**—very small tabby tom
APPRENTICE, FLAMEPAW (ginger tom)

WARRIORS **OAKFUR**—small brown tom
APPRENTICE, TIGERPAW (dark brown tabby tom)

ROWANCLAW—ginger tom

SMOKEFOOT—black tom
APPRENTICE, OWLPAW (light brown tabby tom)

IVYTAIL—black, white, and tortoiseshell she-cat
APPRENTICE, DAWNPAW (cream-furred she-cat)

TOADFOOT—dark brown tom

CROWFROST—black-and-white tom
APPRENTICE, OLIVEPAW (tortoiseshell she-cat)

KINKFUR—tabby she-cat, with long fur that sticks out at all angles

RATSCAR—brown tom with long scar across his back
APPRENTICE, SHREWPAW (gray she-cat with black feet)

SNAKETAIL—dark brown tom with tabby-striped tail

    APPRENTICE, SCORCHPAW (dark gray tom)

WHITEWATER—white she-cat with long fur, blind in one eye

    APPRENTICE, REDPAW (mottled brown and ginger tom)

TAWNYPELT—tortoiseshell she-cat with green eyes

QUEENS   **SNOWBIRD**—pure-white she-cat

ELDERS   **CEDARHEART**—dark gray tom

                    TALLPOPPY—long-legged light brown tabby she-cat

WINDCLAN

LEADER   **ONESTAR**—brown tabby tom

DEPUTY   **ASHFOOT**—gray she-cat

MEDICINE CAT   **BARKFACE**—short-tailed brown tom

                    APPRENTICE, KESTRELPAW (mottled gray tom)

WARRIORS   **TORNEAR**—tabby tom

                    CROWFEATHER—dark gray tom

                    OWLWHISKER—light brown tabby tom

                    WHITETAIL—small white she-cat

                    NIGHTCLOUD—black she-cat

                    GORSETAIL—very pale gray-and-white cat with blue eyes

WEASELFUR—ginger tom with white paws

HARESPRING—brown-and-white tom

LEAFTAIL—dark tabby tom with amber eyes
APPRENTICE, THISTLEPAW (long-haired white tom)

DEWSPOTS—spotted gray tabby she-cat
APPRENTICE, SEDGEPAW (light brown tabby she-cat)

WILLOWCLAW—gray she-cat
APPRENTICE, SWALLOWPAW (dark gray she-cat)

ANTPELT—brown tom with one black ear

EMBERFOOT—gray tom with two dark paws
APPRENTICE, SUNPAW (tortoiseshell she-cat with large white mark on her forehead)

HEATHERTAIL—light brown tabby she-cat with blue eyes

BREEZEPELT—black tom with amber eyes

ELDERS

MORNINGFLOWER—very old tortoiseshell queen

WEBFOOT—dark gray tabby tom

RIVERCLAN

LEADER

LEOPARDSTAR—unusually spotted golden tabby she-cat

DEPUTY

MISTYFOOT—gray she-cat with blue eyes

MEDICINE CAT

MOTHWING—dappled golden she-cat
APPRENTICE, WILLOWSHINE (gray tabby she-cat)

WARRIORS

BLACKCLAW—smoky black tom

VOLETOOTH—small brown tabby tom
APPRENTICE, MINNOWPAW (dark gray she-cat)

REEDWHISKER—black tom

MOSSPELT—tortoiseshell she-cat with blue eyes
APPRENTICE, PEBBLEPAW (mottled gray tom)

BEECHFUR—light brown tom

RIPPLETAIL—dark gray tabby tom
APPRENTICE, MALLOWPAW (light brown tabby tom)

GRAYMIST—pale gray tabby

DAWNFLOWER—pale gray she-cat

DAPPLENOSE—mottled gray she-cat

POUNCETAIL—ginger-and-white tom

MINTFUR—light gray tabby tom
APPRENTICE, NETTLEPAW (dark brown tabby tom)

OTTERHEART—dark brown she-cat
APPRENTICE, SNEEZEPAW (gray-and-white tom)

PINEFUR—very short-haired tabby she-cat
APPRENTICE, ROBINPAW (tortoiseshell-and-white tom)

RAINSTORM—mottled gray-blue tom

DUSKFUR—brown tabby she-cat
APPRENTICE, COPPERPAW (dark ginger she-cat)

QUEENS

ICEWING—white cat with blue eyes, mother of Beetlekit, Pricklekit, Petalkit, and Grasskit

ELDERS   **SWALLOWTAIL**—dark tabby she-cat

STONESTREAM—gray tom

CATS OUTSIDE CLANS

SOL—white-and-brown tabby long-haired tom with pale yellow eyes

SMOKY—muscular gray-and-white tom who lives in a barn at the horseplace

FLOSS—small gray-and-white she-cat who lives at the horseplace

PURDY—elderly, plump tabby loner with a gray muzzle

JINGO—dark brown tabby she-cat

HUSSAR—broad-shouldered gray tom

SPECKLE—flecked brown she-cat, nursing four kits

FRITZ—black-and-white tom with a torn ear

POD—scrawny brown tom with a gray muzzle

JET—long-haired black tom

MERRY—ginger-and-white she-cat

CHIRP—pale gray tabby tom

OTHER ANIMALS

MIDNIGHT—a star-gazing badger who lives by the sea

CAT VIEW
TWOLEG NEST
GREENLEAF TWOLEGPLACE
TWOLEG PATH
TWOLEG PATH
CLEARING
SHADOWCLAN CAMP
SMALL THUNDERPATH
HALFBRIDGE
GREENLEAF TWOLEGPLACE
HALFBRIDGE
ISLAND
STREAM
RIVERCLAN CAMP
HORSEPLACE

ABANDONED
TWOLEG NEST

MOONPOOL

OLD THUNDERPATH

THUNDERCLAN
CAMP

ANCIENT OAK

LAKE

WINDCLAN
CAMP

BROKEN
HALFBRIDGE

TWOLEGPLACE

THUNDERPATH

KEY
To The
CLANS

THUNDERCLAN

RIVERCLAN

SHADOWCLAN

WINDCLAN

STARCLAN

NORTH

HAREVIEW
CAMPSITE

SANCTUARY
COTTAGE

SADLER WOODS

LITTLEPINE ROAD

LITTLEPINE
SAILING
CENTER

TWOLEG VIE

LITTLEPINE
ISLAND

RIVER ALBA

WHITECHURCH ROAD

KNIGHT'S
COPSE

PROLOGUE

Moonlight washed over the stone hollow, bright as day, but beneath the bushes and at the edges under the cliffs, dark shadows seemed to uncoil like claws. Leafpool crouched over Ashfur's limp body. The pale light turned his gray fur to silver as she groomed it for his burial. Beside her, Jayfeather helped, smoothing Ashfur's tail and fluffing it up as it dried.

Leafpool raised her head to gaze up at the icy glitter cast by her warrior ancestors. "May StarClan light your path, Ashfur." She let her voice fall softly into the cold air as she repeated the words used by medicine cats for more seasons than any cat could count, whenever a Clanmate died. "May you find good hunting, swift running, and shelter when you sleep."

The words that should have comforted her, promising a long and happy life for the fallen warrior, instead hurt her, sharper than thorns. Her mind filled with the moment she had discovered the neat teethmarks in Ashfur's neck. Too small for a dog, too clean for a fox, too sharp for a badger. Only a cat could have left them. But which cat? Who hated Ashfur enough to kill him in cold blood, leaving no signs of a struggle? Had it been an honest clash over borders or stolen prey? *Could it have been a WindClan cat, or a passing rogue? Please, Star-Clan, let it be that!*

The thought that a ThunderClan cat might have murdered Ashfur made Leafpool cold to her bones. Ashfur had been outspoken and strong-willed, yes, but a loyal and respected warrior as well. Surely none of his Clanmates had any reason to want him dead?

Bending over his body again, Leafpool began to clean earth and grit out of the dead warrior's pads. Something soft and light fluttered against her muzzle; she drew back to see a tuft of fur snagged in Ashfur's claws.

No! This can't be true! Leaning closer, Leafpool sniffed the fur. *I know that scent!*

Desperately she tried to convince herself that the clump of fur had come from one of the cats who had carried Ashfur back to the camp from where he had been found, floating in the stream on the WindClan border. But the smell of river water was too strong to have come from a cat with dry fur, and besides, Ashfur's claws were soft and limp now. They would flex rather than pull out a tuft of hair if they brushed against another cat.

The only cat this tuft of fur could have come from was Ashfur's killer.

Breathless and shaking, Leafpool gently teased out the fur and carried it into her den. She forced her trembling paws to place the tuft on a leaf, which she folded into a tight wrap. Then she pushed it right to the back of her store, deep into the cleft in the rock, behind the last bundle of herbs. The truth about Ashfur's death must never come out.

In more pain than she had ever imagined she could feel without dying, she asked herself: *Was all this my fault?*

With a snarl, Yellowfang leaped on Bluestar, bowling her over and pinning her down in the lush grass of the forest where StarClan walked. "This is all your fault!" she spat. "None of this would have happened if you hadn't left that wretched secret to fester in ThunderClan."

Bluestar battered at Yellowfang's belly with her hind paws, but couldn't dislodge the former medicine cat's grip. "What's wrong with you?" she hissed. "Don't forget that I was your Clan leader."

All the respect that Yellowfang had once felt for the former ThunderClan leader had vanished. Their shared history crumbled to dust in the face of the terrible future she foresaw for the Clan she had made her own.

"Your secret has been like a maggot eating away inside an apple," Yellowfang growled, her bared fangs close to Bluestar's ear. "ThunderClan is rotten to the core—and more blood will be shed before the truth comes out."

"You can't know that," Bluestar protested, straining to throw off her opponent.

"A blind rabbit could see it! The truth *will* come out. Midnight told Sol *everything*. And we both know that Sol will return to ThunderClan."

Summoning her trained warrior reflexes, Bluestar butted her head into Yellowfang's chest and managed to slip to one side. Suddenly giving up, Yellowfang sprang away. She stood shaking her ruffled gray pelt.

Bluestar scrambled to her paws and stood, panting. "What's the point of fighting?" she rasped when she had caught her breath. "The damage has been done—and whatever you say, this is *not* my fault."

Yellowfang grunted.

"I still can't believe Midnight betrayed us," Bluestar went on. "I trusted her to watch over the Clans."

"It's not Midnight who was the traitor," Yellowfang pointed out, her pelt bristling. "The betrayal began with the first lies, with the secret that you have kept for all these moons. ThunderClan has been living a lie! If these three cats are as powerful as the prophecy says they are, they would have been able to cope with the truth. Unless you think we've been wrong about them all along."

"Never!" Bluestar retorted. "Who else could the Three be? I didn't want to lie!" she added, her voice rising to a wail. "But when could I have told them? They have been happy. Squirrelflight and Brambleclaw are good parents. What good would it have done to tell them what really happened?"

"We'll find out soon enough," Yellowfang growled. "Old secrets can't stay buried forever." She lashed her tail and began to stalk away; then she paused, glancing back over her shoulder. "And if these three cats are not strong enough to deal with the truth," she added, "then you, Bluestar, will have destroyed the Clan you love so much. . . ."

CHAPTER 1

❧

Dead bracken rustled beneath Lionblaze's paws as he stalked through the forest. Above the leafless trees, the sky was dark and empty. Terror raised the hairs on the young warrior's neck, and he shivered from ears to tail-tip.

This is a place that has never known the light of StarClan.

He padded on, skirting clumps of fern and nosing under bushes, but he found no sight or scent of other cats. *I've had enough of this,* he thought, tugging his tail free from a trailing bramble. Panic sparked in his mind as he stared at the darkness that stretched away between the trees. *What if I never find my way out of here?*

"Looking for me?"

Lionblaze jumped and spun around. "Tigerstar!"

The massive warrior had appeared around the edge of a bramble thicket. His tabby pelt shone with a strange light that reminded Lionblaze of the sickly glow of fungus on dead trees.

"You've missed a lot of training," Tigerstar meowed, padding forward until he stood a tail-length from the ThunderClan warrior. "You should have come back sooner."

"No, I shouldn't!" Lionblaze blurted out. "I shouldn't have come here at all, and you never should have trained me. Brambleclaw isn't my father! You're not my kin!"

Tigerstar blinked once, but he showed no surprise, not even a flick of his ears. His amber eyes narrowed to slits, and he seemed to be waiting for Lionblaze to say more.

"You . . . you knew!" Lionblaze whispered. The trees seemed to spin around him. *Squirrelflight isn't the only cat who kept secrets!*

"Of course I knew." Tigerstar shrugged. "It's not important. You were willing enough to learn from me, weren't you?"

"But—"

"Blood isn't everything," Tigerstar snarled. His lip curled, showing the glint of sharp fangs. "Just ask Firestar."

Lionblaze felt his neck fur begin to bristle as fury coursed through him. "Firestar's a finer warrior than you ever were."

"Don't forget that he's not your kin, either," Tigerstar hissed softly. "There's no point defending him now."

Lionblaze stared at the dusk-lit warrior. *Does he know who my real father is?* "You knew all along that I wasn't Firestar's kin," he growled. "You let me believe a lie!"

Tigerstar twitched one ear. "So?"

Rage and frustration overwhelmed Lionblaze. Leaping into the air, he threw himself at Tigerstar and tried to push him over. He battered at the tabby warrior's head and shoulders, his claws unsheathed, tearing out huge clumps of fur. But the red haze of fury that filled his head made him clumsy, unfocused. His blows landed at random, barely scratching Tigerstar's skin.

The huge tabby tom went limp, letting himself drop to one side and hooking one paw around Lionblaze's leg to unbalance him. Lionblaze landed among the bracken with a jolt that drove the breath from his body. A heartbeat later he felt a huge paw clamp down on his shoulders, pinning him to the ground.

"I've taught you better than that, little warrior," Tigerstar taunted him. "You're out of practice."

Taking a deep breath, Lionblaze heaved himself upward. Tigerstar leaped back and crouched a fox-length away, his amber eyes burning.

"I'll show you who's out of practice," Lionblaze panted.

He forced his anger down, summoning a cold determination—all the fighting moves he had ever learned were at the tips of his claws. When Tigerstar sprang at him, he was prepared; he dived forward and hurled himself underneath his opponent's belly. As soon as Tigerstar's paws hit the ground, Lionblaze whipped around and landed a couple of blows on the tabby tom's hindquarters before leaping out of range.

Tigerstar spun to face him. "Better," he meowed, mockery still in his voice. "I have mentored you well."

Before Lionblaze could reply, the huge tabby darted toward him, veering aside at the last moment and lashing out with one forepaw as he passed. Lionblaze felt Tigerstar's claws rake along his side, and blood begin trickling out of the scratches. Fear stabbed at him. *What happens if he kills me here? Will I be really dead?*

His mind cleared. Tigerstar was hurtling toward him again.

Lionblaze scrambled aside; he aimed a blow, but felt his claws slide harmlessly through the tabby's pelt.

"Too slow," Tigerstar spat. "You'll have to work harder, now you know that prophecy wasn't meant for you. That was for *Firestar's kin*, wasn't it?"

Lionblaze knew that the tabby tom was trying to make him too angry to fight. *I won't listen! All I need to do is win this battle!*

He sprang at Tigerstar again, twisting in the air as he had been taught during those long nighttime visits, and landed squarely on the massive tabby's broad shoulders. Digging in with his claws, he stretched forward and sank his teeth into Tigerstar's neck.

Tigerstar tried the same trick of going limp and pulling Lionblaze down with him, but this time Lionblaze was ready. He wriggled out from underneath the heavy body, battering with his hind paws at Tigerstar's exposed stomach fur.

"I'm not falling for that trick twice!" he hissed.

Tigerstar struggled to get up, but blood was pouring from a gash in his belly; he stumbled down again, rolling onto his back. Lionblaze planted one forepaw on Tigerstar's chest and held the other, claws extended, against his neck.

The tabby glared up at him; for a heartbeat, fear flashed in his blazing amber eyes. "Do you really think you could kill me?" he growled. "You'd never do it."

"No." Lionblaze sheathed his claws and stepped back. "You're already dead."

He turned and stalked away, his pelt still bristling and all his senses alert in case Tigerstar followed and leaped on him again. But there was no sound from the dark warrior, and soon he was left behind among the endless trees.

Lionblaze's mind whirled. He had beaten Tigerstar! *Maybe I do have power after all . . . but how can I, if I'm not one of the Three?*

He paused, scarcely seeing the tangling undergrowth and the trees of the dark forest all around him. *Do I want to know who my parents really are?* he wondered. *Does it even matter?* Maybe it was best to let his Clanmates accept him for who they thought he was, so he could go on striving to improve his fighting skills. *I'm already the best fighter in ThunderClan. I know I can be a great warrior.*

"Ashfur is dead," he meowed out loud. "And Squirrelflight won't reveal her secret to any other cats. It would hurt her Clanmates far too much if they knew she'd been lying to them for so long. Why not let everything stay the same?"

Lionblaze woke to the sun on his face. Most of the cats had already left the den; Lionblaze spotted only the gray-and-white pelt of Mousewhisker, who had kept guard over the camp the night before.

Lionblaze's jaws stretched in a yawn. "Thank StarClan I wasn't on the dawn patrol," he muttered.

When he tried to get up, every muscle in his body shrieked a protest; he felt as if his body was one huge ache, from his head to his paws. Down one side, his golden tabby fur was matted with blood.

I hope no cat has noticed that! he thought as he bent his head and began cleaning up his pelt with swift, rhythmic licks.

The fight with Tigerstar had been a dream, hadn't it? Lionblaze didn't understand why he should feel just as much pain and exhaustion as if it had really happened. And he had been cut, as if a living warrior had raked his claws across Lionblaze's flank. . . . He tried not to think about it. *It doesn't matter, because I'll never go back to that place,* he told himself. *It's over.*

He felt better after his grooming, with his fur fluffed up to hide the gash in his side. When he finished, he could hear the voices of several cats just outside the den, though not close enough for him to make out what they were saying. Curious, he rose to his paws, arched his back in a delicious stretch, and pushed his way through the branches into the clearing.

Thornclaw was standing a couple of fox-lengths away; Spiderleg sat close by, while Cloudtail paced up and down in front of them, the tip of his white tail twitching. Cloudtail's mate, Brightheart, watched him anxiously from where she sat with Ferncloud, Brackenfur, and Sorreltail. Honeyfern and Berrynose were crouched nearby, their eyes fixed on Thornclaw.

"Ashfur was killed by a WindClan cat!" the golden brown tom was declaring. "It's the only possible answer."

A few of his listeners nodded in agreement, though Lionblaze saw others exchanging doubtful glances.

"Firestar said he thought that one of us did it," Honeyfern mewed, sounding nervous to be contradicting a senior warrior.

"Clan leaders have made mistakes before," Cloudtail meowed. "Firestar isn't always right."

"I'm sure none of us would kill Ashfur," Ferncloud added more gently. "Why would we want to? Ashfur had no enemies!"

I wish that was true, Lionblaze thought.

However much he tried to forget, that night of fire and storm was seared into Lionblaze's memory. He could hear the roar of the flames on the cliff top, and could see them licking hungrily around him and his littermates as Ashfur blocked the end of the branch they needed to scramble toward safety. Squirrelflight's confession rang in his ears again: She had told Ashfur that Lionblaze, Hollyleaf, and Jayfeather were not her kits. It was the only way to save their lives, by pretending she did not care what happened to them, but she had handed Ashfur a weapon more terrible than any flaming branch. Lionblaze knew that the gray warrior would have announced the truth to all the Clans at the Gathering; only death had closed his jaws forever and kept the secret safe.

"Lionblaze! Hey, Lionblaze, are you deaf?"

Lionblaze dragged his thoughts back to the hollow to see Spiderleg waving him over with his tail.

"You were Ashfur's last apprentice," the black warrior prompted as Lionblaze padded reluctantly up to the group. "Do you know if he'd quarreled with any cat?"

"Especially any WindClan cat?" Thornclaw added, with a meaningful twitch of his whiskers.

Lionblaze shook his head. "Uh . . . no," he replied awkwardly. He couldn't lie and say that Ashfur had quarreled with a WindClan cat, even though he wished with every hair on his pelt that it was true. Letting his Clanmates believe such a thing could cause an all-out war between ThunderClan and WindClan. "I hadn't seen much of Ashfur just before he died," he added.

To his relief, no other cats questioned him.

"We'd know if Ashfur quarreled with a ThunderClan cat," Brackenfur insisted. "It's impossible to keep a secret around here."

If only you knew! Lionblaze thought.

"Brackenfur's right." Sorreltail touched her nose to her mate's ear. "But all the same, we can't be sure that a Wind-Clan cat—"

"Ashfur died on the WindClan border," Spiderleg interrupted. "What more do you want?"

Sorreltail turned to face him, her neck fur bristling at his scathing tone. "I want a bit more evidence than where his body was found before I start blaming any cat."

Honeyfern and Brackenfur murmured agreement, but Lionblaze could see that most of the cats were convinced that a WindClan warrior was responsible for Ashfur's death. However much he worried about what that could lead to, he couldn't bury a guilty sense of relief.

"Are we going to let WindClan get away with this?" Thornclaw demanded, his ears lying flat as he dug his claws into the earth.

"No!" Berrynose leaped to his paws. "We have to show them they can't mess with ThunderClan."

Lionblaze's belly churned as he saw the warriors cluster more closely around Thornclaw. They were behaving as if the golden brown tom was their leader, and seemed ready to follow him into battle to avenge their Clanmate's murder.

"It would be best to attack by night," Thornclaw began. "There'll be enough moonlight to see by, and they won't be expecting trouble."

"We'll see they get it, though." Spiderleg lashed his tail.

"We'll head for the WindClan camp," Thornclaw continued. "It'll be best to split up: One raiding party can attack from this direction—"

"What?" The low growl came from just behind Lionblaze.

Startled, Lionblaze glanced over his shoulder to see Brambleclaw; he, along with all the other cats, had been so intent on what Thornclaw was planning that he hadn't heard the Clan deputy approach.

"We're going to raid WindClan," Spiderleg explained, bunching his muscles as if he was planning to launch himself out of the camp right away. "One of them killed Ashfur, and—"

"There will be no raid on WindClan," Brambleclaw interrupted, a glow of anger springing up in his amber eyes. "There is no evidence that a WindClan cat killed Ashfur."

Lionblaze gazed at the cat he had always believed was his father. *Does he know the truth?* he wondered, remembering all the times that Brambleclaw had play wrestled with him and his littermates when they were kits, and how many times he had helped them or advised them as they grew older. Squirrelflight had told Ashfur that Brambleclaw didn't know the truth, but Lionblaze had no reason to trust her now. *If he does know, he's a very good liar.*

As good as Squirrelflight.

Brambleclaw didn't wait for a response. He stalked off in the direction of the tumbled rocks that led up to the High-ledge, only to halt after a couple of paces and glance back, twitching his ears to beckon Lionblaze to him.

"Are you okay?" The deputy's voice was full of sympathy. "Ashfur was your mentor, after all."

But we weren't close. Lionblaze didn't want to say the words aloud, but he had always known there was something wrong between himself and Ashfur; they had never known the true bond between a mentor and apprentice. Had Ashfur hated him the same way he had hated Squirrelflight? What a waste: Lionblaze wasn't even Squirrelflight's son.

"I'm fine," he mumbled.

Brambleclaw rested his tail-tip on Lionblaze's shoulder. "I can see you're not," he mewed. "Is there anything you want to tell me? You know you can always come and talk to me."

For a couple of heartbeats Lionblaze froze. *Does Brambleclaw suspect me of killing Ashfur?*

"It's hard to lose a cat you were close to," Brambleclaw went on. "But I promised you before, his death will not go unavenged."

He unsheathed his long, curved claws and sank them into the floor of the hollow. Lionblaze flinched, imagining those claws tearing into the throat of the guilty cat. . . .

"If I find the cat who did this," Brambleclaw growled softly, "they will regret taking the life of a warrior and my Clanmate."

He turned away, padding toward the Highledge, but before he reached the foot of the rock fall, Firestar appeared from his den. He paused for a moment, looking down into the clearing; the pale sun of leaf-bare touched his pelt, turning it to flame. Then he bounded lightly down the stones to join Brambleclaw and Lionblaze. He nodded to the group of cats surrounding Thornclaw.

"What's happening?" he queried.

"Some of the Clan want to lead an attack on WindClan," Brambleclaw reported. "I didn't know we had so many mouse-brains in ThunderClan."

Firestar twitched his ears. "It's hard to accept the death of a warrior," he meowed loudly. "But this isn't the time for an attack. I will lead a patrol to speak with Onestar, to see if he knows anything."

"Of course he knows!" Spiderleg had turned to face them, his neck fur bristling aggressively.

"We should attack now, before we lose more warriors," Thornclaw declared.

Firestar shook his head. "There's no point in stirring up trouble when there's no need," he warned.

"But there *is* need." Thornclaw padded forward until he stood nose to nose with his Clan leader. "A warrior is dead!"

Yowls of agreement rose up from the cats around him.

"Ashfur must be avenged!"

"He was a fine warrior!"

"The whole Clan respected him! No ThunderClan cat would have killed him!"

Lionblaze couldn't join in; it was hard enough to hide his fear and anxiety from his Clanmates. They remembered Ashfur as a brave and loyal warrior; they knew nothing of the cat who had been prepared to destroy his Clan to take revenge on Squirrelflight for choosing Brambleclaw instead of him.

Firestar raised a paw for silence, but he was still waiting for the yowling to die down when Lionblaze spotted cats emerging into the camp from the thorn tunnel: a hunting patrol led by Sandstorm. Dustpelt, Squirrelflight, and Hollyleaf followed her into the clearing and went to drop their prey on the fresh-kill pile before padding over to join the cats around Firestar.

"What's all this?" Hollyleaf asked as she reached Lionblaze's side.

Lionblaze stared at Squirrelflight, at the agony in her face as she listened to her Clanmates' praise of Ashfur. He knew that she must be sharing his own thoughts, of the darkness in the gray warrior that was so well hidden from the rest of his Clan. *How much do you know about how he died?* he asked himself, not wanting to meet her gaze.

"Lionblaze, what's happening?" Hollyleaf repeated her question in a sharper tone, prodding him in the side with one paw.

Lionblaze glanced at her. His sister's green eyes were haunted, and she looked as if she hadn't slept for a moon. *She looks just like how I feel,* he thought.

"Thornclaw and some of the others want to attack WindClan because of Ashfur's death," he replied.

Hollyleaf's eyes widened. "Do they really think it was a

WindClan cat?" she asked, a tinge of surprise in her voice.

"Some of them do. But Firestar—"

Lionblaze broke off as the Clan leader darted back to the tumbled rocks and leaped up onto a boulder. "Let all cats old enough to catch their own prey join here beneath the High-ledge for a Clan meeting!" he yowled.

The cats already in the clearing followed him and settled themselves at the foot of the boulder. Lionblaze could see that some of them were still arguing among themselves, but they kept their voices low.

The two apprentices, Foxpaw and Icepaw, emerged from the elders' den under the hazel bush, pushing an enormous ball of moss between them. Mousefur and Longtail followed them out and crouched down in a patch of sunlight. Mouse-whisker pushed his way out of the warriors' den, yawning and flicking bits of moss off his pelt.

Graystripe and Millie appeared from the nursery, with their kits tumbling around their paws. They were followed more slowly by Birchfall and Whitewing; the white she-cat was heavy with kits, and Birchfall kept close to her side. Daisy was the last to appear; she sat in the nursery entrance, giving her chest fur a thorough wash, while Toadkit and Rosekit rolled around beside her, play fighting.

Leafpool and Jayfeather emerged from the medicine cats' den and stayed just outside the bramble screen, away from the rest of the Clan. Lionblaze tried to catch his brother's attention, but Jayfeather refused to respond, resolutely facing Firestar instead.

"I know you're all wondering what to do about Ashfur's death," the Clan leader began. "I promise you that the cat who killed him will be punished. But there's no proof that Wind-Clan was involved."

"There's enough proof for me," Spiderleg grunted.

Firestar ignored the interruption. "I will lead a patrol to speak with Onestar. Not to accuse him or attack his Clan. Ashfur died on the WindClan border, and it's possible that one of Onestar's warriors saw something."

There were murmurs of disagreement from some of the listening cats; Thornclaw was flexing his claws in and out, but he didn't speak up.

"Brambleclaw, you'll come with me," Firestar went on. "And Brackenfur, Sorreltail, and Lionblaze. We'll leave right away."

Lionblaze felt a jolt in his belly when Firestar spoke his name. For a heartbeat, he wanted to protest; he hated the thought of being involved in the investigation of Ashfur's death. But he knew that if he said anything, he would only draw attention to himself. He had no reason to refuse to go to WindClan; as far as the other cats knew, he was as shocked by Ashfur's death, and as determined to get vengeance, as they were.

"Good," Hollyleaf breathed into his ear. "And you've got to tell me what happens when you get back."

"Okay," Lionblaze muttered. "But I'd rather stay out of it."

Firestar leaped down from the boulder and padded through the groups of cats with Brambleclaw just behind him.

Brackenfur and Sorreltail joined them.

Cats who didn't want to attack WindClan, Lionblaze realized. *Firestar isn't taking any risks.*

Firestar led them toward the thorn tunnel; before they left, he turned and summoned Graystripe with a flick of his tail. "Keep an eye on Thornclaw and the others," he murmured to the gray warrior. "Make sure they don't try to launch their own attack."

Graystripe nodded grimly. "Don't worry. I'll stick closer than their pelts."

Lionblaze and the others followed Firestar as he headed through the woods, making for the WindClan border. Fallen leaves rustled as the cats brushed through them; in the shade of the trees, where the leaf-bare sun didn't penetrate, every leaf was still rimmed with frost. The bare branches traced delicate patterns against the sky.

The patrol padded behind Firestar in solemn silence; Lionblaze brought up the rear. He could tell that the rest of the cats were uneasy, halting every few paw steps to taste the air. Sorreltail spun around, her tail lashing, at the sound of an acorn dropping into the undergrowth.

"It doesn't feel like our territory anymore," she mewed disgustedly when she realized her mistake. "There could be anything lurking about. Suppose it was a rogue who killed Ashfur?"

"It might have been." Brackenfur touched his mate's shoulder with his tail-tip. "But you're safe with us. One cat can't take on a whole patrol."

"That crow-food-eating menace Sol could still be hanging around," Sorreltail went on. "No cat knows where he went after ShadowClan threw him out."

Firestar, who had paused to wait for his Clanmates, pricked his ears with interest. "It's an idea. We should all stay alert for any signs of him. I'll announce it to the rest of the Clan when we get back."

"Sol doesn't strike me as the sort of cat who would kill," Brambleclaw commented thoughtfully. "Getting other cats to do his dirty work is more his style."

Firestar nodded. "True. But maybe Ashfur caught him trying to do something to harm ThunderClan."

"Ashfur might have attacked Sol just for being on our territory," Brackenfur meowed. "He would have taken on a badger to protect his Clan."

"He was a loyal warrior," Brambleclaw agreed.

Miserably Lionblaze wished he could feel what they did, and mourn his Clanmate sincerely. Ashfur's famous loyalty wouldn't have stopped him from ruining ThunderClan's reputation by revealing Squirrelflight's secret at the Gathering. He had confessed that he had plotted with Hawkfrost to make Brambleclaw kill Firestar. His obsession with Squirrelflight had destroyed his commitment to ThunderClan. But now that he was dead, his Clan was determined to make him into a hero. Lionblaze longed to yowl out the truth to every cat in the forest, but he knew the destruction that would follow. When the patrol set off again, he could only plod along at the rear, hating the need for silence and hating himself.

"Are you okay?" Brambleclaw had dropped back to pad beside him. "I know you must be missing Ashfur."

Fury at Brambleclaw's misunderstanding flooded through Lionblaze. "I'm fine!" he snapped, knowing he was being illogical. "Stay out of my fur, will you?"

Brambleclaw's eyes widened, but he said nothing, just nodded and quickened his pace again to catch up with Firestar.

"You shouldn't claw his whiskers off," Sorreltail mewed, padding up to Lionblaze and touching his ear with her nose. "Brambleclaw is bound to be worried about you; that's what fathers do." Her amber eyes gleamed with affection. "My kits are warriors now, but they'll always be my kits."

Lionblaze gave her an awkward nod, but he couldn't reply. His secret trapped him like rising floodwater, cutting him off from every cat in his Clan. *He's not my father!* Lionblaze wanted to yowl. *Everything you've been told is a lie!*

CHAPTER 2

A *chilly wind was blowing from* the moor when Firestar and his patrol reached the stream that marked the border with Wind-Clan. Lionblaze's paws tingled as he padded up to the edge of the bank. This was close to where they had found Ash-fur. He tried to shut out the memories of Ashfur's slick gray body, wedged behind a rock and bobbing in the current. Yet he could not regret Ashfur's death.

Each cat leaped across the stream and raced into WindClan territory without even checking for scent. Lionblaze guessed that they, too, were spooked by the memory of the dead warrior. Firestar led them on, still at a run, until the stream was hidden behind them by rocks and reeds.

Lionblaze tasted the air and shivered. There was a tang of snow that must have come from the mountains. A dark haze like storm clouds crouched on the horizon; Lionblaze knew he was looking at the distant home of the Tribe of Rushing Water. *How are they managing?* he wondered. Leaf-bare would be even harder where snow lay thick on bare rock and prey was scarce. *But I wish I could go back,* he added to himself, knowing he meant not just back to the mountains, but back in time as well. *When I was with the Tribe, I knew who I was and where my destiny was leading.*

"There are WindClan cats nearby," Firestar meowed.

Lionblaze jumped guiltily; thinking about the Tribe, he had never noticed the WindClan scent, though it was strong and fresh. For the first time he started to wonder how their mission would turn out. There was still hostility between ThunderClan and WindClan; Onestar was bound to see an accusation behind Firestar's questions.

The ThunderClan leader headed across the moor toward the WindClan camp with his warriors at his flanks. Wind buffeted their fur, and a strong gust nearly carried Sorreltail off her paws.

"I can't imagine why cats would choose to live here!" she hissed as she struggled to regain her balance.

"We like it here!" A loud meow rang out across the moorland.

Lionblaze looked up to see a WindClan patrol appearing over the shoulder of the hill. Tornear, the cat who had spoken, was in the lead, followed by Crowfeather, Whitetail, and Heathertail.

Meeting Heathertail's gaze, Lionblaze saw nothing but cold contempt in the eyes of the cat who had once been his friend—and even more than that. Bitter regret surged through him. As he looked back, those times had been the happiest and easiest of his life, even though he had broken the warrior code to meet Heathertail in the tunnels beneath the forest. Now she looked as if she would have killed him for a couple of mousetails; Lionblaze shuddered as he pictured his own body lying in the stream.

"Greetings, Tornear." Firestar dipped his head as the WindClan patrol approached.

"What are you doing here?" Tornear sounded wary but not hostile, though Crowfeather's neck fur was bristling and Whitetail had unsheathed her claws.

"I need to speak with Onestar," Firestar explained. "May we visit your camp?"

Tornear hesitated, narrowing his eyes in suspicion, then gave a brusque nod. "Very well, but we'll escort you. And you'd better not start anything."

"We only want to talk," Firestar promised.

Taking the lead, Tornear headed farther up the hill in the direction of the WindClan camp. Crowfeather and Whitetail flanked the ThunderClan patrol on either side, while Heathertail brought up the rear. Lionblaze was acutely conscious of her, padding just behind him, and felt her gaze pierce him like a thorn.

At last Tornear led them up the long slope toward the circle of gorse bushes that surrounded the WindClan camp. Pushing through the thorns, Lionblaze paused to look down. It was a bleak place: a wide hollow of rough moorland grass where stones poked up through the thin soil. Twisted thornbushes gave the only shelter, except for the disused badgers' set that was now the elders' den.

Lionblaze spotted Onestar sitting near the middle of the hollow, talking to Barkface, the WindClan medicine cat. A few other WindClan cats—including the deputy, Ashfoot, and Crowfeather's son, Breezepelt—stood around listening.

Lionblaze's paws pricked with curiosity as he recognized the urgency in Barkface's stance and expression; Lionblaze couldn't hear what he was saying, but it looked as though he was sharing grave news with his Clan leader.

What's all that about? Lionblaze wondered. *They can't know anything about Ashfur!*

Onestar glanced up as Tornear raced down the slope to announce the visitors. Seeing Firestar and the others, he hesitated for a few heartbeats, then spoke quickly to Barkface. The medicine cat nodded, and at last Onestar signaled with his tail to let Firestar bring his warriors down into the camp.

"Greetings, Onestar." Firestar halted in front of the WindClan leader and bowed his head. "Thank you for allowing us to talk to you."

The look Onestar gave to Firestar showed none of their old friendship. "Say what you have to say," he mewed cautiously.

His edgy tone made Lionblaze wonder if all was well in WindClan. *Maybe there's something he doesn't want us to know about.* Glancing around, he saw that all the WindClan cats looked skinny and underfed, but that was just as usual for WindClan.

"I'd like to speak to you in private," Firestar began.

Onestar's neck fur rose and he shook his head. "Anything you have to say can be said in front of my Clanmates."

While he was speaking, Ashfoot padded up and stood by her leader's side. She said nothing, just surveyed the

ThunderClan cats with calm, clear eyes.

"Well?" Onestar prompted.

"If that's how you want it." Lionblaze's belly churned as Firestar continued: "On the night of the Gathering, we found Ashfur's body in the stream that marks our border. There was a gash in his throat; we think a cat killed him."

Instantly the WindClan warriors began to bristle, and Breezepelt let out an indignant yowl.

Onestar lashed his tail and dug his claws hard into the ground. His eyes blazed with anger. "How dare you assume we had anything to do with it?" he hissed. "We have nothing to gain from killing one of your warriors."

"None of us had any quarrel with Ashfur," Whitetail put in.

"*This* Clan is loyal to the warrior code," Crowfeather growled, his lip curling in a snarl.

Lionblaze braced himself, ready for the fight he was sure would break out at any moment. But Firestar remained calm; not even his tail-tip twitched.

"No cat is accusing you," he insisted. "We came to ask if you saw anything on the border that night."

"What, like one of my warriors killing Ashfur?" Onestar's fur was still fluffed up with anger. "Look to your own Clan-mates first, Firestar. Question their loyalty to the warrior code, not ours."

Lionblaze felt the fur rising on his neck and shoulders; Brackenfur and Sorreltail were bristling, too, while Bramble-claw flexed his claws in and out at the veiled insult. *So what if there are cats of mixed blood in ThunderClan?* Lionblaze thought fiercely. *We're all loyal.* He pictured Ashfur's body again, soaked and limp. *All except one.*

He spotted Heathertail standing off to one side, her gaze fixed on him. She seemed to be daring him to strike out so that she would have an excuse to jump on him and sink her claws into his fur. Breezepelt had padded so close to her that their pelts were brushing, and he met Lionblaze's stare with a challenge in his eyes. *Heathertail is mine now,* he seemed to be saying.

You're welcome to her, Lionblaze glared back.

"Then you saw nothing?" Firestar pressed; his voice had hardened, insisting on an answer.

"Nothing." Onestar spat out the word like a piece of crow-food. "Now get out of our territory. Ashfoot, take a couple of warriors and escort them to the border."

His deputy gave him a brisk nod and waved her tail to beckon Tornear and Breezepelt, who padded up to the ThunderClan patrol with truculent stares.

Firestar dipped his head toward the WindClan leader. "Thank you, Onestar. If you learn anything more, will you please send us a message?"

Onestar didn't reply. Following Firestar's lead, Lionblaze tried to stay dignified as he and the others were herded up the side of the hollow and through the barrier of gorse bushes onto the open moor.

None of the WindClan cats spoke as they conducted Firestar's patrol back to the border. Ashfoot set a brisk pace, but

Lionblaze would have liked to go racing ahead, to return to the woods, away from the cold eyes of these hostile cats. Yet there was no safety in the woods, either—nowhere he could hide from the death of Ashfur and all it meant for his Clan.

On the hillside above the stream, Ashfoot halted. "You can go back to the camp," she ordered Breezepelt and Tornear. "I'll see them the rest of the way."

"Why?" Breezepelt demanded.

"You're needed for a hunting patrol," the WindClan deputy replied. "Or do you think the rabbits will come running into the camp on their own?"

Breezepelt let out an annoyed hiss, and Tornear looked uneasy, stopping once to glance back as both cats climbed to the top of the hill and vanished over it in the direction of the camp.

Ashfoot silently watched until they were out of sight, then turned to Firestar with a sigh. "I wanted to talk to you alone, Firestar. There's something I have to tell you."

Lionblaze's belly lurched. Had Ashfoot been by the stream that night? Could she put a name to the cat whose teeth had torn out Ashfur's life? But the WindClan deputy looked too calm for a cat who had been a witness to murder.

"Go on," Firestar meowed.

"A few sunrises ago," Ashfoot continued, "I was leading the dawn patrol along the stream when I spotted Sol—you remember, the cat who took over ShadowClan for a while?"

"Sol?" Firestar's green eyes stretched wide. "I thought he had left the lake."

"No—or at least, he was here a few days ago."

"Then why didn't Onestar tell me about him?" Firestar's shock was giving way to anger.

Ashfoot shrugged, looking uncomfortable. Lionblaze knew that she was a fair-minded cat; she couldn't be happy about the tensions between her own Clan and ThunderClan. But her loyalty to Onestar wouldn't let her speak openly.

"Ashfur's death is your problem, not ours," she pointed out. "You can't expect Onestar to be happy when you come barging into his camp accusing his cats of murder."

"We didn't—" Brambleclaw began indignantly, his amber eyes blazing.

Firestar raised his tail for silence. "Let's end this misunderstanding now," he meowed to Ashfoot. "We are *not* accusing WindClan of anything. We just want to find out anything we can about Ashfur's death. Now tell us what you know about Sol. Where did you see him? When?"

"It was about a quarter moon ago," Ashfoot replied. "He was near the lake, in the woods on your side of the stream. I don't think he saw us; he was too busy eating some fresh-kill."

"Prey-stealing!" Sorreltail hissed.

"That's not the day Ashfur died," Brackenfur murmured thoughtfully. "But it's close to the place where we found his body."

"Very close," Firestar agreed. "Thank you, Ashfoot. That's the most useful thing we've learned so far."

Ashfoot dipped her head. "I'm glad to be of help. I wish you and your Clan well, Firestar."

Lionblaze could see the sympathy in her eyes. *She can tell we're in trouble,* he realized. *If only she knew how much!*

Sunhigh was past and long black shadows were beginning to creep across the hollow when Firestar's patrol returned. The queens and Birchfall were drowsily sharing tongues outside the nursery, while Cloudtail, Brightheart, and Hazeltail were crouched beside the fresh-kill pile. Foxpaw and Icepaw were practicing fighting moves outside their den. Lionblaze heard Icepaw screech, "WindClan murderer! I'll rip your pelt off!"

Firestar sighed. "We'd better put a stop to *that.* I'll call another meeting right away."

Brambleclaw's whiskers twitched in surprise. "Shouldn't we discuss it with the senior warriors first?"

Firestar shook his head. "No. The whole Clan is involved in this. I want them to know about Sol right now, before some of these hotheads manage to sneak off and attack WindClan."

He bounded across the clearing toward the tumbled rocks, but before he reached them Hazeltail spotted the returning warriors and leaped to her paws. "Hey!" she yowled. "Firestar's back!"

Heads popped out from between the branches of the warriors' den. The queens sat up and pricked up their ears, while all five kits tumbled out of the nursery, tripping over one another's paws. Jayfeather poked his head out from behind the bramble screen, a bundle of herbs in his jaws. By the time

Firestar reached the Highledge, there was no need for him to summon the Clan; every cat in the camp had gathered to hear what WindClan had to say. Lionblaze, with Brambleclaw and the rest of the patrol, padded over to sit at the back of the crowd.

"What did you find out?" Thornclaw called from where he sat at the foot of the tumbled rocks. "When do we attack?"

"We don't," Firestar replied. "WindClan did *not* murder Ashfur."

An uneasy muttering spread among the cats, but Firestar didn't wait for an argument to break out. Quickly he went on: "Onestar and his warriors knew nothing about Ashfur's death until I told them. And Ashfoot gave me one very useful piece of information: She saw Sol a few sunrises ago, by the stream near the lake."

Spiderleg shot upright, his tail waving. "That's where Ashfur's body was found!"

Yowls of shock and anger broke out; several cats leaped up, eyes blazing and fur bristling, as if they wanted to attack the rogue cat right away.

"Sol killed Ashfur!"

"Filthy murderer!"

"We should find him and teach him what happens when rogues attack a warrior!"

Firestar raised his tail for silence. "We still have no proof," he went on when he could make himself heard. "But—"

"What proof do we need?" Mousefur rasped. "Look at what he did to ShadowClan!"

"He didn't kill any ShadowClan cats," Dustpelt reminded her. "What reason would he have for killing Ashfur?"

Mousefur let out a disgusted hiss. "I wouldn't put anything past that mangy piece of crow-food."

"But he must have had a reason," Brackenfur meowed, backing up Dustpelt. "Not many cats kill just for fun."

Lionblaze recalled the stories he had heard about Scourge, the leader of BloodClan who had tried to take over in the old forest. He sounded like a cat who had enjoyed killing. But Lionblaze didn't think Sol was like that.

"Maybe Ashfur caught Sol on our territory," Brightheart suggested. "They could have fought—"

"But Ashfur hadn't been fighting," Sandstorm interrupted. "There were no wounds on him except for the marks on his throat. Isn't that right, Leafpool?"

Heads turned to look at the medicine cat, who was sitting outside her den, away from the crowd around the Highledge. She replied to Sandstorm with a curt nod, but said nothing.

"Well, then," Cloudtail meowed, "maybe Sol caught Ashfur unawares, and took the chance to stir up trouble between ThunderClan and WindClan."

"That sounds like Sol," Squirrelflight agreed with a flick of her tail. "Set cat against cat, and then step in to seize power for himself."

"I think we need to know more," Graystripe mewed quietly. "It's useful to know that Ashfoot spotted Sol, but that doesn't set Sol's teeth in Ashfur's neck."

"You're right." Firestar nodded toward his former deputy.

"Can any cat tell us more about Sol?"

To Lionblaze's surprise, Hollyleaf tentatively raised her tail. "I . . . I saw him, Firestar. By the lake, not long after he was driven out of ShadowClan."

She never told me about that! Uneasiness stirred in Lionblaze's belly. But he and Jayfeather hadn't told their sister about the catmint they had fetched from WindClan, either. *When did we start keeping secrets from one another?*

"Tell us what happened," Firestar prompted.

"Nothing much," Hollyleaf replied. "He said the Clans needed him, and he promised he'd be back."

Cloudtail lashed his tail. "That's a threat, if ever I heard one!"

"Why didn't you report this?" Firestar asked Hollyleaf.

Hollyleaf ducked her head. "I didn't think it mattered," she told him. "I thought it was just talk because he was angry about losing control of ShadowClan. And he was heading along the lakeshore toward WindClan territory. I thought he was leaving."

"You still should have mentioned it," Firestar told her, though his voice was mild. "I could have told the patrols to keep a lookout for him."

Hollyleaf studied her paws. "I'm sorry, Firestar."

"Is there anything else we ought to know?" the Clan leader asked.

"I—I'm not sure," Hollyleaf meowed hesitantly. "Sol mentioned that he had met Midnight the badger, but I can't see what that has to do with killing Ashfur."

"It might tell us how to find him," Brambleclaw pointed out. "If Sol knows Midnight, he might have come from the sun-drown-place!" The Clan deputy's eyes were glowing; Lionblaze could tell that he was remembering his heroic journey from the old forest to find the badger who would tell the Clans where they would live from now on.

"So what are we going to do?" Dustpelt asked Firestar.

"Why are you even asking?" Thornclaw growled. "We go and deal with Sol, of course!"

Lionblaze remembered how certain Thornclaw had been that morning that a WindClan cat had murdered the gray warrior. It hadn't taken much to change his mind. But at least no cat was suggesting that a ThunderClan cat was the killer anymore.

They're glad to accuse Sol because he's a rogue, he realized.

"We can't be sure that Sol killed Ashfur," Firestar meowed over the chorus of agreement that met Thornclaw's words. "But we need to find out. We'll send a patrol to the sun-drown-place, to get Sol and bring him back here. Then we can question him, and if he *did* kill Ashfur, he'll be punished."

Prickles ran up and down Lionblaze's spine at the thought of confronting Sol. He didn't know whether he wanted to go on the patrol or not. The rogue cat knew more than was natural—more about *him* than any other cat had ever seemed to know; maybe the answers to Firestar's questions would be things no cat wanted to hear.

"Brambleclaw, you know the way to the sun-drown-place," Firestar announced. "You'll lead the patrol. Brackenfur,

Hazeltail, and Birchfall can go with you."

Lionblaze spotted Birchfall giving Whitewing a regretful look and leaning over to lick her ear. He guessed that Birchfall didn't want to leave his mate when she was so close to giving birth to her kits.

"This could be dangerous," Brambleclaw meowed to Firestar. "It might be better to have one or two more cats."

"True." The Clan leader glanced around. "Lionblaze and Hollyleaf, then. You can leave at dawn."

Lionblaze glanced at his sister; Hollyleaf's neck fur was standing on end and her green eyes glittered, but whether it was from fear or excitement, he couldn't tell.

Hazeltail leaped to her paws and padded across to Hollyleaf. "Isn't this great?" she mewed. "We're really going to do something to help our Clan."

Hollyleaf flicked her ears; Lionblaze couldn't hear what she said in reply. The rest of the Clan were crowding around the chosen cats, congratulating them and offering advice. Every other cat seemed fired up to track down and destroy a murderer; he was the only one reluctant to avenge Ashfur's death.

A few moments before, he had been relieved that suspicion had moved away from ThunderClan. But laying the blame at Sol's paws was no better. He didn't want to be reminded of the Clan cats' instinctive mistrust of outsiders, of cats who weren't Clanborn.

What if I'm a rogue, too? Will they all turn against me?

CHAPTER 3

Jayfeather sat still while the rest of the Clan swirled around him, buzzing with tension and excitement.

"I'm scared." Jayfeather recognized Bumblekit's voice close by. "What if Sol comes into the camp and gets us?"

Jayfeather heard the rasp of a tongue, and pictured Millie giving her son a comforting lick. "Sol is far away, little one," she murmured.

"And there are big, strong warriors here to guard us," Daisy added. "Do you think that your father would let any cat lay a claw on you?"

Bumblekit's tone brightened. "No! Graystripe is the best!"

Jayfeather wished he could be reassured as easily as the kit. He knew bad times were coming. Fear, suspicion, and accusation crashed over him from all sides, as if his Clanmates were hurling rocks at him. He felt sick and dizzy, and the ground under his paws didn't seem solid anymore.

Beside him, he heard Mousefur heaving herself to her paws with a gusty sigh. "If Ashfur's killer meant to stir up trouble, mission accomplished. That cat has stuck a nose into a nest of bees by taking one of our warriors."

And that cat will get stung. But Jayfeather didn't want to think about what might happen to Ashfur's murderer.

He picked out Lionblaze from the mingled scents of ThunderClan cats, but his brother didn't slow down as he padded past.

"So you're going to find Sol," Jayfeather called to him.

Lionblaze halted. "Yes."

Jayfeather was desperate to talk to his brother as they always did: easily, with nothing left unspoken. But the secret they had shared since the night of the storm made it impossible.

The awkward silence was broken by Hollyleaf padding up to them.

"You never told us you'd seen Sol," Jayfeather meowed.

He could imagine his sister's shrug. "It didn't matter then."

"Even so, you should have said something." Lionblaze sounded upset. "You know Sol was supposed to help us with the prophecy."

"What prophecy?" Hollyleaf snapped. "There isn't a prophecy, as far as we're concerned."

"You didn't know that when you saw Sol."

Jayfeather winced as he listened to them bicker. There was no point to their argument, except that it stopped them from discussing the only thing that mattered: whether any of them believed that Sol had killed Ashfur.

I'm glad I'm not going, he told himself. *I don't want to listen to them all the way to the sun-drown-place and back!*

Leafpool's voice cut across his thoughts. "Jayfeather, there you are! I want you to come help me prepare herbs for the patrol."

"Okay, coming."

He rose to his paws and followed his mentor back to the medicine cats' den, leaving Hollyleaf and Lionblaze to their squabbling. As soon as he brushed past the bramble screen, his mouth filled with the scent of the traveling herbs.

"I've laid everything out," Leafpool told him. "We just have to make them into leaf wraps."

It was a relief to have something to distract him, but the task was soon done, and he emerged into the clearing again with a leaf wrap for Brambleclaw clamped between his jaws. By now the excitement over the patrol was beginning to die down, and the cats were returning to their dens. Distinguishing Brambleclaw's scent from the tang of the herbs he carried was difficult, but Jayfeather finally located him with Squirrelflight near the fresh-kill pile.

"I wish you were coming with us," Brambleclaw was mewing to his mate as Jayfeather padded up. "We have so many good memories from that journey."

Jayfeather caught the wistful note in his voice. It was as if the Clan deputy was looking back to a good time that was over, and regretting everything that had gone wrong since.

I wonder if he knows how wrong?

"I wish I was coming, too," Squirrelflight replied, her voice subdued. "But I'm probably not fit enough for a long journey, after the wound I took in the battle."

"There's no need to worry about Sol, you know," Bramble-claw reassured her. "I'll keep you safe."

"I know." Squirrelflight sighed.

Jayfeather's pelt prickled. Squirrelflight had never needed another cat to keep her safe! Once she would have clawed the ears off any cat who suggested it. But now she sounded . . . broken; waves of guilt and longing were coming from her, so strongly that Jayfeather almost felt sorry for her.

He brushed past her and set the wrap of herbs down at Brambleclaw's paws. "Here," he announced. "Traveling herbs. Eat them all, and get plenty of rest before tomorrow."

"Thanks, Jayfeather."

"Hey, Brambleclaw!" Graystripe's voice came from across the clearing; Jayfeather heard his paw steps as he bounded up. "Firestar wants me to act as deputy while you're away. Can I have a word with you about border patrols?"

"Sure." Brambleclaw gulped the herbs down quickly. "What do you want to know?"

"Well, I think a few cats are still worried about Wind-Clan. . . ."

The voices of the two toms faded as they padded across the clearing. Jayfeather had turned back toward his den when Squirrelflight intercepted him.

"Jayfeather, I want to talk to you."

"There's nothing left to say," Jayfeather snapped. *And I don't want to hear anything you might have to tell me.* He veered around the cat he had thought was his mother and headed toward his den. He felt hollow, as if a vast emptiness had opened up inside him. For so long he had depended on the prophecy to tell him who he was and what his destiny would be; without it, was he going to be just a medicine cat for the rest of his life? *And where's the cat who gave birth to us? What happened to her?*

Jayfeather hated feeling that he wasn't in control anymore. Unsettled, he blundered into the brambles that screened the medicine cats' den. His paws tangled in a long tendril; thorns raked through his pelt and scratched his nose. He let out a startled yowl.

"Jayfeather!" Leafpool was instantly by his side. "Keep still. I'll get you out."

"I'm fine," Jayfeather growled. He'd *never* made a mistake like that, not even when he was a kit! He tugged himself free of the brambles and felt a clump of fur tear out as he stumbled into the den.

"Are you all right?" Leafpool's voice was anxious. "Your nose is bleeding. I'll get some cobweb."

"I said, I'm *fine*." Jayfeather shrugged her away, giving one paw a swift lick and swiping it over his nose. The scratch stung, but he couldn't stand being fussed over.

Why can't she leave me alone? he thought angrily as he stalked toward the store to get more herbs. *She doesn't have to worry about me. We're not even kin!*

When he had delivered all the traveling herbs, Jayfeather found a few moments to snatch prey from the fresh-kill pile. As he gulped down his vole, he heard Berrynose's raised voice a couple of tail-lengths away.

"Well, I don't trust ShadowClan! After all that trouble with Sol, Blackstar would do anything to prove his Clan is still strong."

Dustpelt's annoyed hiss followed immediately. "Are you mouse-brained? Are you actually suggesting that a Shadow-Clan warrior trekked all the way across our territory to kill Ashfur?"

"It could happen," Berrynose mumbled.

"And hedgehogs could fly," Dustpelt retorted scathingly.

Swallowing the last of his prey and swiping his tongue around his jaws, Jayfeather headed back to the den. *I'm sick of cats wondering who killed Ashfur!*

But when he took tansy to Millie and Briarkit, who were recovering from greencough, he couldn't help overhearing Cloudtail, Brightheart, and Daisy, sitting close to the nursery entrance.

"Don't worry about a thing, Daisy," Cloudtail assured the cream-colored she-cat. "Some of the warriors are leaving, but there are plenty of us left to protect you and the kits."

"Graystripe said we can double the guard on the camp," Brightheart added.

"I know you'll all help." Daisy still sounded worried. "But is it right to bring that murderous cat back here?"

Jayfeather didn't want to listen to yet another discussion about Sol. Pushing his way through the brambles into the nursery, he found the kits swarming like ants whose nest has been disturbed.

"Now you be the killer!" Rosekit squealed, batting

Blossomkit on the ear with one paw. "And we'll all come and catch you!"

Blossomkit let out a screech of excitement; Jayfeather almost tripped over the other kits as they bundled on top of her in a writhing heap.

"Stop that right now!" Millie's voice was shocked. "This isn't fun. A brave ThunderClan warrior is dead."

Ashfur was never this important when he was alive, Jayfeather thought.

The kits calmed down a little as Jayfeather set down the tansy and left. On his way back to his den, he passed Firestar with Sandstorm, Graystripe, and Brackenfur.

"We can't assume the problems are over," Sandstorm was meowing. "If I were you, Firestar, I'd warn all cats to stay away from the WindClan border, except for patrols."

"Right," Graystripe agreed. "We don't want to find another warrior dead in the stream."

Jayfeather stifled a sigh. *What's the point of patrols and guards? The killer is here.*

A night breeze had sprung up when Jayfeather padded over to the fresh-kill pile where Lionblaze and Hollyleaf were eating with the rest of the Sol patrol. Earlier in the day, he hadn't known what to say to them, and it was no better now.

"Hi," he meowed. "Ready for tomorrow?"

"As ready as we'll ever be," Hollyleaf replied.

"It's weird, going without you." Lionblaze brushed his muzzle against Jayfeather's shoulder. "This will be the first time we've ever been separated."

Jayfeather nodded. He had even managed the long journey to visit the Tribe in the mountains, but this time he had to stay behind. In spite of his earlier impatience with his littermates, it felt wrong to be split from them, especially when he knew that the tendrils of the secret that bound them together could not be broken by any distance.

"Well . . . I guess it's good-bye," he muttered.

"I guess," Lionblaze meowed.

Jayfeather touched his nose to his brother's, and then to Hollyleaf's.

"Bye, Jayfeather," she murmured.

There ought to be more to say, Jayfeather knew, but tension quivered among the three of them like the strands of a spider's web. In the end, he ducked his head, mumbled, "May StarClan light your path," and headed back to the medicine cats' den.

Jayfeather opened his eyes to see bleak rocks stretching to either side of him and a plunging precipice just in front of his paws. Startled, he leaped back. Wind swept across the mountaintop, ruffling his fur. As he recovered from the first shock of finding himself here, he recognized the place where he had met Midnight the badger.

Looking up, Jayfeather saw the stars whirling around the sky, so fast that they became blurred trails of light. He tried to dig his claws into the thin soil where he stood, terrified of falling upward into the gaping emptiness.

Then he heard the scrape of claws on rock. Wrenching his

gaze from the swirling stars, he whipped around to see the bulky body and white-striped head of Midnight.

"What do you want?" he demanded, trying not to sound as scared as he felt.

"Sol not kill Ashfur," Midnight rumbled. "This you know. These cats chasing wild geese." She lumbered closer to Jayfeather, starlight glittering in her small black eyes. "Truth must come out."

"Why?" This time Jayfeather couldn't stop his voice from quivering.

Midnight's words fell like stones into a deep pool. "Anything else will destroy your Clan forever."

"But—" Jayfeather began to protest, but the wind rose, whipping away Midnight's words and his own, and the badger's looming form, until he felt that he and Midnight and the stars themselves were being swept into a vast whirlpool.

He seemed to hit the ground with a jolt, and opened his eyes in the darkness of his own den. The air bore the scent of frost, and Jayfeather guessed that dawn was near.

Leafpool was shifting around in the bracken of her nest close by. "It's time for the patrol to leave," she meowed. "Do you want to come say good-bye?"

Jayfeather had said his farewells the night before, but he scrambled out of his nest and followed his mentor into the clearing. Most of the Sol patrol were bunched together near the opening of the thorn tunnel along with Firestar, Graystripe, and Squirrelflight.

A fox-length or so away, Jayfeather located Birchfall and

Whitewing; their mingled scents told him they were pressed close together.

"You take care of yourself and get plenty of rest," Birchfall told his mate. "Eat lots of fresh-kill, and tell Leafpool if you feel anything. . . ."

"Shh," Whitewing murmured lovingly. "I'll be fine. I'm not the only cat who ever gave birth!"

Jayfeather padded past them and found himself close to Squirrelflight, who was saying good-bye to Brambleclaw. Unlike Whitewing, she was keeping her emotions firmly under control; Jayfeather couldn't tell what she was feeling.

"Be careful at the sun-drown-place," she warned the ThunderClan deputy. "Don't get too close to the edge of the cliffs. They might give way again."

"I know. I don't want to go for another swim." Brambleclaw was trying to sound cheerful, but Jayfeather could tell that it was forced.

"Brambleclaw, just remind me about hunting patrols," Graystripe broke in. "The best places are by the old Twoleg nest and near the dead tree, right?"

"Right," Brambleclaw replied. "Make sure the patrols remember that if they're hunting by the dead tree they've got to be careful not to cross the ShadowClan border."

"You'll be fine, Graystripe," Firestar assured the gray warrior. "You know the territory well enough by now."

The cats who were staying behind edged backward as the patrol got ready to leave. A solemn silence spread over them. Jayfeather was aware of a sudden heightening of tension; no cats had ever set out on an expedition like this before.

"May StarClan light your path," Firestar meowed. "You are going to find the truth."

No! The truth is here! Jayfeather clamped his jaws shut so that he didn't yowl out loud. Midnight had told him what he already knew: Sol did not kill Ashfur. The patrol was heading toward danger for nothing. Why couldn't his Clanmates see that they had to look among themselves to find the truth?

He wondered whether they would find Sol and what would happen if they did. His paws tingled as he thought about what Sol could tell them.

He knows about the prophecy. . . .

CHAPTER 4

❧

Frost lay thick on the ground as Brambleclaw's patrol headed through the forest toward the lake. The cats trotted in silence through the silver bracken, their breath clouding around their muzzles. Above Hollyleaf's head the sky was lightening to a pale dove-gray.

Hollyleaf felt as though her paws would freeze to the ground at every step. Icy claws seemed to rake through her fur; the bitter cold numbed the tips of her ears. She felt light-headed—ever since Squirrelflight's revelation, she had found it hard to choke down even the smallest piece of fresh-kill. All that kept her going was a burning need to find out what Sol knew.

Lionblaze trotted alongside her, grim-faced and strong, his amber gaze fixed on the forest ahead. His presence comforted Hollyleaf, though she felt Jayfeather's absence like the stab of a thorn.

Maybe it's best that he stayed behind, she thought. *It's not like he can look for Sol himself.*

Brambleclaw led the way to the stream, and they followed it downhill until they reached the edge of the lake, where the water was still and shallow, with a delicate covering of ice.

Are we mouse-brained, to set out on a long journey in leaf-bare?

But in spite of the cold, tension within the patrol ebbed as they headed along the shore on the edge of WindClan territory. Hazeltail dropped back to pad along beside Hollyleaf, her eyes shining.

"Isn't this great?" She gave a little bounce, like an excited kit. "We're going somewhere no cats have been before."

"Actually they have," Hollyleaf pointed out, not wanting to listen to Hazeltail's chatter. "Brambleclaw and Squirrelflight went to the sun-drown-place with the other cats chosen by StarClan."

"That must have been so exciting!" Hazeltail sighed. "Your mother and father have traveled farther than any cats, ever. They're so adventurous!"

No, they're just liars, Hollyleaf thought bitterly.

There was no sign of any WindClan cats as they skirted the territory, but as they approached the horseplace Hollyleaf began to pick up a strong WindClan scent. Brambleclaw halted, raising his tail to tell his patrol to do the same. He stood with head raised, his jaws parted to taste the air.

Aware of the pelts bristling around her, Hollyleaf realized how jumpy they all were. They weren't doing anything to break the warrior code by keeping close to the edge of the lake, but a single whiff of WindClan scent had them all unsheathing their claws. *Ashfur's death has done this to us.*

"Why should there be any trouble?" Hazeltail asked, puzzled. "We're allowed to walk beside the lake, aren't we?"

Before Hollyleaf could respond, a gray she-cat appeared at the top of the bank and padded down toward the patrol.

"Ashfoot!" Brambleclaw relaxed. "Greetings."

"Greetings, Brambleclaw." The WindClan deputy dipped her head as she reached the group of ThunderClan cats. "I wondered if you would go looking for Sol. That is why you're here, isn't it?"

Brambleclaw nodded. "Whether or not he killed Ashfur, he has questions to answer."

"Then I've something to show you," Ashfoot meowed. "Follow me."

She led the way along the edge of the lake until they reached the Twoleg fence around the horseplace; the mesh shone like a huge cobweb in the strengthening daylight.

"There." Ashfoot flicked her ears toward a rough place on the mesh where a long, silky strand of reddish fur was caught.

Brambleclaw padded up to it and sniffed it, then turned to the patrol with his amber eyes wide. "Sol."

Hollyleaf's heart pounded harder in her chest. The evidence of Sol's presence brought his memory back to her more strongly than ever. He had seemed to know so much, had prophesied so much . . . and yet he had turned out to be a traitor.

"Then he went this way!" Brackenfur exclaimed, his eyes gleaming. "We're on the right track."

"The scent's stale," Brambleclaw warned, "but not that old. Sol certainly passed this place not many sunrises ago."

Ashfoot took a pace back, toward her own territory. "Goodbye, then, and good luck."

"Thanks, Ashfoot," Brambleclaw responded. "You've helped us a lot—what made you do it?"

Ashfoot twitched her ears. "I want my own Clan to be safe. Sol must be dealt with before he causes more trouble." Without waiting for a reply, she padded back up the bank and disappeared over the shoulder of the hill.

"Or else she wants us to stop blaming WindClan," Birchfall muttered as soon as she was out of earshot.

"That may be," Brambleclaw mewed. "But we don't need to bother about that now. All of you, get a good sniff of this fur, and fix the scent in your minds. Then we can be on our way."

Sliding under the Twoleg fence, he led the way across the field. The ground was hard as stone, and the grass crunched underneath their paws. Their route led them close to the wooden horse nests. Hollyleaf felt her neck fur begin to bristle as she caught the scents of Twoleg and dog, but nothing moved and there was no sound.

She expected Brambleclaw to pass by quickly, but instead he halted at the entrance to the horse nest. "Why are we stopping?" she asked.

"We won't stay long," Brambleclaw replied, "but there are some cats here I want Hazeltail to meet. Hello!" he called softly through the opening.

Hazeltail looked up, puzzled, but before she could speak, two cats appeared from the shadows. In the lead was a muscular gray-and-white tom, with a smaller, paler she-cat just behind him.

"Brambleclaw!" The tom sounded surprised but welcoming.

"What are you doing here—and all these others? I hope there's no trouble in your Clan."

"Nothing that need worry you," Brambleclaw replied.

"Who are they?" Hollyleaf whispered in Lionblaze's ear.

Lionblaze shrugged. "No idea."

"Smoky, Floss," Brambleclaw went on, "this is Hazeltail, Daisy's daughter." He twitched his ears to draw Hazeltail to his side, in front of the stable cats. "Hazeltail, this is Smoky . . . your father."

Hazeltail's eyes widened in astonishment. "Daisy brought us here when we were kits. Father!"

She rushed forward and rubbed her muzzle against Smoky's chin. Purring loudly, Smoky bent his head and gave her a lick around the ears. "I've missed you all," he murmured.

With the touch of his tail on her shoulder, he urged the small she-cat forward. "Do you remember Floss?" he prompted Hazeltail. "She helped Daisy look after you, when you were first born."

Hazeltail looked uncertain. "I don't remember that," she mewed, dipping her head to Floss. "But I do remember seeing you here when Daisy brought us back."

"How is Daisy?" Smoky asked Brambleclaw. "And the other kits . . . Berry and Mouse?"

"They're all fine," Hazeltail assured him, her eyes sparkling. "They're Berrynose and Mousewhisker now. We're all warriors of ThunderClan. Berrynose lost half his tail in a fox trap—"

Floss interrupted with a gasp. "Was he badly hurt?"

"Not too badly," Hazeltail replied. "Leafpool—she's our medicine cat—looked after him. He's a strong warrior now, and so is Mousewhisker."

"And Daisy?" There was a shadow of sadness in Smoky's eyes as he looked to Brambleclaw for an answer. "Is she happy in the Clan? She was so scared, that time she brought our kits back here after the badger attack."

Brambleclaw nodded. "She has found her place. She will never be a warrior, but she is a true cat of ThunderClan."

"She has two more kits!" Hazeltail broke in. "Rosekit and Toadkit. They're so cute!"

"I can see she has moved on," Smoky murmured. Then he gave his pelt a shake, as if dismissing memories. "So you're a warrior now," he meowed to his daughter. "Show me what you've learned."

"Okay." Hazeltail dropped into the hunter's crouch and began to glide forward. "Now I'm stalking a mouse," she explained. "You have to set your paws down light as clouds, because the mouse will feel the vibrations through the earth. Then when you're ready—" She paused, waggling her rump. "You pounce!"

She leaped into the air and landed with her front paws gripping the tip of Birchfall's tail.

Birchfall jumped a tail-length off the ground. "Hey! That hurt!"

Hazeltail's eyes gleamed. "Attack me, then!"

Hollyleaf watched as Birchfall sprang for Hazeltail; she dodged to one side and fetched him a blow across the shoulder with her claws sheathed. Birchfall whipped around and leaped on top of her with a screech; the two young cats wrestled together on the ground.

We were like that once, Hollyleaf thought. *Not a care in the world.* Seeing the pride in Smoky's eyes, she felt a wave of jealousy sweep over her. *Would my father be proud of me?* she wondered. *Does he even know I exist?*

"I'm impressed," Smoky meowed, as Hazeltail and Birchfall broke apart and sat up, shaking scraps of earth and debris out of their fur. "ThunderClan certainly teaches cats to look after themselves."

Floss stepped forward, looking shy but friendly. "Would you like to stay with us for the rest of the day?"

"Good idea." Smoky stepped back and waved his tail toward the inside of the horse nest. "It's warm in here, and there are plenty of mice if you're hungry."

"Thanks, but no," Brambleclaw replied. "We have to keep going."

"We're on the trail of a killer!" Hazeltail added.

Floss and Smoky exchanged an alarmed glance, their neck fur beginning to fluff up. "What—who did they kill?" Floss asked nervously.

"It's a long story." Brackenfur padded up, giving Smoky a calming touch on the shoulder with the tip of his tail. "And you don't have to be frightened about anything. We just need to speak to a cat who may have seen what happened."

Smoky relaxed, the fur on his neck and shoulders beginning to lie flat again. "What cat is this?" he asked.

"A white-and-brown tabby tom," Brambleclaw replied, "with very long fur and pale yellow eyes."

Floss caught her breath. "I saw a cat just like that! He was heading across the field, very early, a couple of sunrises ago."

"Then we're hard on his paws," Brambleclaw purred. "Let's go."

Hazeltail padded up to her father and touched noses with him. "Good-bye," she mewed. "I'll come to see you on the way back."

"Come any time," Smoky told her. Hollyleaf could see how sad he was to let his daughter go so soon.

"I will!" Hazeltail promised.

As they headed across the field, following in Sol's paw steps, Birchfall veered to pad beside Hollyleaf. "It must be weird to be half-Clan," he murmured, too quietly for Hazeltail to hear him. "Imagine never seeing your kin."

Hollyleaf didn't reply. *It's better than what I am,* she thought bleakly. *I'm nothing Clan!*

Chapter 5

As the patrol crossed the next field, snow began to fall in soft feathery flakes that melted as soon as they touched the ground. Lionblaze sneezed as one landed upon his nose.

At the opposite side of the field they came to a wide stretch of whitish stone, with huge red nests at one side. The snow was heavier by now, and a wind had risen, whipping the flakes across the open expanse as they ventured onto the hard surface. Lionblaze padded along beside Hollyleaf, trying to protect her from the worst of the wind.

Suddenly a loud snorting sound came from one of the nests. Terror gripped Lionblaze's limbs and he leaped forward, racing across the stone with the snow brushing his belly fur. Hollyleaf hurtled beside him, with Hazeltail on his other side.

The sound came again, followed by a yowl from Brackenfur. "It's okay! It's only horses!"

Only horses! Lionblaze's flying paws propelled him onward as he imagined the gigantic creatures with their heavy feet that could break a cat's spine with one blow. A Twoleg gate loomed up out of the swirling snow; he wriggled underneath it and bunched his muscles to leap forward again. Hollyleaf and Hazeltail were just behind him.

"No!" Brambleclaw screeched. "Stop! Thunderpath!"

Lionblaze slammed to a halt as yellow beams sliced through the flurries of snow. A monster with glaring eyes swept past, buffeting Lionblaze's fur and soaking his paws with a wave of dirty snowmelt. He and his Clanmates shrank back; Lionblaze's heart was pounding with fear as he waited for Birchfall, Brackenfur, and Brambleclaw to join them.

"You call yourselves warriors?" Brambleclaw's voice was scathing. "That was pure panic. The horses were inside their nests. There was no danger until you decided to hurl yourselves into the path of a monster."

"Sorry," Lionblaze muttered. Searing shame swept over him, hot as a forest fire. Brambleclaw's harsh words stung all the more painfully because he knew the deputy was right. They had acted like apprentices on their first venture out of the camp.

Hazeltail's head was hanging in shame, and Hollyleaf had turned away, lifting each paw in turn to shake the dirty water off her fur. Lionblaze knew how much it meant to her to uphold the warrior code; she must be furious with herself for being spooked like that. *And what about you?* he demanded silently. *The bravest warrior in ThunderClan, scared of a horse that isn't even loose?*

Brambleclaw let out a long sigh and relaxed. "All right. Let's see about getting across here."

Lionblaze heard the roar of another monster as the Clan deputy padded forward cautiously to the edge of the

Thunderpath. The gleaming creature leaped past in a blaze of light; from the other direction, an even bigger monster came barreling along with a throaty growl, its round black paws as big as boulders.

How are we ever going to cross? We'll be squashed flat!

He could see that Hazeltail and Hollyleaf were still scared, their fur on end and their eyes wide with alarm. He knew he must look just the same. He braced himself to force his paws to carry him across the hard, black surface of the Thunderpath.

"Come up here beside me," Brambleclaw directed them calmly. "We'll cross one at a time. Brackenfur, you can go first, to show them how it's done."

Brackenfur twitched his ears in acknowledgment. "It's not so bad," he told the younger cats kindly. "The Thunderpath in the old forest was much bigger than this."

Birchfall's fur bristled. "Then I'm glad we don't live there anymore!"

Brackenfur padded up beside Brambleclaw and waited for another monster to sweep past. Its roar died away in the distance.

"Okay, go," mewed Brambleclaw.

Brackenfur leaped forward, his golden brown pelt almost vanishing in the swirling snow. When he reached the other side, everything was still quiet.

"Hollyleaf, go!"

Taking a gulp of air, Hollyleaf hurled herself across the Thunderpath. Lionblaze dug his claws into the ground, trying to stop himself from shaking, until he saw her reach

Brackenfur's side safely.

The growling of another monster was approaching through the snow. Lionblaze flinched back as it came into sight: a huge creature in glaring colors. His heart raced even faster when he saw several Twolegs in its belly as it flashed past.

Did it eat them? Will it eat us?

"Lionblaze, now you go."

Summoning all his courage, Lionblaze stepped up beside Brambleclaw and launched himself forward. For a few heart-beats his world was full of the choking stink of the monster that had just passed by, and the black stuff scraped his pads as he raced across. Then he was standing on a narrow strip of grass between the Thunderpath and a prickly hedge, and Hollyleaf was pressing her pelt against his.

"We did it," she murmured.

"You know, Birchfall is right," Lionblaze whispered back, as his heartbeat gradually calmed. "If the old Thunderpath was worse than this, I wouldn't want to live near it, either!"

A moment later Hazeltail joined them, and then Birch-fall. A stream of monsters followed, leaving Brambleclaw marooned on the other side. Finally the last of the monsters disappeared, though Lionblaze could still hear their roaring in the air.

Brambleclaw bounded out onto the Thunderpath, racing for the other side. Another monster appeared in the distance, and Birchfall screeched, "Look out!" The Clan deputy didn't break stride. Long before the monster swept past, he was safely across, among his Clanmates.

"See, nothing to it." He flicked an ear dismissively. "Now let's keep going."

The wet leaves and debris under the branches of the hedge plastered themselves to Lionblaze's belly fur as he flattened himself to crawl into the next field. A strong scent flooded over him as he struggled to his paws on the other side. He felt as though he ought to remember it, but the memory slipped away from him like an elusive piece of prey.

"What are those?" Hazeltail asked nervously, angling her ears toward the center of the field.

Lionblaze peered through the snowflakes. Ahead of them, clustered together in small groups, were several huge animals with black-and-white pelts. As he examined them, one of them raised its head and let out a low, mournful sound.

"Cows!" Hollyleaf exclaimed, coming to stand beside her brother. "You remember, Lionblaze. We saw them on the way to the mountains."

"Cows—of course." Lionblaze's mind flew back to the time when they had encountered the old loner, Purdy. He had shown the cows to them as they passed a farm; his mother— no, *Squirrelflight*—had told them the massive creatures weren't dangerous, provided they didn't step on you.

"The cows are okay," Brambleclaw reassured Hazeltail, as he emerged from the hedge. "They won't attack us."

Hazeltail gave him a doubtful look, and as Brackenfur took the lead across the field, Lionblaze was inclined to share her concern.

The cows gathered around them, gazing down at them with huge liquid eyes. Lionblaze was far closer to their stony feet than he wanted to be, and he didn't like the looks of the big curved claws sticking out of their heads. Fighting techniques wouldn't be much use against animals this size. The cows bent down and sniffed at the cats' fur with hot, wet breath; Lionblaze thought he was going to choke on the strong reek of their scent, and their doleful moaning almost deafened him.

As Brackenfur led them calmly through the forest of legs, one of the long, swishing tails gave Hollyleaf a stinging slap in the face. She leaped backward, cannoning into Lionblaze.

"Fox dung!" she snapped.

Lionblaze steadied her until she got her balance.

"I'm starting to wonder if this is such a great adventure," she muttered, with a glance at Hazeltail, who nodded vigorously in agreement. "The journey to the mountains was much easier than this, even with the dogs in the barn."

And there was some point to that journey, Lionblaze added silently. *We weren't just looking for a cat I know isn't a murderer.*

Leaving the cows behind, the cats trekked through the snow toward the other side of the field. Lionblaze tasted the air for Sol's scent, but he couldn't pick up a trace of it.

I can't smell anything except cow, he grumbled silently. *I can barely find my own Clanmates!*

To his relief, he soon made out the next hedge, looming black against the swirling snow. The patrol plodded up to it and halted in the shelter of the thickly packed thorns.

"We'll never get through there!" Birchfall exclaimed, his

eyes wide with dismay. "We'll be ripped to pieces."

"No, we won't," Brambleclaw mewed. "We just need to look for a place where the hedge is thinner."

He began to lead the way along the bottom of the hedge. *I hope we don't have to go back,* Lionblaze thought miserably, trying to shake the snow off his pelt.

His heart fell even further when he made out the roar of another Thunderpath, somewhere on the other side of the hedge. "Not again!" he muttered.

At last Brambleclaw halted. "This might do." He pointed with his muzzle at a spot in the hedge where two arching branches left a tiny gap between them. "Lionblaze, will you give it a try?"

Lionblaze nodded and stepped forward, testing the width of the gap with his whiskers. Then he flattened himself to the ground and dragged himself forward. Thorns raked across his back, and he felt his fur snag on them as he struggled through to the other side and scrambled to his paws.

"It's okay," he called.

As Hollyleaf and Birchfall followed, Lionblaze looked out over a vast white landscape. The ground sloped gently down to the Thunderpath he had heard: It was much wider than the first one, with monsters roaring up and down in both directions. Glaring Twoleg lights edged it on both sides.

We'll never get across that! he thought despairingly.

A startled yowl distracted him; spinning around, he saw Hazeltail emerging from the hedge and pawing frantically at her muzzle.

"I've got a thorn in my nose!" she wailed.

"Let me see." Hollyleaf padded up to her. "Keep still, and stop clawing at it."

Hazeltail sat down, her eyes filled with pain. The thorn was a huge one, firmly embedded in her nose. Bright blood welled out around it.

Lionblaze watched his sister using the medicine cat skills she had learned long ago from Leafpool. Hollyleaf licked the area around the thorn and got a good grip on it with her teeth. Pulling firmly, she drew out the thorn and spat it onto the ground. More blood gushed out of Hazeltail's nose and splashed onto the snow.

"Ouch!" Hazeltail protested.

"We really need some water to rinse the blood away and close the wound," Hollyleaf meowed.

Lionblaze glanced around, ready to fetch some for her, but there was no sign of any streams. . . .

"Press your muzzle into the snow," Hollyleaf instructed Hazeltail. "That will stop the bleeding."

Blinking doubtfully, Hazeltail dipped her head and buried her nose in a patch of clean white snow. "It's very cold!" came a muffled meow.

"Stay there a bit longer," Hollyleaf urged. "I promise it will help."

I hope it will, Lionblaze thought, *or Hollyleaf could just be freezing Hazeltail's nose off.* He could see how worried his sister looked as she watched her Clanmate.

Hazeltail kept her face pressed into the snow for several

long moments, then lifted her head. Clumps of white clung to her face, making her look as if she were turning into Cloudtail, with his long, snow-colored pelt. "I-it doesn't h-hurt so much now," she reported through chattering teeth.

Hollyleaf bent forward to inspect the wound left by the thorn. Carefully she brushed the snow away with her paw. The injury looked like a neat, clean hole, almost sealed up already. "I think that did the trick," she meowed.

"Well done." Brambleclaw's rumbling purr sounded behind Hollyleaf. Lionblaze saw him blinking warmly at her with the same fatherly pride in his eyes that Smoky had shown when he was watching Hazeltail.

Hollyleaf turned away; Lionblaze knew how much she must want to respond, but she couldn't. Once Brambleclaw's approval had meant so much to all of them. But not anymore. *Whatever skills we have, they didn't come from you.*

The snow was starting to ease off, but the cloud covering the sky made it impossible to tell where the sun was. *Maybe it's nearly sunset,* Lionblaze thought, shivering. Straight ahead lay the huge Thunderpath, and beyond it the land stretched flat as far as they could see, unbroken except for a small copse in the middle of the openness. Beyond it, over to one side, Lionblaze made out a mass of twinkling lights.

"What's that?" he asked, pointing with his tail. "It looks as if a lot of stars have fallen down to earth."

"No, that's lots and lots of Twoleg nests, all together," Brackenfur explained.

Hazeltail gasped. "I didn't think there were as many

Twolegs as that in the whole world!"

"I hope we don't have to go near them," Birchfall added.

Hazeltail nodded, while Lionblaze muttered, "We're *not* kittypets." He felt as if he was trying to convince himself.

Brambleclaw and Brackenfur led the way down to the Thunderpath and crouched at the edge, one at each end of the line of cats. Monsters growled past, their blazing lights reflecting off the wet black surface.

"This time we'll all cross together, once there's a big enough gap," Brambleclaw decided. "When I say run, run as if a whole tribe of badgers was after you."

Lionblaze tried desperately to hide his fear as he waited for the deputy's signal. This was far worse than the Thunderpath they had crossed earlier. It seemed as if the stream of monsters would never end!

Next to him, Hazeltail was quivering too, and beyond her, Birchfall's fur was bristling as if he faced a horde of enemies. On Lionblaze's other side, Hollyleaf worked her claws furiously in the ground, her eyes fixed on Brambleclaw as she waited for the command to cross.

Why do I have to be brave all the time? Lionblaze asked himself miserably. *I shouldn't have to be, not now we know the prophecy wasn't about us. As far as we know, we could be kittypets!*

Horror and shame swept over him at the thought. He was so wrapped up in his dismay that he almost missed Brambleclaw's yowled signal: "Now!"

CHAPTER 6

Hollyleaf leaped forward with her Clanmates. As they reached the middle of the Thunderpath, she heard the roar of another monster in the distance, rapidly growing louder. Dazzling light angled across her as the huge creature seemed to leap out of nowhere. Hollyleaf ran even harder, pushing with her paws against the hard surface to drive herself faster and faster to the other side.

A terrified screech split the air. When Hollyleaf gained the safety of the grass beyond, she spun around to see Hazeltail rigid with fear, crouching in the middle of the Thunderpath in the path of the monster.

"No!" Hollyleaf yowled. "Hazeltail, run!"

Hazeltail was too panic-stricken to move. With a snarl of fury, Brambleclaw darted back onto the Thunderpath and grabbed her by the scruff, almost under the paws of the oncoming monster.

"It'll kill them both!" Birchfall wailed.

The monster's blazing eyebeams raked across the two warriors as Brambleclaw dragged his Clanmate across the black surface. Hazeltail's legs dangled at first, as if she were dead; then in a heartbeat she scrambled to her paws and fled. Brambleclaw dashed after her, the monster almost on top of his haunches. For a heartbeat, Hollyleaf was certain that he would be crushed under the monster's whirling paws; then it was roaring past them, and Brambleclaw was still running. Hazeltail collapsed onto the grass and Brambleclaw skidded to a halt beside her.

He let out a disgusted snort. "That was an example of how *not* to cross a Thunderpath."

"I'm sorry." Hazeltail sounded like a frightened kit. "I'm so sorry!"

The rest of the cats flopped down, panting. Even Lionblaze looked ruffled. *Sol must be braver than any of us realized,* Hollyleaf thought as she tried to calm her breathing. *He made this journey all by himself!*

Brackenfur padded up to Hazeltail and gave her a comforting lick. "It's okay," he murmured. "We all make mistakes."

"But I could have gotten Brambleclaw killed!" Hazeltail's eyes were wide with horror. "Thank you, Brambleclaw. You saved my life!"

The fury in Brambleclaw's eyes faded, and he blinked. "Just make sure I don't have to do it again."

"I promise you won't."

After allowing them a few moments to rest, Brambleclaw urged the patrol members to their paws again. "We can't stay here," he meowed. "Let's head for the trees. There might be some prey there."

The cats followed him as he struck out across the prickly

grass. The snow had stopped, but it still lay thickly on the ground, clogging Hollyleaf's paws as she limped after her Clan deputy. *My fur's so cold I think I'm turning into an ice cat,* she thought, trying to shake the cold white clumps off her feet. A cold wind was blowing into their faces, catching up the loose snow and flinging it into her eyes. "Mouse dung, that stings!" she muttered.

As they drew closer to the copse, she could see that the trees were shorter than the ones on ThunderClan territory, and twisted into strange shapes. They looked like the bushes on WindClan's moorland territory, bent double like hunched Twolegs. But as she tasted the air, Hollyleaf realized that the smells were more familiar than anything she had scented since she left the forest. The reek of the Thunderpath was dying away, and in its place she could pick up the scents of leaf and bark; water flooded her jaws as she recognized mouse, rabbit, and squirrel.

"We'll stay here to eat and rest," Brambleclaw announced when the cats reached the edge of the trees. "We won't find anywhere better to spend the night."

Birchfall's ears perked up, and Hollyleaf exchanged a hopeful glance with Lionblaze at the thought of not having to plod any farther through the snow.

"It can't be sunset yet," Brackenfur objected, eyeing the gray clouds that still shouldered their way across the sky.

"No, but we're all tired and cold," Brambleclaw replied. "And when we can't see the sun, we can't be sure that we're heading the right way to the sun-drown-place."

Brackenfur shrugged, agreeing, and all six cats headed deeper into the copse. There wasn't as much snow under the shelter of the trees, and Hollyleaf felt her paws starting to warm up. The ground was uneven, sloping roughly down to where a small stream trickled among the roots of the trees.

"Catch your prey and then rest," Brambleclaw ordered. Hollyleaf thought he sounded tense—perhaps he was unhappy about where their journey would take them next. *Does he know there's something dangerous up ahead?*

Brackenfur vanished into the undergrowth, and Lionblaze and Birchfall headed off together.

"Would you like to hunt with me?" Hollyleaf asked Hazeltail; her Clanmate still looked shocked by her panic at the Thunderpath.

"That would be great!" Hazeltail's ears flicked up. "Where should we start?"

"Right here's as good as anywhere."

Both she-cats tasted the air; Hollyleaf picked up a strong scent of squirrel, and a moment later she spotted one scuffling among the debris at the foot of a twisted thorn tree. Angling her ears, she pointed it out to Hazeltail. Her friend nodded, eyes gleaming.

Hollyleaf signaled to Hazeltail to stay where she was, then dropped into a hunter's crouch and worked her way in a wide circle around to the other side of the tree. She had carried out this hunting move so often in ThunderClan territory that it almost felt as if she were home again. Approaching the squirrel from the other side, she crept closer and closer, sliding her paws through the rough grass. When she thought she was close enough, she let out a fearsome yowl and leaped. Panicked, the squirrel darted away, only to run straight into Hazeltail's claws. Hazeltail dispatched it with a swift bite to the neck.

"Great catch!" Hollyleaf exclaimed.

"You set it up," Hazeltail mewed; she looked a lot more cheerful now.

As Hollyleaf padded over to her friend, Lionblaze came bounding out from behind a bramble thicket. "Birchfall and I got a really fat rabbit."

Birchfall appeared as he spoke, staggering as he dragged the rabbit between his forepaws. Dropping it with a gusty sigh, he stumbled into the low-growing branches of a hazel bush. A load of snow slid down and covered him; he emerged hissing with disgust, shaking snow from his pelt.

Hollyleaf couldn't suppress a small *mrrow* of laughter. "Watch out, or we'll have to call you Snowfall," she purred.

The four young cats dragged their prey into a sheltered hollow beside the stream, where the ground was covered with a drift of dead leaves. Soon Brackenfur appeared with another squirrel, and Brambleclaw with a couple of mice. As they ate, the warmth of their bodies spread throughout the hollow; with the branches of the bushes straggling overhead, Hollyleaf thought it almost felt like a den.

Full and comfortable, she swept her tongue around her jaws. "I could sleep for a moon," she announced drowsily.

"Fine," meowed Brambleclaw, "but we'd better set a watch."

"I'll go first," Lionblaze offered.

"Okay." Brambleclaw stretched his jaws in an enormous yawn. "Wake me when you're ready, and I'll take the next one."

As Hollyleaf settled down to sleep, the last thing she saw was her brother's golden tabby shape, his ears pricked as he stared through the trees.

A paw prodding into her side woke Hollyleaf. Blinking in confusion, she thought at first she was in the warriors' den. *But where's all the moss and bracken? And why can I hear running water?*

Then she remembered she was on the journey to the sun-drown-place, with Brambleclaw and the others. The ThunderClan camp lay a day's travel behind them, and everything here was new and strange.

Hazeltail was gazing down at her. "It's your watch," she mewed. "You're the last."

Hollyleaf staggered to her paws and arched her back in a stretch. Lionblaze, Birchfall, and Brackenfur were all curled up close by. "Where's Brambleclaw?" she yawned.

"He woke up while I was on watch," Hazeltail explained. "He said he was going to scout ahead." She settled herself comfortably among the leaves and wrapped her tail over her nose. "I'm going to get some more sleep while I can," she murmured.

Hollyleaf groomed the scraps of dead leaf out of her pelt, then padded the two or three paw steps to the edge of the stream. Before she bent to lap, she let her gaze travel over the trees that surrounded her; she could just make out their branches against the sky, which was beginning to fade from black to gray. Everything was quiet.

She took a long drink of the icy water; as she shook the drops from her whiskers, she heard a loud alarm call and caught a glimpse of a blackbird shooting upward. A moment later Brambleclaw came stalking through the trees, carrying a rabbit in his jaws.

"The hunting is good here," he remarked, dropping his prey at Hollyleaf's paws.

The rich scent of the fresh-kill made Hollyleaf's mouth water. "Should I catch some more?" she suggested. "One rabbit won't go far between six of us."

"Fine," Brambleclaw replied. "But don't go out of the copse. I'll wake the others. Next time, you can take first watch," he added. "But right now we need to keep moving."

Hollyleaf followed the stream, bounded up beside a small waterfall, and practically fell over a vole just before it could slip into its hole in the bank. Scratching earth over its limp body, she climbed the bank and stood tasting the air, her ears alert for the tiny sounds of prey. Soon she spotted a mouse nibbling seeds under a bush. Her paws lighter than air, Hollyleaf glided over the ground and broke the mouse's neck with a swift blow of her paw. Then she went back to collect the vole, and returned to the hollow with both pieces of fresh-kill.

She would have been proud of her hunting skills once, especially when she could show Brambleclaw how fast she could bring back prey. Now she couldn't even meet the deputy's gaze as he congratulated her. All her training, everything she thought she knew, was nothing but dust if she wasn't even a real Clan cat.

All six cats were awake. They ate quickly and followed Brambleclaw to the edge of the copse. "We're not far from Midnight's home now," he meowed. "Be careful, and keep close to me."

The land ahead was flat and empty, except for the Twoleg nests, with no shelter in sight. The sky was clear but for a few ragged, scudding clouds, and behind the patrol it shone milky-pale with dawn. The wind hit Hollyleaf in the face as soon as she left the shelter of the trees. It felt cold and sharp, with an unfamiliar tang, like the scent of frozen blood.

"It's going to blow my fur off!" she heard Birchfall complain.

Hollyleaf's eyes and mouth stung, and her pelt felt sticky. She screwed up her eyes and ducked her head, keeping close to Lionblaze as they trekked on and on across the brittle grass until, beneath the whistling of the wind, Hollyleaf could make out a dull roaring, like nothing she had ever heard before.

Suddenly Lionblaze halted; unable to stop in time, Hollyleaf bumped into him. Hissing in annoyance, she staggered as Hazeltail collided with her from behind. Raising her head, Hollyleaf saw that Brambleclaw and Brackenfur were standing side by side at the head of the patrol, staring at something. Hollyleaf padded up to them, the rest of the cats falling into a line alongside.

Great StarClan! They had reached the very edge of the land!

CHAPTER 7

Jayfeather stood in the clearing after the Sol patrol had left, sniffing the tang of snow on the dawn wind. He could hear rustling as several cats pushed their way through the branches of the warriors' den. There was a strange sense of tension among his Clanmates.

"Dawn patrol." Graystripe's voice came from close by Jayfeather. "Sandstorm, you can lead. Take Foxpaw and Squirrelflight with you. And take care along the WindClan border."

"Do I have to go with them?" Jayfeather heard the dismayed voice of Foxpaw. "I don't like WindClan."

"Shh." Ferncloud sounded shocked. "You know there's nothing to be frightened of anymore."

Jayfeather winced; it sounded as if most of the Clan believed that Sol was the murderer, and there was nothing more to worry about. *But they're wrong! They're completely wrong!*

"Foxpaw, you're my apprentice," Squirrelflight meowed with an edge of annoyance in her voice. "Of course you come with me. Or if you'd rather, you can go and search the elders for ticks."

"Uh . . . no, I guess I'll come."

"You'll be fine," Firestar assured the apprentice; Jayfeather hadn't heard him come down from the Highledge. "Who have we got for hunting patrols, Graystripe?"

"I thought I'd lead one," the gray warrior meowed. "I'll take Sorreltail and Mousewhisker." In a lower voice he added to Firestar, "If you or I do the border patrols, every cat will think there's something to be scared of."

"Good thinking," Firestar agreed.

"Dustpelt, will you lead another hunting patrol," Graystripe went on more loudly. "Cloudtail and Brightheart can go with you. Try the ShadowClan border, but remember what Brambleclaw said about being careful not to cross it."

"I wasn't born yesterday, thanks," Dustpelt snapped, irritation sparking from him.

"Should we take Icepaw?" Brightheart asked. "She doesn't get out much, now that Whitewing is in the nursery."

"Sure," Graystripe meowed. "Icepaw! Stop batting that bark around and come over here."

Jayfeather heard the scampering of paws and excited mews as the other apprentice bounded up. "You're going hunting with Dustpelt, Cloudtail, and Brightheart," Graystripe told them. "We're counting on you to bring back a lot of fresh-kill."

"I'm sure you will," Firestar assured her. "You're doing so well."

Jayfeather could feel the apprentice's happy pride as she padded over to join the senior warriors.

"It won't be long before we'll be holding another warrior ceremony," Firestar remarked to Graystripe.

Although his words sounded cheerful, Jayfeather picked up the doubt buzzing beneath them. He knew that his Clan leader's thoughts were with the patrol of Clanmates who were heading off to find Sol.

Did Sol really kill Ashfur? Was I right to send so many warriors to look for him? Will my Clan be vulnerable without them? Jayfeather could hear his leader's thoughts as clearly as if Firestar had spoken them aloud. To his surprise, he realized that Firestar still felt weak after the attack of greencough that had taken one of his nine lives. Lurking in his mind was the fear that the sickness would return.

And maybe he's right, Jayfeather thought. He could hear Spiderleg wheezing over by the nursery, as his kits tumbled all over him.

"That's right," their mother, Daisy, meowed. "You can practice your fighting moves with your father. Spiderleg, can't you be a scarier badger than that?"

"Badgers . . . don't"—Spiderleg was finding it hard to catch his breath—"get . . . greencough," he finished painfully.

Nearby Millie was grooming her three kits, breaking off every now and then to cough. "Don't stay out if it gets too cold," Graystripe warned her, bounding over to her side. "And you three kits—don't play too rough with your mother."

Jayfeather heard Blossomkit's high-pitched mew. "We won't."

"Right, the patrols can go now," Graystripe announced as

he returned. "Keep a good lookout, and report anything you see that's at all strange."

The stone hollow was quiet after all the patrols had left; the remaining warriors returned to their den to get out of the cold. Daisy and Millie rounded up the kits.

"It's time for some exercise," Daisy meowed. "Running around will keep you warm. Who can fetch me a twig from the thorn barrier and get back here first?"

"I can!" all the kits yowled together, and they pelted across the clearing. Jayfeather jumped back to avoid being knocked over and retreated into his den.

As soon as he set paw behind the bramble screen, the dust from churned-up moss and bracken hit him in the nose. "What's going on?" he asked, stifling a sneeze.

"I'm changing the bedding," Leafpool explained. "Can you come over here and roll up this moss, please?"

Jayfeather padded over, his paws sinking into the heaps of moss and bracken that Leafpool had already clawed together. "I think it's going to snow," he pointed out. "All the fresh stuff will be soaked with it."

"We can squeeze the water out," Leafpool replied. "This old bedding is disgusting. How can we ask sick cats to sleep in it?"

I'd rather sleep in it, Jayfeather thought, *than go outside to get freezing cold and wet.*

He was starting to push the piles together, half burying himself in dried fronds of fern and clumps of moss, when he heard a cat brush past the brambles. He picked up Firestar's scent above the dusty smell of the bedding.

"How are you, Leafpool?" Firestar meowed.

"Fine, thanks." Leafpool's tone was brisk, and she didn't stop raking out the remains of the bedding.

"There's something I want to ask you. . . ." Firestar's voice trailed off, and Jayfeather picked up strong waves of anxiety coming from him. He crouched among the ferns, trying not to sneeze again and hoping that whatever Firestar had to say didn't need to be said in private.

"Well?" Leafpool prompted.

"It's just—" Firestar broke off again.

Spit it out! Jayfeather urged him silently.

"I know it's not my place to tell a medicine cat how to speak with StarClan," Firestar meowed, sounding more awkward with every word. "But I wondered . . . have you thought of finding Ashfur in StarClan and asking him who killed him?"

What? Jayfeather nearly choked on a piece of moss.

For a long moment Leafpool was silent; when she spoke at last, her voice was as icy as leaf-bare snow. "It's not my choice whom I meet in StarClan. Our ancestors approach me; I cannot search them out. If Ashfur comes to me and wishes to talk, then I will listen."

It wasn't only shock and anger she felt as she answered Firestar, Jayfeather realized. There was something else behind that: Could it be . . . fear?

"I'm sorry," Firestar apologized. "I didn't think . . ."

"I'll do all I can, I promise," Leafpool added more gently.

"I want to know who killed Ashfur as much as you do."

So why am I finding it hard to believe her? Jayfeather asked himself.

Later that day, after Jayfeather had cleared out all the old bedding and delivered tansy to the cats still suffering from the after-effects of greencough, he padded over to the fresh-kill pile and chose a vole. A thick flurry of snow had swept across the clearing earlier, but now a weak ray of sunlight warmed his fur.

While he was eating, he scented Leafpool emerging from the elders' den with Mousefur and Longtail padding behind her.

"Jayfeather?" Leafpool called to him. "When you've finished there I want you to go out for a stroll with Mousefur and Longtail. It'll be the first time they've been out of the camp since the greencough."

Jayfeather gulped down a mouthful of vole. "Okay."

"We're not kits, you know," Mousefur grumbled. "We can be trusted to get to the lake and back without some cat guiding our paws."

"I know," Leafpool replied patiently. "But I want Jayfeather to look for herbs. We're getting very low on tansy. We could do with chervil and yarrow, too. There might still be something growing under the trees near the lake."

Mousefur's only response was an exaggerated sigh; Jayfeather pictured the skinny brown elder rolling her eyes.

Leafpool padded up to Jayfeather, close enough to brush his pelt. "I want you to take special care of Mousefur," she whispered. "Make sure she doesn't go too far, and check her breathing." More loudly she added, "Mousefur, maybe you and Longtail could help Jayfeather carry back any herbs he finds."

"I think we might just about manage that," Mousefur growled.

Jayfeather swallowed the last of his vole and led the way across the clearing and through the thorn tunnel. Mousefur followed him, guiding Longtail. The forest seemed very quiet now that most of the leaves had fallen from the trees. Jayfeather had to push his way through mounds of dead leaves on the ground and keep alert to avoid drifts of snow that still remained under the trees. The air tingled with frost.

The scent of water led him toward the lake. He kept one ear pricked for Mousefur and Longtail, who padded beside him, and sensed before Mousefur the branch that had fallen across their path.

"This way," he mewed to Longtail, laying his tail over the blind tabby's shoulders to guide him around the obstacle. "It's okay, you won't get your paws tangled."

"I think you see better than any of us." Mousefur didn't sound as grouchy as usual; she almost seemed impressed.

I wish I did, Jayfeather thought. *Right now I can't see far enough.* He wanted to know what had happened to the prophecy, and whether Rock knew anything about the secret Squirrelflight had revealed. Most of all, he wanted to know who his real parents were.

The trees thinned out and cold wind hit Jayfeather in the

face as the three cats neared the lake.

"You go off and do whatever you have to," Mousefur meowed. "Longtail and I are going to find a nice patch of sun to snooze in."

"Yes, there should be plenty of herbs—"

"Look," the skinny brown elder interrupted, "I know Leafpool only sent you along with us to be sure we made it to the lake without keeling over. You'll be lucky to find enough herbs to fill your own mouth this far into leaf-bare!"

"It's not like that," Jayfeather protested.

"Go on, we'll be fine," Longtail insisted.

"And if *you* need *our* help, just call," Mousefur added. "I might be a bit unsteady on my feet, but there's nothing wrong with my ears."

"Fine." Relieved to be free of his duty, Jayfeather pelted along the lakeshore until he reached the twisted tree roots where he had hidden the stick. The cold wind from the lake blew his fur the wrong way as he tugged it out and dragged it under an elder bush. Then he lay down with his paws resting on the scratches.

Come on, Rock. I need to talk to you.

Alarm trickled down his spine as he realized he might find himself back with the Ancient Clan. Something inside him was drawing him back—desire to see the friends he had made there, curiosity about how they had coped on the journey to the mountains—but he had to fight against it. He knew that the Ancient Clan sharpclaws couldn't help him now.

Jayfeather concentrated as hard as he could, trying to

picture the underground cave where Rock waited, but he could still feel grass under his belly and a twig tickling his ear.

"There's no need for that," a voice behind him rumbled. "The stick isn't the answer to everything."

Jayfeather's eyes flew open, and he realized that he could see. He was still under the elder bush; turning, he saw Rock standing behind him, almost transparent against the grass and trees. Rock crept under the bush to join Jayfeather, his hairless body smelling of stone and the endless dark of the tunnels.

Jayfeather suppressed a shiver. "Did you know all along that Squirrelflight was lying to us?" he demanded.

Rock's bulging, sightless eyes turned toward him. "The answers lie within your own Clan," he replied, "if you can find them."

"That's no answer," Jayfeather mewed irritably. "I need your help!"

"I cannot give the kind of help you want," Rock warned him.

"Then what about the prophecy? If we're not Firestar's kin—"

"Make your own future, Jayfeather," the spirit-cat interrupted. "Don't expect it to be dropped at your paws like a piece of fresh-kill."

Every hair on Jayfeather's pelt prickled with annoyance. How was he supposed to make his own future if no cat would *tell* him anything? He dug his claws into the earth.

"Jayfeather!" Mousefur's voice came from the edge of the lake. "Jayfeather!"

Darkness slammed down over Jayfeather's vision. The scent of Rock vanished.

"Jayfeather, where are you?"

He crawled out from under the elder bush, kicking dead leaves and debris over the stick. He would have to come back later and hide it properly.

"What are you doing under there?" Mousefur asked, padding up to him. "We're ready to go back now. We wondered if you have any herbs for us to carry."

"Er . . . no, I haven't found any," Jayfeather stammered.

Mousefur sighed. "Maybe you're not looking in the right place. Last I heard, herbs don't grow well under elder bushes. There's a huge clump of tansy just behind you," she added.

Jayfeather's pelt grew hot with embarrassment. He should have taken time to grab a few herbs before he tried to speak with Rock. He had been so intent on finding the spirit-cat that he hadn't even noticed the sharp scent of the tansy.

"Thanks," he muttered.

He was aware of Mousefur's irritation as he and the skinny elder picked the herbs together. There wasn't enough for Jayfeather to need help carrying it, and he scented no other herbs as all three cats headed back toward the camp.

"Is that all?" Leafpool asked; she was waiting outside the den when Jayfeather arrived with the tansy. "What about the yarrow and chervil I asked for?"

"I couldn't find any," Jayfeather mumbled around the bunch of stems.

Leafpool snorted. "Didn't look, more likely. Jayfeather, I

didn't send you out there to waste time. You have to do what you're supposed to!" Her voice deepened to a snarl. "If every cat did that, there wouldn't be any problems."

Who put ants in her fur? Jayfeather wondered. It wasn't like Leafpool to be so short-tempered. For once he didn't want to argue with her, so he just headed for the den to put the tansy away.

Leafpool brushed past him. "Leave that! I'll do it." She almost snatched the herbs out of his jaws; fury rolled off her as she carried them into the cave.

Jayfeather backed out of the den and padded across to the fresh-kill pile. But he had eaten earlier, and even a freshly caught mouse couldn't tempt him. There were pangs in his belly sharper than hunger: Already he missed Lionblaze and Hollyleaf more than he would have thought possible. They had never been separated for this long before.

In the dream Midnight had said that the patrol was chasing wild geese and Rock had told him that the answers lay inside ThunderClan itself. But Jayfeather didn't know how he was going to find them on his own. What kind of power was it, to walk in other cats' dreams, when you woke up still blind? There was no way he was going to find out anything when he was trapped in darkness at every step.

CHAPTER 8

❧

Lionblaze forgot to breathe as he stared across the vast gray water. Sharp, cold wind buffeted his fur; he felt as though it could sweep him off his paws at any moment and hurl him down the cliffs to the rocks far below.

"This way," Brambleclaw ordered. He led the patrol along the edge of the cliff to a narrow gully lined with scrubby grass. Lionblaze gasped in relief as he stepped out of the wind.

"Midnight the badger lives near here," Brambleclaw went on, once the patrol was clustered around him at the bottom of the gully.

"How did you know where to find her?" Hollyleaf asked curiously.

"We didn't," the Clan deputy admitted. "We didn't even know we were looking for a badger." He twitched his tail-tip. "I found Midnight's den by falling into it."

Hazeltail's eyes stretched wide. "Were you hurt?"

"Weren't you scared of Midnight?" Birchfall added.

Brambleclaw flicked one ear as if he were trying to get rid of a fly. "This isn't the time for stories. We have to keep going."

He led his patrol through the gully, every so often climbing the slope to pop his head out and see how far along the cliff they were. Lionblaze and the others stayed crouching in the dip, listening to the blast of wind overhead.

At last Brambleclaw beckoned them with his tail to join him at the top. "We're almost there," he told them. "Follow me closely."

Lionblaze and the rest of the patrol flattened their bellies to the short, bristly grass as they padded after Brambleclaw toward the edge of the cliff.

Is he going to jump over? Lionblaze wondered, as each paw step took them closer to the sheer drop.

But just before the land vanished from under their paws, Brambleclaw jumped down into a much deeper, narrower gully, sloping steeply through a dip in the cliffs. Brackenfur and the other cats followed him, with Lionblaze bringing up the rear. The sharp stones that covered the bottom of the gully dug into his pads or skidded from under him, nearly carrying him off his paws. Birchfall slipped, crashing into Hazeltail, and Brackenfur had to block the two younger cats before they hurtled down any farther.

"Thanks!" Birchfall gasped.

"Just watch where you're putting your paws," Brackenfur mewed.

The gully led down to a rocky shore, the sand almost completely covered with pebbles. Lionblaze had seen waves on the lake when the wind blew hard, but these waves were much bigger, crashing onto the rocks with spurts of foam. Hazeltail stared at them, wide-eyed, so scared that she could scarcely put one paw in front of another.

"I hate this," Hollyleaf muttered, backing away toward the cliff face. "My fur's getting all wet and sticky." She turned her head to give her shoulder a lick. "Yuck!"

Lionblaze felt the same stickiness in his pelt; his nose wrinkled at the unfamiliar tang in the air. *This is no place for cats,* he told himself.

With a wave of his tail, Brambleclaw jumped onto a rocky outcrop and instantly disappeared under the edge of the cliff.

"Where did he go?" Birchfall asked, bewildered.

Lionblaze spotted the deputy's amber eyes glowing from the shadows at the bottom of the cliff.

"Come on!" Brambleclaw called.

Reluctantly the rest of the patrol followed him beneath the jagged, teethlike rocks and into a low-roofed cave. Lionblaze gazed around at the pale sandy walls and the floor strewn with large, smooth stones. High above them, gray light slanted down from a small hole in the roof.

"Is that where you fell?" Lionblaze guessed, remembering how Brambleclaw had said he first found Midnight.

Brambleclaw nodded. "The cave was full of water, and I nearly drowned. Your mother saved my life."

A cold pang swept through Lionblaze, harsh as the booming water outside. *She's not my mother.* The words almost forced themselves out of his jaws, but he bit them back. If Brambleclaw didn't know, this wasn't the place to tell him.

Hollyleaf hadn't heard the exchange between Lionblaze and Brambleclaw. She was sniffing curiously around the cave, padding over to where the floor sloped upward at the back, turning soft and sandy. Some branches were tucked in it at the top.

"What are those doing there?" Hollyleaf asked.

"This is Midnight's den," Brambleclaw explained.

For the first time Lionblaze noticed the scent of badger underlying the smell of the water. His neck fur bristled, but he made himself relax. The scent was stale, and besides, Brambleclaw had told them that Midnight was friendly to cats.

"Will she come and find us?" Hazeltail mewed nervously.

"I hope she does," Hollyleaf replied. "Jayfeather told us all about her. She knows so much."

Her green eyes flashed at Lionblaze from the shadows. *Is that what she really wants?* he wondered. *Does she think Midnight can tell us who our parents are?*

"Midnight isn't here." Brambleclaw sounded disappointed. "And her scent is stale, so there's no point in waiting for her. She's been gone for several days. We'd better get back."

When they emerged from the cave, the water had risen even farther up the shore. A wave crashed onto the rocks and licked over the pebbles; Lionblaze jumped back as water swirled around his paws before retreating with a rattling hiss.

"Back to the gully, quickly," Brambleclaw ordered.

He took the lead as the patrol scrambled back across the rocks. Lionblaze staggered as water foamed around him as high as his belly fur, but he managed to stay on his paws and drag himself to safety, up the steep slope of the gully where Brambleclaw and Hazeltail had already taken refuge.

Hollyleaf dragged herself after him, her black pelt soaked and flattened to her sides from the spray.

"I hate this place!" she spat as she tried to shake herself dry. "Midnight must be mouse-brained to live here."

A sharp cry of alarm cut through her words. As Birchfall tried to leap up into the gully, a huge wave crashed over him. Hollyleaf stretched out a paw, but before she could grab him, the wave swept him back out of reach. Lionblaze caught a glimpse of him struggling in the gray water, his jaws wide in a yowl of terror, before his head went under.

"He'll drown!" Hollyleaf screeched.

At the same instant a dark shadow flashed over Lionblaze's head; Brambleclaw had leaped down into the water and was swimming strongly to where Birchfall had disappeared. Brackenfur, still precariously balanced on the rocks below, launched himself after the Clan deputy.

Lionblaze bunched his muscles to leap down and join them, only to find Hollyleaf blocking his way. "You can't," she rasped. "More cats will die!"

"There must be something we can do," Lionblaze meowed desperately.

Glancing around, he saw a straggling bush growing between the rocks a couple of tail-lengths above them.

"Hazeltail," he called. "Can you break a branch off that bush?"

The young she-cat was staring at the sun-drown water, frozen with horror as she watched her Clanmates struggling in the waves. She started as Lionblaze spoke, then turned and began tugging at the longest branch.

Lionblaze scrambled up to help her. To his relief the bush was dry; the branch cracked away from the main trunk, so that he and Hazeltail could claw it free and drag it down the gully to the edge of the water. Lionblaze let out a gasp of relief when he saw that Birchfall had resurfaced; Brambleclaw had his teeth fastened in the younger warrior's neck fur, while Brackenfur swam on his other side, trying to push him toward the cliff.

Dropping the branch at the bottom of the gully, Lionblaze beckoned his sister with his tail. "Grab the end," he directed. "Sink your teeth and claws in, and don't let go."

Hollyleaf obeyed, pushing the branch so that it stuck out into the water as far as it would go. Lionblaze and Hazeltail crouched beside her, all three cats hanging on to the end of the branch, trying to keep it steady among the crashing waves. More water swirled around them.

We can't keep this up for long, Lionblaze thought grimly. *We'll be swept away as well.*

He narrowed his eyes to peer across the roaring water and spotted his Clanmates bob above the surface as a wave drove them inshore. The short leaf-bare day was drawing to an end; the sinking sun flooded the surface of the water with scarlet so that the cats' heads were just shadows bobbing in a sea of blood.

The wave swept them closer still; Brackenfur reached out and managed to sink the claws of one paw into the end of the branch. "Grab it!" he yowled to Birchfall.

The young tom looked frozen with fear, his eyes staring vacantly, but as Brambleclaw let go his scruff, he clutched wildly at the branch and dragged himself along it until he could scramble onto the rocks at the bottom of the gully. Lionblaze let go of his end of the branch to haul Birchfall's limp body up higher; water streamed from his pelt and he vomited up a huge mouthful of liquid.

Brackenfur clawed his way along the branch to safety, and stood shaking the water out of his ginger fur. "Brambleclaw!" he yowled. "Brambleclaw, where are you?"

Cold horror flooded over Lionblaze as he realized that the deputy had disappeared. *He can't have drowned. What will we do without him?*

Then he spotted Brambleclaw's dark head break the surface a couple of fox-lengths away from the end of the branch. He was trying to swim, but his efforts were much feebler now.

Waves were tugging at Hollyleaf and Hazeltail as they clung to the branch. Hollyleaf's tail streamed out into the water.

"Get back, but don't let go!" Lionblaze ordered, his heart pounding as hard as the waves on the shore. Then he raised his voice to a yowl. "Brambleclaw! Over here!"

The deputy heard him and seemed to find new strength. Struggling to keep afloat, he let the next wave carry him up to the branch, then struck out toward it. He managed to fasten his claws into it and haul himself out before the retreating wave swept him back again.

"Fox dung!" he spat, standing on the stones of the gully

with water eddying around his paws. "I thought I was on my way to StarClan for sure."

The cats began to retreat from the hungry water. Brambleclaw scrambled up the gully until he stood beside Birchfall, who was still slumped on the stones with his eyes closed. Only his heaving chest showed that he was alive.

Brambleclaw prodded him with one paw. "Birchfall?"

The young tabby's eyes opened and he let out a shuddering sigh. "I might have drowned." His voice shook with fear. "I might never have seen Whitewing again—or our kits!"

"But you're fine now." Brambleclaw's voice rasped in his throat, rubbed raw by the bitter water. "It's time we started moving."

The Clan deputy didn't allow his patrol to rest until they reached the shallow gully that ran along the top of the cliff. Out of the wind, with the waves booming against the cliffs below, they could collapse and try to groom the water out of their fur. Lionblaze winced at the bitter taste of salt, and saw that his Clanmates were making faces as they licked.

"Thanks, Brambleclaw and Brackenfur," Birchfall mumbled. "You saved my life back there."

Brackenfur touched the young tom's shoulder with the tip of his tail. "It's all over, and thank StarClan, no cat died. Brambleclaw, what do you think we should do next, seeing that Midnight isn't here?"

Brambleclaw accepted his Clanmate's tactful change of subject with a flick of his ears. "We'll keep looking for Sol.

There'll be cats in the Twolegplace who have seen him."

The hair on Brackenfur's neck lifted at the mention of Sol's name. "Yes, he had a look of kittypet about him."

That cat's no kittypet. Lionblaze didn't dare say the words out loud, in case some cat asked him how he knew so much about Sol. He exchanged a doubtful glance with Hollyleaf. He wasn't sure that he wanted to visit the Twolegplace, and he could tell that his sister felt the same. Hazeltail was looking nervous, too, but it was Birchfall who spoke what they were all thinking.

"Do we have to go so close to Twolegs? It's not right for Clan cats."

"We've got no choice," Brambleclaw growled. "We're not going back to ThunderClan without Sol!"

I wonder whether Brambleclaw would be so keen to hunt down Ashfur's killer if he knew that Ashfur had tried to destroy Squirrelflight? Lionblaze thought.

But Brambleclaw also didn't know that Squirrelflight had lied to him. *She let him believe he was our father. Would he be so loyal to her if he found out the truth?*

Lionblaze shook his head, trying to clear it of all the lies. He had to fix his mind on the one thing he could control: being the best warrior for ThunderClan that he could possibly be. *I know I can still fight without being hurt. I just need a chance to prove it. . . .*

"What's the matter?" Hollyleaf muttered into his ear. "Have you heard something?" Her black pelt was bristling.

Lionblaze realized that he had sunk his claws into the

ground as if he were about to attack. "No, it's okay," he replied, forcing himself to relax. "I was just thinking about Sol."

Brambleclaw hadn't heard their exchange. "This is what we're going to do," he announced. "There's nowhere for cats to live near the edge of the cliff, and nowhere to catch prey. So we'll have to head for the outskirts of the Twolegplace and look for any cats who might have seen Sol."

"So long as we *stay* on the outskirts," Hollyleaf muttered.

The patrol slunk cautiously over the edge of the gully and made for the red blur of Twoleg nests on the far side of the open stretch of cliff. Lionblaze felt thankful that the noise of crashing water was dying away behind him, though the wind still thrust at him.

The sun had vanished, swallowed up by the sun-drown-place, and shadows were stretching across the grass. Lionblaze's stomach growled, and he remembered that he hadn't had so much as a sniff of fresh-kill since early that morning.

"We'll look for prey as soon as we get to the Twolegplace," Brackenfur promised when he heard the rumble of Lionblaze's belly.

And what sort of prey will we find there? Lionblaze wondered. *I'm not eating kittypet food!*

As they drew closer to the Twoleg nests, Lionblaze grew more and more anxious; he could tell from his Clanmates' bristling fur and flickering glances that they felt the same. Something black swooped down on them with a high-pitched chittering sound; Lionblaze threw himself to the ground and rolled over, his teeth bared and his claws extended, in time to spot a bat fluttering away and vanishing into the growing darkness.

Birchfall suppressed a small *mrrow* of laughter. "I wish you'd caught it," he mewed. "Then we might all have had a bite to eat."

"A pretty small bite for the six of us," Lionblaze growled.

Lights were beginning to appear in the Twoleg nests, and the sky above them was lit by an eerie orange glow. Lionblaze wrinkled his nose against the strange scents and felt his neck fur bristle at the harsh, unfamiliar sounds.

Beside him, Hollyleaf's eyes were glowing and her tail was fluffed out to twice its size. Even Brambleclaw and Brackenfur were moving more cautiously as the huge Twoleg dens loomed up ahead.

"I don't think Sol lives with Twolegs," Brambleclaw meowed, "so we're more likely to find him—or cats who have seen him—near the edge."

He led the way across a stretch of softer grass, and halted in front of a tall fence made out of flat strips of wood. Lionblaze tasted the air; among many smells he couldn't identify, he picked up the scents of Twoleg and dog.

"Each Twoleg nest has a small piece of territory attached to it," Brambleclaw explained. "It's enclosed by a fence made of wood or red stones. I think that's the Twoleg way of marking their borders."

"How does he know so much about it?" Hollyleaf muttered suspiciously.

"There was a Twolegplace in the old forest," Brackenfur

told her. "Right up against our territory. Don't you remember the story of how Firestar wandered away from his Twolegs and met Graystripe in the forest?"

Hollyleaf shrugged. "I guess."

Brambleclaw led the way alongside the fence, toward a gap that was flooded by orange light. Before they reached it, loud barking exploded from the other side of the fence; Lionblaze jumped as two dogs slammed their bodies against the flimsy wood. He exchanged an alarmed glance with Hollyleaf. *What if the fence gives way?*

"Run!" Brambleclaw yowled.

The patrol bolted along the fence and swerved through the gap. As soon as he set paw on the hard black stone at the end of the fence, Lionblaze was engulfed in a beam of piercing white light. A monster was charging straight for them!

Some cat let out a screech of terror. For a heartbeat, Lionblaze spotted his Clanmates outlined against the glare from the monster's eyes. Then he leaped back to the side of the Thunderpath, landing with a thump in the middle of some thorns.

When he dared to look up, the monster had slowed down and was turning into a gap behind one of the Twoleg nests. Sharp orange light shone down from tall stone trees standing in lines along both sides of the Thunderpath. Just opposite, Lionblaze spotted Birchfall sprawled at the foot of the fence, and Brackenfur balanced on top of it, his back arched and his tail straight up and bristling. Hollyleaf and Brambleclaw emerged side by side from the deep shadows under a tree.

"Birchfall?" Lionblaze called softly. "Are you okay?"

To his relief, the young tabby tom scrambled to his paws and gave his whiskers a shake. "I've got all the warriors in StarClan inside my head," he meowed. "That thing was *fierce!*"

The thorns where Lionblaze had landed grew beside another gap in the Twoleg fence. His belly lurched when he spotted another monster in front of the Twoleg den. Then his breathing steadied and his heart slowed down as he realized that this monster was asleep.

On the other side of the gap, a shiny Twoleg thing had tipped over, spilling out a pile of rubbish. Lionblaze's nose wrinkled at the scent of crow-food. Then the heap heaved and Hazeltail emerged from the middle of it, shaking debris from her pelt.

"I knocked the thing over," she complained, "and now I'm covered with all this yucky stuff."

Lionblaze padded across to help her. Clinging to her pelt were scraps of something that smelled like a plant, but they were cold and slimy, like herbs picked and left in the rain to rot. Cautiously he stretched out a paw to knock them off; Hollyleaf and Brambleclaw bounded up to help.

"They taste vile." Hazeltail licked her shoulder and swiped her tongue around her lips as if she was trying to get rid of a disgusting taste. "I'd rather eat fox dung."

Brackenfur padded up and stood at the edge of the Thunderpath, keeping watch for more monsters. His fur still hadn't settled down; Lionblaze noticed that Brambleclaw looked just as ruffled as he helped Hazeltail clean her pelt.

Seeing the senior warriors' confidence shaken made Lion-blaze feel a bit braver. "There can't have been dogs in the Twolegplace near the old forest," he murmured to Hollyleaf. "Even Brambleclaw was surprised."

"I wonder what else will surprise us," Hollyleaf responded.

Meanwhile Birchfall had crossed the Thunderpath and was nosing around in the heap of debris that had fallen out of the shiny Twoleg thing. "Hey, look at this!" he meowed. "Brambleclaw, can we eat it?"

Lionblaze wasn't sure at first what his Clanmate was drag-ging out of the pile of rubbish. It was smooth and pale and smelled a little like fresh-kill, though it was no kind of prey that he had ever seen before. The stink of Twolegs clung to it as well; Lionblaze knew he didn't want to eat it, but at the same time his belly growled at the thought of food.

Brambleclaw sniffed the thing carefully and nibbled a bit from one side. "It tastes a bit like blackbird," he reported after a moment. "I don't think it will hurt us to eat it, and we need food."

"I guess that means he doesn't think we'll catch much prey around here," Hollyleaf whispered into Lionblaze's ear.

Brambleclaw clawed the Twoleg prey into fair shares for each cat. Birchfall checked the rubbish again, but he didn't find any more prey.

"This isn't bad," Lionblaze mumbled to Hollyleaf around a mouthful of the stuff, "if you ignore the scent of Twolegs."

Hollyleaf was crouched over her share, eating it in neat, rapid bites. "Huh! Give me a good plump vole any day."

With the edge taken off his hunger, Lionblaze felt stronger, but as Brambleclaw led them farther into the Twolegplace, he started to feel trapped. The red stone nests reared up on either side, closer than the walls of the hollow and higher than the trees in the forest. His pads ached from walking on the hard stone. *How can any cat live here?*

The orange glare from the stone trees cast the cats' shadows huge and wavering on the wall beside them as they slunk along the edge of the Thunderpath. Suddenly Hollyleaf stiffened, flicking out her tail to touch Brambleclaw on the shoulder. "There's something up ahead!" she hissed.

Lionblaze froze as Brambleclaw raised his tail for the patrol to halt. He half expected the roar of another monster, but nothing broke the silence except for the patter of approaching paws.

Hazeltail drew closer to his side; Lionblaze could feel her pelt quivering. "What if it's a dog?" she murmured.

"Then we fight it." Lionblaze flexed his claws.

He relaxed with a sigh as a small black-and-white cat appeared from around the next corner. It halted and stared at the patrol in horror, its back arched and every hair on its pelt standing on end.

Almost immediately the newcomer started to back away, its terrified gaze still fixed on the forest cats. Before it could turn and flee, Brambleclaw took a single pace forward.

"We're not going to hurt you," he called, lifting one forepaw to show his claws were sheathed. "We just want to talk to you."

"That's what *he* said!" The little cat looked almost frightened out of its fur. "And look what happened!"

Before Brambleclaw could ask what it meant, the black-and-white cat spun and fled back around the corner where it came from. Brambleclaw launched himself after it, with the whole patrol hard on his paws, but when they rounded the corner, the Thunderpath was empty. Nothing moved under the harsh orange light.

"Mouse dung!" Brambleclaw spoke through gritted teeth.

"What in the name of StarClan was he talking about?" Brackenfur asked, looking mystified.

Lionblaze exchanged a glance with Hollyleaf. He could see she shared the idea that had instantly flashed into his mind: *Sol!*

"I wonder who 'he' is," Brambleclaw mused aloud, his ears twitching as he surveyed the silent Thunderpath. "Could it be Sol, do you think?"

"I bet a moon of dawn patrols it is!" Birchfall mewed excitedly.

"We don't look anything like Sol," Brambleclaw continued, his tone thoughtful. "But we're strangers, just as Sol must have been."

"And what happened?" Hazeltail shivered. "From the way that cat behaved, it must have been something bad."

No cat replied. Lionblaze's belly fluttered. His Clanmates were looking edgy, their eyes wide with fear, as if they expected to find Sol under the next fallen leaf.

Finally Brambleclaw broke the silence. "It's too late to go

on looking now. Let's get some rest and start a proper search in the morning."

He led the way back around the corner and along the Thunderpath, past the fence where the dogs had tried to attack. Everything was quiet now, though the scent of dog was still strong; Lionblaze slid out his claws, ready to rip them along the vicious creatures' pelts. But there was no sound from behind the fence. Eventually they reached the stretch of soft grass and trees they had crossed on their way to the Twolegplace.

Lionblaze and Hollyleaf settled into a makeshift den among the roots of one of the trees; the rest of the patrol found places nearby.

"I'm so tired my paws could drop off," Hollyleaf mumbled, stretching her jaws in a huge yawn.

"Mine, too." Lionblaze had been afraid that his worries and the strangeness of their surroundings would keep him awake, but when his aching body curled up among the dead leaves, he felt exhaustion pressing on him like a heavy pelt. As he drifted into sleep, he could still hear the distant roaring of the sun-drown-place.

CHAPTER 9

Jayfeather woke when a cold breeze ruffled his fur. "We need more bedding in here," he grumbled to himself as he scrambled out of his bare nest. "It's as drafty as sleeping on top of the ridge in WindClan territory!"

He lifted his head to sniff the scents of early morning. There was a strong tang of herbs in the air; as Jayfeather bent his head to give his pelt a quick grooming, he located Leafpool in front of the storage cave. She was making up leaf wraps of tansy, and beside her there was a fresh mixture of juniper berries and daisy leaves to ease the pain of Mousefur's aching joints.

"Should I take those for you?" Jayfeather offered, padding up behind his mentor.

Leafpool jumped. "Don't creep up on me like that! You frightened me out of my fur." She carefully patted the herbs together, then added, "No, I can manage. I want you to go over to the nursery and check every cat there, and the bedding, for fleas. I spotted Briarkit scratching yesterday."

Jayfeather turned away, resentment seething beneath his skin. "Am I a medicine cat or an apprentice?" he muttered, loud enough for Leafpool to hear, but the she-cat did not respond.

He called a greeting as he pushed through the brambles into the nursery, and then he started to check for fleas.

"Oh, thank you, Jayfeather," Millie meowed. "I'm sure I've a couple in my pelt somewhere. It'll be such a relief to get rid of them."

"You need a change of bedding," Jayfeather told her, tracking down a flea in Briarkit's neck fur and spearing it with a claw. "I'll get Foxpaw and Icepaw to deal with it." *Unless Leafpool expects me to do that as well,* he added grumpily to himself.

"Right, you're done," he told Briarkit. "Blossomkit, I'll—"

He broke off with a startled yelp as claws stabbed into his tail. Wrenching it free, he spun around and picked up the scent of Toadkit.

"I pretended your tail was a mouse," the little tom told him proudly. "I caught it, too!"

Jayfeather bared his teeth. "Just keep your claws to yourself!"

"There's no need for that," Daisy protested. "He was only playing."

Jayfeather bit back a sharp retort and went to check Blossomkit and Bumblekit for fleas. Toadkit wriggled away from Daisy and bounced up to him, interest sparking from him as Jayfeather parted Blossomkit's pelt.

"Can you eat fleas?" he mewed. "Do they taste yucky?"

"Why don't you try one and find out?" Jayfeather suggested.

"You be a flea and I'll eat you!" Blossomkit squeaked, pulling away from Jayfeather and leaping on top of Toadkit. Jayfeather staggered as the two wrestling kits piled into him.

"Stop that!" he snarled. "Blossomkit, do you want your fleas fixed or don't you?"

The little tortoiseshell kit instantly broke away from the play fight and stood quietly in front of Jayfeather again. Toadkit pushed up close to them; Jayfeather could feel the kit's breath on his ear.

"Do you like being a medicine cat?" Toadkit asked. "I wouldn't want to do it if you only get to look for fleas."

StarClan, give me patience! "That's not all medicine cats do," Jayfeather replied through clenched teeth. "We have to know about herbs and—"

"Do you think I'd be a good medicine cat?" Toadkit persisted. "I'd be good at finding herbs. I can scent out anything. Can I be a medicine cat? Can I?"

"You'll be lucky to make warrior if you don't shut up," Jayfeather muttered.

"Daisy!" Toadkit let out a wail as he scampered away through the bracken that covered the floor of the nursery. "Daisy, Jayfeather was mean to me!"

"Honestly, Jayfeather!" Daisy's irritated voice came from the other side of the den. "I think you've got ants in your fur this morning. You should go away and come back later when you can be more pleasant."

Jayfeather ignored her, and went on searching for fleas in gloomy silence. He wanted Hollyleaf and Lionblaze to come back. They belonged together—especially now, when they had no idea where they had been born, who their parents were, or why Squirrelflight had lied to them for so long.

When Jayfeather finally left the nursery, he paused for a few heartbeats, letting out a long sigh as the weak rays of the leaf-bare sun soaked into his fur. A paw step behind him and the scent of his Clan leader made him turn.

"Good morning, Jayfeather," Firestar meowed. There was concern in his voice. "Are you okay? Any problems?"

"I'm fine." Jayfeather dipped his head awkwardly. He didn't want to tell his leader that all his problems came from his Clanmates. After all, Firestar had never lied to him, as far as he knew.

He felt a pang of regret that he didn't share his Clan leader's blood after all. His respect for the flame-colored tom had nothing to do with the prophecy, and everything to do with the way Firestar led his Clan, even losing a life to greencough for their sake.

"Good," Firestar murmured. Jayfeather sensed that the Clan leader didn't entirely believe him. "You know, you can always tell me if there's anything bothering you."

"Yes . . . fine." Jayfeather felt even more uncomfortable. *Firestar, you don't want to know the things I could tell you!*

To his relief, Firestar padded off toward the fresh-kill pile. Left alone at the edge of the hollow, Jayfeather scanned the clearing. He located Mousefur and Longtail sharing tongues outside their den, and heard the skinny brown elder complain,

"Leaf-bare was never as cold as this in the old forest."

Outside the apprentice den, Foxpaw and Icepaw were trying out a new fighting move; Jayfeather reminded himself to tell them about the nursery bedding. Cloudtail and Brightheart were padding toward the thorn tunnel. "I think we should try for prey near the old Twoleg nest," Cloudtail suggested.

"Stupid furball!" Brightheart's voice was full of affection. "We scared off all the prey when the cats with greencough stayed there."

"There's been time for them to come back. . . ." Their friendly bickering died away as they left the camp.

In spite of the feeble warmth of the sun, cold pierced Jayfeather through and through. He had never felt so alone. Rock had told him that the answers lay with his Clanmates. *But what if I don't have Clanmates?*

"Do I have to do this?" Jayfeather protested as he emerged from the trees into the mossy clearing where the apprentices trained. "It's a waste of time when we have to look for herbs."

"The herbs won't run away," Leafpool responded tartly. "You know as well as I do that *every* cat gets basic fight training, even medicine cats."

Jayfeather bit back another complaint. He hated learning to fight, because he knew he would never be any good at it. But there was no point in arguing with Leafpool; she always seemed to be in a bad mood these days.

"Right," Leafpool began, leading the way into the center of

the clearing. "Let's start with some defensive moves. I'm going to attack you, and I want you to dodge to one side and get a blow in as I pass you."

"Okay," Jayfeather muttered. "The sooner we start, the— *ow!*"

While he was speaking, Leafpool leaped past him and landed a stinging blow on his ear.

"I wasn't ready!" he yowled.

"You think a ShadowClan warrior is going to give you any warning? You have to be alert *all the time*, Jayfeather."

On the last words, Leafpool sprang at him again. This time Jayfeather was more prepared; he jumped to one side and swiped at where he thought his mentor was, but his paw barely grazed her pelt.

"Better," Leafpool admitted. "But not good enough. Let's do it again."

Jayfeather managed to land a blow or two, but his paws felt heavy and clumsy, and his senses weren't as sharp as usual. Even though his mentor kept her blows light and her claws sheathed, he began to feel battered and exhausted. Finally, as he leaped aside, he lost his balance on a rough patch of ground and collapsed, paws flailing, without touching Leafpool at all.

"I'm over here, Jayfeather." Leafpool's voice came from the opposite side of the clearing. "Honestly, you've got no more fighting sense than a baby rabbit! I don't think you're trying at all."

"I am!" Jayfeather spat.

"I know what your problem is." His mentor's voice was

cold. "You expect Lionblaze and Hollyleaf to protect you, so you can't be bothered to learn to defend yourself."

"That's not true!"

"I think it is. But Lionblaze and Hollyleaf won't always be around. They're not around now. You need to be able to look after yourself."

Jayfeather didn't reply. *She doesn't understand,* he thought mutinously, as he scrambled up and tried to shake the moss out of his pelt. *It's not the same for her and Squirrelflight. If they were so close, she'd know Squirrelflight lied about us being her kits. Leafpool would never have let her do something like that. I wonder what she'd do if she knew what her sister was really like?*

Jayfeather limped back to the medicine cats' den through the damp scents of twilight. His legs ached and his head throbbed where he had grazed it colliding with a tree. He was too exhausted to look for any herbs to treat himself. "I hope Leafpool's happy," he grumbled as he curled up in his nest. "I'll probably be too stiff to do anything tomorrow."

He closed his eyes—and then opened them a heartbeat later to find himself in deep, lush forest, with starlight dancing on the leaves. His aches and pains had vanished and a warm, scent-laden breeze soothed his fur. Leaf-bare in the waking forest was only a distant memory.

A narrow path wound ahead of him through arching clumps of fern. Jayfeather began to follow it, ears pricked as he glanced around for any familiar cats. He could hear rustling in the undergrowth on either side and he caught glimpses of furry pelts, as if there were cats all around him, but none of them emerged to greet him.

"Who's there?" he called out. "Yellowfang? Bluestar? Can any cat hear me?"

There was no reply. Becoming more frustrated with every paw step, Jayfeather followed the track until it reached a clearing covered with soft grass. A small pool was at the center, reflecting the stars. There were still no cats in sight.

"Where are you?" Jayfeather wailed, stepping out into the open. "Why won't you talk to me?"

Fronds of bracken dipped and rustled at the opposite side of the clearing, and Spottedleaf appeared. Jayfeather's rush of relief died when he saw how warily she was regarding him, her tail kinked high over her back.

"Spottedleaf . . . ?" he began uncertainly.

"We can't give you the answers you're seeking," the tortoiseshell she-cat interrupted. "Go back to your Clan. That is where the truth lies."

"But—you *must* tell me more than that!" Jayfeather begged. "Did StarClan know all along that Squirrelflight and Brambleclaw weren't our parents?"

Anger flared in Spottedleaf's amber eyes. "When will you realize that StarClan doesn't know everything?" she snarled, lashing her tail. "Sometimes we have questions, too! Sometimes we're just cats, like you!"

Without giving Jayfeather a chance to reply, she whipped around and vanished into the ferns.

Jayfeather sprang forward to pursue her, only to feel the

ground give way beneath his paws. He jolted awake in his own den, opening his eyes onto darkness. He stretched his jaws wide, longing to wail like a kit abandoned by its mother.

They've all left me: Hollyleaf and Lionblaze, all the rest of my Clan-mates, and now StarClan as well. I'm completely alone.

Even his belief in the prophecy, which had once seemed to promise so much, had been built on a lie.

I may as well be blind in my sleep, too. What am I going to do now?

CHAPTER 10

Hollyleaf shifted uneasily in the makeshift nest under the tree roots. Beside her, Lionblaze's ears and tail were twitching, as if his sleep was disturbed by dark dreams. Hollyleaf wasn't sure how he managed to sleep at all, so close to the Twolegplace. Even in the middle of the night, monsters growled, Twolegs shrieked, and dogs barked.

I've never been in such a noisy place, she thought, trying to find a comfortable spot among the dead leaves. *How do the kittypets stand it?*

Toward dawn she slipped into a fitful doze, only to be woken again as Lionblaze scrambled out of the nest. Yawning hugely, Hollyleaf followed him.

The orange glow in the sky above the Twolegplace had given way to the pale light of dawn; the roofs of the Twoleg dens were black outlines against the sky. A cold breeze was blowing, and every blade of grass was edged with frost. Brambleclaw and the other Clan cats stood gazing across the grass to the outlying dens of the Twolegplace.

"We need to go back into the Twolegplace," Brambleclaw began, "and look for that cat we met last night. He has to explain what he meant."

Hazeltail's whiskers twitched nervously. "They obviously don't like strangers around here."

Birchfall touched her ear with his nose. "There are enough of us here to outnumber a few jumpy kittypets!"

Hollyleaf exchanged a glance with her brother. "I think we're on Sol's trail," Lionblaze murmured, clawing at the grass. "I'll bet you the fattest vole on the fresh-kill pile that he's the reason that black-and-white cat was so scared of us."

Hollyleaf nodded. Curiosity gave her more confidence as she followed Brambleclaw back across the grass and into the gap between the Twoleg nests. She could see that her Clanmates felt the same, padding along with bright eyes and tails held high. *We're warriors!* she reminded herself. *We don't have to be afraid of anything.*

The breeze strengthened to a bitterly cold wind that swept through the world of hard, red stone as the patrol padded deeper into the Twolegplace. There was barely enough light to make out the right direction, and no sun to melt the ice that covered the puddles beside the Thunderpath.

"I'm so thirsty!" Hollyleaf whimpered. "My tongue feels like a mouse's pelt."

While Brambleclaw paused to taste the air, she crouched down beside one of the puddles and touched the ice with her tongue, grateful for the tingling freshness.

"Come on," the Clan deputy meowed. "This way."

Hollyleaf tried to jump up, only to stop with a strangled cry of dismay. Her tongue had frozen to the ice; a sharp pain shot through it as she tried to wrench herself free.

"What's the matter?" Lionblaze asked.

"My tongue . . ." Hollyleaf could hardly get the words out. "It'th thtuck!"

Lionblaze snorted as he suppressed a *mrrow* of laughter. Birchfall stooped down until he was nose to nose with Hollyleaf; irritation swelled inside her when she saw amusement dancing in his eyes.

"It'th not funny!" she mumbled as clearly as she could with her tongue plastered to the ice.

"Stand back." Brackenfur's calm voice came from behind Hollyleaf. "Let me have a look." He leaned beside Birchfall, gently shouldering the younger cat out of the way. "Well, you're certainly stuck," he went on. Hollyleaf could tell that he was struggling not to laugh, too. "I suppose we could break off the ice. Then you'd have to carry it until it melts."

"Hey, you've discovered a new way to fetch water for the elders!" Hazeltail put in.

Her pelt itching with frustration, Hollyleaf tried again to wrench her tongue free, only getting another stab of pain for her efforts. "It hurt-th! Do thomething!"

She pictured herself crouched on the hard ground with her tongue stretched out, and suddenly she felt laughter bubbling up inside her. *I guess I do look pretty funny.* She couldn't remember the last time she had found anything to laugh at.

"Hollyleaf." Brambleclaw was at her side; his amber eyes sparkled, but his voice was gentle as he touched his nose to her ear. "Breathe out hard. Your warm breath should melt the ice."

He crouched down next to her and let out a long breath at the patch of ice where she was stuck. A trickle of warmth spread through Hollyleaf; it was good to be cared for. But the warm feeling turned to ice as Brambleclaw broke off to add, "You know, you're just like your mother. She was always getting stuck in things, too."

She's not my mother!

Hollyleaf let out a fierce breath and tugged at her tongue again, gasping as it came free at last. The frozen puddle was glossy with melted water where Brambleclaw had breathed on it. But she wasn't going to thank him. "Right," she meowed, straightening up. "I'm okay. Let's—"

She broke off as a low growl sounded behind her. Every cat spun around. A couple of fox-lengths away, a line of dogs was standing on the other side of the Thunderpath, blocking their way. There were five of them, all different shapes, from a small, rough-coated brown-and-white one to a huge black-and-tan brute. Vicious hatred glared out of their eyes.

Hollyleaf heard Hazeltail whisper, "Oh, no . . ."

"Back away." Brambleclaw's voice was quiet but steady. "Don't turn and run."

Fear froze Hollyleaf's paws to the ground harder than the ice had trapped her tongue. She couldn't move. It was too easy to imagine the dogs' teeth ripping into her pelt, her blood streaming out. . . .

She staggered as Lionblaze gave her a hard nudge. "Come on!" he hissed.

Suddenly Hollyleaf found she could move again. All her

instincts were screeching at her to turn and flee, but she forced herself to retreat paw step by paw step; the line of dogs advanced, keeping the same distance between them and the cats. The big black-and-tan dog opened its jaws to show dripping yellow teeth. A drawn-out snarl came from its throat.

Not much farther, Hollyleaf told herself. *Once we're away from this Twolegplace, we can climb the trees.*

Then every hair on her pelt stood on end as she heard another growl from behind. Glancing over her shoulder, she saw that two more dogs had appeared, cutting off their escape route. They looked as vicious as the first dogs, with gaping jaws and lolling tongues.

"We're fresh-kill," Birchfall murmured.

At the same instant, the first set of dogs leaped forward.

"Run!" Brambleclaw yowled.

His hind legs pumping, he headed for a narrow gap with Twoleg nests on one side and a high wooden fence on the other. Hollyleaf and the rest of her Clanmates raced after him, with the dogs yelping at their paws. Hollyleaf had never been more terrified in her life, not even when Ashfur had held them prisoner on the burning cliff top. She expected sharp yellow teeth to pierce her flank at any moment. Her paws felt as if they were on fire from running on the hard stone, and her breath tore from her chest.

Lionblaze was pelting along beside her, his fur fluffed up so he looked twice his normal size. Hollyleaf knew that he wanted to turn and face the dogs. *No! They'll tear you apart!*

"Don't leave me!" she gasped between panting breaths.

Yet more dogs appeared ahead of them, crowding down the narrow alley. Brambleclaw swerved through another gap onto a path between thick hedges; his Clanmates stayed hard on his paws, but the dogs were catching up.

Hollyleaf realized that their enemies were running steadily, not putting out all their strength, as they waited for the cats to tire so they could be picked off easily. *That's how Crowfeather taught Breezepaw to catch rabbits, when we were on the journey to the mountains,* she recalled. *But we're the prey now!*

Suddenly Brambleclaw halted and squeezed through a narrow gap at the foot of the hedge, his hind paws scrabbling as he forced his body through. "Come on!" he panted. "They can't follow us through here!"

Brackenfur shoved Hazeltail through next, then Birchfall. "Hollyleaf—quick!" he meowed.

Hollyleaf didn't want to leave her brother, but there was no time to argue. She pushed her way through the prickly bushes; Brackenfur followed and Lionblaze scrambled after him, so quickly that he left some of his golden fur behind on the thorns.

"Mangy crow-food eaters!" he yowled back through the hedge.

Her chest heaving, Hollyleaf glanced around. She was standing on a smooth stretch of bright green grass, surrounded by low-growing bushes. At one side was a Twoleg den; all the doors and windows were shut, and there was no sign of any Twolegs.

"Maybe now we can—" Brambleclaw began.

He broke off, and Hollyleaf stared in horror as she saw that the hedge stopped near the wall of the Twoleg nest, leaving just a low wooden fence to fill the gap. The dogs were leaping effortlessly over the fence, and bounding across the grass toward the patrol. Their eyes were gleaming with hunger and scorn, and their growls had changed to joyful yelping.

They're enjoying this! Hollyleaf realized as she turned to flee.

Suddenly the door to the den burst open. A Twoleg rushed out, screeching and shaking a long stick at the dogs. Another Twoleg followed with a yowl, something shiny in his hands. He swung it toward the dogs; water cascaded out of it, but the dogs just shook it off.

The far side of the Twoleg territory was also bordered by a wooden fence. Brambleclaw raced toward it, waving his tail for the others to follow. Breathlessly they scrambled up the slippery wood. Hazeltail started to slip back; Brackenfur gave her a shove from below, and Brambleclaw grabbed her scruff to haul her the rest of the way. Hollyleaf realized as she clambered to safety that her paws had left smears of blood on the wood.

For a few heartbeats the dogs jostled one another at the foot of the fence, whining and scrabbling as they tried to reach the cats. Brambleclaw gazed down at them, his back arched and his fur bristling with a mixture of terror and anger. "Leave us alone, flea-pelts!" he hissed.

Suddenly the huge black-and-tan dog broke away from the rest and raced back across the grass to the low part of the fence near the den. The rest of the pack streamed after him and began jumping, back into the alley.

"They're coming to get us!" Birchfall gasped.

"We can't stay here." Brambleclaw's voice was tense. "Follow me."

He leaped down as the first of the dogs appeared around the corner, and took off down the alley, his tail streaming out behind him and his belly fur brushing the stones. Hollyleaf and the others pelted after him.

We can't keep this up much longer! Hollyleaf thought.

Brambleclaw swerved into another gap and immediately halted. The rest of the patrol piled into his back. Hollyleaf gazed ahead, terror pounding through her. This alley was a dead end. Straight in front of them was a high wall built of the same red stone as the Twoleg nests, and almost as tall. *We'll never climb that!*

Brambleclaw leaped up at the wall but fell back, his straining paws nowhere near the top. Hollyleaf knew that Hazeltail would never manage it. And the hedge on either side looked too thick to get through.

"You go on," Hazeltail mewed bravely, even though she was shaking with fear. "Don't worry about me."

Brackenfur touched her shoulder with his tail-tip. "We can't keep going," he murmured. "We're all too exhausted. There's nowhere left to go."

"What about there?" Hollyleaf had spotted a group of tall, shiny objects like very smooth boulders, standing together in one corner. Scents of Twoleg rubbish hung around them. She gestured toward them with her tail. "We can hide."

Brackenfur glanced around for other cover, but there was

none. He nodded swiftly. "Go!"

Brambleclaw guided Hazeltail into hiding and shoved Birchfall after her into the narrow space beside the shiny boulders. Hollyleaf and Lionblaze followed, leaving Brackenfur and Brambleclaw to crouch on the outskirts of the space, their ears and whiskers twitching as they waited for the dogs to appear.

Hollyleaf was crowded up against Hazeltail; she could feel her Clanmate trembling and hear the whimpers of terror that she tried to stifle.

"I know I'll never see my kits," Birchfall murmured. "I just hope Whitewing is okay."

Pounding footsteps and loud yelping announced that the dogs had reached the alley. Hollyleaf could smell their stink even over the scents of the Twoleg rubbish. *I guess that means they'll be able to scent us, too.*

Then she felt Lionblaze pushing his way past her, toward the opening where Brackenfur and Brambleclaw were crouching. With a shock like a rush of icy water, she realized that he was going out to fight the dogs.

"No! You can't!" she hissed.

"I can!" Lionblaze insisted, turning glowing amber eyes on her. "I won't get hurt, you know I won't."

He pushed his way to the edge of the silver boulder, squeezing past Brambleclaw and Brackenfur, and ignoring the Clan deputy when he asked what in StarClan's name Lionblaze thought he was doing.

"Lionblaze, no!" Hollyleaf screeched. "Stop!"

CHAPTER 11

❧

Lionblaze heard his sister screeching, but he ignored it. He *knew*, with every hair on his pelt, that he could fight the dogs. He could feel his blood pumping hot and fierce through his veins, and every fighting move he had ever learned was at his claw-tips.

The dogs seemed to approach in slow motion. He had all the time he needed to watch the drool waving from their lips and their paws pounding over the ground. His gaze flicked from one to another.

I'll take out that black-and-tan one first. When it falls, it'll trip the thin gray one, and the white one too, if I'm lucky. Then I'll go for that yapping little horror with the black paws....

He was dimly aware that his Clanmates were yowling behind him, but he still didn't respond. *This is* my *fight. I'm the only one who can save them!*

Lionblaze braced himself to leap, spotting the surprise in the leading dog's yellow eyes. "You didn't think a cat would turn and fight!" he taunted. "Well, now's your chance to learn!"

His last words were drowned by a shattering crash; he glanced behind to see that one of the silver boulders had toppled over, sending a silver disc spinning across the ground. It rolled into the pack of dogs; they swerved to avoid it, the rush of their attack halted.

To Lionblaze's surprise, a dark brown tabby she-cat popped up from behind the fallen boulder, closer to the fence than the terrified Clan cats were. "Quick!" she meowed. "Help me push this one over."

She reared up, resting her forepaws against the side of the next shiny boulder. Brambleclaw sprang up beside her, and together they pushed. The boulder crashed over like the other one, the silver disc on top of it spinning away. Twoleg rubbish spilled out from inside.

The dogs were yelping in frustration, scrabbling at the boulders in their efforts to get around them and sink their jaws into their prey.

"Come on!" the strange she-cat ordered. "It won't hold them off for long."

She dove through a narrow gap at the bottom of the hedge that had been hidden by the silver boulders, and the patrol followed her at full pelt, racing across a wide stretch of pale gray stone.

Renewed barking made Lionblaze glance over his shoulder as he fled. The small brown-and-white dog and the thin gray one had pushed their way through the gap and were bounding across the expanse of stone.

"They're coming!" he gasped.

"This way!" the she-cat mewed tersely. She led them down a narrow path between two high fences and halted beside a small hole with jagged edges. "Through there."

Birchfall bundled through first, followed by Hazeltail and Hollyleaf, and Lionblaze squeezed through after them. He let out a yowl of alarm as he crashed hind legs over head into brittle grass. Head spinning, he staggered to his paws to see Brambleclaw already beside him and the strange she-cat scrambling through the hole.

"Brackenfur?" he asked anxiously.

A screech answered him as the golden brown tom hauled himself through the fence, paws flailing as he tugged at his tail. "Fox dung!" he gasped, collapsing on the grass. "That flea-ridden brute bit me!"

Brambleclaw gave his Clanmate's tail a quick sniff; Lionblaze could see that some of Brackenfur's fur had been stripped off, but there didn't seem to be any blood.

"You'll be okay," the deputy decided. "Where now?"

The she-cat's reply was drowned out by a flurry of barking. The fence creaked and bent as the dogs flung themselves against it.

In the Twoleg nests around them, lights began to appear in the dark holes in the walls. Lionblaze heard a Twoleg shouting angrily, but the dogs went on barking and pounding at the fence. His belly lurched when he saw that the small brown-and-white dog had stuck its head through the gap and the wood around it was starting to splinter.

The dark tabby she-cat darted forward and slashed her claws at the dog's nose. Yelping, it pulled back.

"That'll teach you," she meowed with satisfaction. To the

cats she added, "Quick, follow me!"

They raced after her to the entrance of a Twoleg nest. Brambleclaw skidded to a halt.

"We can't go in there!" he protested. "It's a Twoleg nest."

"Fine!" the tabby snapped. "Stay out here and get eaten." She squeezed through the skinny gap at the side of the flat piece of wood blocking the opening and disappeared.

Brambleclaw and the rest of the patrol exchanged confused glances; then the deputy shrugged and raised his tail, signaling his Clanmates to follow. Lionblaze paused to look back across the grass, and saw that the small dog was still scrabbling at the gap. It had managed to get its shoulders and one paw through the hole.

Lionblaze felt his fur bristle and grow hot again as he braced himself to fight. He could almost taste the blood and hear the terrified yelping as his claws ripped into his enemies' pelts.

Then he heard a crash and a Twoleg shouting; it sounded much closer than before. The dogs' fierce barking turned to frightened yelps; the little dog struggled backward to free itself from the hole in the fence, then vanished.

Lionblaze's fur lay flat again as the noise died away. He started to feel disappointed that he hadn't managed to try out his battle skills against the dogs, then jumped as Brackenfur nudged him.

"Come on," mewed the ginger tom, angling his ears toward the entrance to the nest. "What are you waiting for?"

The other cats had already gone inside. Lionblaze pushed his way through the gap, with Brackenfur close behind him.

He found himself in a small, straight-sided den; his Clan-mates huddled together in the middle, casting nervous glances around them. He tasted the air: There was a strong scent of cat, but only a very faint, stale trace of Twoleg.

"That's unusual," he began. "Why . . . ?"

The brown tabby she-cat paid no attention to him. "This way," she mewed briskly. "Since you're here, you may as well meet the others."

She led the way through an archway into a larger den. Light streamed into it from a long slit in the wall. As Lionblaze padded hesitantly forward, the smell of cats grew overpoweringly strong; it was almost like coming back into the camp after a patrol in the forest. Hollyleaf kept close to him, their pelts brushing, while Brambleclaw and Brackenfur stayed on the outside of the group. Lionblaze knew they were ready to protect the younger cats if they needed to. *And so am I. If we have to fight our way out, I'm ready.*

Brambleclaw signaled for his patrol to halt in the center of the den. A broad-shouldered gray tom sat on a shallow ledge just below the gap in the wall, while a she-cat with a flecked brown pelt was curled up on something like a soft boulder in bright Twoleg colors. Four kits suckled at her belly. On the other side of the den, another cat was barely visible as he peered out from underneath some wooden Twoleg thing.

Lionblaze caught his breath as he recognized the black-and-white tom sitting on top of another soft-looking boulder. He was the cat they had met the night before, who had run away from them.

"I'm Jingo," the tabby she-cat announced, before Lionblaze could speak. "Over there is Hussar"—she waved her tail at the gray tom sitting on the ledge—"and the queen with kits is Speckle."

"Hi, there," Hussar meowed, with a lazy wave of his tail. Speckle just twitched her ears; she looked wary, as if she was afraid the newcomers might harm her kits.

"Over there's Pod," the tabby she-cat went on. The cat underneath the wooden structure blinked at them. "Come out, Pod, no cat is going to hurt you. And I think you've already met Fritz."

As she finished speaking, she leaped up onto the squashy boulder beside the black-and-white tom. He stared at the Clan cats, wide-eyed, and didn't speak.

Brambleclaw stepped forward. "Who did you think we were?" he asked Fritz. When the tom didn't reply, he turned to Jingo. "When we met him last night he seemed to think we were connected with another cat, one who talked to you but ended up causing you trouble. Do you know who that was?"

"We don't trust strangers around here anymore." Jingo's voice was solemn. "Not since Sol."

Lionblaze felt a jolt in his belly. *We were right! Sol has been here!*

"Sol?" Brackenfur's neck fur rippled. "You know him, then?"

Jingo nodded. "He came here last leaf-bare, but no cat knows where from. He lived on the edge of Twolegplace for a while, then when the weather turned colder he moved into this abandoned Twoleg nest and invited some other cats without housefolk to join him."

"I was one of the first." Pod emerged from underneath the wooden thing, revealing himself to be a scrawny brown tom, his muzzle gray with age. "Speckle and Fritz came with me."

"And I joined later, with Hussar," Jingo went on. "I heard about the community of cats that had made a home for themselves, and it sounded like a good idea."

"Did Sol act like he was your leader?" Lionblaze asked. The patch-pelted loner had tried to take over ShadowClan; maybe that wasn't the first time he'd been in control of a group of cats.

"Yes, did he ever tell you to believe anything in particular?" Hollyleaf added.

Jingo looked puzzled. "Not exactly. Only that we could live however we wanted to, because that's what we deserved. Life was good, he said. . . ."

"Life was not good!" Pod snapped. He sat down and lifted a hind leg to scratch behind his ear. "We had to do whatever Sol told us to, like bring him food and feathers for his nest. And he scared the little cats by telling them that they'd die without him."

"It wasn't that bad!" Jingo protested. "You're just thinking of what happened later."

"And why wouldn't I?" Pod stopped scratching to glare at her. "That mouse-brained idiot nearly got us all killed!"

Fritz nodded vigorously, giving his whiskers a nervous twitch, but still didn't speak.

Lionblaze glanced at Hollyleaf; she looked as shocked as

he felt, her eyes glittering and her claws working on the hard Twoleg floor. *When Sol had lived in the forest, he never wanted cats to die,* Lionblaze thought. *Is Hollyleaf wondering if he really could have killed Ashfur?*

He was distracted by Speckle's four kits, who left their mother and scrambled down, one after another, from the soft boulder. Speckle sat up, watching nervously as the biggest of the four, a tom with a flecked brown pelt like his mother, bounced up to Brambleclaw.

"I'm Frisk," he announced. "What's your name? Are you coming to live here?"

Brambleclaw shook his head. "We're just passing through. I'm Brambleclaw," he added, addressing all the cats. He went on to introduce the rest of the patrol. "Thanks for helping us," he finished, dipping his head to Jingo. "The dogs would have ripped us to pieces without you."

"We'd help any cat in danger from those dogs," Jingo responded. "And you're welcome to stay as long as you like."

"Thank you." Brambleclaw bowed again. "Now, can you tell us what Sol did?"

Jingo settled herself on the soft boulder, tucking her paws underneath her chest. Hussar sprang down lightly from the ledge and padded over to sit beside Pod. For the first time, Lionblaze noticed that he had a long scar along his side, where the fur hadn't grown back. Glancing around, he noticed that the others had signs of injury, too: One of Fritz's ears was torn, Pod's muzzle was scarred, and the tip of Jingo's tail was missing.

"These cats have been fighting hard," he muttered to Hollyleaf.

He sat down on the hard Twoleg floor, longing for the grass of the forest or the soft moss of his nest in the warriors' den. Hollyleaf sat beside him, her claws still flexing restlessly, and their Clanmates gathered around.

"Sol didn't cause any trouble at first," Jingo began. "He kept to himself and stayed out of kittypet territory."

"He was the first cat to find this abandoned Twoleg den," Hussar put in. "He started inviting other cats to live here with him—cats without housefolk of their own, to start with."

"He said he wanted to keep us all safe," Speckle mewed, creeping a bit closer to the edge of the soft boulder.

Pod snorted. "More likely he wanted us to do things for him. Lazy lump. He had an easy life here."

"That's not fair!" Speckle protested. "We're safer here than wandering about in the open, sleeping under bushes."

"So what happened next?" Brambleclaw prompted, before Pod could continue the argument.

"More and more cats joined him here." Jingo took up the story again. "I lived with housefolk then, but I liked the sound of what Sol was doing, so I came to give it a try."

"I joined soon after her," Hussar added. "I liked the freedom. I could come and go without waiting for my housefolk to let me in and out."

"And catching our own prey was better than eating that dry Twoleg food," meowed Jingo.

"But why did the Twolegs let you stay?" Brackenfur asked

curiously. "Don't they want this nest?"

"Obviously not," Hussar replied with a shrug.

"Twoleg kits used to come here now and again," Jingo explained. "They never tried to chase us out, though, and they don't come anymore."

"Sol told us what to do if adult Twolegs came," Speckle explained. "There's a dark space right at the top of the nest, with a pointed roof. Sol told us to hide up there."

"They did come once or twice." Fritz spoke for the first time. "So we all hid."

"And the Twolegs never found us," Speckle added proudly.

Even though he had good reasons for not trusting Sol, Lionblaze realized that what he had done here wasn't all bad. The cats had shelter here and support from one another. He wasn't sure why kittypets would want to come, but it was certainly better for loners than trying to survive in the open through the harsh moons of leaf-bare. It was like a Twoleg-place version of a Clan.

"So what went wrong?" he meowed.

"Can't you guess?" Jingo replied bleakly. "The dogs found us. They couldn't get in here, because most of them are too big to get through that narrow gap at the entrance."

"A little one pushed his way in, once." Hussar extended his claws, the beginnings of a snarl in his throat. "He didn't try it twice."

"But they lay in wait for us whenever we came out," Fritz continued with a shudder. "And then they chased us."

"Clumsy, oafish brutes!" The tip of Pod's tail twitched.

"If we did manage to hunt, they stole our prey," Jingo continued. "And they killed Flower." Her eyes clouded with sorrow and guilt. "She was a beautiful young cat. Her housefolk had the den next to mine, and I persuaded her to come here."

She bowed her head, and Fritz nudged her shoulder.

"So how did Sol react to that?" Brackenfur asked, after a moment's respectful silence.

"He told us we needed to show the dogs that we had the right to live here." Hussar took up the story. "So he made a plan. He found a small unused den beside that stretch of stone where the monsters sleep. He said if we could lure the dogs in there they wouldn't be able to get away while we fought them."

Fritz shuddered, letting out a frightened mewling sound, and sank his claws into the soft boulder underneath. Jingo pressed up against him comfortingly.

"It didn't work?" Brambleclaw guessed, though Lionblaze already knew the answer to that question.

"What do you think?" Pod spat.

"Sol showed us how to fight," Jingo went on. "We spent a lot of time training—"

"Which meant there wasn't enough time to hunt," Pod interrupted. "My belly thought my throat was clawed out."

Jingo ignored the interruption. "Then Sol said we were ready. He chose a tom called Pepper to go out and catch some prey, and then get the dogs to chase him to the small den. We were all lying in wait, ready to follow the dogs in and fight them. Sol was with us, and when—"

"Why are you talking about that piece of fox dung?" A new voice spoke from behind Lionblaze, who glanced over his shoulder to see a black tom standing in the entrance to the den. His fluffed-out fur made him look twice his size, and his tail whipped from side to side.

Lionblaze's muscles tensed; a cat who looked like that was ready to attack. But then he realized that the black tom's anger wasn't directed toward him or his Clanmates.

"It's okay, Jet," Jingo replied. "These cats asked about—"

"It's not okay," Jet hissed. "It'll never be okay. I don't want to *think* about that cat ever again!" Still bristling, he whirled around and disappeared.

"I'm sorry if we've upset him . . ." Hazeltail mewed, gazing after the black tom.

"It's not your fault," Jingo assured her. "Pepper was his littermate, and now he can't bear for any cat to mention Sol."

"Pepper died?" Hollyleaf asked.

Hussar nodded, his eyes clouding. "Before we ever made it into the den. We were hiding on the roof of one of the other dens, and we saw Pepper streaking across the stone space with the dogs on his tail. I've never heard such a racket as they were making! Then we heard this awful shriek—"

Lionblaze's paws tingled as a yowl sounded from outside the den, almost as if Hussar's words had called it up. It was followed by an outbreak of barking, drawing rapidly closer. All the Clan cats crouched closer to the ground, frozen by fear, their claws scraping on the hard floor. Pod whisked back underneath the Twoleg thing, while Speckle gestured urgently with her tail. "Kits—come here quickly." The four kits scrambled back onto the soft boulder, and Speckle circled them protectively with her legs and tail.

Only Jingo and Hussar seemed calm. Jingo meowed, "They can't get in."

Lionblaze jumped at the sound of scrabbling just outside the den. Hussar leaped to his paws, only to relax a moment later as a ginger-and-white she-cat poked her head through the entrance; a mouse dangled limply from her jaws. Just behind her, a young gray tabby tom peered over her shoulder.

"Oh, it's you, Merry." Hussar arched his back in a stretch, then sat down again. "And Chirp. Come and meet these new cats."

Merry took a step into the den, her green gaze flickering from one Clan cat to another. Then she shook her head, mumbled something inaudible around the mouthful of prey, and retreated; Lionblaze heard the sound of her paw steps fading.

Chirp, however, padded into the den and sat down. But he stayed near the door and kept casting nervous glances over his shoulder.

"We're all jumpy since the fight with the dogs," Hussar commented.

"And can you blame us?" Pod emerged again and gave his chest fur a few licks, as if trying to pretend he hadn't shot so quickly into hiding.

"Tell us what happened," Lionblaze prompted. "After you heard the shriek . . ."

"We all raced into the den," Jingo went on, digging her claws into the soft boulder. "Pepper was already dead. The dogs were tossing his body about. We attacked, but there were too many of them, and they were too big and fierce for us. Every cat was injured. The dogs ripped Frosty to pieces, and Jester was so badly wounded that he died after we brought him back here."

Lionblaze felt sick. Sol had made a terrible mistake. Every cat could have died in that single battle, and it was obvious the dogs were still causing trouble.

"Ask me if Sol joined in the fight," Pod rasped.

Brambleclaw cocked his ears. "Well?"

"He didn't raise a single claw to help us," the old tom growled. "He wasn't even there to watch! He just strolled in here while we were licking our wounds."

"What happened then?" Brackenfur asked.

Jingo twitched her ears. "If he'd admitted he was wrong, it might have been different. But he insisted that we were the ones who decided to fight, and it wasn't his fault that we lost. Then he sat down and started washing himself, and asked Jet to bring him some food."

"If I hadn't held Jet back, he might have ripped Sol to pieces," Hussar added.

Birchfall's whiskers twitched. "I wish he had!"

Jingo looked surprised, but she didn't ask the young warrior what he meant. "So we asked Sol to leave," she meowed. "We would have driven him out if we had to, but he just told us we were making a mistake and went without a fight." She sighed. "Maybe he was right. I don't know anymore."

"No, she was right," Birchfall muttered into Lionblaze's ear. "They're better off without Sol, and so are we!"

Jingo rose to her paws, yawned and stretched, then sat down again. "That's all we can tell you. Now tell us what you know."

Brambleclaw and Brackenfur exchanged a glance; it was Brackenfur who spoke first. "Sol came to the forest where we live," he began. "It must have been after he left you. He went to stay with ShadowClan—a group of cats who live near us—and he persuaded them to stop believing in the warrior code and the spirits of their warrior ancestors."

The Twolegplace cats glanced blankly at one another. Clearly they had never heard of StarClan or the warrior code.

"He can be very powerful when he's trying to persuade you," Jingo murmured.

Lionblaze flashed a glance at Hollyleaf. They knew better than most cats how persuasive Sol could be. *Maybe Sol was right,* Lionblaze couldn't help thinking, in spite of his horror at what the dogs had done. *Maybe these cats shouldn't blame him because they lost the battle.* He flexed his claws, imagining what he would do if he came face to face with one of the dogs. *Maybe they should have trained harder.*

"So are you looking for Sol because of what he did to . . . to ShadowClan?" Jingo asked.

"No, it's because another warrior—" Birchfall began eagerly. Lionblaze's belly churned at the thought of discussing Ashfur's murder.

Brambleclaw raised his tail to silence the younger warrior. "We just need to talk to Sol about something that happened recently," he stated calmly. "Have you seen him?"

"No, and we don't want to," Pod growled.

Hussar muttered an agreement, but Lionblaze noticed that Speckle was looking wistful, as if she had better memories of Sol.

"I haven't seen Sol." Chirp, who had remained quietly by the door, spoke suddenly, startling Lionblaze. "But I heard he's back."

Hussar scraped his claws hard against the floor. "He wouldn't dare!"

"Not here," Chirp explained, "but on the other side of Twolegplace. Where a cat called Purdy used to live."

"We know Purdy!" Lionblaze exclaimed, remembering the old loner who had guided them on part of their journey to the mountains.

"Thanks, that's a great help," Brambleclaw meowed. "We'll go and look for him there."

"It's too late to go now." Jingo rose to her paws and leaped lightly off the soft boulder to land beside Hussar. "You can stay here for the night."

Brambleclaw dipped his head. "Thank you."

"You can eat with us," Jingo continued. "Come on, Hussar, help me carry the prey."

The two cats left and returned a moment later loaded with fresh-kill, which they shared among all the cats. Speckle jumped down from her boulder to join them, and her kits scrambled after her; she picked out a mouse for them and they squabbled happily over it.

"This isn't what Sol would have taught them," Lionblaze murmured to Hollyleaf as he crouched to eat a blackbird. "Remember how he told ShadowClan that every cat should feed themselves? He said it was a sign of weakness for any cat to depend on another."

Hollyleaf nodded. "These cats obviously have a fresh-kill pile somewhere, and they hunt for cats who can't hunt for themselves. They're almost like a Clan."

"It looks like they're better off without Sol." But as Lionblaze spoke, he knew that some of these cats wouldn't agree with him. He had felt the pull of Sol's charm, his quiet authority and sense that he knew exactly the right thing to do. Jingo and the others must have felt it too, and missed the loner when he was gone. Lionblaze thoughtfully ate his blackbird. It was plump and juicy, but it had a taint of the Thunderpath about it, and he would have found it hard to choke down if he hadn't been so ravenous.

When they had finished eating, Speckle's kits started to bat a scrap of leaf around, squealing and tumbling over one another in their excitement. Frisk, the biggest and boldest of the four, batted the leaf toward Lionblaze.

Some of Lionblaze's tension melted away as he batted the leaf back to the kit. This was almost like playing with the kits back in the stone hollow. Speckle's litter were big and strong, almost ready to become apprentices.

Soon they should be learning to fight and hunt, he thought. *Do these cats have the skills to teach them properly?*

Hollyleaf joined in the game, too, chasing the leaf and pouncing on it until all four kits collapsed, panting, beside their mother.

"They're fine kits," Lionblaze gasped, flopping down on the floor in front of Speckle. "They'll grow up to be strong cats."

"I hope so," Speckle murmured. She bent over Frisk, licking his rumpled fur. Then she looked up again. "Whatever you think Sol has done, you're wrong."

Lionblaze's belly lurched as he glanced at his sister; Hollyleaf's green eyes were wide with alarm. *How much does this cat know?*

He was too startled to reply. After a couple of heartbeats, Speckle went on quietly: "Sol never gets his own paws dirty. If something has happened, another cat did it—maybe at Sol's bidding, maybe not. You won't be able to accuse him of anything."

There was a yearning in her voice; even though she knew the damage Sol had done here, she clearly wanted him back.

"Is Sol the father of your kits?" Hollyleaf asked, reaching out her tail to touch the brown queen's flank.

Speckle shook her head. "Their father left when the dogs started to become a problem." She hesitated, then added almost defiantly, "I wanted them to be Sol's. I know that the other cats say he betrayed us, but we were the ones who decided to fight the dogs. Sol didn't force us to do anything."

No, he just made it seem as if you couldn't do anything else. Lionblaze couldn't speak the words aloud to Speckle. It was obvious she was still deeply in love with the loner.

He and Hollyleaf exchanged another glance. Neither of them had mentioned Ashfur, but Lionblaze knew that the gray warrior's death must be weighing on his littermate's thoughts, just as it was on his own.

Speckle bent her head and went on grooming Frisk. "If Sol came back," she mewed between licks, "I'd be very glad to see him."

CHAPTER 12

❧

Jayfeather shifted uncomfortably on the bare earth. How was any cat supposed to sleep without a proper nest? But Leafpool had kept him so busy the day before that there had been no time to search for fresh moss. "It'll do the den good to be aired out," Leafpool had said. *Huh!* Jayfeather wriggled again, feeling a cold dawn wind ruffle his pelt.

The sound of a cat brushing past the bramble screen brought him properly awake. He picked up Leafpool's scent, and the smell of the moss she carried in her jaw. *At last! But why didn't she ask me to help?* Jayfeather's paws itched with irritation that Leafpool seemed determined to do even the most basic tasks without him. *Does she think I'm too incompetent even to carry moss?*

But there was no point in protesting. Jayfeather stumbled out of the scoop where his nest should have been and helped Leafpool arrange the moss near the trickle of water, where sick cats slept.

"Do you want me to fetch more?" he offered.

His mentor's only reply was a grunt that could have meant anything. Jayfeather wanted to ask her what was biting her, but he knew she wouldn't tell him anything. *She'd probably claw my ears off just for asking,* he muttered to himself. *The only way I'll get any answers—about my own past and what's going on with Leafpool—is if I look for them myself.*

While he pushed the moss tidily into place, Jayfeather cast his mind back to his earliest memories. His littermates' absence stabbed him like a claw. *We might find out a lot more if we could share what we remember!*

He recalled a long, cold journey, stumbling through snow that reached up to his belly fur, following his mother's scent. *No*—Squirrelflight's *scent!* Pausing with a pawful of moss, he tried to think himself back into that snowbound forest. He strove to distinguish each individual scent: his own, Lionblaze's, Hollyleaf's, Squirrelflight's . . . and there was another! Another adult cat, a warm and bulky shape. He'd never remembered this detail before, but another cat was definitely there, just ahead of Squirrelflight, forcing a way through the snow. . . .

Who was that? Jayfeather wondered. *Did two cats bring us back to the hollow?*

He needed to ask another cat, one who had been in ThunderClan when Squirrelflight brought her kits to the hollow. But it had to be a cat who wouldn't get suspicious about his questions or tell the rest of the Clan what he had been asking.

Well, there's one cat who doesn't gossip. . . .

"I'll go get more moss," he meowed, rapidly shoving the last pawful into place.

Without giving Leafpool a chance to protest, he brushed past the bramble screen and into the clearing. But instead of heading for the thorn tunnel, he darted across to the elders' den under the hazel bush.

"Mousefur!" he called, ducking under a trailing strand of honeysuckle.

The skinny brown elder was curled up near the trunk of the hazel. "I hope your tail's on fire or foxes are invading the camp," she rasped, stifling a yawn. "Or that you've got another really good excuse for waking me up."

"Sorry," Jayfeather mumbled. *Mouse dung! That's a great way to start. . . .*

"Don't worry," Longtail mewed peaceably. The blind elder was sitting by Mousefur's side; Jayfeather heard the rasp of his tongue as he gave himself a thorough wash. "Mousefur has been asleep for ages. It's time she woke up."

Mousefur let out an annoyed hiss. "Well, what do you want?"

"I've come to check you for fleas," Jayfeather explained, thinking fast. "One of the apprentices brought some back from patrol." He hoped neither of the elders would think to mention his lie to any other cat.

"I haven't been scratching," Mousefur meowed. "But you can check my pelt anyway." She settled herself comfortably with her paws tucked underneath her. "Be careful you don't miss any," she added as Jayfeather began probing her thick, ungroomed fur. "You've been Leafpool's apprentice for long enough."

Jayfeather bit back an irritated retort as he realized this could be the opening to the conversation he wanted. "That's true," he mewed. "It was the middle of last leaf-bare when I was born, wasn't it?"

"The coldest leaf-bare I remember," Longtail agreed. "I remember how thick the snow was. The whole Clan was stunned when Squirrelflight came back to the hollow with three kits! She said they'd been born earlier than she expected, which is why she didn't have a chance to get back to the nursery, but even still, what queen plans to have kits in the dead of leaf-bare?"

"Thank StarClan she had Leafpool with her," Mousefur added, twitching her ears as Jayfeather parted the fur on her head. "She'd have been in big trouble otherwise."

Leafpool! Jayfeather stopped running his claws through Mousefur's pelt. So Leafpool was the second cat he hadn't been able to identify. She'd never said anything to him about being with Squirrelflight when he was born. . . .

Locating a bit of twig on the ground, he snatched it up behind Mousefur's back and cracked it in his teeth. "That's one flea you don't need to worry about," he meowed. Trying to sound as if the answer didn't matter very much, he added, "Do you remember anything else about Squirrelflight bringing us home?"

"Not a lot," the elder replied. "It was so cold and snowy, we spent most of our time asleep that leaf-bare. I do remember how surprised every cat was that Squirrelflight hadn't realized how close she was to having her kits when she went away. But then, she was always scatterbrained, right from when she was a kit."

"Did you notice anything . . . odd about that time?" Jay-feather asked, cracking the twig again. He hoped Mousefur wouldn't think she was infested with fleas.

"Odd?" Mousefur snorted. "Most of what the Clan does these days seems odd to me."

"I remember," Longtail put in. "It was around then that Leafpool fed you that funny-tasting herb."

Jayfeather's ears pricked. "What funny herb?"

"Oh, how should I know?" Mousefur muttered. "Leafpool brought me some tansy, as usual. I think she expects me to live on the stuff every leaf-bare. And this weird-tasting stuff was mixed in with it."

A tingle in Jayfeather's paws told him that the strange herb was important. "Did Leafpool tell you what it was?"

Mousefur stretched, shaking her pelt. "No. I never asked her. When I complained about the taste, she just took away what was left. She said it hadn't been meant for me anyway."

"What was it like?" Jayfeather pressed, moving across to Longtail to check his pelt.

"Odd, but not unpleasant," Mousefur mewed. "I'd have clawed Leafpool's ears off if she fed me something disgusting! It tasted cold, like frost on fur, and fresh like grass, even though it was dry and dusty—from right at the back of Leaf-pool's store, I'd guess."

"How weird." Jayfeather gave the twig another crack. "It's not like Leafpool to get herbs muddled up."

Mousefur snorted. "She was all over the place, trying to help Squirrelflight care for you kits! The fuss she made, any cat would think Squirrelflight was the first queen ever to give birth!"

"Really . . ." Jayfeather murmured.

Quickly finishing his examination of Longtail's fur—and finding a real flea, which he crunched between his teeth— he said good-bye to the elders and headed into the forest to gather moss. As he tugged mouthfuls of it from between the roots of a tree, he wondered what Mousefur's mystery herb could have been. It was strange that Leafpool hadn't told Mousefur what the herb was or who it had been meant for. And stranger still that Leafpool, who was always so careful, had made a mistake.

I need to find out what the herb was, Jayfeather thought, gathering up his moss to carry it back to the camp.

When he returned to the medicine cats' den, he found that Leafpool had already gathered more bedding while he was talking to the elders. "Did you go to RiverClan to find that moss?" she demanded. "Or have you been mooning about in the forest again?"

"Uh . . . no." Jayfeather dropped his bundle and started to arrange it in his own nest. "I thought I'd check on the elders first." When Leafpool didn't respond, he added, "Mousefur told me a weird story. She said you gave her a funny-tasting herb once, mixed up with her tansy."

A pulse of alarm came from Leafpool, but she mewed, "I don't remember that. When was this?"

"Oh, a long time ago." Something told Jayfeather not to be too specific. He didn't want his mentor to know that he had been asking questions about his birth. "Do you know what it was?"

Leafpool let out an annoyed hiss. "How am I supposed to know that? For StarClan's sake, do you think I don't have more important things to worry about?"

"I was just—"

"If you're so bored that you have to start asking about something that happened last leaf-bare, I can soon find you something to do. We're still short of moss in here, so you can get on with that."

"Okay." Jayfeather was glad to leave. *But I never mentioned last leaf-bare,* he thought as he padded across the clearing. He had sensed his mentor's fear, too. *Leafpool was lying. She knows what the herb was, and she knows it's important. I must be getting close to the truth— and Leafpool doesn't want me to find it.*

CHAPTER 13
♣

Hollyleaf blinked in surprise when she woke among the stone walls of the Twoleg nest instead of under the branches of the warriors' den in the ThunderClan camp. Then she remembered their journey to find Sol, and how Jingo had brought them to this abandoned Twoleg nest to save them from the dogs.

As Hollyleaf sat up, her brother yawned and stretched. "I don't like this place," he muttered. "It's time we left."

Hollyleaf murmured agreement. It wasn't right for warriors to be so close to all this Twoleg stuff, even though there were no Twolegs here.

The pale light of dawn flooded into the den through the gap in the wall. Looking around, Hollyleaf saw that Birchfall and Hazeltail were still asleep. Brackenfur was perched on the ledge under the gap where Hussar had sat the night before. There was no sign of Brambleclaw, but a moment later he sprang up from outside and squeezed through the gap to sit beside Brackenfur.

"All's quiet," he reported. "But there's a strong smell of dog."

Hollyleaf twitched her whiskers; she could pick up the rank scent even here.

"We have to get moving," Brackenfur meowed. "Have you seen Jingo?"

Brambleclaw shook his head. Speckle and her kits were curled up in a furry heap on one of the soft boulders, while Fritz and Pod were sleeping on the other. There was no sign of the other Twolegplace cats.

"She'll be here somewhere." Brambleclaw jumped down inside the nest. "I think we can trust her."

He padded over to prod Birchfall and Hazeltail awake. As the two younger warriors were blinking sleep away, Jingo padded in through the entrance to the den.

"Good, you're ready," she mewed, with a brisk nod of greeting. "Let's go."

She led the way into the Twoleg territory through the gap in the wall. "This journey's going to be a bit different," she warned the Clan cats when they were all in the raw, damp air of the leaf-bare morning. "We won't be setting paw to the ground until we get where we're going."

Hollyleaf shot a startled glance at her Clanmates, and saw that they were all looking equally surprised. How could they get anywhere if their paws didn't touch the ground? Was Jingo expecting them to *fly*?

"It's not safe to walk around on the ground since the battle with the dogs," Jingo explained. "The dogs lie in wait for us and hunt us like prey."

Shuddering, Hollyleaf leaned closer to Lionblaze. "That's exactly what happened to us yesterday."

Her brother nodded; his amber eyes were gleaming and his

claws flexed as if he was imagining his chance to slash a dog that attacked him or his Clanmates. *Better to stay out of their way,* Hollyleaf thought.

"So we've found a different way of moving around our territory," Jingo went on. Gracefully she leaped up onto the top of the Twoleg fence. "Ready?" she called, glancing over her shoulder at the Clan cats.

Brambleclaw quickly leaped up beside her, followed by the rest of the patrol. Jingo set off, balancing easily on the narrow fence, then turning a corner to pad past several Twoleg dens, with a small Thunderpath on the other side.

Hollyleaf stiffened as the door to one of the Twoleg nests opened and a little white dog bolted out; its high-pitched yapping filled the air.

"It's okay," Jingo reassured the Clan cats. "That's a housedog. It's a stupid nuisance, just like all the others, but it's not dangerous like the wild dogs."

Hollyleaf had to take her word for it, but as she watched the dog bounding along the bottom of the fence and scrabbling about in the earth under a bush, she was glad that she wasn't down below where it could get at her. She dug her claws more firmly into the narrow strip of wood under her paws and focused on the tip of Lionblaze's tail.

The fence came to an end at a row of small dens with flat roofs. "These are monster nests," Jingo told them, leaping up onto the nearest roof.

"Monsters have *nests*?" Hazeltail exclaimed.

"Sure." Jingo waved her tail to where a Twoleg was

approaching at the edge of the Thunderpath. "Watch."

The Clan cats jumped up onto the roof beside her and watched the Twoleg as it opened the door of one of the dens and vanished inside. A moment later they heard the throaty growl of a monster. It nosed its way out of the den and headed down the Thunderpath, with the Twoleg in its belly.

"Great StarClan, this is where they sleep!" Birchfall's neck fur was bristling.

"Yes, but they can't climb up here," Jingo meowed. "Let's get on."

The patrol easily bounded across the flat roofs until the cats came to another fence and more Twoleg dens. Daylight was strengthening and a stiff wind had sprung up; Hollyleaf gripped with her claws at every step, scared that she would be blown off her skinny perch. So this was what Jingo meant by not setting paw on the ground. Not flying, but staying high up, out of reach of the wild dogs. She tried to imagine not daring to set paw on the ground in the forest, and having to leap from tree to tree to avoid being chased and killed.

No cat should be forced to live like this.

At the next corner, the fence gave way to a wall built of red stone; the top was wider and it was easier to pad along. The Thunderpath here was wider too, with stone trees growing at both edges, and a few monsters prowling along it. Every so often the wall was interrupted by a lower section of wooden fence; Jingo slid down onto it, padded quickly across, and leaped up onto the wall on the other side. The Clan cats followed. Hollyleaf's pelt prickled with fear as she remembered how the dog pack had leaped the low fence the day before; but no dogs appeared, and every cat reached the other side of the wooden fence safely.

Farther along the wall, Jingo halted; peering past her, Holly-leaf saw that one of the wooden sections had been swung back, leaving a gap between their stretch of wall and the next. As if at a signal, a flurry of barking broke out somewhere behind them, and a gust of wind brought the scent of dogs.

"We'll have to jump," Jingo decided. "Get back a bit; leave me space for a running start."

Once the Clan cats had shuffled backward, Jingo bounded along the wall and took off from the end in a powerful leap, landing neatly on the other side. The Clan cats glanced at one another; Hollyleaf could see that Hazeltail and Birchfall were both looking nervous.

"I'll go next," she meowed, deciding it would be better to get this over with than to watch her Clanmates go ahead of her. She hurtled along the wall and into the air before she could think about the wide gap and the nearby dogs.

Her paws hit the red stone of the wall and Jingo jumped forward to steady her.

"Well done," the brown tabby mewed. "Move along to give the others space."

Hollyleaf squeezed past her, turning in time to see Brack-enfur leaping easily across the gap. Birchfall followed him; the young warrior's front paws landed on the wall, but his hind paws dangled down. His eyes were huge with fear as the bark-ing grew louder and two dogs raced round the corner. Quick as lightning, Brackenfur grabbed Birchfall's scruff in his teeth and hauled him the rest of the way; his tail whisked up just in time, out of reach of the leading dog's teeth.

Birchfall shuddered. "Thanks, Brackenfur. I thought I was dog food for sure."

Hazeltail was shivering on the other side of the gap, gazing down in terror at the barking dogs as they reared up on their hind legs and scrabbled at the wall. "I can't, Brambleclaw," she whispered. "I just can't. I know I'll fall."

"No, you won't," the Clan deputy assured her. "You're good at jumping. You'll be fine."

"If you fall, I'll leap down and fight the dogs," Lionblaze promised.

With a despairing look at both of them, Hazeltail moved back a couple of fox-lengths and bounded up to the end of the wall. Both dogs hurled themselves at her as she leaped, but she cleared the gap with a tail-length to spare, and was welcomed on the other side by a quick lick on her ear from Birchfall.

Lionblaze followed and then Brambleclaw, and the cats set off again, with the dogs pacing alongside a fox-length below, whining and yelping in frustration at not being able to reach their prey. Hollyleaf wondered if there was any way of shaking them off. The Twolegplace wouldn't last forever. Sooner or later they would have to come down to the ground, and then they would be ripped to pieces.

"Where do you think you're going?"

A new voice came from up ahead: Hollyleaf spotted a huge blue-furred tom standing nose to nose with Jingo. He had the sleek, well-fed look of a kittypet, but his neck fur was beginning to fluff up and his blue eyes were unfriendly.

"Just passing through," Jingo replied calmly.

"Well, get a move on," the kittypet growled. "I'm going home for some sleep. I don't want to listen to that racket all day. Those dogs wouldn't even be here if you hadn't brought them."

Anger lit up Lionblaze's eyes, and he began to push forward along the edge of the wall to stand beside Jingo. Hollyleaf's fur prickled. Starting a fight here would probably end with both cats falling off the wall into the waiting jaws of the dogs.

Brambleclaw raised his tail to halt Lionblaze. "Stay out of it, unless the kittypet attacks," he ordered. "Let Jingo handle it."

Lionblaze obeyed, but he kept his furious gaze fixed on the kittypet.

"You're the one who's holding us up," Jingo replied, still calm. "If you weren't stuck there in the way, we'd be long gone."

The blue-furred tom let out an angry snort, but said nothing more. Instead he leaped down into the Twoleg territory, raced across to the nest, and vanished through a small hole in the door.

Hollyleaf relaxed; they had more important things to do than teach kittypets some manners. Still with the dogs following, they padded farther along the wall until they came to another corner.

"This is where we can get rid of the dogs," Jingo told them.

Turning the corner, she led the way along a narrow wooden fence between two Twoleg dens. There was no way for the dogs to follow, even though they tried to push themselves into the gap at the foot of the fence. Their frustrated yelping sounded behind Hollyleaf as she and her Clanmates approached the nest.

"This way—and watch where you're putting your paws." Jingo sprang up onto a narrow, flat area above the entrance to the Twoleg nest, then clawed her way up a creeper that grew alongside it until she reached the edge of the Twoleg roof. "It's not hard!" she called down, beckoning with her tail.

"And hedgehogs can fly!" Birchfall muttered.

But when it was Hollyleaf's turn to climb, she realized that Jingo was right. The creeper had thick, twisted stems that created plenty of paw holds, and it was strong enough to bear even the weight of Brambleclaw and Lionblaze. But the edge of the roof felt unsteady, and Hollyleaf tried unsuccessfully to dig her claws in, terrified that the wind would blow her off.

"Where now?" Brambleclaw panted as he hauled himself over the edge to stand beside Jingo.

As an answer, the brown tabby she-cat began scrambling up the steep slope of the roof. "This is a good shortcut," she meowed.

"We can't go up there!" Hazeltail gasped. "We'll fall!"

"If Jingo can do it, we can do it," Brackenfur declared firmly. "Up you go, Hazeltail. I'll be right behind you."

Slipping and scrabbling, the Clan cats clawed their way up the slope to where Jingo was sitting with her tail curled round her paws, at the very top of the roof next to a couple of tree stumps made of stone.

"It's great up here," she mewed as Hollyleaf struggled up the last fox-length to join her. "Sometimes I come just to look."

You come up here even if you don't have to? Hollyleaf felt as if her claws had been worn away in the desperate climb. A sharp ridge stretched away in both directions; it felt far too narrow to balance on. Wind buffeted her fur and plastered her whiskers to the side of her face.

Not wanting to let Jingo know how uneasy she was, she forced herself to look up from her clinging claws. Instantly she forgot to be scared. She could see *forever*! All the way across the tumbled roofs of the Twolegplace, to the flat stretch of rough grass that covered the cliffs above the sundrown-place. And beyond that, over the gray, heaving waves as far as the horizon.

"Look!" Lionblaze yowled, dragging himself up to balance on the ridge beside Hollyleaf. "You can see the mountains!"

Hollyleaf twisted around to stare in the opposite direction. After the edge of the forest, the mountains lay like a smudge of cloud on the horizon. She could make out gray slopes and cliffs, and peaks tipped with snow reaching up to the sky.

"Do you think we're as high as we were in the mountains?" she asked wonderingly.

"Of course not." There was a hint of scorn in Lionblaze's voice. "It took us ages to climb up to the waterfall."

Hollyleaf realized he was right, and yet the mountains seemed so close she could almost imagine leaping off the roof and landing on the ledge that led behind the waterfall to the cave where the Tribe of Rushing Water lived.

"I wonder what they're doing," she murmured, half to herself. "Will we ever see Stormfur and Brook again?"

No cat answered her. As soon as the rest of the patrol had reached the roof ridge, Jingo rose to her paws. "For this next bit, you have to be extra careful," she warned. "Going down is far harder than going up. If you slip . . . well, just don't slip, that's all."

Cautiously, in a half-crouch, Jingo led the way down the other side of the roof. Hollyleaf's paws skidded on the smooth stone of the roof; there was nothing to hold on to, and the downward slope seemed to end in empty air. When she was halfway down, a big white bird swooped past her, letting out a raucous cry and filling the air with the beating of its wings. Hollyleaf froze, trying to dig her claws into the stone, until it was gone.

"I'm *never* doing this again!" Birchfall hissed behind her.

Hollyleaf was shaking by the time they reached the edge of the roof and perched on a narrow channel half choked with leaves and other debris. A couple of fox-lengths below was a flat roof, and just beyond that, a narrow Thunderpath.

"Is that another monster nest?" Hazeltail asked.

Jingo nodded. "We'll have to come down to the ground here," she meowed, "because we have to cross that Thunderpath. But I think we're safe now. The wild dogs don't often come this far."

When she reached the grass beside the Thunderpath,

Hollyleaf tasted the air. She could pick out the mingled scents of several dogs, but none of them were close by. And no monsters appeared as Jingo paused to listen, then waved her tail for the Clan cats to cross.

Once on the other side, Jingo jumped up onto another wall, this one built of gray stone. Padding along it, Hollyleaf saw that the Twoleg nests here were smaller, with narrower strips of grassy territory behind them. A couple of tiny Twoleg kits were playing on one of the patches of grass, but they didn't notice the cats as they padded past.

"Is it much farther to Purdy's nest?" Brackenfur asked. "I think every cat is getting tired and hungry."

Hollyleaf muttered agreement. Every muscle in her body was aching, and her belly felt like a giant hole. The sky was covered with cloud, but she sensed it was long past sunhigh, and no cat had eaten since the fresh-kill in the abandoned Twoleg nest the night before.

"Not far now," Jingo responded. "We can—"

She broke off as a gust of wind swept across them, bringing with it a slap of icy rain. Birchfall let out a yowl of alarm. Hollyleaf flattened herself to the top of the wall, terrified that the wind would blow her off.

"This way!" Jingo ordered.

She ran along the top of the wall to the fence dividing the Twoleg territories. A bushy pine tree grew close to the wall; Jingo sprang up onto the nearest branch and forced her way in among the needles. Peering out, she called, "Come on! We need to shelter."

Unbalanced by the buffeting wind, the Clan cats stumbled along the wall and climbed into the tree. Hollyleaf's pelt was soaked by the time she reached it. The pine needles raked through her fur as she plunged into the branches, clawing for paw holds so she could climb higher.

"What does she think we are, squirrels?" Lionblaze gasped as he struggled upward. The branches dipped and swung under his greater weight, and Hollyleaf suddenly felt the whole tree spinning around. She drove her claws hard into the branch and closed her eyes until the dizzy sensation faded.

"I thought you came from a forest," Jingo meowed, a tail-length above where Hollyleaf was clinging. "Aren't you used to trees?"

"We don't climb that often," Brambleclaw replied. He had stayed lower down in the tree, just above the spot where it overhung the wall. "If we're caught in the rain in the forest, we'd rather shelter among the roots of a tree, or under a bush."

"Well, you learn something new every day," Jingo responded, sounding amused.

By the time the rainstorm was over, Hollyleaf could tell that the daylight was beginning to fade. *I hope we reach Purdy's den before nightfall. I don't want to be wandering around this Twolegplace in the dark.* Scrambling out of the tree after her Clanmates, she tried to groom the pine needles from her fur, but the whole of her pelt was clumped and messy. *I might as well be a rogue,* she thought crossly, *not a Clan cat at all.*

Then a deeper pang shook her. *Maybe that's what I am.*

The patrol followed Jingo along more walls and fences, and over the roofs of another set of monster nests, until twilight began to spill from the shadows. Eventually Jingo halted at the corner of a wall.

"See that holly bush?" she meowed, waving her tail in the direction of a dark, bushy mass poking over a fence on the other side of a small Thunderpath. "Purdy's den is just beyond it."

"Thank you, Jingo," Brambleclaw meowed. "We would never have found it without you."

"You're welcome," the she-cat replied. "You'll be able to hunt and spend the night there. But be careful," she added more seriously. "Sol has a way of making cats believe in him. I know, because I believed in him, too. Enough to leave my housefolk, where I was happy." In the gathering dusk, her eyes shone with sadness.

"Why don't you go back to your housefolk?" Birchfall asked.

"Because the other cats need me," Jingo replied. "Every cat needs a leader—someone to follow, someone to make the hard decisions. That's why we listened to Sol. But it's my job now. I can't leave them."

Loneliness throbbed in her voice. Hollyleaf felt desperately sorry for her. A Clan leader was chosen through the warrior code and given nine lives by StarClan. It was a huge honor, and the leader had the support of the Clan deputy, the medicine cat, and the senior warriors. But Jingo had no one.

The tabby she-cat gave herself a shake, as if getting rid of useless regrets. She touched noses with each of the Clan cats.

"Good-bye and good luck," she meowed. "Come and see us if you ever pass our nest again."

"We will," Brackenfur promised. "Good-bye and good luck to you, too."

Jingo dipped her head as the other cats added their good-byes, and turned to pad along the wall, back the way she had come. Her head and her tail were lifted high.

"Good-bye, Jingostar," Brambleclaw whispered, too softly for the retreating she-cat to hear him. "May StarClan light your path."

Hollyleaf crouched just behind Brambleclaw in the shadows underneath the holly bush. The Twoleg den beyond looked even more abandoned than the one where Jingo and the others lived. Dark holes gaped in the walls and roof.

"Remember when we met Purdy on the way to the mountains?" Lionblaze murmured into his sister's ear. "He said his Upwalker had died."

"Maybe Purdy won't be here at all," Hollyleaf suggested. She wasn't sure whether she would be glad or sorry. She looked forward to meeting the cranky old cat again, but she was afraid of what the encounter with Sol would bring.

"There's only one way to find out," Brambleclaw meowed. He began to pick his way through the straggling bushes that surrounded the nest. Hollyleaf's jaws flooded as she picked up a strong smell of mouse.

"Prey!" Hazeltail's voice was sharp with hunger. "Brambleclaw, may we hunt?"

The Clan deputy hesitated for a heartbeat. "Okay," he mewed. "But let's make it quick. And don't leave this bit of territory."

The patrol scattered among the bushes. Hollyleaf soon pinpointed a mouse scurrying through dead leaves, and killed it with a swift blow. "Thanks, StarClan," she mumbled through the first delicious mouthful. It felt as if she hadn't eaten for a moon. She had just finished gulping down her fresh-kill when she heard Brambleclaw calling the patrol together. As she slipped through the bushes, another mouse practically ran across her paws. She held it down and bit its throat, then carried the limp body back to her Clanmates.

The others were waiting for her. Lionblaze was swallowing the last of his prey while Birchfall swiped his tongue around his jaws with a satisfied expression.

"Everyone fed?" Brambleclaw asked. "Hollyleaf, are you going to eat that?"

Hollyleaf shook her head. "I already ate," she explained around the mouse. "I thought we could give this to Purdy."

Brambleclaw nodded approvingly. "Good idea. Let's go, then."

Cautiously, stopping every few paw steps to listen and to taste the air, he led the way up to the Twoleg nest and through the dark, gaping entrance hole. Hollyleaf shivered as she stepped inside. It was even colder here than outside: a raw cold that struck upward from the damp stone floor. Brambles grew through the gaps in the walls, as if the territory outside was invading the nest. There was a musty smell made up of stale prey, rotting leaves, and mold. But there was a smell of cats, too, stronger and fresher than the other scents.

"Purdy?" Brambleclaw called.

There was no reply. The deputy padded forward, with the patrol clustered tightly together behind him. Every hair on Hollyleaf's pelt prickled. There was something strange about this place, something chilly and unwelcoming.

Then a new voice spoke behind them. "Are you looking for me?"

CHAPTER 14

❦

Hollyleaf whirled around. Behind her, in an arched opening, a tall, well-muscled cat was outlined against the dusk. The white patches on his pelt shone very brightly.

"Sol!" Hazeltail's gasp was amazed and terrified all at once.

She really thinks Sol is the killer! Hollyleaf thought.

She was aware of bristling pelts and stiff limbs around her. But as soon as she looked into Sol's glowing amber eyes, Hollyleaf felt herself relaxing. How could she have forgotten how wise he was, how calm and certain he was about the future? Nothing troubled him, because he already knew what to expect.

"Greetings, Sol." Brambleclaw stepped forward. "Yes, we're looking for you. You need to come back to ThunderClan."

Sol looked into the eyes of each cat in turn. "Something has happened."

Hollyleaf felt a jolt in her belly, as if a stone had struck her. *What does he know about Ashfur?*

"We just need you to come with us," Brambleclaw meowed. "Firestar wants to talk to you."

Sol's eyes narrowed. "Something has happened that you think concerns me. Something bad. You wouldn't come all this way to thank me." He paused thoughtfully. "A cat has died...."

Behind Hollyleaf, Birchfall caught his breath.

"No," Sol corrected himself. "A cat has been killed. And you think I'm responsible." The tip of his tail twitched, but he betrayed no other emotion.

I'd be terrified if any cat accused me, Hollyleaf thought, scraping her claws against the cold stone. But Sol just surveyed the patrol calmly and waited for them to speak.

"He must be guilty!" Hazeltail whispered to Hollyleaf. "He didn't even ask who died!"

"Sol? Is that you?" A frail voice broke the silence, and Purdy appeared in the entrance, dragging a scrawny rabbit behind him. He was thinner than when Hollyleaf had last seen him, and his tabby pelt looked messier than ever.

"Look what I got!" Purdy dropped the prey and looked up. He blinked in astonishment as he recognized the Clan cats. "If it ain't Brambleclaw!" he exclaimed. "And Hollypaw and Lionpaw! I hope you two young 'uns are behaving yourselves."

"Yes, we are," Lionblaze replied, padding forward to touch noses with the old loner. "And we're warriors now. Lionblaze and Hollyleaf."

"Well, who'd have thought it?" Purdy's eyes gleamed. "Well done, youngsters."

For a few heartbeats, Hollyleaf felt like an apprentice again.

She should have been insulted, that Purdy still thought of her and her brother as young cats who were always getting into mischief. Instead she yearned for the days when everything had seemed so simple, and all she had to do was make herself the best warrior she could.

"How's that brother o' yours?" Purdy asked.

"He's Jayfeather now," Hollyleaf replied. "He's a full medicine cat."

Purdy shook his head again. "Who'd have thought it?" he repeated.

Brambleclaw padded forward and dipped his head to the old loner. "Greetings, Purdy. It's good to see you again. Come and meet my other Clanmates. This is Birchfall, and this is Hazeltail and Brackenfur."

"Good to know you," Purdy mumbled, looking a bit embarrassed to be among so many strangers.

"I'm sorry, Purdy." Sol stepped forward, to stand in front of the old cat. "I have to go."

Purdy blinked in astonishment. "What? Why?" When Sol didn't reply, he added, "I know you've only been here a couple o' days, but I reckoned we were getting on fine. This old nest don't feel half as empty wi' you around. And look—" He waved his tail toward the rabbit he had dragged in. "I found us some prey. It's a bit old and scrawny, but it could make a good meal. . . ." His voice trailed off, and he hunched his shoulders.

"You enjoy the rabbit, Purdy," Sol mewed gently, his amber eyes glowing. "I think the ThunderClan cats want to leave at once."

"What's all the rush?" Purdy turned to Brambleclaw. "Why do you need Sol to leave with you right now? Couldn't you all stay here a bit longer? You'd be right welcome."

Let Sol stay here. Hollyleaf wanted to speak the words aloud. *We don't need to take him back. Purdy needs him more than we do.* But she knew that was impossible.

"We'll stay for the night," Brambleclaw decided. "But we'll have to leave at dawn."

"Fine!" Purdy's ears perked up. "Have some o' this rabbit," he invited proudly.

"Thank you," Brambleclaw replied, his voice gentle, "but we can catch our own to add to your fresh-kill pile."

"I brought you a mouse," Hollyleaf added, snatching up her prey and dropping it at Purdy's paws.

The old tabby's eyes shone. "That's right kind of you." He crouched down and tucked in.

The Clan cats headed for the entrance to the den. Brackenfur glanced back at Sol, who was still standing in the middle of the den.

"Don't worry," Sol meowed. "I'll be here when you get back."

Brackenfur still looked uncertain; as they padded through the entrance, Brambleclaw shouldered his way toward him and murmured into his ear. "Stay on guard. But keep out of sight."

Brackenfur gave him a relieved nod and crept underneath the low-growing branches of a nearby bush, where he crouched with his gaze firmly fixed on the den.

Darkness had fallen while the cats were inside. The harsh orange light of the Twolegplace covered the sky, blotting out the stars. Hollyleaf wished she could have seen the spirits of the Clan's warrior ancestors, to know that they were still watching over her.

Once outside, she headed for the thicket of shiny green leaves where she had caught her mice. Hazeltail padded along beside her.

"I'm so glad we found Sol," she murmured. "Now we can go home."

Hollyleaf nodded. "I feel bad about taking Sol away from Purdy," she confessed.

"But Sol is a murderer!" Hazeltail halted, her eyes wide with shock. "What if he kills Purdy, too?"

"He wouldn't do that," Hollyleaf replied.

"How do you know?" Hazeltail persisted. "We need to get him back to the camp fast, before he does any more damage. Firestar will know what to do with him."

Hollyleaf shook her head helplessly. There was no way to reply to Hazeltail's questions. Besides, if Sol didn't come back to ThunderClan with them, what would happen in the hunt for Ashfur's killer? Would Firestar be forced to look closer to home? Hollyleaf's belly felt cold at the thought of accusations flying around her Clan.

She plunged into the thicket to hunt, but this time prey didn't come so easily to her paws. In the end she had to be content with a single shrew; she padded back to Purdy's den feeling embarrassed, but the rest of the patrol had only found thin pickings, too.

"Prey's pretty scarce 'round here," Purdy admitted as they crouched down to eat. "But I can find enough to feed me and Sol through leaf-bare. I ain't never starved before!"

He must be so lonely if he's willing to share this much prey with a stranger, Hollyleaf thought sadly, swallowing her morsel of shrew.

Once she had eaten, she settled down to sleep. The stone floor of the den was damp and cold, and wind whistled through the gaps in the walls. Huddling next to Lionblaze for warmth, Hollyleaf wished for the thick moss and bracken of her nest in the camp, and for the sheltering branches of the warriors' den.

Hollyleaf slept fitfully, and woke to see the cold light of a leaf-bare dawn angling across the floor. Brambleclaw and Brackenfur were already on their paws; Hazeltail and Birchfall were stirring drowsily, while Purdy slept in a rumpled heap in the opposite corner.

Sol was curled up in a sheltered niche where a couple of stones had fallen from one of the inner walls of the den. Brambleclaw padded over and prodded him awake.

"It's time to leave," he meowed.

Sol lifted his head, his amber eyes blinking, then rose to his paws. "If you wish."

"He creeps me out," a voice whispered in Hollyleaf's ear.

Hollyleaf started and turned to see Birchfall. "Don't sneak up on me like that!" she snapped, annoyed with herself because Sol was spooking her, too. "He's just a cat."

As she finished speaking, Sol padded past her toward the entrance to the den. "I told you I would come back," he murmured, quietly enough that she was the only cat to hear.

Struggling to shrug off her feelings of uneasiness, Hollyleaf roused Lionblaze, and the sound of voices woke Purdy, who stumbled sleepily over to the remains of the rabbit. "You got to eat something before you go," he meowed.

"But you need it more than we do," Brackenfur protested.

"I can catch another," Purdy retorted, his neck fur beginning to bristle. "You need to keep your strength up if you're goin' on a long journey."

The ThunderClan cats exchanged glances; clearly Purdy would be insulted if they refused, so they crowded around the last of the prey and forced down a few gristly scraps. Purdy watched them, while Sol just waited in the entrance, his gaze lifted to the sky.

"Don't go near them monsters," Purdy instructed. "They'll flatten you as soon as look at you. And there's dogs give trouble sometimes. They know not to mess wi' me, but youngsters like you . . ."

"We met the dogs, Purdy," Hazeltail told him. "You're right, they are dangerous. We'll be careful."

The old tabby tom gave his chest fur a lick, as if he was pleased to have been helpful. Every mouthful of prey felt like dust to Hollyleaf. She wished there was something they could do, so that Purdy wouldn't be left alone.

When all the cats had finished eating, Hollyleaf said goodbye to Purdy. The old cat was still trying to stay cheerful, but

Hollyleaf could see the loneliness and fear in his eyes. She touched noses with him gently. "May StarClan be with you, Purdy," she murmured. "I hope we'll meet again."

"Mebbe we will." But Hollyleaf could tell Purdy didn't believe they would. "You take care now, you hear?"

Brambleclaw led the way to the entrance of the den. Sol rose to his paws and fell in beside the Clan deputy as the cats emerged into the garden. By this time the sun was up; the sky was the clear, pale blue of leaf-bare, and a faint breeze rustled the leaves on the bushes.

Halfway to the fence, Brambleclaw stopped and looked back at Purdy, who stood watching them from the nearest gap in the wall.

"Come with us, Purdy," he meowed urgently. "There's room for you in the elders' den. Firestar will welcome you."

Purdy stared at him. "Well, I . . . I dunno what to say."

As sorry as she felt for the old cat, Hollyleaf felt herself bristling inside. *This can't be right! Purdy isn't a Clan cat. What will the other Clans say?* Then she suppressed a shiver. *I might not be a Clan cat, either. Does that mean I should live alone, without any friends to help me hunt?*

Sol was looking on expressionlessly. *Does he care about Purdy at all?* Hollyleaf wondered.

"Well?" Brambleclaw prompted the old cat.

"No, I'll be fine." Purdy gave his rumpled pelt a shake. "There ain't no need to feel sorry for me. I've survived more than one leaf-bare on my own."

"We'd appreciate your help getting around this

Twolegplace, you know," Brackenfur meowed, padding back toward the den. "You know the area far better than we do."

"And once we're back in the camp, you'd have a lot to teach our apprentices," Brambleclaw put in. "I don't suppose Holly-leaf and Lionblaze have forgotten how you saved them from the dogs."

Lionblaze nodded, while Hollyleaf suppressed a shudder at the memory of the dogs who had trapped them in a barn on their way to the mountains. Without Purdy's quick thinking, she and her brother and Breezepelt would all have been torn to pieces.

"Elders have a lot of influence in the way the Clan is run," Brambleclaw went on. "It would be an honor to have you live with us, with all your experience, and all you know about Twolegs—I mean, Upwalkers."

Hollyleaf dug her claws into the earth. She knew that the two senior warriors were lying. Bringing another loner into the Clan wouldn't be easy, and they didn't need to know about living among Twolegs, because there were so few of them by the lake. *Why not leave Purdy where he is, if he's happy? Why do Clan cats always think they know best?*

"Well, okay." Purdy scrambled through the gap in the wall and padded over to join the patrol. "I'll come along as far as the edge of Twolegplace, at least. Reckon you might need a bit o' help findin' your way." Turning to Sol, he added, "I never finished tellin' you that story about the fox. . . ."

Brambleclaw led the way to the gap in the fence where the patrol had entered the night before. Here he paused, his head raised and his ears pricked, while he tasted the air. The rest of the patrol waited in silence; Hollyleaf closed her eyes, concentrating until she felt the tug at her paws that told her the direction of the lake.

"Do you know which way to go?" Hazeltail fretted, obviously not trusting her own inner guide.

Brambleclaw nodded. "I think so. I'm trying to remember what we saw from that rooftop."

"I'm not going up there again!" Birchfall wailed.

"No, there's no need," Brambleclaw assured him. "But one of us can climb a tree soon to check whether we're going the right way. Let's get moving."

Hollyleaf squeezed through the gap in the fence, hard on the Clan deputy's paws, and found herself on a grass shoulder beside a Thunderpath. They had crossed here the night before, when all was dark and quiet. Now monsters were rushing up and down. Their bright colors dazzled Hollyleaf's eyes; the air was filled with their growling and their acrid stink.

"I hate this," she muttered to Lionblaze. "I don't care how many times we've done it, I'm still afraid some cat will get squashed."

Brambleclaw padded up to the very edge of the Thunderpath until his fur was ruffled by the wind of passing monsters. "When I say run, run as if a whole pack of dogs were behind you."

Lionblaze sighed. "Well, we've had plenty of practice."

Hollyleaf noticed that Brackenfur had positioned himself next to Purdy, as if he intended to keep an eye on the old cat when the time came to cross. Sol stood on Purdy's other side, his gaze fixed on the opposite side of the Thunderpath.

A huge monster swept by, the rumbling from its belly louder than a whole Clan of cats growling at once. As it faded into silence, Brambleclaw glanced sharply up and down the Thunderpath. "Now! Run!"

Hollyleaf leaped forward, aware of Lionblaze on one side of her and Birchfall on the other. The surface of the Thunderpath was hard under her flying paws. Then she was across, stumbling thankfully onto the grass on the other side.

Turning, she saw that all the cats had crossed safely, except for Purdy, who was weaving erratically across the middle of the Thunderpath, and Brackenfur, who padded beside him, trying to urge him on.

"Take it easy, youngster," Purdy meowed. "There ain't no monsters coming."

"But—" Brackenfur began desperately.

He broke off at the sound of a monster approaching. As it roared into sight around the corner, he gave Purdy a massive shove from behind. The old tabby stumbled forward with a startled yowl and flopped safely onto the grass as the monster swept past, snarling, barely a mouse-length away. Brackenfur had sprung to safety beside him with a heartbeat to spare.

"Purdy, never scare us like that again!" Brambleclaw hissed in exasperation.

The old cat picked himself up, blinking. "What? There weren't no problem. And there weren't no need to go pushin' me around," he added to Brackenfur in an injured tone.

Brackenfur sighed. "Sorry."

"Always panickin', you young cats," Purdy muttered.

Hollyleaf rolled her eyes. "This journey is going to be interesting," she whispered to Lionblaze.

Brambleclaw gathered the patrol together with a wave of his tail and set off along the edge of the Thunderpath. Soon Hollyleaf picked up the sound of many Twoleg kits, their voices shrill in the crisp morning air. "What's that?" she asked, her paws tingling with suspicion.

"Nothin' to worry about," Purdy reassured her. "You'll see."

Hollyleaf wasn't sure she could trust the old cat's judgment. Rounding the next corner, she saw a huge Twoleg nest with a wide expanse of stone on the ground all around it. A fence of narrow, shiny trees cut it off from the Thunderpath. Crowds of Twoleg kits—more Twolegs than she had ever seen together at one time—were running and yowling and throwing things at one another.

"What is this place?" she meowed curiously.

Purdy shrugged. "Dunno. They come here most days."

Hollyleaf's belly clenched with shock as the old cat trotted up to the fence and stuck his nose through a gap. At once several of the Twoleg kits ran up to him, stretching out their hands.

"What's he *doing*?" Brackenfur muttered. "Purdy!"

Purdy took no notice. The Twoleg kits were reaching through the fence to stroke him; his purr was loud enough to reach the rest of the patrol where they stood a few tail-lengths away.

"Remember, he used to be a kittypet," Birchfall murmured. "It must make him act weird sometimes."

Brambleclaw said nothing, just twitched his tail to guide the patrol past the shiny fence at a safe distance. They waited for Purdy a few fox-lengths down, alongside the Thunderpath. As they padded past, Hollyleaf noticed one of the kits pull something out of its pelt and hold it out to Purdy, who licked it up enthusiastically.

Has he no sense?

Eventually a harsh clanging sounded from inside the Twoleg den, and all the kits ran over toward it and stood in a line to go through the entrance. Purdy turned away and came bounding up to the patrol.

"What're you all starin' at?" he demanded, puffing.

"Purdy, was that a good idea?" Brambleclaw asked. Hollyleaf could tell he was trying to keep irritation out of his voice. "What did that kit feed you?"

"Dunno." Purdy's eyes gleamed as he swiped his tongue around his jaws. "It was real tasty, though."

Brambleclaw sighed. "Right, let's go."

A little farther on, the Twoleg dens became more widely spaced; then they stopped altogether as woodland took over on either side of the Thunderpath. Relief flooded through Hollyleaf from ears to tail-tip as Brambleclaw veered away from the Thunderpath to pad under the trees. Before they had ventured more than a couple of tail-lengths into the wood, he halted.

"This would be a good place to check our direction," he

meowed. "Who feels like climbing a tree?"

"I will!" Lionblaze offered instantly.

"No, I will," Hazeltail argued. "I'm lighter. I can get up higher."

Brambleclaw nodded. "Okay, Hazeltail."

Lionblaze looked disgruntled while Hazeltail leaped up the trunk of the nearest tree, digging her claws into the bark. Hollyleaf's heart thumped as she watched her friend clambering through the leafless branches, higher and higher, until she reached the top of the tree and clung there, swaying in the breeze. Hollyleaf couldn't stop thinking about how Cinderheart had fallen, back in the forest, and injured her leg.

What do we do if Hazeltail is hurt, when we have so far to go?

But a few heartbeats later, Hazeltail began to scramble down; soon she reached the lowest branch and jumped down beside her Clanmates.

"I could see so far!" she exclaimed.

"Are we on the right track?" Brambleclaw asked.

"Yes!" Hazeltail's fur was fluffed up with excitement. "I couldn't see the lake, but I could tell where it is, behind Wind-Clan's ridge. We need to go this way"—she gestured with her tail into the trees—"and we'll get there without going through any more Twolegplaces."

"That's great news." Brambleclaw gave the younger warrior an approving nod. "Well done, Hazeltail."

Hazeltail's eyes shone with pride as the patrol set off again. Now that the path was wider, Hollyleaf noticed that Bracken-fur and Birchfall were walking one on each side of Sol.

The loner glanced at each of them, his amber eyes glinting with amusement. "You don't need to put me under guard, you know," he mewed. "I'm not going to run away."

Purdy halted, staring at Sol with a baffled look. "Under guard? What's all that about?"

Brambleclaw was forced to halt, too; his whiskers twitched with irritation as he glanced back. "It doesn't matter. We have to keep moving."

"ThunderClan thinks I've done something," Sol replied to Purdy, ignoring Brambleclaw. "That's why they want me to go back with them."

"Wha'?" Purdy gaped. "That's fluff-brained!" Turning to Brambleclaw, he added, "You're wrong, you know. Sol's a decent cat. He wouldn't do nothin' bad."

Brambleclaw didn't try to explain. He just waved his tail, signaling for the patrol to continue, and almost immediately disturbed a pheasant, which came scrambling out of a clump of bracken with a raucous alarm call. At the same moment a squirrel, obviously spooked by the pheasant, dashed out of cover and raced for the nearest tree. Springing forward, Hollyleaf intercepted it and brought it down with a swift blow of her paw.

"Neat catch!" Birchfall called.

All the patrol gathered to share the unexpected prey, and Purdy's awkward questions were pushed to the back of every cat's mind. But Hollyleaf knew he would ask again. *And which one of us is going to tell him the truth?*

The patrol headed on through the forest, but not long after

sunhigh Hollyleaf noticed that Purdy was getting tired, stumbling and blundering into bracken or brambles. She padded beside him, trying to guide him with her tail, but it was clear that he wouldn't be able to keep going until nightfall.

Sprinting ahead, Hollyleaf caught up to Brambleclaw. "It's Purdy," she mewed. "He's so tired. What are we going to do?"

Brambleclaw glanced back. "Mouse dung! We can't just leave him here." Clearly the Clan deputy was regretting that he had asked Purdy to join them. "Okay, we'll stop soon," he decided. "Do what you can to help him, Hollyleaf."

"Sure." Hollyleaf waited for Purdy to stagger up to her, then padded beside him again. "Do you want to lean on my shoulder?" she offered.

Purdy glared at her. "You think I can't manage on my own? Jumped-up young whippersnapper!"

"Sorry." Hollyleaf guessed he was angry because he knew he needed help, but pride wouldn't let him accept it. She fell back a couple of paw steps so she could keep an eye on him, and was relieved when Brambleclaw called a halt.

"So soon?" Lionblaze asked, gazing up at where the sun still angled through the trees. "We could go a lot farther before it gets dark."

"I know," Brambleclaw meowed, with a glance at Purdy. "But we all had a tough time in the Twolegplace, and we need to hunt and rest. There should be plenty of prey here."

The place Brambleclaw had chosen to stop was a small clearing among huge oak trees. Dead leaves covered the ground. At one side, a tiny spring trickled between moss-covered stones into a pool. Purdy stumbled over to it, took a few laps of water, and flopped down in a rumpled heap. Heartbeats later, loud snores came from him.

Sol padded across to a sunny patch of ground and sat down with his tail curled around his front paws. His amber eyes glowed in the golden light. He clearly had no intention of hunting for himself.

Hollyleaf headed into the undergrowth. The scents were strong, and she soon caught a mouse and a thrush. *Maybe it's not a bad idea to stop early,* she thought as she kicked earth over her fresh-kill. *It's warmer now, so the prey is out and about.*

When she had added another mouse to her catch she hurried back to the clearing to find that her Clanmates were already building a fresh-kill pile near the pool.

Birchfall dragged up a huge rabbit, his tail raised proudly. "There are more over there." He gestured with his tail. "We'll eat well tonight."

Dropping a mouse and the thrush onto the pile, Hollyleaf took the other mouse over to Purdy and prodded him awake.

The old tabby gave a startled snort, looking around wildly. "What is it? Foxes? Let me get at 'em!"

"It's okay, Purdy." Hollyleaf rested her tail on his shoulder. "I brought you a mouse."

Purdy blinked. "That's right good of you." He began devouring the mouse in famished gulps, then stopped and moved back awkwardly. "Here—you have some, too."

"No, it's for you," Hollyleaf mewed. *How long has it been since Purdy had a decent meal?* "There's plenty more."

When all the cats had eaten—Brambleclaw made sure Sol was given a share of the catch—they settled down to sleep among the trees. By now the sun had gone and twilight was gathering. A cold breeze clattered the bare branches.

Hollyleaf noticed that Purdy was shivering. She beckoned Hazeltail over with a wave of her tail. "Purdy really can't look after himself," she murmured into her Clanmate's ear. "Let's sleep beside him and keep him warm."

"Okay," Hazeltail mewed, though she looked doubtful. "I hope he hasn't got fleas."

I'm sure he's got fleas, Hollyleaf thought, as she and Hazeltail clawed together a heap of dry leaves to make a nest. *And ticks. We'll have to give him a good going-over with mouse bile before we let him go anywhere near Mousefur!*

When Hollyleaf woke, it was still dark. She could just make out the trace of bare branches against the sky, but stars still glittered overhead. Purdy was snoring louder than ever, and Hazeltail was curled up beside him with her tail wrapped over her ears.

Hollyleaf knew she wouldn't be able to go back to sleep. Very quietly, so as not to disturb any cat, she rose to her paws and peered around, blinking to clear her bleary eyes. Brambleclaw, Brackenfur, and Birchfall had all made nests close together on the other side of the pool. All three of them were sleeping peacefully; Birchfall's tail twitched as if he was dreaming.

Three cats . . . not four . . . Sol's gone! Hollyleaf swept her gaze around the clearing, but there was no sign of the distinctive tortoiseshell-and-white pelt. Tasting the air, she picked up his scent; it was still fresh, but faint.

Hollyleaf's first impulse was to wake Brambleclaw. But some inner command sent her paws in the other direction, following the wispy thread of Sol's scent. She padded as silently as she could through the trees, flinching as her paws crunched in the brittle leaves. She soon began to hear the sound of running water. It grew louder until she came to a spot where the trees thinned out a little, and the ground fell away to where a stream gurgled along over stones. Sol was sitting at the top of the slope, his back to her, his gaze fixed on the paling stars.

"Do you still think they hold all the answers, Hollyleaf?" he asked without turning his head.

Every hair on Hollyleaf's pelt rose, until she realized that she was standing upwind of the stream and Sol must have scented her approach. "I . . . I don't know," she replied. "I don't know anything anymore."

Now Sol turned to her, his amber eyes blinking sympathetically. "Why is that?"

Hollyleaf sighed. "Everything was so much easier when I could trust what other cats said." Even as she spoke, she couldn't believe she was telling this to any cat. She hadn't even shared her doubts with her littermates.

"You must learn to trust yourself, Hollyleaf," Sol meowed, in the deep, rich voice that seemed to inspire confidence. "Only you know what is right."

"I get so confused sometimes." Hollyleaf's voice shook. "I don't want to have to decide everything on my own."

"It gets easier, little one." Sol rose to his paws. "Come on, let's go back to the others."

Hollyleaf's belly churned as she followed Sol back to the clearing. *He almost destroyed ShadowClan! Every cat thinks he killed Ashfur! So why do I feel that I can trust him with my life?*

When they reached the clearing, the rest of the patrol were stirring. Brambleclaw looked up from grooming his pelt, a surprised expression in his amber eyes. But all he said was, "I wondered where you'd got to," as he padded over to check on Purdy.

The old tabby heaved himself out of his nest. "I'm fit as a squirrel," he insisted, shaking dead leaves from his back. "No need for you youngsters to be fussin'."

After they had finished up the previous night's fresh-kill, the cats set out again. Passing the place where she had met Sol, Hollyleaf realized they were coming to the edge of the woods. Soon they stood beneath the forest's outermost trees, gazing across fields dotted with gray-white puffs that Hollyleaf realized were sheep.

"I don't like this," Purdy grumbled as they crossed the fields, giving the sheep a suspicious glance. "What are them creatures, anyway?"

"Sheep, Purdy," Hollyleaf replied, padding beside him. "Didn't they have any on that farm where we met you last time?"

Purdy sniffed. "Never seen 'em before." He jumped, fur fluffing up, as one of the sheep ambled away from the others and trotted closer to the cats. "Quick—run!"

"It's okay," Hollyleaf mewed; the sheep halted and began to crop a new patch of grass. "They're not taking any notice of us."

"There's too much . . . space around here," Purdy complained, flattening himself to the ground. "No trees. No Upwalkers—Twolegs, you call 'em."

"You mean you *want* Twolegs?" Hollyleaf's exasperation spilled over like rain from a leaf. "That won't do if you're going to live in ThunderClan."

"Hey, take it easy." Lionblaze veered over and rested his tail on Purdy's shoulders for a heartbeat. "Purdy can't help not being a Clan cat."

Nor can we! Hollyleaf almost flashed the words back at her brother, but stopped herself in time. *How long before one of us gives away the secret?*

With a massive effort she made herself relax. "I know. Sorry, Purdy."

By sunhigh, Hollyleaf could see that the old cat was tiring again, and soon Brambleclaw called a halt in the shelter of some trees surrounded by gorse bushes. Purdy collapsed on his side, breathing hard. Sol padded away a few paw steps and sat down, peering out over the field.

"Hey, look at this!" Hazeltail was sniffing at a clump of something that looked like thistledown stuck on one of the gorse bushes. "What is it?"

Hollyleaf padded up to look. Birchfall followed curiously. "It smells of sheep," Hollyleaf meowed. Glancing around, she spotted more of the clumps on other bushes. "Their pelts must get snagged on the thorns when they brush past."

"It's very soft." Hazeltail tugged at the clump with her teeth and came away with a mouthful of it. "I'm going to take some back for the nursery."

Birchfall suppressed a *mrrow* of laughter. "You look as if you've swallowed a thistle!" He ducked as Hazeltail swatted at him with her tail. "It's a good idea," he added hastily. "I'll collect some, too, for my kits."

Hollyleaf left them pulling the sheep pelt off the bushes, and padded back to Purdy. The old cat was reviving, and looked calmer now that the sheep were a safe distance away.

"Do we have we time to hunt?" she asked Brambleclaw.

The Clan deputy's ears twitched in surprise. "Are you hungry already?"

"No," Hollyleaf replied, lowering her voice. "I just want one mouse, for the mouse bile. We'll never hear the last of it if we let Purdy into the camp with all his fleas and ticks." Raising a hind paw to scratch her side, she added, "I think I might have picked something up from him already."

"Okay." There was a glint of amusement in Brambleclaw's eyes. "But don't be long. I want to keep going. We're not far from the lake now. I can feel it in my paws."

Dusk was falling as the patrol left the fields behind and came to a small Thunderpath. Tasting the air, Hollyleaf breathed in the scent of horses. "The horseplace!" she exclaimed. "We're nearly home!"

Brambleclaw led the way, slipping under the shining fence

and across the expanse of whitish stone, past the Twoleg nest and the horse nests. As they emerged into the field, Hollyleaf looked around for the horses, but there was no sign of them. "They must be shut up in their wooden nests," she murmured to Lionblaze.

She couldn't see Smoky or Floss, either, though she picked up their scents. Her paws prickled with urgency; she wanted to be back in the warm familiarity of the stone hollow, and yet she knew that there was no real safety there.

Or anywhere else, she reflected sadly. *Where will all the lies and betrayal end?*

CHAPTER 15

"Thanks, Jayfeather," Whitewing purred as Jayfeather dropped a leaf wrap of ragwort in front of her.

The nursery was warm and quiet. Daisy and Millie had taken their kits out for some exercise, leaving the white queen to get some rest.

"Make sure to eat it all," Jayfeather instructed her. "Your kits will be born soon, and you need all the strength you can get."

"I know." Whitewing sighed. "I hope it's not much longer. I feel *huge!*"

"You're fine," Jayfeather assured her. He said good-bye and pushed his way out of the nursery. The morning was crisp but he could feel the weak rays of leaf-bare sun, melting the night frost.

"Now," he muttered to himself, "if only Leafpool's still out looking for yarrow. . . ."

He couldn't pick up his mentor's scent when he brushed past the bramble screen into the den, but another cat was there, irritation coming off him in waves.

Mouse dung! Jayfeather thought. *Now I'll have to deal with him.*

"Berrynose," he mewed. "What can I do for you?"

"It's my tail," the young warrior told him. "It hurts. And it smells funny."

Jayfeather sniffed at the stump of Berrynose's tail, and almost recoiled at the rotting scent. "You've got an infection," he reported.

"How?" Berrynose sounded indignant. "Leafpool said that it healed after I caught it in the fox trap."

"It did," Jayfeather agreed. "You must have opened up the wound again. Can you remember catching it on anything lately?"

Berrynose hesitated. "I got stuck in some brambles when I was chasing a rabbit," he admitted at last.

"That could do it," Jayfeather mewed. "But there's nothing to worry about. You need a poultice of marigold, that's all. Wait there a moment." He padded into the cave where the herbs were stored, and located the marigold. Chewing up the leaves, he returned to Berrynose. "Keep still while I plaster this on," he mumbled around the mouthful.

"Can I be excused from duties?" the cream-colored warrior asked hopefully.

Jayfeather was unsympathetic. "No. You don't patrol or catch prey with your tail. But come back here tomorrow and I'll put a fresh poultice on."

"Okay," Berrynose mewed. "Thanks, Jayfeather. It does feel better."

Right, Jayfeather thought when he had gone. *Now for my plan* . . . He went back into the cave and collected a few leaves of chervil, dandelion, and borage. Bounding across to the elders' den, he set the leaves down in front of Mousefur.

"Are any of these the herb?" he demanded.

Mousefur let out an annoyed hiss. "What herb?"

Without the bunch of leaves in his mouth, Jayfeather could smell fresh-kill, and he guessed he had interrupted the elders' meal. "The herb you told me about, the one Leafpool mixed with your tansy."

"Oh, that." The skinny elder still sounded grumpy. "What do you want to know for?"

"Just curious." Jayfeather realized he had sounded too urgent. He didn't want Mousefur to tell Leafpool what he was doing. "You never know, it might be useful."

Mousefur let out a grunt and gave the herbs a suspicious sniff.

"Let me try, too," Longtail offered. "I didn't taste the stuff, but I might remember the scent."

"Well?" Jayfeather asked, when both elders had given the herbs a good sniff.

"No, it wasn't any of those," Mousefur meowed. "I know these herbs. Leafpool uses them all the time for fever and infected wounds."

"That's right," Longtail added. "Sorry."

Jayfeather suppressed a frustrated sigh. "Not even this one?" he asked, pushing forward the chervil.

"What part of 'no' didn't you understand?" Mousefur growled, giving his ear a stinging flick with her tail.

"Okay." Jayfeather gathered up the herbs again. "Thanks.

I'll bring some more later."

"Give us the chance to finish this rabbit first!" Mousefur called after him as he left the den.

Jayfeather returned to his own den, intent on finding more herbs for Mousefur and Longtail to try. But he had just replaced the chervil, dandelion, and borage in their proper places when he heard Leafpool enter the den behind him. A strong scent of yarrow came with her.

"Jayfeather, what are you doing?" she asked sharply. "Why do you smell as if you've been sleeping in our supplies?"

"Uh . . . I fell over in the store," Jayfeather stammered. "I got herb dust on my pelt."

Leafpool let out a long sigh. "Really, Jayfeather, it's like having a kit in here! And why were you poking around in the store anyway?"

Jayfeather felt his pelt rising at the anxiety and fear that was flooding from his mentor. *Why doesn't she want me looking in the store?* he wondered. *I've as much right to be in there as she has! What is she hiding now?*

"I wasn't *poking around,*" he retorted. "And I cleaned the stuff up."

Leafpool sniffed. "Put this yarrow away, then," she ordered. "I want to go check on Millie's breathing. She's out there romping around with her kits, and it might be too much for her."

Once Leafpool had gone, Jayfeather tidied away the yarrow and slipped out a daisy leaf and a sliver of burdock root. *If it's either of these, I'm a mouse!* Making sure that Leafpool was over by the nursery with Millie, he hurried back to the elders' den.

"You again!" Mousefur muttered. "What is it this time?"

She sniffed briefly at each of the herbs Jayfeather put in front of her, and tasted the daisy leaf. "No," she mewed. "It wasn't them."

Longtail came over for a sniff, but he didn't recognize the herbs either.

Jayfeather sighed. "Okay, we'll keep trying."

"I think you've got bees in your brain," Mousefur meowed as she settled down for a nap.

Jayfeather was eating a vole near the fresh-kill pile when he heard Firestar padding past him, on his way to the medicine cats' den. Gulping down the last couple of mouthfuls, he followed, standing just outside the bramble screen so that he could hear what the Clan leader had to say.

"Leafpool, I wanted to ask you . . ." Firestar sounded almost embarrassed.

"Yes?" Leafpool prompted, an edge to her tone.

"I just wondered whether you've had a chance to speak with StarClan yet." Jayfeather could tell that the Clan leader wanted to sound casual, as if the question didn't really matter, but he was failing miserably.

Jayfeather's belly clenched as he wondered what Leafpool's answer would be; then he made himself relax. *The whole Clan would know about it if Leafpool had spoken to Ashfur!*

"No!" Leafpool snapped. "If I do, you'll be the first to know."

"Oh, okay . . . thanks." Firestar edged out of the den, paused, and then bounded off, not even noticing Jayfeather.

Why doesn't Leafpool want to talk to StarClan? Jayfeather wondered. *What is she so afraid of?*

His paws itched to get out of the camp, maybe go down to the lake, find the stick, and see if Rock would talk to him again. But Rock had told him to look for answers here, among his own Clan. *StarClan, why aren't you helping me?* Jayfeather demanded silently. *Isn't that your job, to guide the Clans?*

As if in answer to his unspoken plea, Sandstorm padded across the clearing and halted beside him. "Do you want to go for a walk in the forest with me?"

Jayfeather twitched his ears in surprise. "What for?"

Sandstorm let out a faint purr of amusement. "Can't I just want your company? No, you're right," she added. "I do need to talk to you, somewhere we won't be interrupted."

"Okay," Jayfeather agreed. "But I'll have to ask Leafpool first. She's . . . well, she's a bit touchy just now."

"I know," Sandstorm told him. "Wait there." She brushed past the bramble screen, and Jayfeather heard her meow, "Leafpool, I'm borrowing Jayfeather for a bit. We're going into the forest."

"All right," Leafpool replied, though she sounded grudging as she gave permission. "Tell him to fetch some tansy back with him."

Jayfeather's paws tingled as he followed Sandstorm through the gorse tunnel and along the trail that led toward the WindClan border. He had always respected the ginger she-cat, and even though he now knew that she wasn't his kin, he still trusted her.

Sandstorm said nothing particularly helpful as she followed the stream that marked the border with WindClan. Jayfeather listened impatiently to her comments about how the prey was running and whether WindClan was likely to make a raid across the border. But he didn't object; he knew the she-cat wouldn't talk until she was ready.

Eventually they reached the spot where the trees gave way to moorland, and a cold wind came whistling down from the ridge that stretched all the way to the Moonpool.

"Let's rest for a while," Sandstorm suggested, sitting at the edge of the stream.

Jayfeather padded over to join her, turning until the wind was in his face, enjoying the snow-scented blast that flattened his pelt to his sides.

"Jayfeather," Sandstorm began, "do you think Leafpool is all right? She seems very tense lately."

So that's what it's about! "I've noticed that too," he replied cautiously.

"Is it the strain of dealing with the greencough?" Sandstorm guessed. "Or something worse? Do . . . do you think it's possible she's blaming herself for Ashfur's death?"

Jayfeather sank his claws into the grass to steady himself. *I didn't see that coming!* He wanted to tell Sandstorm that the death of Ashfur had *nothing* to do with Leafpool. *I can guarantee it!* But he knew how stupid it would be to voice his certainty. It would provoke questions from Sandstorm—questions that he had no way of answering without bringing the whole of ThunderClan crashing down around his ears.

"I don't think so," he murmured.

"Perhaps she feels she ought to have predicted his death, or stopped it somehow," Sandstorm went on. "Or maybe she thinks she should be able to visit him in StarClan and find out the truth."

Jayfeather froze. *So Firestar hasn't told Sandstorm that he asked Leafpool to find Ashfur and talk to him. How many more cats have secrets from one another?*

"I think Leafpool's tired from dealing with the green-cough," he mewed, knowing he would have to say something to explain his mentor's strange mood. "And I know she's worried about Whitewing's kits being born in such a cold season. Besides, every cat is still grieving for Ashfur." *Well, maybe not every cat . . .* Jayfeather curled up his claws as the lie slipped out.

"You could be right," Sandstorm sighed. "Firestar and I are both worried about her. After all she's not just our medicine cat, she's our daughter, too. Brambleclaw and Squirrelflight would feel just the same about you if you were in trouble."

Or not . . . Jayfeather found it hard to nod seriously, hoping that his expression showed none of the turmoil he felt.

"You'll tell me if you find out anything else?" Sandstorm mewed.

"Of course." *Of course not!* As he followed the ginger she-cat back to the camp, Jayfeather wondered which cat would be the next to probe his secrets, and how long the terrible things he knew could stay hidden.

* * *

"Into the nursery now, kits," Daisy mewed gently. "It's time you were asleep."

"But WindClan is attacking us!" Rosekit protested. "And I'm going to be Clan leader and fight them off!"

"You can be Clan leader tomorrow," Daisy promised.

Jayfeather listened as the kits tumbled into the nursery, their high-pitched voices fading. A chill night breeze ruffled his fur; stretching, he padded off toward his den.

Two sunrises had passed since his conversation with Sandstorm. Leafpool was still touchy, and Jayfeather still didn't know why. His mentor was afraid of something, that much he was sure of, but he didn't dare ask for an explanation.

He had just reached the bramble screen when he heard a yowl from Cloudtail, who was on guard duty at the end of the thorn tunnel. "Brambleclaw! Brackenfur! Hey, they're back!"

Rustling came from the warriors' den as cats bounded out into the open. Several of them raced past Jayfeather to greet the returning patrol. Jayfeather followed, but hung back, trying to make sense of the mingled scents as the cats slipped through the thorn tunnel and into the camp. Brambleclaw was in the lead, followed by Brackenfur. A shiver passed through Jayfeather's pelt as he recognized the scent of Sol. The loner stepped calmly out of the tunnel and paused at the entrance before padding forward into the camp. Confidence radiated from him; this was no prisoner dragged back to answer for his crimes.

A flurry of excited speculation broke out among the Clan cats.

"That's Sol!"

"They found him!"

"He looks so calm," Brightheart mewed, sounding confused. "Surely he wouldn't look like that if he had killed Ashfur?"

"I wouldn't put anything past that cat," Dustpelt growled. "Look what he did to ShadowClan."

"What's Firestar going to do with him?" That was Fox-paw's voice, quivering with excitement. "I think he should rip his pelt off and leave him for the crows."

"No." Graystripe's voice rose strongly above the babble. "That isn't how Firestar does things. He'll talk to Sol and find out the truth."

I hope not, Jayfeather thought.

Another cat followed Sol into the clearing, with a scent Jayfeather couldn't place, though he knew he should remember it. Hazeltail followed, and last of all came Hollyleaf and Lionblaze. Jayfeather relaxed as he realized that his litter-mates had made it home unhurt.

The Clan cats fell silent as Firestar padded past Jayfeather, their pelts almost brushing. "Greetings, Sol," he meowed. His tone was cool but polite. "Thank you for coming."

"Anything I can do to help," Sol replied, with equal polite-ness.

"I'll let you rest for tonight," Firestar went on. "You must be tired after your journey. Berrynose, Honeyfern!"

"Yes, Firestar?" The two young warriors bounded up.

"Make a nest for Sol, would you? That bush between the medicine cats' den and the warriors' den would be a good place. It's nicely sheltered, tucked under the cliff."

And there's a narrow entrance, so it's easily guarded, Jayfeather added silently.

"Well done, Brambleclaw, and all of you," Firestar continued, when Honeyfern and Berrynose had hurried off. "I know how difficult this must have been."

"More than we expected," Brambleclaw admitted. "We found Sol in a Twolegplace, with—"

"Wi' me!" An angry voice interrupted Brambleclaw, and Jayfeather suddenly remembered who the cat was whose scent he hadn't been able to identify. *Purdy! What's he doing here?*

"An' I'd like to know why you've dragged Sol all this way!" the old cat went on. "I hope you're not accusin' him of somethin' he hasn't done!"

An astonished murmur broke out among the listening cats. Jayfeather wasn't sure whether Purdy's mere presence or his fierce defense of Sol had provoked it.

"Brambleclaw, who's this?" Firestar asked, surprise in his voice.

"His name is Purdy," Brambleclaw replied. "He's the loner we met on our first journey to the sun-drown-place. Purdy, this is our Clan leader, Firestar."

"Welcome, Purdy." Jayfeather pictured the flame-colored tom dipping his head to welcome the old tabby into the camp. "You can stay in the elders' den. Foxpaw, will you go with him and introduce him to Mousefur and Longtail?"

"Thanks, Firestar," the loner meowed. "Sol, just you give me a call if you need me, okay?" He padded after Foxpaw as the apprentice led the way toward the elders' den.

As the old loner retreated, Leafpool padded up and gave Sol's pelt a thorough sniff. "Were you hurt at all on the journey?" she asked. "Any stiffness in your legs?"

"No." Sol's voice was tinged with amusement. "I'm used to traveling long distances."

Yes, because no cats want you around for very long. The sarcastic words rose to Jayfeather's lips, but he had more sense than to let them out.

"Come on, Sol, I'll take you to your nest," Brackenfur announced.

As the two of them padded off, Firestar called quietly to Spiderleg. "You can take the first watch over Sol," he murmured. "Bring him some fresh-kill, then make sure he stays in the den until morning."

"No problem, Firestar." Spiderleg bounded over to the fresh-kill pile.

Firestar headed back to his own den, leaving the rest of the Clan clustered together near the camp entrance.

"I'm sure he's a killer!" Poppyfrost exclaimed. "Did you see those eyes? He looks as if he could see right through you."

"I'm too scared to go to sleep," Icepaw mewed. "What if he murders us in our nests?"

"Right," Mousewhisker added. "I don't know why Firestar let him in here."

"Firestar needs to find out the truth," Brightheart meowed.

"And I'm sure there's nothing to worry about," Sorreltail

added briskly. "Spiderleg will make sure that Sol doesn't get out of his den."

In spite of the she-cats' reassurance, Jayfeather's paws tingled and the fur rose on his pelt as if a thunderstorm were about to break over the clearing. The air was tense with fear and uncertainty, as if every cat knew that something huge was hanging overhead.

Trying to ignore his jitters, Jayfeather padded over to where Hollyleaf and Lionblaze had flopped down together beside the thorn barrier.

"Hi," he mewed. "How was the journey?"

"Long." Lionblaze's voice was bleak. "I thought we'd never get back."

"We met some other cats," Hollyleaf added. "They were having trouble with dogs, and Sol had encouraged them to fight. Several of them were killed, and since then the cats have to battle the dogs every time they set paw outside their den." She let out a weary sigh. "More damage that Sol's done."

"He's a troublemaker," Lionblaze agreed, with a yawn.

The question Jayfeather wanted to ask—*Do you think he killed Ashfur?*—stayed unspoken. All he could pick up from his littermates were sensations of weariness, fear, and misery; he didn't allow himself to probe deeper into their minds.

"It's good to have you home," he told them.

Neither Lionblaze nor Hollyleaf responded. Jayfeather realized that although he had missed his brother and sister with pangs sharp as claws, now that they were back, the murdered body of Ashfur still came between them.

"Come and eat," he suggested, pushing the thought away. "Then you both need a good sleep."

I wonder if we'll get a chance to talk to Sol, he thought as he followed his littermates over to the fresh-kill pile. *After all, he's the only other cat who knows about the prophecy.* A new thought occurred to him: *Sol talked as if we were definitely the Three referred to in the prophecy. But we can't be, because Squirrelflight's not our mother!*

Was this something that Sol didn't know? Or had he been lying to them as well?

CHAPTER 16

Lionblaze woke to the sound of excited mewing and movement around him. He lifted his head to see his Clanmates pushing their way out of the warriors' den and into the clearing. He staggered to his paws, wincing at the stabs of pain from his aching muscles, and shouldered his way through the branches after them.

The sky was clear, but the sun hadn't risen far enough to penetrate the hollow. Deep shadows hung over the dens and blanketed Spiderleg in near darkness where he crouched, on watch outside Sol's nest. But even though it was so early, it looked as if most of ThunderClan was gathered in the clearing. Daisy, Millie, and Whitewing were sitting outside the nursery. Lionblaze saw that they had their tails curled protectively around the kits, who gazed out across the stone hollow with wide, scared eyes. Foxpaw and Icepaw bounded across to join the warriors, feeling the need to be close to the older, more experienced cats.

Hollyleaf was already up, standing with Hazeltail and Brackenfur. She didn't glance at Lionblaze, and somehow his paws wouldn't carry him over to her.

It's as if part of us, part of what we used to be, died with Ashfur!

Firestar emerged from his den on the Highledge and ran lightly down the tumbled rocks to join Graystripe at the bottom. At the appearance of the Clan leader, the excitement in the clearing mounted.

"Here's Firestar!"

"Now something's bound to happen!"

Lionblaze flexed his muscles, trying to work the stiffness out of them. He heard a flurry of paw steps, and the dawn patrol raced back into the camp with Thornclaw at their head.

"What's going on?" the golden brown warrior panted as he skidded to a standstill in the middle of the clearing. "Have we missed anything?"

Brambleclaw padded over to him. "What are you doing here so early?" he demanded. "You can't have been all the way along the ShadowClan border."

"Oh, everything's quiet," Berrynose mewed, peering over Thornclaw's shoulder. "There's nothing to worry about."

Brambleclaw's tail-tip twitched. "All right," he growled. "But take longer over it next time." He turned back to the cluster of warriors outside their den. "Hunting patrols," he announced. "Sandstorm, will you lead one, please. And Brightheart, you can— " He broke off, his tail flicking with irritation when he realized that no cat was listening to him.

He glanced frustratedly at Firestar, who padded up to him with Graystripe at his side. "They won't settle," Brambleclaw meowed. "No cat even wants to eat."

Graystripe nodded, and leaned over to murmur into Firestar's ear. Lionblaze just caught the soft words: "You may as well get this done now."

Firestar's ears pricked. "You're right. Brambleclaw, go and fetch Sol."

Every cat's gaze was fixed on the deputy as he padded across to the bush where Sol had slept. He exchanged a quick word with Spiderleg, then vanished under the branches. A few heartbeats later he emerged again with Sol behind him.

As the loner padded over to Firestar, the first rays of the sun slid over the rim of the hollow and shone on his fur. He looked as sleek as if he had spent the last moon grooming his pelt, instead of trekking through the Twolegplace and across open country to reach the camp. Lionblaze felt tired and scruffy in comparison.

As Brambleclaw escorted Sol to the center of the clearing, the ThunderClan cats drew back on either side, their eyes wide and their fur fluffed up.

What's wrong with them? Lionblaze wondered with a flash of irritation. *Sol's just a cat! Why are they acting like a lot of cowardly rabbits?*

"Sol! Wait for me!" Purdy's yowl echoed around the hollow as he erupted from the elders' den, with Mousefur and Longtail following. They halted just beyond the outer branches of the hazel bush, while Purdy lumbered farther into the clearing. His fur was sticking up on end, covered with scraps of moss, and his eyes blazed with anger.

Brackenfur intercepted him before he could reach Sol.

"Take it easy, Purdy," he mewed quietly. "No cat is harming Sol. Just keep back with the others."

Purdy gaped in shock, but before he could reply, Hazeltail padded up to him and nudged him over to sit beside her and Birchfall.

Firestar stood face to face with Sol in the middle of the circle of cats. "Do you know why we've brought you here?" he asked.

Sol tilted his head to one side. "A cat has been murdered, and you think I'm responsible." He confidently met Firestar's gaze. His fur gleamed in the pale, cold sunlight.

"You killed Ashfur!" Thornclaw snarled at him.

"Yes," Cloudtail growled. "You were seen on the Wind-Clan border. Don't try to deny it!"

"Why did you kill him?" Sorreltail demanded. "What had he ever done to you?"

Sol ignored the hostile yowling and kept his gaze fixed on Firestar as the Clan leader waved his tail for silence.

"One of our warriors was found in the WindClan border stream, with bitemarks in his throat," Firestar meowed when the clamor had died down. "Do you deny it was you?"

Sol stared at him without blinking. "Think about what you are saying, Firestar. The truth will be known when it is time."

Lionblaze caught a flash of frustration in Firestar's green eyes. Sol had neither confirmed nor denied the accusation.

"Make him confess!" some cat hissed from the back of the crowd.

Firestar ignored the fierce words, his gaze still fixed on Sol. "What were you doing on the WindClan border?" he asked.

Sol shrugged. "How should I remember? It was many sunrises ago."

"Did you see Ashfur there?" Lionblaze could tell how hard Firestar found it to keep his voice even and calm as he questioned the loner.

"Ashfur . . . ?"

"A powerful tom with thick gray fur." There was an edge of irritation in Firestar's tone; Lionblaze guessed that Sol knew very well who Ashfur was.

Sol shook his head. "I didn't see any cat there."

"Did you scent any?"

Lionblaze caught a gleam of amusement in Sol's eyes, as if the mysterious loner had picked up Firestar's increasing desperation. "I scented ThunderClan and WindClan," he replied. "But I didn't recognize any particular scents."

"Did you hear any sound of fighting?"

Sol blinked slowly. "No."

Firestar paused, the tip of his tail twitching in frustration. A cold claw seemed to touch Lionblaze's belly as he realized that even his Clan leader couldn't penetrate Sol's secrets.

"Go and get something to eat," Firestar mewed eventually. "But don't think this is over," he warned Sol. "We will speak of this again. Cloudtail, will you take over guard duty, please?"

"It'll be a pleasure," the white warrior growled. He padded after Sol and Brambleclaw as the deputy escorted Sol to the fresh-kill pile and then back to the nest, and settled himself under the outermost branches of the bush, his face grim and his pelt bristling.

When Sol had gone, Brambleclaw was able to organize the hunting patrols, and cats began to leave.

"All the cats who went to find Sol can have the morning to recover," the deputy meowed to Lionblaze. "Make sure you all get a good rest."

Lionblaze wasn't sure that would be possible. His Clanmates crowded around him and the other cats who had made the journey, demanding to know what had happened.

"Was it hard, trying to bring Sol back?" Poppyfrost asked.

"Yeah, did he try to escape?" Foxpaw added excitedly.

"No," Lionblaze replied. "He was willing to come. He did exactly what we wanted."

And that's strange, he added to himself. *Does he have a reason of his own for agreeing to come here?* Every hair on his pelt prickled. *Does he think he can do to us what he did to ShadowClan?*

"Were you scared?" Mousewhisker whispered, his eyes wide as if he was imagining all kinds of disasters. "That cat might do anything."

"You watch what you're saying, young 'un!" Purdy's voice rang out loudly as the elder came bustling up to the group of cats. "You don't know what you're talkin' about. Sol is a good cat. He's my friend."

Mousewhisker jumped back, alarmed by the old tabby's fierce protest.

"But he was seen—" Cinderheart began.

"Sol would *never* hurt another cat," Purdy insisted, looming over the younger cats. "Have you all got fluff in your heads?"

"Look, Purdy," Lionblaze began, trying to think of how he could convince the old cat.

Sandstorm interrupted him. "It's okay, Purdy. No cat will harm Sol if he's innocent. Come on, let me show you the fresh-kill pile."

Mumbling something under his breath, Purdy glared at the younger warriors before allowing the ginger she-cat to lead him away.

"Phew!" Lionblaze glanced at Hollyleaf. "I thought he was going to knock me out with his dog-breath."

Hollyleaf was more sympathetic. "Well, he's the only one defending Sol just now. Every other cat has already decided that he's guilty."

Lionblaze opened his mouth to ask, *What do you think?* But Hollyleaf was already padding away, and the question remained unspoken. Thinking it over, Lionblaze wasn't sure that he wanted to know the answer.

He was heading back to the warriors' den to rest when he heard a call from Firestar, and spotted the Clan leader at the foot of the tumbled rocks, beckoning with his tail to gather his remaining warriors around him. As he padded up to the Highledge, Lionblaze thought that Firestar looked edgy; he was flexing his claws as if he wanted action but wasn't sure what it should be.

"Leafpool," the Clan leader began, spotting the medicine cat at the edge of the group, "do you know of any way we can be sure whether Sol killed Ashfur?"

The medicine cat shook her head.

"What about the bitemarks?" Sorreltail suggested. "Could we get Sol to bite on a leaf, and then measure his teethmarks against Ashfur's wound?"

"Brilliant!" Firestar meowed, giving the tortoiseshell she-cat a warm look of approval. "I'll—"

"It won't work," Leafpool interrupted. "Ashfur has been buried for too long."

"There's something else we need to think about," Gray-stripe added. "Remember when ThunderClan kept Brokentail prisoner, back in the old forest? He ended up befriending Tigerclaw and attacking ThunderClan from within. We can't trust Sol while he's inside our camp!"

"Then we've got to punish him." Birchfall lashed his tail. "We can't let him cause any more trouble."

"Let's make him collect mouse bile!" Poppyfrost's eyes gleamed; clearly she was remembering the tasks she had to do when she was an apprentice.

"We could make him hunt prey for the Clan," Brackenfur suggested.

"But then he might escape," Lionblaze pointed out.

"We can't punish him until we're sure he's guilty," Firestar meowed. "All we can do is wait. Leafpool, will you watch for any signs from StarClan? Surely our warrior ancestors know the truth." He raked his claws across the ground, leaving deep marks in the wet earth. "Why haven't they shown us something already?"

Leafpool's expression was guarded. "StarClan will tell us

what it wants us to know in its own good time."

Firestar dipped his head, accepting what his medicine cat told him. "Then Sol will stay here under guard until we have more evidence," he decided. With another glance at Leafpool, he added, "Until StarClan decides to help us."

In the days that followed, ThunderClan settled into an uneasy routine of feeding Sol, watching him stretch his legs when he was allowed out into the clearing, and escorting him to make dirt. Sol never lost his air of calm, and he treated every cat with the same friendliness.

Lionblaze waited frustratedly for the chance to talk to him alone. He was desperate to discuss the prophecy. He couldn't forget the sense of power and control he had felt when facing the dogs, which convinced him still that he was one of the Three. But Sol was never left alone, and only the senior warriors were assigned to guard him.

The weather stayed sunny and dry, even though each morning the trees were rimmed with frost. Sometimes it was even warm enough by sunhigh to bask on a couple of flattish rocks at the base of the cliff. Mousefur especially liked to stretch out there, soaking up the sunlight.

"The elders should be allowed to bask here whenever we want," she had announced. "Our old bones need it." She sighed, twitching her ears. "Back in the old forest, we had Sunningrocks. All the Clan's cats could bask there together, if they wanted."

Since Purdy's arrival, she had taken to lying on the rocks

with him. Lionblaze was surprised at their friendship, but he figured that they talked about things like how rude young cats were these days and how much tastier prey used to be.

Around sunhigh, several days after the patrol's return, Lionblaze was strolling back to the camp with Honeyfern and Berrynose. They had spent the morning training with Squirrelflight and Brackenfur and the two apprentices; Brackenfur had taken over as Icepaw's mentor since Whitewing was so close to having her kits.

"They're doing so well," Honeyfern purred. "Did you see how high Icepaw can leap?"

"And Foxpaw can dodge really quickly," Lionblaze agreed. "Squirrelflight made them practice that move over and over again, and they've both got it now."

Berrynose paused to stretch his jaws wide in a yawn. "I feel like lying in the sun for a bit to catch my breath. I wonder if Mousefur will let us have a turn on the basking rocks."

"Good idea," mewed Lionblaze.

Pushing his way through the thorn tunnel, he saw that Mousefur, Purdy, and Longtail were all snoozing on the flat-topped rocks. Berrynose bounded over to them eagerly; Lionblaze followed with Honeyfern.

But Purdy wasn't dozing after all. "So my Upwalker," he was meowing as they approached, "he says to me, 'Purdy,' he says, 'there's only you can get rid of this mouse, and—'" He broke off, blinking as he spotted the younger cats.

Lionblaze noticed that Mousefur and Longtail, to whom Purdy was telling his story, were both fast asleep.

"Hi, Purdy," he greeted the old tabby. "We were wondering if we could bask here with you for a bit. We've been training all morning, and we're tired."

"Young cats today—no stamina," Purdy grumbled, but he rose to his paws, stretched, then prodded Mousefur and Longtail awake.

"Wha'?" Mousefur woke with a start.

"These young 'uns want to bask," Purdy explained.

The tip of Mousefur's tail twitched, but to Lionblaze's surprise she didn't object. "I suppose so," she muttered. "We'll even leave the rocks to you, providing one of you brings a bit of fresh-kill to our den. I could just eat a good plump vole."

"I'll do that," Honeyfern offered, bounding off to the fresh-kill pile.

Mousefur laid her tail on Longtail's shoulders to guide him down from the rocks, and the three elders headed off toward their den under the hazel bush.

"Thanks!" Lionblaze called after them.

"You fell asleep and missed some of the story," Purdy mewed to Mousefur as they retreated. "I'd better start it all over again. There was this mouse, see . . ."

Lionblaze and Berrynose climbed up onto the basking rocks, and Honeyfern joined them a few heartbeats later. The flat surface was warm where the elders had been lying, and bright yellow sunlight spilled down on it. Lionblaze stretched out and let the heat soak into his fur. *I wish I could lie like this forever,* he thought, *and never have to worry about anything again.*

On the rock next to him, Berrynose and Honeyfern were

sharing tongues and watching Millie's kits playing in the clearing close by.

Berrynose bent his head close to the tabby she-cat's ear. "We'll have kits like that one day," he purred.

Honeyfern looked up at him, blinking shyly. "I'd like that."

Lionblaze was surprised at how gentle Berrynose sounded; he was used to the older warrior being a bossy nuisance, ordering around other cats if he thought he could get away with it. Maybe having Honeyfern as a mate would be good for him.

At least he might stay out of my fur.

The cream-colored warrior rasped his tongue over Honeyfern's shoulder. "You'll make a wonderful mother."

Watching them together, a pang of loneliness gripped Lionblaze's belly. *Who is my mother? Why didn't she want me?* Closing his eyes, he wondered what she had been like, and whether she ever thought about the kits she had abandoned.

"Watch me! Watch me!" Blossomkit's voice came from a little way across the clearing. "I can leap higher than any cat!"

"No, you can't, I can!" Bumblekit argued.

Lionblaze opened one eye to see all three of Millie's kits leaping and tumbling around, a couple of fox-lengths from the rocks where he and his Clanmates lay. Briarkit fell over and rolled so that she was next to a crack in the rock wall; leaping up, she balanced on her hind legs with her forepaws stretching up into the air.

"I bet you can't do this!" she boasted.

In the same instant, Lionblaze spotted a long, dark shadow emerging from the rock behind the kit. It reared up against the gray stone, but Briarkit was too excited to notice. Lion-blaze sat bolt upright.

Snake!

He bunched his muscles to spring, but Honeyfern was quicker. Leaping down from the rock, she bundled Briarkit out of the way. The snake arched its neck; before Honeyfern could move it struck down and buried its hooked fangs in her shoulder.

Honeyfern sprang backward with a screech of pain. "Help!"

CHAPTER 17

♣

Hollyleaf pushed her way through the thorn tunnel with a vole and
two mice dangling from her jaws. Her hunting patrol had
done well, but her nose and paws were numb with cold as she
padded over to the fresh-kill pile. The leaf-bare sun didn't
penetrate the shadows under the trees, and the ground there
was still frozen.

She was dropping her prey on the pile when she heard a
shriek from the base of the cliff, on the far side of the medicine cats' den. Whirling around, she saw Lionblaze bolt into
the middle of the clearing, his pelt bristling as if a whole Clan
of enemies were on his tail.

"Help! Come quick!" he screeched. "Honeyfern's been bitten by a snake!"

Icy terror coursed through Hollyleaf's blood as she rushed
across the clearing. They'd never had a snake in the hollow
before! When she reached the cliff, she saw Briarkit cowering
at the base of the rocks; the little kit was trembling, her eyes
wide with shock. Millie bounded up and drew her away with
her tail wrapped protectively around the kit.

Berrynose crouched beside Honeyfern, who was lying on

her side with her paws splayed out; her breath came fast and shallow, and her eyes were full of terror. A thin line of blood on her shoulder showed where the snake had struck.

Sorreltail and Brackenfur raced across from the warriors' den with the same look of horror in their eyes when they saw their wounded daughter. Cinderheart, Honeyfern's littermate, was hard on their paws.

As they skidded to a halt, Sorreltail pressed her muzzle into Brackenfur's shoulder. "No . . . oh, no . . ." she whispered. "I can't lose another kit! Not after Molepaw! Please, Star-Clan . . ."

"Where's Poppyfrost?" Hollyleaf muttered to Lionblaze as her brother came running back. Sorreltail needed all her kits right now.

"Out on patrol," Lionblaze replied. "She—"

He broke off as Leafpool pushed her way through the knot of cats. "Stand back and give me some room," she ordered.

Berrynose glared at her. "I'm not leaving," he snarled.

Ignoring him, Leafpool crouched beside Honeyfern and rested one paw on her shoulder. "Try not to move," she meowed.

Hollyleaf waited expectantly for Leafpool to start helping Honeyfern. Surely she would know what to do? But she hadn't brought any herbs with her, and she wasn't doing anything more than sitting beside the trembling tabby warrior.

Leafpool looked up, her gaze sweeping over the crowd of cats and coming to rest on Cinderheart. There was a pleading look in her eyes, so desperate and hopeful that it made

Hollyleaf wince. *I don't understand,* she thought. *What does she want from Cinderheart?*

"Help me!" Honeyfern had begun to twitch and writhe in pain. "My blood is on fire! Help me, please! It hurts so much!"

Berrynose stared at Leafpool. "Do something!" he begged. His gaze swept over the cluster of cats. "One of you, do something!"

Leafpool didn't seem to hear him; she just dragged her gaze away from Cinderheart and looked down at Honeyfern as she struggled for breath.

Sorreltail slid out her claws, her disbelieving gaze fixed on the medicine cat. "Why aren't you doing anything?"

Leafpool bowed her head. "I'm so sorry," she whispered. "There's nothing I can do. The poison has taken hold of her."

Sorreltail raised her head and let out a yowl of anguish, while Brackenfur wrapped his tail around her shoulders and drew her close.

Honeyfern's legs folded into her belly, and her back arched in agony. When the spasm passed she lay limply, her chest hardly moving to show that she was still breathing. Her legs continued to twitch; her eyes had begun to glaze over.

In silence, Hollyleaf and the rest of the cats shuffled backward to give Berrynose space to help Honeyfern on her journey to StarClan. The cream-colored tom crouched over her, stroking her fur with one paw. "We would have had wonderful kits together," he murmured. "Just as strong and beautiful as you. And one day I'll see you in StarClan."

Honeyfern's jaw moved and a rasping sound came from her throat, as if she was trying to reply.

"You saved Briarkit's life," Berrynose went on, bending his head to lick the dying she-cat's head. "Every cat in StarClan will honor you."

A long sigh came from Honeyfern. Hollyleaf watched helplessly as her friend's limbs grew still and the rise and fall of her chest faded away. Finally, her blue eyes stared sightlessly into the sky.

Pain as sharp as the snake's bite pierced Hollyleaf. She gazed at Cinderheart's horrified expression, trying to imagine how she would feel if she lost one of her littermates.

No! Hollyleaf dug her claws into the earth. *That must never happen!*

Leafpool moved toward Honeyfern's body, but Brackenfur stopped her. Instead he padded up to Berrynose and rested his tail on the young warrior's shoulder. "She's gone," he told him. "She hunts with StarClan now."

As gently as if he were Berrynose's father, Brackenfur nudged him to his paws and led him away, then nodded to Leafpool. The medicine cat crouched beside Honeyfern with a paw on her chest to check for any signs of breathing. Shaking her head slightly, she mewed to Lionblaze, "Find some warriors to help carry her body into the clearing. We need to get her away from the cliff in case the snake is still around."

"I'll help," Hollyleaf offered instantly.

Lionblaze beckoned with his tail to Spiderleg and Thornclaw, and together the four cats lifted Honeyfern's limp body and carried it to a shaded spot not far from the warriors' den.

As they were crossing the clearing, Graystripe appeared through the thorn tunnel, his jaws full of prey. Poppyfrost and Mousewhisker followed him into the camp. As soon as she saw her sister's body, Poppyfrost dropped her fresh-kill and raced over.

"What happened?" she wailed. "Honeyfern, wake up!"

Sorreltail padded up to her and guided her along after Honeyfern's body, their pelts brushing, until the warriors set the dead she-cat down and her kin could huddle together around her, comforting one another as they kept vigil.

The sun still shone, but Hollyleaf felt as if ice were creeping through the hairs on her pelt, and she couldn't stop shivering. "Are you okay?" she asked Lionblaze. "You saw it all happen."

Lionblaze gave her a bleak nod but didn't speak.

"Honeyfern will be a great loss to her Clan."

Hollyleaf started as she heard Sol's voice, and turned to see that the loner had left his nest. Thornclaw must have left him unguarded when he came to see what was happening. Sol's amber eyes shone with sadness and his head was bowed as if he genuinely grieved for the young she-cat.

"It's hard when a life is cut off so early," he added.

Hollyleaf knew she should send him back to his nest, but she couldn't summon the energy. All the other cats seemed too distracted by their grief to worry about what Sol was up to.

He might as well stay, she thought. *What harm is he doing?*

Purdy and the elders had appeared, too, padding up and mingling with their Clanmates.

"There's nothin' worse than losin' a young cat," Purdy

meowed. "She'd all her life stretchin' in front of her."

"She was a fine cat," Mousefur agreed. "The last thing she ever did was fetch me some fresh-kill."

All the cats were milling around in the center of the clearing, unsure what to do. Hollyleaf was relieved when Graystripe strode into the middle of them, raising his tail for silence.

"Mousewhisker," he directed, "go and fetch Firestar. He took a hunting patrol toward the old Twoleg nest. Brambleclaw is on a border patrol, so we'll have to wait for him to come back, as I don't know where he'll be right now," he added as Mousewhisker pelted off. "Leafpool, can you check Briarkit, to make sure she's okay?"

Leafpool nodded; she looked glad to have something to do. Millie guided her kit over to the medicine cat and waited, her claws scraping the ground and her eyes frantic with worry. Daisy followed, keeping a watchful eye on all the other kits, who seemed as shocked as Briarkit.

As Leafpool sniffed the kit all over, Hollyleaf murmured to Lionblaze, "She *must* be all right. Honeyfern can't have died for nothing."

Finally Leafpool nodded. "She'll be fine," she told Millie. "I'll give her a poppy seed so she gets a good night's sleep."

"But what about the snake?" Daisy wailed. "We've never had one in the camp before."

"Yes, what about it?" Millie added. "We've got to do something. More cats might die."

Graystripe turned to Lionblaze. "Show me exactly where the snake struck."

Hollyleaf followed her brother and Graystripe across the

clearing toward the basking rocks. She admired the way the gray warrior had taken over; he must have been a good Clan deputy back in the forest, she realized.

"That's the crack that the snake came out of." Lionblaze pointed with his tail toward a deep cleft in the cliff face. "I didn't see if it went back in there."

Very cautiously, Graystripe approached and sniffed along the cliff, peering into every crack. "No sign of it," he reported, returning to Lionblaze. "But it could be anywhere. Some of these cracks are very deep. There's plenty of room for it to hide."

Hollyleaf's paws tingled with fear. How could they go on living in the stone hollow, when death might come sliding silently out of the cliff at any moment and strike down another cat?

"Millie's right," she meowed. "We have to do something."

Before Graystripe could reply, there was a flash of flame-colored fur at the entrance to the tunnel, and Firestar raced back into the camp. Graystripe bounded over to meet him. Hollyleaf watched as her leader's expression changed from anxiety to horror, and he padded over to Honeyfern's body, where he crouched down beside her grieving kin.

Hollyleaf was just close enough to hear what he said. "I'm so sorry." Firestar's voice was shaking. "Honeyfern should have been safe here. I promise you I'll never let anything like this happen again."

But how can you stop it? Hollyleaf wondered. *It's not your fault. You couldn't have known there was a snake hiding under the cliff.*

Mousewhisker had followed Firestar into the camp, along with Dustpelt and Birchfall, the rest of Firestar's patrol. They were soon joined by Brightheart and Jayfeather, each carrying a bunch of catmint. Their dazed expressions told Hollyleaf that Mousewhisker must have met them, too, and passed on the terrible news. Last of all, Brambleclaw's patrol returned from checking the WindClan border; their cries of shock and anguish echoed around the hollow. Hollyleaf longed to go back to her nest in the warriors' den and bury herself in the moss and bracken with her eyes shut tight. Perhaps Honeyfern's death would turn out to be just a terrible dream.

Before her paws could carry her there, she saw Firestar bounding up the rocks to stand on the Highledge. "Cats of ThunderClan!" He raised his voice to carry to every part of the stone hollow. "A dreadful thing has happened, but we must stay calm. Honeyfern died a warrior's death, protecting a kit of her Clan. We will mourn her, not just tonight, but for all the moons to come. And we must make sure that the snake doesn't come back to hurt any other cats."

"Tell us what to do, and we'll do it," Brambleclaw called out.

Firestar dipped his head to his deputy. "To begin with, we'll make a barrier of brambles across that part of the cliff. Dustpelt, will you take charge of that?" The brown tabby warrior gave a curt nod. "No cat must go near it. Millie and Daisy, make sure that your kits understand. And it's best we don't use the basking rocks anymore. Snakes usually sleep during leaf-bare, but I think this one must have been disturbed by cats sunning themselves on the stones."

Hollyleaf saw Purdy and Mousefur exchanging a shocked glance. "That might have been us!" Purdy exclaimed.

Mousefur hung her head, and her eyes filled with sorrow. "Better it had been me, than that poor young cat," she murmured.

"Okay," Firestar meowed. "Get on with your duties, all of you. Tonight we will keep vigil for Honeyfern." He ran lightly down the rocks again and bounded across to Brambleclaw.

"Lionblaze!" Dustpelt called. "Help me with the barrier, please. You can take Foxpaw and Icepaw into the forest to collect brambles."

"Coming," Lionblaze replied. He paused briefly to touch noses with Hollyleaf, then raced off to round up the two apprentices.

Daisy and Millie were gathering their kits together and bundling them back toward the nursery. "Don't any of you *dare* go near that part of the cliff," Millie meowed sternly. "You heard what Firestar said."

"We won't." Blossomkit's mew was high-pitched with fear, and all the kits looked unusually subdued.

Whitewing was following them back to the nursery when Birchfall bounded over to her and pressed his nose into her shoulder. "You will be careful, won't you?" he fretted.

The white she-cat blinked at him, her eyes full of love. "Of course I will. You don't have to fuss."

Birchfall angled his ears toward Berrynose, still crouched silently over the body of Honeyfern. "I won't lose you to Star-Clan," he insisted. "Not for a long, long time."

Whitewing and Birchfall leaned into each other, their pelts brushing and their tails twined together.

Hollyleaf stood still as the rest of the cats moved away. She didn't know what to do. She wanted to go and comfort Cinderheart, but she didn't dare disturb Honeyfern's grieving kin. She had begun to pad uncertainly toward the warriors' den when Leafpool trotted up to her.

"Hollyleaf, could you help Brightheart to put the herbs away?" she asked. "Jayfeather and I are going to check the queens and kits for signs of shock."

"Sure." Hollyleaf was relieved to have something to do. She retrieved Jayfeather's share of the catmint and carried it to the medicine cats' den, where Brightheart was already sorting through her bundle of stems. Hollyleaf joined her; it was good to breathe in the scent of herbs that drifted around the den; it reminded her of when she had been Leafpool's apprentice. *I used to get worried when I couldn't remember which herb was which. If only that was all I had to worry about now!*

"I wish we knew an herb to cure snakebite," Brightheart murmured sadly as her forepaws flicked through the leaves, deftly stripping off any that were shriveled or damaged.

Hollyleaf nodded, but she knew that no amount of wishing would bring Honeyfern back. Her ears flicked up at the sound of a cat brushing past the bramble screen; she glanced over her shoulder to see Leafpool coming in.

"I need some poppy seeds for Daisy," the medicine cat explained. "She's getting hysterical."

"I can't say I blame her," Brightheart mewed. "If I had

kits now, I'd be terrified."

Leafpool collected the seed in a leaf wrap and was about to leave the den when Firestar put his head around the brambles.

"Yes?" Leafpool asked; there was an edge to her tone that Hollyleaf didn't understand.

"We need to make sure the snake isn't a threat to us," Firestar meowed quietly.

Leafpool blinked, puzzled. "What do you want me to do? I can't summon the snake out of its hole."

"No," Firestar replied, "but you can make sure that it never reaches the main part of the camp. I want you to put deathberries around the place where the snake came from."

Hollyleaf felt her paws freeze to the ground as soon as the Clan leader mentioned deathberries. She exchanged a shocked glance with Brightheart. Every cat knew that Leafpool refused to have deathberries in the camp because they were so dangerous.

"Firestar, you know—" the medicine cat began.

"Explain to the kits, and to every single cat, what the berries are and why they mustn't be touched or eaten," Firestar interrupted her. "They'll understand. We have to do this. I will *not* lose another cat this way."

Leafpool hesitated, then nodded reluctantly. "Very well. Jayfeather and I will collect some today. But I don't like it," she added more forcefully. "If the deathberries don't kill the snake within one moon, we'll have to try something else."

CHAPTER 18

Lionblaze led Foxpaw and Icepaw into the forest to collect brambles. He felt numb; the terrible scene kept repeating itself endlessly behind his eyes.

Was there anything I could have done? If I'd been quicker . . . maybe if I'd leaped for the snake I could have killed it first.

Both the apprentices were still trembling with fear, spooking at every leaf rustle, as if they thought that a snake might be hiding in every hollow. *And for all I know, they're right. . . .*

"I can't believe we've got Sol *and* a snake in the camp," Icepaw mewed, jumping aside with her fur bristling as an oak leaf drifted to the ground beside her.

"I wonder if Sol summoned the snake to kill Honeyfern," Foxpaw added, his voice shaking.

"Don't be ridiculous!" Lionblaze's voice came out louder than he'd intended; both apprentices jumped backward. "The snake was just there. It could easily have bitten Sol instead of Honeyfern."

"I wish it had," Foxpaw muttered.

Lionblaze didn't say anything. Hadn't there been enough death in the Clan already?

He led the apprentices to a bramble thicket near the

beginning of the old Thunderpath and crawled underneath to bite the long, thornless stems at the bottom. The two apprentices hesitated at the edge of the stone, blinking nervously.

"Come on!" Lionblaze urged them. "What's the matter?"

"Are there any snakes in there?" Icepaw whimpered.

"If there are, I'm dead," Lionblaze replied irritably. "Okay," he added with a sigh. "I'll bite through the stems, and you drag the tendrils out."

For a while they worked steadily, and the pile of bramble tendrils began to grow. Then Foxpaw stopped with the end of a stem in his mouth.

"What's wrong?" Lionblaze asked. "I need you to get that out of the way so I can reach the next one."

Foxpaw dropped the tendril. "I can smell WindClan!"

Icepaw let go the stem she was dragging to the pile and tasted the air. "No, it's RiverClan!" she exclaimed.

Quickly Lionblaze wriggled his way out of the thicket and took a deep breath. "You're both right," he meowed, his neck fur beginning to rise. "And there's ShadowClan scent as well."

Foxpaw laid his ears flat and crouched low to the ground. "Are we being invaded again?" he shrieked.

"I don't think so." Lionblaze forced himself to stay calm. "The scents aren't strong enough for lots of cats." Gesturing with his tail, he added, "Stay behind me. And don't do *anything* unless I tell you."

The two apprentices huddled together, close to his hind paws, while Lionblaze faced the undergrowth from where the scents were approaching. A clump of bracken quivered, and Blackstar of ShadowClan stepped into the open, followed by Rowanclaw. A heartbeat later Leopardstar and Reedwhisker appeared, and hard on their paws came Onestar and Tornear.

All three leaders! Lionblaze stared at them, his heart racing. *What kind of patrol is this?*

"Greetings, Lionblaze." Blackstar dipped his head. "We need to speak with Firestar."

"O-okay," Lionblaze meowed. "Follow me. Foxpaw, Icepaw, bring back the brambles, please."

Leaving the apprentices to their task, he led the visitors back to the stone hollow and through the thorn tunnel. The clearing was quieter than when he had left. Honeyfern's body still lay in the shade. Her family crouched around it, keeping vigil alone until nightfall. Sol had disappeared; Thornclaw was back on guard duty outside his nest. The queens and kits had retreated into the nursery.

Firestar was standing in the middle of the clearing, talking to Graystripe and Brambleclaw. All three cats looked up in surprise as Lionblaze emerged with his unusual patrol following.

"Greetings," Firestar mewed, dipping his head courteously to the other Clan leaders. His tone was wary, and his neck fur had begun to bristle. "What can I do for you?"

Blackstar didn't bother to return his greeting. "Is Sol here?" he demanded.

"And is it true that he killed Ashfur?" Leopardstar added.

Onestar bared his teeth in a snarl. "When were you going to tell us that you're keeping a murderer captive?"

Firestar's ears pricked and his tail-tip twitched from side to side. Lionblaze could see shock in his green eyes. "How did you find out so quickly?" he asked.

"One of my patrols saw your cats returning with Sol along the edge of the lake," Onestar replied, his voice tense with anger. "They told a RiverClan patrol, and RiverClan passed on the news to ShadowClan."

Firestar's gaze flicked from one leader to the next. "Since when was this any of the other Clans' business?" he meowed icily.

"Since you put *our* Clans in danger," Leopardstar retorted.

"You *know* how much of a threat that cat is," Onestar added, his forepaws kneading the ground. "And yet you brought him back into our territories!"

Blackstar took a pace forward. Lionblaze could hardly believe that he would attack Firestar in the ThunderClan camp, but he braced his muscles ready to defend his leader if any of the other cats so much as raised a paw.

"Have you forgotten what Sol tried to do to ShadowClan?" Blackstar hissed. "He tried to force us to stop believing in StarClan!"

And I'm a mouse! Lionblaze thought cynically. A look flashed between Graystripe and Brambleclaw, telling Lionblaze that the senior warriors shared his thought. Blackstar wasn't prepared to admit any responsibility, though at the time he had been only too willing to listen to Sol.

"What are you going to do with him?" Leopardstar demanded.

Firestar hesitated. He was looking increasingly harried, but he kept his claws sheathed. "I haven't decided," he admitted. "We're still trying to find out exactly what happened."

Onestar's nostrils flared and he narrowed his eyes. "Sol is too dangerous to keep anywhere near the lake. You should send him away *now*."

"You should have left him where he was," Leopardstar growled. "Any cat with a flea's worth of sense would see that."

"Then Ashfur's murder would have gone unpunished," Firestar argued.

"Vengeance isn't everything," Onestar spat. "You have put all our Clans in danger by bringing Sol back. Whatever happens next, you will not have our support."

The other two leaders nodded in agreement, and a threatening murmur came from their three followers. A chill ran through Lionblaze, though hot blood was pounding in his veins; he wanted to slice his claws through the fur of these arrogant cats. *They have no right to interfere in ThunderClan's business like this!*

Blackstar raised his chin. "Sol must be gone from Clan territory by the next Gathering," he insisted. "Or we will unite our three Clans to get rid of him ourselves."

CHAPTER 19

Jayfeather padded in Leafpool's paw steps as she climbed to the ridge where the trees thinned out and pine needles prickled under paw. He felt the ground grow damp and his paws slipped as he scrambled down the other side into a tangle of undergrowth. As he regained his balance, he picked up the tang of yew bark and berries.

"Here we are," Leafpool meowed. "I'm going to climb the tree and bend down a branch so you can reach it." She nudged him forward a couple of paw steps. "Stand just there."

Jayfeather listened to his mentor scramble up the tree, and a few heartbeats later felt the touch of the yew branch on the top of his head. His fur bristled at the overwhelming scent of deathberries.

"Reach up as high as you can." Leafpool's voice came from just above him. "There's a stem with berries just there. Be very careful."

Like you need to tell me! Jayfeather thought.

He stretched upward, his front paws lifting from the ground, until a feathery twig poked him in the face and he felt the heavy clump of deathberries touch his fur. He managed to fasten his teeth into the stem where it met the branch, and felt Leafpool's muzzle press close to his as she helped him bite it through.

Waves of unhappiness were flooding from the medicine cat, shocking Jayfeather so much that he almost lost his balance. He had to shuffle his hind paws, wedging them more firmly among the damp pine needles, before he could go on nibbling at the twig with its deadly load. Leafpool was filled with gnawing anxiety about bringing more death into the hollow; she was saturated with sorrow, so full of grief that she could hardly move.

Yet her voice was steady as she mewed, "That's it," and Jayfeather felt the twig fall to the forest floor just beside his paws. He relaxed, rolling his shoulders to get rid of the strain of stretching, then picked up the clump of berries by the end of the twig, careful not to let any of the deathberries touch his mouth.

A light thump beside him told him that Leafpool had leaped down from the tree. "If you carry that," she told him, "I'll follow behind and make sure that none of the berries fall off. It doesn't matter so much up here, but I don't want to scatter any of them near the camp."

When they emerged from the thorn tunnel, the clearing seemed full of cats, their voices buzzing like an angry swarm of bees. Jayfeather located Lionblaze and padded up to him, setting the deathberries down for a moment to ask, "What in StarClan's name has happened now?"

"The other three Clan leaders were here." Lionblaze's voice was a low, furious growl. "They told Firestar he has to get rid of Sol by the next Gathering, or they'll get rid of him themselves."

"What?" Jayfeather lashed his tail. "What right do they have to tell ThunderClan what to do?"

He could feel sparks of anger coming from Lionblaze. "They don't care that Ashfur was killed," his brother snarled. "They're like scared rabbits, convinced that Sol is going to leap out and tear them apart. Firestar *can't* give in to them!"

Jayfeather murmured agreement, but his paws tingled with unease. He didn't like that the other Clans knew all about Ashfur's murder. The ripples of the gray warrior's death were spreading farther and farther, and there was no sign that the effects would fade away.

He tried to shrug off the uneasy feeling as he heard Leafpool calling him. "Jayfeather, put the berries on this leaf. We have to make sure that all the kits know how dangerous they are."

She set a flat leaf down in front of Jayfeather, who laid the clump of deathberries on top of it. Then he followed his mentor as she dragged the leaf across the camp to the nursery. "Fetch Foxpaw and Icepaw, too," she added.

Jayfeather tasted the air and located the two apprentices near the cliff where Dustpelt was building the barrier. "Foxpaw! Icepaw!" he called, jerking his head. "Leafpool wants you."

"Coming!" Icepaw called.

Jayfeather caught a grumble from Dustpelt. "I *suppose* we'll get this barrier built this side of greenleaf. Come right back when Leafpool's finished with you!" he ordered the two apprentices.

"Millie! Daisy!" Leafpool called when Jayfeather caught her up outside the nursery. "Bring the kits out here, please."

"Why?" Daisy's voice was drowsy from the poppy seeds.

"There's something I need to show all of you."

Leafpool and Jayfeather waited while the two queens herded their kits outside; Whitewing followed them, crouching in the entrance tunnel.

"Now," Leafpool began, "do you see these berries?"

Jayfeather could feel the kits' curiosity, though they were still subdued and didn't answer Leafpool.

"They look tasty," Bumblekit ventured after a heartbeat.

"No! They're not tasty!" Leafpool's voice quivered with anger and disgust. "These berries are *evil*. They're called deathberries, and if you eat just one of them, you won't just get a bellyache, you'll *die*. There won't be anything a medicine cat can do for you."

Jayfeather knew that wasn't entirely true. Mousefur had told him that Cinderpelt had saved Sorreltail after she ate deathberries by making her sick, but it had been a close call. Leafpool had to scare the kits thoroughly, though, so they wouldn't dream of going near the deathberries.

"Then why have you brought them into the camp?" Daisy fretted.

"Because Firestar wants to use them to kill the snake," Leafpool replied. "I need to make sure that every cat knows not to go near them."

"Did you hear that?" Millie asked the kits sharply. "Take a good look, so you'll recognize them again."

"We'll be careful," Rosekit mewed, sounding scared. The rest of the kits murmured agreement.

"Foxpaw? Icepaw?" Leafpool prompted.

"We'll remember," Foxpaw meowed. "We won't touch them."

"We'll keep a lookout for them when we're out in the forest, too," Icepaw added.

"Good. Then you can go. But don't forget what I said." Leafpool began to drag the leaf with its deadly load back across the camp, but halted and turned to Jayfeather. "Bring me a mouse from the fresh-kill pile, please."

Jayfeather bounded off, returning with the mouse to the medicine cats' den. "It's a good plump one," he meowed.

"I'm not going to eat it," Leafpool told him. "This is for the snake. I'm going to stuff it with deathberries. Put it down and keep your paw on it to hold it steady."

"You'll get poison on your paws!" Jayfeather exclaimed.

"No, I'm going to use a stick to push the berries down the mouse's throat."

As he clamped his paw firmly over the mouse, Jayfeather could feel his mentor's revulsion at what she was doing. He could almost read her thoughts. *I'm a medicine cat! I'm supposed to cure, not kill!* But he said nothing while Leafpool went on shoving the deadly berries into the body of the mouse.

I'll only get my fur clawed off if I try to talk to her.

Finally Leafpool let out a sigh. "There, that should do. I've poked some thorns in there, too. They'll cut the snake from inside and send the poison more quickly around its body."

Jayfeather nodded. He was surprised by how much his mentor hated using her skills like this, seeing as her victim was the snake that had killed Honeyfern. He had been fascinated to discover that there were plants that would harm instead of heal. *I wonder if there are others. . . .*

Leafpool laid the prepared mouse back on the leaf and dragged it out into the clearing again, over to where Dustpelt was building the bramble barrier around the snake's hole. Lionblaze and the two apprentices were helping him.

Jayfeather padded over to his brother, while Leafpool explained to Dustpelt what she had done.

"Good idea," the brown tabby warrior grunted. "I'll put it behind the barrier near the hole."

"Be careful," Leafpool warned him.

"I'll be fine," Dustpelt meowed, sounding unusually gentle as he reassured the medicine cat. "Look, I'm picking it up by the tail." Jayfeather heard him leap across the barrier and a moment later leap back. "There," he meowed. "All done. Right, what are you waiting for?" he added, swinging around to face his helpers. "Let's get this barrier finished."

Back in their den, Jayfeather and Leafpool wrapped the rest of the deathberries in the leaf. "We'd better store them in case the mouse doesn't work the first time," Leafpool explained. "I don't like it, but—"

A loud wail interrupted her. "Leafpool! Leafpool!"

"What now?" Jayfeather groaned.

He picked up Birchfall's scent as the young warrior crashed past the bramble screen. "Leafpool, you've got to come at once!" he panted. "Whitewing has pains in her belly."

"All right, don't panic." Leafpool rose to her paws. "I'm sure it's nothing serious. Maybe her kits are coming. Jayfeather, put that leaf wrap away," she instructed as she brushed past him. "Right at the back of the store where no cat will pick it up by mistake."

Gingerly Jayfeather pushed the leaf wrap in front of him and crept all the way to the back of the store, among a litter of old folded leaves and piles of shriveled herbs. "We need to clear this lot out," he muttered as he pushed the deathberries into the farthest corner.

Crawling back into the den, he twitched his whiskers with disgust. His pelt was covered with herb dust and clinging stems. He had just begun to groom one shoulder when Leafpool returned.

"Whitewing's fine," she reported. "It's just a bellyache. I'll take her a couple of juniper berries." She ducked quickly into the store and out again with the berries in a leaf wrap. "I've just remembered," she mumbled around her mouthful. "With all this trouble, I forgot to check on Purdy's sore pads. Can you go and do it now?"

"Sure," Jayfeather sighed, resigning himself to putting up with a messy pelt for a bit longer. He fetched the ointment of yarrow from the store and padded over to the elders' den.

As he crawled under the outer branches of the hazel bush, he heard Purdy's voice. "What I don't understan' is why you're all against Sol. Those other leaders who came here today, they want Firestar to get rid of him!" The old tabby sounded flustered. "Why won't any of you listen when I tell you he's a good cat?"

"Purdy, you're not listening when other cats tell you what Sol did here." Mousefur sounded as if her patience was wearing thin.

And there was never that much of it anyway, Jayfeather thought as he paused at the edge of the den.

Purdy snorted. "Some nonsense about tellin' other cats what to believe in. They didn' have to listen if they didn' want to."

True! Jayfeather suppressed a *mrrow* of amusement. *Purdy's not as stupid as some cats seem to think!*

"StarClan is very important to us, Purdy," Longtail murmured. "You'll understand if you stay with us."

"Cats in the sky!" Purdy snorted again. "Hedgehogs will fly before I believe that. Anyway," he went on, "that's nothin' to do with how Firestar is treatin' Sol now. It's not natural, keepin' a cat penned up like that. Firestar needs to come to his senses an' let Sol live with the rest of the Clan."

Jayfeather padded forward; he could sense Mousefur's anger growing and wanted to prevent a quarrel. Spotting him, Mousefur let out a hiss of annoyance and went to crouch in the farthest corner of the den.

"Hi, Purdy. I've come to look at your pads," Jayfeather announced.

"About time," the old cat grumbled. "My paws feel as if they're burnin' off." He lay down on his side, sticking out his paws for Jayfeather to examine.

Jayfeather felt carefully over all four of the elder's feet. They were cracked—probably from his long journey—and they felt hot and swollen. "This ointment will help," he mewed, beginning to smooth it on. "Try to stay off your paws as much as you can. The apprentices will bring you fresh-kill."

Purdy let out a long sigh. "That's much better, young 'un. You may be a scrawny young piece o' nothin', but you know what you're doin'."

"Thanks a bunch," Jayfeather muttered. "I'll come every day and—" He broke off as Longtail stretched out his neck to sniff the young cat's pelt.

"Jayfeather, that herb . . ."

"What herb?"

"Sticking to your pelt, I'm not sure, but I think—Mousefur, come over here," the blind elder called.

"What?" Mousefur still sounded grouchy, but she padded back to Jayfeather and sniffed at his fur. Then he felt her lick off one of the stems he must have picked up when he crawled into the back of the store. She chewed slowly.

"What are you *doing*?" Jayfeather asked.

"That's it!" Mousefur's voice was shrill with surprise. "Jayfeather, that's the herb Leafpool mixed in with my tansy!"

CHAPTER 20

Jayfeather wriggled around and sniffed where some scraps of the herb still clung to his pelt. The scent was sharp, and as he pushed his nose against the dried leaves, he felt a crinkled edge. He had no idea what the herb was. Leafpool must hardly ever use it; she certainly had never told him about it.

Rapidly he finished spreading yarrow ointment on Purdy's pads. "That should be fine," he meowed. "I'll fetch you some more tomorrow."

He whirled around and slipped out of the den, ignoring Purdy's plaintive cry of "What was all that about?"

Racing back to his own den, he found Leafpool curled up in her nest. "Leafpool, what—?" he began, skidding to a halt beside her. Then he broke off. He remembered how defensive Leafpool had been the first time he had questioned her about the mysterious herb. *Better keep quiet, and find out what I can by myself.*

"Jayfeather, why are you rushing around like that?" Leafpool mewed; she sounded bone-weary. "I want to have a quick nap before sunset. The Clan is sitting vigil for Honeyfern tonight."

"Sorry," Jayfeather mumbled. To his relief, Leafpool didn't ask him what he had been about to say.

"This is the night we should travel to the Moonpool," she went on. "You'll have to go by yourself. I can't leave the vigil."

Jayfeather nodded. "Okay." He made himself sound calm, but he wanted to bounce up and down like an excited kit. Without Leafpool, surely he could find out something about the mystery herb from the other medicine cats?

A brisk evening breeze rattled the bare branches as Jayfeather padded through the forest. His earlier excitement had faded; he set his paws down confidently, but inwardly he was full of doubt. What would the other medicine cats say about Sol?

When he reached the top of the ridge, he found Barkface and Kestrelpaw waiting for him beside the stream. Just as he reached them, Littlecloud came bounding up from the direction of ShadowClan. Jayfeather's ears pricked with surprise as he picked up another cat's scent along with him. "Flamepaw!" he exclaimed.

"You remember me!" Flamepaw was bubbling over with excitement, like a pool in a rainstorm. "I saw you when Tawnypelt brought me to your camp with Tigerpaw and Dawnpaw. We're kin," he added proudly.

No, we're not. A pang of regret shook Jayfeather. He liked the three eager young apprentices.

"Flamepaw is my apprentice now," Littlecloud announced.

"Tonight I'll introduce him to StarClan."

"Congratulations," Jayfeather meowed, touching the young cat on the shoulder with his tail. He remembered how disappointed Flamepaw had been when he and his littermates came to the ThunderClan camp, because Sol had convinced Blackstar that ShadowClan didn't need a medicine cat. It was great to hear that he was happy now, following the path Star-Clan had laid out for him. This wasn't the right time to tell him that they weren't kin after all.

There won't ever be a right time, Jayfeather thought.

By the time the other cats had exchanged greetings, there was still no sign of Mothwing and Willowshine from River-Clan.

"We won't wait," Barkface decided. "We've a lot to get through tonight."

"Maybe they'll catch up," Littlecloud meowed.

And maybe Mothwing doesn't feel like trekking all the way to the Moonpool just to catch up on her sleep, Jayfeather thought. *She usually sends Willowshine, though.*

The medicine cats were beginning the last scramble up the steep slope toward the bushes that surrounded the Moonpool, when they heard a breathless yowl from behind them. "Wait! Wait for us!"

Jayfeather turned and caught the scent of Mothwing and her apprentice, growing rapidly stronger as the two cats raced to catch up.

"Sorry," Mothwing panted as they reached the bottom of the rocks. "We got held up. Petalkit got a thorn in her eye."

"Poor little thing," Barkface murmured. "I hope you got it out."

"Yes, it just took a good lick," Mothwing replied. "I left her asleep in the nursery."

"I don't know if you've tried this," Littlecloud meowed, "but I've always found celandine good for damaged eyes. Just trickle a bit of the juice into her eye to ease the pain."

"Oh, thank you!" Mothwing exclaimed. "I didn't know that. I'll try it as soon as we get back. Willowshine, do we have any celandine in the store?"

"I think so," the younger cat replied. "There's not much left, but it should be enough."

"Let's keep going," Barkface mewed. "We're wasting moonlight."

Jayfeather clawed his way up the rocky hillside and pushed through the bushes to the rim of the hollow where the Moonpool lay. He could hear the gentle splash of the waterfall, and pictured the surface of the water dappled with the light of countless stars.

"I've something to say," Barkface announced as the cats settled down beside the pool. "Jayfeather, I know our leaders visited your Clan to talk about Sol."

Jayfeather's belly clenched; he braced himself for what he thought was coming.

"I want to say that it must have been a very hard decision for Firestar to make," the old medicine cat went on. "I don't think any of us should say that it was the right or the wrong thing to do."

The other medicine cats murmured their agreement.

Jayfeather's ears twitched; that was the last thing he had expected to hear, and he was surprised and touched by his companions' sympathy. "It—it's in the paws of StarClan," he stammered.

"And it's time for us to share tongues with StarClan." Jayfeather heard Littlecloud rise and pad to the very edge of the water. "But first, I must present Flamepaw to the spirits of his warrior ancestors. Flamepaw, are you ready?"

"Yes." The word came out as a squeak; Jayfeather felt Flamepaw's embarrassment mingled with his awe.

"Flamepaw," Littlecloud went on, slipping into the words of the age-old ritual, "is it your wish to enter into the mysteries of StarClan as a medicine cat?"

"It is." Now the young cat had control of his voice, though excitement still vibrated through it.

"Then come forward."

Flamepaw padded past Jayfeather until he stood in front of his mentor.

"Warriors of StarClan," Littlecloud meowed, "I present to you this apprentice. He has chosen the path of a medicine cat. Grant him your wisdom and insight so that he may understand your ways and heal his Clan in accordance with your will." He paused, then added in a whisper, "Crouch down and drink from the pool."

As Flamepaw obeyed, Jayfeather and the rest of the medicine cats stretched out their necks, too, and lapped a few drops of water from the Moonpool. As the icy liquid trickled down his throat, Jayfeather curled up and tried to relax. *Please, Star-Clan,* he begged, *show me something useful. My Clan is tearing itself apart.*

His eyes opened and he found himself on a narrow forest path, with lush ferns arching over his head on either side. Sunlight warmed his fur and dappled the grass around his paws. But he couldn't see any other cats, and when he tasted the air all he could pick up was the scent of green, growing things.

"Where are they all?" he muttered to himself, beginning to pad forward.

Suddenly he heard a rustling from the undergrowth ahead of him, and the fern fronds dipped and swayed. Jayfeather sniffed eagerly, but the scent he picked up wasn't any of the ones he had hoped for.

"Flamepaw!" he exclaimed, as the young apprentice burst into the open and stood gazing around with wide eyes, his fur fluffed up in a mixture of excitement and fear.

"Jayfeather, it's you!" he exclaimed. "Where are we? Is this what's supposed to happen?"

"Calm down," Jayfeather responded. "Everything's fine."

Mouse dung! he added inwardly. *I'm in his dream! What good will that do?*

"I was hoping to meet Tigerstar," Flamepaw confessed, gazing up and down the path with bright, curious eyes. "He's my kin, and I've heard so much about him!"

"I'm not sure where Tigerstar is," Jayfeather replied, careful not to tell the new apprentice about the dark forest. "You should be glad to meet any warriors of StarClan."

"I know, but . . . will they be glad to meet me?" Flamepaw crouched down, looking very small and scared. "I don't know what to say to them!"

Jayfeather touched the apprentice's shoulder with the tip of his tail. "When you see them, you'll be fine," he promised. "You just have to listen."

Flamepaw gave him a doubtful look, but he rose determinedly to his paws and set off down the path. "See you later, then," he mewed.

Right now, I'd be happy to see any of the StarClan warriors, Jayfeather thought. *Are they deliberately hiding from me?*

He padded down the path in the opposite direction from Flamepaw until he reached a clearing where sweet-smelling herbs grew around a small pool. He remembered finding this place before, when he had spoken with Spottedleaf, but there was no sign of the tortoiseshell she-cat now.

Bounding over to the pool and looking down into the water, Jayfeather froze with shock. Though the sun still shone, the green depths glittered with countless stars.

"What are you doing down there?" he yowled, clawing at the grass. "Come talk to me!"

The only answer was a thick, stifling pelt of darkness falling over him; disoriented, he staggered and found his claws scraping on stone instead of grass. He was awake again, back beside the Moonpool. The other medicine cats around him were beginning to rise to their paws.

Still frustrated and troubled by his dream, Jayfeather stood up with the other cats and climbed back up the spiral path.

When they had scrambled down the rocky slope to the moorland, he found himself padding next to Littlecloud.

"I think Flamepaw managed very well for his first time," the ShadowClan cat meowed. "He met Nightstar, who was our leader back in the old forest."

"That's good," Jayfeather murmured, not mentioning that he had seen the young apprentice in his dream.

"I think he'll be a great medicine cat," Littlecloud went on. "He already knows a good number of herbs."

Herbs! In his desperation to meet with StarClan, Jayfeather had forgotten about the question he had meant to ask.

"I came across this herb," he began, "and I don't know what it is." *Please, StarClan, don't let him wonder why I haven't asked Leafpool!*

"What sort of herb?" Littlecloud queried.

"It has a sharp scent, and the leaves feel crinkly," Jayfeather meowed, wishing he could have told the ShadowClan medicine cat what it looked like; even if he had been able to see it, the shriveled stalk wouldn't have given him much of a clue to the fresh herb. "It tastes cold, like frost on fur, and even the dried leaves taste fresh like grass," he added, remembering what Mousefur had told him.

"Hmm . . ." Littlecloud padded on thoughtfully for a few heartbeats. "It sounds like parsley to me. Its leaves have a very distinctive shape, like tiny shallow claws around the edge, and it tastes the same fresh or dried."

"And what's that used for?" Jayfeather struggled to keep the excitement out of his voice.

"Not much," Littlecloud replied. "But it's good for stopping milk in nursing queens if their kits die."

Jayfeather stopped dead.

Or if their kits didn't die, but were given to a different cat!

His heart was pounding so hard that he thought it would burst out of his chest. All the separate scraps of knowledge that he had gathered about his birth suddenly tumbled together into a terrifying pattern.

"Are you okay?" Littlecloud asked anxiously.

"What? Oh—yes, fine."

Jayfeather forced his paws forward again. His mind was spinning and filling with flashes of light, and he hardly remembered to say good-bye to the other medicine cats when they reached the border of their territories.

He had always been told that Squirrelflight had no milk, so Ferncloud and Daisy had nursed him and his littermates. Which meant Squirrelflight wouldn't have needed to take parsley. *So maybe our real mother had to eat it to hide that she'd just given birth!*

Jayfeather's memory carried him back to when he was a tiny kit, struggling through the snow. *He had to remember! Think about the scents,* he told himself. That's where the answers lie. His sense of smell had never before let him down when it was important. It couldn't fail him now.

There was a cat close to him, walking slowly through the snow with the scent of milk clinging to her fur. It wasn't Squirrelflight—it *couldn't* be Squirrelflight. Suddenly, Jayfeather took a deep breath. He knew exactly which cat's scent it was.

Everything added up. Which cat could depend on Squirrel-flight's loyalty, knowing she would carry out the deception for moons and moons, even if it meant lying to her own mate? Which cat had always poured out love and concern around him and his littermates? Which cat could never admit that she had borne kits?

Leafpool! Leafpool is our mother!

CHAPTER 21

❧

Hollyleaf blinked wearily in the misty dawn as the elders and Purdy carried Honeyfern's body out of the camp. The sun had vanished and the sky was covered with thick gray clouds. The breeze carried a tang of rain to come. All the Clan stood silently watching while their Clanmate went to her burial.

When the elders had disappeared through the thorn tunnel, Brambleclaw began organizing the day's patrols. Hollyleaf spotted Sorreltail padding sorrowfully toward the warriors' den, her head bowed and her tail trailing in the dust. She bounded after her, catching up to her beside the outer branches of the thornbush.

"I'm so sorry," she meowed. "I'm really going to miss Honeyfern."

"We'll all miss her." Sorreltail's voice was choked with grief. "She was so gentle as a kit. And so quick to learn! She knew most of the hunting moves even before she was apprenticed."

"She was always lots of fun to play with," Hollyleaf told her, touching her nose to Sorreltail's shoulder.

Sorreltail blinked. "She enjoyed being with you and your brothers. And she was always so worried that you wouldn't get enough milk, because Squirrelflight couldn't feed you."

Hollyleaf began to bristle at the mention of the cat she had believed was her mother, and tried hard to make her fur lie flat again. She wouldn't think about that betrayal when it was more important to comfort Sorreltail.

"It wasn't Squirrelflight's fault," the tortoiseshell queen went on, obviously misunderstanding what was bothering Hollyleaf. "And you were well looked after. Ferncloud and Daisy fed you, and I don't think Leafpool was ever out of the nursery, bringing them borage to make their milk come, and all the strengthening herbs she could find!"

"Leafpool did all that?" Hollyleaf asked.

"Oh, yes, she was always fussing over you! Maybe because you were her sister's kits, or maybe because she was with you when you first came to the hollow."

"I didn't know that." Hollyleaf felt a prickling in her fur. *If Leafpool was with us, she must know who our real mother is!*

Sorreltail nodded, then arched her back in a long stretch. "I'm going to see if I can get some sleep," she murmured. "Maybe Honeyfern will walk in my dreams."

As soon as Sorreltail had disappeared into the warriors' den, Hollyleaf looked around for the medicine cat. She had vowed never to ask Squirrelflight anything more about her real parents; she didn't want to speak to the cat who had lied to her ever again. But maybe Leafpool would tell her.

She spotted Leafpool talking to Firestar near the entrance to the thorn tunnel, and padded across to them, hovering a couple of tail-lengths away as she waited for a chance to get the medicine cat alone.

"You've been keeping vigil all night," Firestar was meow-ing. "You're exhausted. Why don't you go out into the forest and get some air? Stretch your legs and maybe find a quiet spot to have a sleep, without any cat to interrupt you."

"I shouldn't leave the Clan . . . ," Leafpool protested.

"Jayfeather's back from the Moonpool," Firestar pointed out. "We can do without you for a little while." He stretched forward and touched noses affectionately with Leafpool. "I could make that an order."

Leafpool yawned. "All right, Firestar, but I'll be back before sunhigh."

"Take as long as you want." Firestar dipped his head and padded away.

Hollyleaf waited until Leafpool had gone out through the thorn tunnel, then followed her into the forest. The medicine cat was out of sight, but Hollyleaf tracked her by her scent until she joined her at the top of a treeless rise overlooking the lake. Leafpool was sitting with her tail wrapped around her paws, gazing out across the water.

She sprang to her paws as Hollyleaf bounded up beside her. "Hollyleaf! Were you looking for me?"

"Yes, I—I wanted to ask you something." Now that the moment had come, Hollyleaf didn't feel so sure about what she was about to do. The answer would change her life for-ever. Was that what she wanted? *I have to know the truth!*

Leafpool's eyes were wary as she mewed, "Go on, then."

She knows we've found out about the lie! Hollyleaf guessed, her belly lurching. *Squirrelflight must have told her what happened that day on the cliff.*

"Well?" Leafpool prompted.

Hollyleaf took a deep breath. "Tell me what you know. All of it. I have to know the truth!"

Leafpool's amber eyes brimmed with sorrow. She took a pace toward Hollyleaf, sweeping her tail around as if to lay it on the younger cat's shoulder, but left the gesture unfinished.

"You don't have to worry," Leafpool meowed. "I will never tell any cat. But please tell me why you did it."

Hollyleaf felt as if a massive piece of fresh-kill were stuck in her throat. This wasn't how she had intended their talk to go. "Did what?" she managed to choke out.

Leafpool let out a long sigh, closing her eyes as if she had to nerve herself for what she was about to say. Then she faced Hollyleaf again.

"Why did you kill Ashfur?"

No! Hollyleaf dug her claws hard into the ground. *That wasn't what she had asked! Leafpool couldn't know!* She opened her jaws to reply, but the words of denial wouldn't come.

"I know, Hollyleaf," Leafpool mewed gently. "When I was preparing Ashfur's body for his vigil, I found a tuft of your fur caught in his claws. But I hid it away where no cat would find it. I think I wanted to hide it from myself." She paused, swallowed, and repeated, "Why?"

"He had to die!" Fury made Hollyleaf hiss through gritted teeth. "You know why!"

"No, I don't."

Leafpool's eyes were genuinely mystified, and Hollyleaf realized that Squirrelflight had never told her about revealing the terrible secret to Ashfur.

"He had to die because he knew!" Hollyleaf snarled. "That night, on the cliff in the storm, Squirrelflight told him that we weren't her kits. He was going to tell all the Clans, at the Gathering, and I couldn't let him do that! They think we're true Clan cats, forestborn like they are. I couldn't let them find out the truth—that Firestar's Clan was even less pure than they thought. Ashfur would have destroyed ThunderClan."

As she spoke, Leafpool's eyes had grown wider with dismay. "Oh, StarClan, no!" she whispered. "This is all my fault. . . ."

Hollyleaf's mind was whirling. She couldn't think beyond this moment; she only knew that the cat who held the truth in her paws was standing in front of her. "Squirrelflight told you about us, didn't she? You were there when we first came to the hollow. You must know who our real mother is."

Leafpool faced her calmly now. "Yes, I know."

"Then you have to tell me—please!"

For several heartbeats, Leafpool didn't reply. She stood blinking, her muscles tensed as if she were about to leap over a vast chasm. Then she spoke.

"I am your mother, Hollyleaf. Squirrelflight was trying to protect me."

For a moment that lasted a heartbeat or a maybe a moon, Hollyleaf stared at her. *No, it can't be!* But she knew that Leafpool had spoken the truth.

Whipping around, she bounded away, her paws slipping on

the dead leaves so that she slid to the bottom of the rise in a tangle of legs and tail. Scrambling to her paws, she pelted toward the deepest places of the forest, as far from the hollow as she could get. She didn't know where she was going, only that she wanted to outrun the lies, and the taste of Ashfur's blood in her mouth.

It was all for nothing! I did it to save us all, but it was no use! Everything has been ruined. . . .

CHAPTER 22

Jayfeather struggled through snow that reached up to his belly fur. Frozen lumps of it stuck between his pads, making every step painful. Just ahead of him was another cat; he recognized her tabby-and-white pelt, and wailed for her to come back and help him, but she never turned her head. Then the snowy ground gave way beneath his paws, and he was falling, falling. . . .

He woke in his own nest, the bedding tossed about by his thrashing limbs. Sitting up, heart still racing from his dream, he heard Leafpool scrabbling about in the depths of the store. A throbbing tide of anguish came from her, so strong that for a heartbeat he thought she was shrieking aloud.

Jayfeather sprang to his paws and padded over to the cave entrance. A flame of desperation burned inside him, to ask the medicine cat if she really was his mother, but he couldn't ignore such deep distress. "Leafpool?" he meowed. "What's the matter?"

Leafpool backed out of the store. "I . . . I told Hollyleaf something I shouldn't have," she confessed.

Jayfeather understood at once; now all the secrets were gushing out like water breaking through a dam. He raised his chin in a challenge. "You told her that you're our mother, didn't you?"

He heard Leafpool's gasp of shock. "How long have you known?"

"I didn't *know*, until just now. But I've been putting things together, and last night everything fell into place. Squirrelflight's loyalty to the cat who gave birth to us. The vague memories I have of that journey through the snow. The way you behave toward the three of us. And the fact that Mousefur remembers parsley accidentally mixed with her tansy about that time. Parsley is used to stop the milk in nursing mothers. You would have needed to take it to stop your own milk."

There was a long silence after he had finished speaking, in which Jayfeather almost thought he could hear his own heart beating.

"If you know so much," Leafpool mewed at last, "then do you know what happens next?"

"No." Jayfeather felt a strong sensation that there was something else Leafpool wanted to say to him, but she kept silent. He thought about entering her mind to find out what it was, but he didn't quite dare. He didn't like the idea of what he might discover.

"You have to help your littermates," Leafpool told him, her voice sharp and urgent. "You *must* learn to live with this, for the sake of the Clan."

You've got no right to tell us what we must *do.* But Jayfeather did not speak the thought aloud. Part of what the medicine cat said was true. Sooner or later, they all had to find a way forward.

"Please," Leafpool mewed, and there was a note of desperation in her voice. "Find Lionblaze and Hollyleaf, before anything else happens."

Is there anything else that could go wrong? Jayfeather wondered. But he nodded and backed out of the den. Leafpool was scared for her kits—all three of them—just as she had always been when trouble came to the Clan.

He scanned the clearing until he located Lionblaze approaching the fresh-kill pile with a mouthful of prey. Jayfeather bounded over to him. "Leave that and come with me," he meowed, jerking his head. "We have to talk."

Jayfeather could feel Lionblaze's confusion, but his brother didn't protest, just dropped his prey on the pile and padded beside him toward the camp entrance.

"Where's Hollyleaf?" Jayfeather asked. The sense of approaching disaster loomed even closer as he realized that this new knowledge would hurt her hardest of all. *The warrior code means so much to her!*

"I've no idea," Lionblaze replied. "I think she left camp, but I haven't seen her since the end of the vigil."

"We have to find her," Jayfeather mewed as they emerged from the tunnel into the forest. "She . . . she's found out something that could upset her."

"What?"

"I'll tell you when we find Hollyleaf." Jayfeather lifted his head to taste the air, searching for a trace of their sister's scent.

"Tell me now," Lionblaze insisted. "Haven't there been enough secrets? Even the three of us hardly seem to talk anymore."

Jayfeather turned to face him. "Leafpool is our mother."

He sensed shock like a bolt of lightning flashing through his brother. "I don't believe it!" Lionblaze gasped. "She's a medicine cat. It's impossible!"

"You'd better start believing it," Jayfeather mewed bleakly. "She told me so herself. And we have to decide what we're going to do about it."

After a long search through the forest, trying to follow confusing traces of their sister's scent, they discovered Holly-leaf at the top of the mossy bank that sloped down toward the lake. Jayfeather sensed her tension as soon as he bounded up to her. "Hollyleaf, we need to talk," he meowed.

"There's nothing to discuss." Hollyleaf's voice was distant. Jayfeather could tell that she hadn't turned to face him and Lionblaze. Instead she was gazing across the water as if the answers were hidden among the waves. "We have to find out who our real father is. And that will be the end of all the secrets."

"What do you mean?" Lionblaze asked, padding up to join them. "No cat knows yet who killed Ashfur, not unless Sol confesses. That's one secret that the Clan won't let rest."

"Too bad." Hollyleaf's voice was dismissive, though Jay-feather detected a new surge of tension within her. "There are more important secrets than that. We *must* know who our father is."

"You're right," Jayfeather agreed, curiosity prickling in every hair on his pelt. "But it's not going to be that easy figuring it out on our own. Did you ask Leafpool?"

"No, and I don't think she would tell us if we did."

Jayfeather realized she was right. He couldn't imagine that Leafpool would want to tell the truth about their father now, when she had kept the secret for so many moons. Once the rest of the Clan found out what she had done—and they would find out, because Jayfeather couldn't see how the secret could be contained any longer—her life would be ruined. She wouldn't want that to happen to another cat as well.

"Wait a moment," Lionblaze meowed. "Do we really want to do this?"

"What do you mean, mouse-brain?" Hollyleaf hissed. "Are you going to live the rest of your life never knowing who fathered you?" Jayfeather heard her claws tearing at the moss. "Because I'm not!"

"Just think about what you're saying." Lionblaze sat down beside Jayfeather. "We never wanted the secret to come out, and now that Ashfur's dead it doesn't have to. Leafpool won't tell any cat the truth."

"I want to *know*!" Hollyleaf's tail lashed through the dead leaves that covered the ground.

"But why?" Lionblaze argued. "If we keep quiet, everything will go back to how it was before."

If you believe that, you'll believe anything, Jayfeather thought, but he said nothing.

"Haven't you realized what this means?" Lionblaze went on, his voice growing excited. "Leafpool's our mother, and Firestar is her father. We're still part of the prophecy!"

CHAPTER 23

Lionblaze *slid out of the camp* through the dirtplace tunnel and skirted the rim of the hollow until he came to the place where he and his littermates had nearly been burned alive on the night of the storm. The grass was still blackened, and debris from charred branches was scattered around. Lionblaze shuddered as he remembered the leaping flames and the mad glare in Ashfur's eyes.

Above his head the moon floated in the indigo sky, waxing toward full and surrounded by the frosty glitter of stars. No clouds blurred their light. *Does that mean you approve of what I'm doing, StarClan?* Lionblaze silently addressed his warrior ancestors. He had made this plan as soon as he realized that he and his littermates were still part of the prophecy, but it had taken him another day to decide to put it into action. *Whatever you think, I have to do this.*

Looking down into the hollow, he could see the thornbush where Sol was a prisoner, and Birchfall, crouched on watch just beyond the outer branches. The thick, criss-crossing growth of the thorn hid Sol from Lionblaze's sight, but Sol's scent drifted up to him as he tasted the air.

"Right," Lionblaze whispered. "Let's go!"

Paw step by paw step, he crept down the cliff face, testing each foothold before he dared put his weight on it. He wasn't just afraid of falling; if he dislodged a stone, or slipped and had to scrabble to save himself, he would alert Birchfall. He froze once as he brushed against a straggling bush growing from a crack, and once when a shower of grit spurted up from under his paws and pattered down into the camp. But Birchfall didn't move.

Snoozing on watch? Lionblaze wondered.

Moons seemed to have passed before he leaped down the last fox-length to land lightly on the ground beside the bush. His legs trembled. With a swift glance toward the slumbering shape of Birchfall, he crawled underneath the branches of the thornbush.

In the dim light that filtered through the twigs, he saw Sol curled up in a mossy nest, his tail wrapped over his nose and his sides heaving with the rhythmic breathing of sleep. Lionblaze crept over to him and prodded his shoulder. Sol's eyes flew open, and for a heartbeat Lionblaze thought he saw surprise flicker in their amber depths. His jaws opened, but Lionblaze slapped his tail over the loner's muzzle before he could utter a sound.

"Quiet!"

Sol nodded, and Lionblaze took his tail away.

"I'm sorry, Lionblaze. For a moment I thought you were that snake." Sol was composed once more, his hushed voice barely reaching Lionblaze's ears. "What can I do for you?"

"I . . . I need to talk to you." Now that Lionblaze had succeeded in coming face-to-face with his Clan's prisoner, it was harder than he had expected to say what he had to say. "I've found out that my mother isn't who I thought she was, and I need to figure out if it affects the prophecy."

"Good," Sol mewed softly. He sat up and began to groom moss out of his fur. "You can start by helping me get out of here."

"I—I can't do that!" Lionblaze only just remembered to keep his voice down.

"Of course you can. You must have climbed down the cliff to get here without Birchfall seeing you. You can show me the way to get back up. I didn't kill Ashfur. You know I didn't."

"As far as ThunderClan is concerned, you're the only cat it could have been," Lionblaze retorted. He wasn't sure what he thought himself. He couldn't forget how Sol had promised to help him fulfill the prophecy—and how much he needed that help now—but he also shrank from betraying his Clan by letting the loner escape.

"Why should I help you if you won't help me?" Sol gave Lionblaze a long look from glowing amber eyes, then calmly licked one paw and started to wash his face.

Lionblaze stared at him in frustration. *I can't make him talk, but I can't show him the way out, either!*

"Okay," he muttered. "I'm leaving. I can't help you escape, it would cause too much trouble."

"For you?" Sol queried.

"For my *Clan*," Lionblaze hissed. It was too easy to imagine what the other Clan leaders would think when they heard Sol was on the loose. They'd blame ThunderClan, that was for sure. He flattened himself to the ground so he could wriggle out under the thorn branches.

"Wait! Don't you want to know who your father is?"

Lionblaze stopped and looked back over his shoulder. "You *know* that?"

"Of course." Sol passed his paw over one ear.

"So who is he?" Lionblaze asked, his belly churning.

Sol's eyes glinted with amusement. "Nothing for nothing, Lionblaze. I'll tell you the truth when you get me out of here."

"And how do I know I can trust you?" The words came out louder than Lionblaze had intended; he froze as a scuffling sound came from outside the den.

"Sol?" Birchfall called. "Are you okay?"

Sol paused, his whiskers twitching. Ants crawled through Lionblaze's pelt and he held his breath as he waited to be discovered. *Firestar will strip my pelt off and throw it out for the crows!*

"Sol?" Birchfall's voice came again, sounding more anxious.

"I'm fine, Birchfall," the loner replied. "Just talking to myself."

"Okay, good night."

Lionblaze relaxed as he heard Birchfall settling down again, though his pelt still felt hot with tension.

"How do you know you can trust me?" Sol went on. He sounded amused. "You don't. But knowledge is power,

Lionblaze, and right now I have more knowledge than any of the Clan cats."

"All right," Lionblaze mewed slowly. "I'll show you how to get out. But you must promise to tell me about my father . . . and advise me about the prophecy."

Sol dipped his head. "You have my word."

Whatever that's worth . . . "Okay, follow me," Lionblaze whispered. "Put your paws where I put mine. It's a tricky climb, and it'll be ten times harder because we mustn't be spotted."

He pushed his way out through the thorns with Sol hard on his paws and began to haul himself up. The cliff seemed to stretch above his head forever, and Lionblaze couldn't believe that no cat would see them splayed out against the rock in the bright moonlight. But no accusing yowls came from the clearing, and at last he pulled himself up to the cliff top and turned to wait for Sol to join him.

The loner huffed out a breath as he hauled himself over the rim of the hollow, then gestured with his tail for Lionblaze to follow him away from the edge. He halted a few fox-lengths away.

"Well?" Lionblaze demanded. "You're free. What about your part of the bargain?"

"Not here," Sol replied. "It's too dangerous. Besides, if you stay away too long, some cat might notice you're missing. You should get back to the warriors' den."

"But you promised!"

"And I'll keep that promise." Sol flicked his ears in the direction of ShadowClan territory. "I'll go to that old Twoleg nest beyond the ShadowClan border, and wait for you there. Come with your littermates as soon as you can."

"Okay." Lionblaze's belly churned with frustration. "But you'd better be there."

Sol flicked his tail dismissively. "I will be." Turning, he bounded off toward the ShadowClan border.

Lionblaze watched him until the undergrowth hid his blotched pelt from sight. Then he slipped down to the thorn barrier and back into the camp the same way he had left it. He hoped no cat would ask why it had taken him so long to make his dirt.

I did the right thing, he argued with himself. *Hollyleaf said we have to find out who our father is. And even more important, Sol is the only cat who can help us fulfill the prophecy!*

"Firestar! Firestar!" Birchfall's yowl dragged Lionblaze from a deep sleep. All around him in the warriors' den, his Clanmates were rousing.

"Is there an attack?" Brightheart's fur bristled. "Birchfall sounds terrified!" She scrambled out of her nest and pushed her way out into the open, with Cloudtail just behind her.

"Firestar!" Birchfall's screech sounded right outside the den.

"What's got into him?" Dustpelt grumbled, rising to his paws and shaking moss out of his fur. "Can't a cat get a decent night's sleep around here?"

More warriors were shouldering their way out, loudly demanding what was going on. Lionblaze knew exactly what was bothering Birchfall, but he realized he had to seem just as concerned as every cat. He sprang up and slid out through the branches into the gray dawn light. Shadows still lay deep around the edges of the clearing, and the ground was dusted with frost.

Firestar was bounding down the tumbled rocks. Birchfall raced across the clearing to meet him at the bottom.

"Firestar!" the young warrior gasped. "Sol has escaped!"

Firestar's ears flicked up. With Birchfall panting behind him, he raced over to the thornbush and thrust his head inside. More of the ThunderClan cats followed him, and Lionblaze crowded up with them, making sure that he left his fresh scent at the bottom of the cliff where he and Sol had begun their climb.

"He's really gone?" Brambleclaw asked, rushing up to join his leader as Firestar backed away from the bush.

Firestar nodded.

"Hey, there are marks on the cliff!" Hazeltail stretched up with her paws to point at a spot where a couple of pebbles had been dislodged. "Sol must have escaped this way."

"Good riddance, if you ask me," Cloudtail growled, giving a single lash of his tail. "It's not like we could have kept him here forever."

There was a murmur of agreement; Lionblaze saw relief in the eyes of more than one cat.

"You're not going to track him down, are you, Firestar?" Sandstorm asked. "He's caused us enough trouble, and we could never have punished him enough for killing Ashfur."

"He's obviously guilty," Spiderleg put in. "He wouldn't have risked his neck climbing the cliff to escape, otherwise."

"That's true," Thornclaw meowed as Firestar looked thoughtful. "He must have been scared of what we would do to him. We sure taught him a lesson!"

Firestar took a couple of paces away from Sol's den and gazed at the cats who stood around him. "You're right," he murmured at last. "Let's hope that Sol has learned the Clans can't be messed around with, and doesn't try to cross any more borders. Brambleclaw, we'll double the patrols for now, until we're sure he's not still in the territory."

"Sure, Firestar," the deputy meowed with a brisk nod.

"What will you tell the other Clans?" Graystripe asked, a worried look in his amber eyes. "If we say he escaped, they'll think we were too weak to hold on to him. And they might blame us for letting him out to cause more trouble."

Firestar twitched his ears. "I'll tell him we banished him from our territories and made him promise never to set paw here again."

"But that's not true." Sandstorm looked uneasy. "Should we really be lying to the other Clans?"

"Like they always tell us the truth!" Cloudtail snapped.

"I think Sandstorm's right," Brightheart put in, with a sharp glance at her mate. "What if Sol *is* still around? What would the other Clans think of us then?"

Firestar hesitated, his gaze fixed on his paws, then raised his head again. "We'll do as I said. It's for the sake of Thunder-Clan," he meowed. "We need to show that we're strong and committed to the warrior code, and that we deal with our own Clan's affairs in our own way. And we'll make sure that Sol *isn't* still hanging about," he finished.

As the cats began to move away, and Brambleclaw began to organize the patrols, Lionblaze spotted Hollyleaf standing at the edge of the clearing. Her eyes were like green flames, but it was impossible to tell what she was looking at.

Slipping between Sandstorm and Hazeltail, he padded to her side. "I have to tell you something," he mewed softly.

Hollyleaf didn't seem to hear him. "He escaped!" she hissed, her claws flexing in and out.

Lionblaze couldn't tell if she sounded glad or sorry. He didn't dare tell her what had really happened with so many of his Clanmates close by. "Where's Jayfeather?" he asked.

Hollyleaf's ears flicked. "How should I know?"

"I'll find him," Lionblaze meowed. "Go into the forest and meet us by the training clearing. Don't argue!" he added as Hollyleaf opened her jaws. "Just do it. It's important."

His sister rolled her eyes, but she set off toward the camp entrance, staying in the shadows. Once he was sure she was on her way, Lionblaze headed for the medicine cats' den, but before he reached it, Jayfeather emerged from the nursery. Lionblaze bounded over to him.

"What's all the yowling about?" Jayfeather demanded.

"Sol has escaped."

"*Has* he?" Jayfeather's eyes stretched wide with surprise. Then the young medicine cat sniffed. "How convenient."

"We have to talk," Lionblaze muttered, glancing back to

where his Clanmates were splitting up into patrols. "Come with me into the forest. We're meeting Hollyleaf beside the training clearing."

To his relief, Jayfeather didn't argue. "I'll tell Leafpool I'm going to look for yarrow. We're running short, and Purdy's pads are still giving him trouble." He trotted off toward his den.

Lionblaze didn't wait for him; it was best if all three of them left the camp separately. Hating the need for deception, he tagged on to the end of a patrol that was just leaving, with Sandstorm at its head. Once out in the forest he dropped back; in case any cat had spotted him he pretended to have picked up a thorn in his pad. As soon as the patrol had vanished, he raced for the training clearing.

Hollyleaf was crouched in the hollow under a tree root. "Well?" she demanded as Lionblaze approached.

"Let's wait for Jayfeather."

Not many heartbeats had passed before Lionblaze heard a rustling in the undergrowth and picked up his brother's scent. Jayfeather shouldered his way out of the long grass and joined them.

"*Now* will you tell us what all this is about?" Hollyleaf meowed.

As briefly as he could, Lionblaze told them how he had managed to get into Sol's den to talk with him, and how he had shown him the way up the cliff. "He's gone to hide in the old Twoleg nest where he stayed before," he finished. "We have to go there so he can tell us who our father is—"

"Have you got bees in your brain?" Hollyleaf growled with a lash of her tail. "You let a ThunderClan prisoner escape?

That's completely against the warrior code! What do you think Firestar will do if he ever finds out?"

"There's no reason why he should find out," Lionblaze replied steadily. "I thought you were the one who wanted to find out the truth about our father! Now we can. Are you coming with me or not?"

Jayfeather was looking uneasy, but he nodded. "We'll come." He nudged Hollyleaf. "There's no sense in complaining about it. You know we've got no choice. We can't live with only half the truth, and this looks like our only chance of finding out."

The sun had risen above the treetops by the time they reached the end of ShadowClan territory and struck out into the unknown forest. It was so long since they had been there that Lionblaze wasn't sure of the way, but Sol's scent trail led them onward.

It looks as if he headed straight for the Twoleg nest. So maybe he does mean to keep his part of the deal.

Eventually the crumbling walls of the old Twoleg nest came into sight, hardly visible among tall clumps of seeding willow-herb, bracken, and thistles. Sol's scent was strong and fresh. Lionblaze led the way up to the entrance and peered inside. Weeds sprouted through cracks in the stone floor, and cobwebs stretched across the corners.

"Sol?" he called. "Are you there?"

"Greetings." The voice came from above Lionblaze's head. He looked up to see Sol sitting on top of one of the walls, half-hidden by the branches of a holly bush stretching in from outside.

The loner rose to his paws and jumped down beside Lion-blaze and his littermates. "Greetings," he repeated. "I see you came—"

"We came to find out the truth!" Hollyleaf shouldered her way past Lionblaze. "Tell us what you know."

Sol blinked. "It won't help you, you know. As long as you're part of the prophecy, why does it matter who your father is?"

"It matters," Hollyleaf growled.

"Wait." Lionblaze stepped forward to stand alongside his sister. "I agree with Sol. I'd like to know the truth about my father, but it's the prophecy that's important."

"But we need to know," Jayfeather argued. "One name, that's all we want."

A gleam of cold amusement lit in Sol's eyes. Lionblaze knew he was enjoying the power he held over them. Suddenly he wasn't sure that Sol knew anything about their father. Perhaps he was just taunting them, knowing they couldn't take him back to the Clan. But he had known who they were from the start, and had offered to help. . . .

"This is our chance to fulfill the prophecy," Lionblaze mewed desperately, turning to his littermates. "Sol knows so much . . . he even knew when the sun was going to vanish!"

Neither of his littermates responded. Jayfeather just looked stubborn, while Hollyleaf had tensed her muscles as if she was about to pounce on Sol and force him to tell the truth.

No! If she lays a claw on him he'll never tell us!

Sol's amber gaze traveled slowly over Hollyleaf; her bristling hostility didn't ruffle a single hair on his pelt. "Think about what I can offer you," he meowed softly. "So much more than merely knowing your ancestors! Real power takes much more than that. Listen to me, and I'll teach you how to truly hold the power of the stars in your paws."

Hollyleaf let out a furious hiss and crouched to spring.

"No!" Lionblaze yowled. He leaped on his sister, gripped her by the scruff and dragged her outside, ignoring her flailing paws and her screeches of outrage. "Are you mouse-brained?" he demanded, releasing her among the dead bracken outside. "If you make Sol angry, he'll never help us."

"Why do we need him?" Jayfeather padded out to join them; his voice was calm, his head tilted on one side. "The prophecy doesn't say anything about needing help. How can Sol be more powerful than we are?"

"We don't have the power of the stars yet, do we?" Lionblaze's belly churned as he tried to make his littermates understand. "Let him teach us what he knows. What harm can it do? And then he'll tell us who our father is."

Frustrated, he realized that there had been no point in coming to the Twoleg nest. Neither Hollyleaf nor Jayfeather was prepared to talk sensibly with Sol. They probably believed he killed Ashfur, like the rest of the Clan. They might as well go straight back to the hollow.

He looked back at the entrance to the nest to see Sol standing there; his glowing amber gaze swept across them. "You are not ready to listen to me yet," he mewed. "When you are, come again. I'll be here, waiting for you."

CHAPTER 24

Hollyleaf's pelt prickled with frustration as she and her brothers headed back toward their own territory. They had been so close to discovering who their father was! But Sol had enjoyed holding his knowledge out of their reach, like a juicy bit of prey that he meant to keep for himself.

I could have made him tell us, if Lionblaze hadn't interfered!

She was so angry that she was hardly aware of her surroundings; suddenly Jayfeather nudged her hard in the side, nearly knocking her off her paws. "What—?" she began.

Lionblaze slapped his tail over her mouth. "ShadowClan!" he hissed. "Hide!"

All three cats dived for cover into a bramble thicket. Hollyleaf spat in annoyance as a thorn pierced one of her pads, and she tried to lick it out as ShadowClan scent wreathed around her.

"Ivytail, Smokefoot, and Owlpaw," Lionblaze reported, peering out through the bramble tendrils. "They're patrolling the border. I hope they didn't scent us."

No challenging yowls came from the patrol, and the scents gradually died away, leaving only the smell of the border markers.

"I guess it's safe to come out now," Lionblaze mewed after a few heartbeats. "Let's get back into our own territory as quickly as we can."

He took the lead, racing over the rough grass, weaving his way around hazel thickets and clumps of fern, until they flashed past their own border markers and drew to a panting halt several fox-lengths into ThunderClan territory.

"We'd better hunt on our way back," he told them. "That way we can pretend we went out to restock the fresh-kill pile."

Jayfeather nodded. "And I'll look for yarrow. If I come back empty-pawed, Leafpool will want to know why."

Though she did as Lionblaze suggested, padding softly through the undergrowth with her ears pricked and her jaws gaping for the first scent of prey, Hollyleaf's pelt crawled with resentment. *We shouldn't have to lie and deceive like this! Why can't we be proud of what we can do?*

While stalking a squirrel, she thought about how she could make Sol tell them the name of their father. *I'd do anything. Anything!* she thought fiercely. She remembered how easily her jaws had met in Ashfur's throat. . . .

No, don't think of that! Ashfur had to die because he would have ruined everything. He's not important now. We're the ones who matter!

Hollyleaf's claws tore at the mossy ground under her paws; alerted, the squirrel started up and shot to safety in the nearest tree.

"Mouse dung!" Hollyleaf spat.

"What's the matter with you?" Lionblaze asked, padding

up with a blackbird in his jaws. "Do you expect the prey to come and throw itself onto your claws?"

Hollyleaf shrugged and turned away. *When our father learns who we are, he'll be so proud of us! Maybe he doesn't even know about us! Maybe he's always wanted kits, and now he has three warriors to be his kin for the rest of his life.*

Closer to the camp, she managed to catch a mouse, though she had to admit to herself that it looked ready to die of old age and hadn't even tried to run. Prey was scarce, and by the time they reached the stone hollow she and Lionblaze hadn't caught anything else, but Jayfeather had found a clump of yarrow and now padded along with a bunch of the herb in his jaws.

When Hollyleaf pushed her way into the clearing, followed by her littermates, she spotted Spiderleg, Birchfall, and Hazeltail clustered together near the fresh-kill pile.

"I don't think Sol's gone," she heard Birchfall meow as she padded across with her prey. "He's lurking about somewhere."

Hazeltail shivered. "I hope not. I knew all along we should never have brought him back."

Spiderleg shrugged. "He can't do any more harm. Let him go where he likes."

"And kill more cats?" Hazeltail's neck fur rose. "That's mouse-brained!"

"If he's here, our patrols will find him," Birchfall reassured her, touching her shoulder with his tail. "And Firestar—"

He was interrupted by a call from Dustpelt, who came

bounding over from the barrier around the snake's hole. "I'm alerting every cat," the brown tabby warrior meowed. "That mouse with the deathberries hasn't been touched. The snake must be still around." He dashed off to warn Brambleclaw and his patrol, who had just appeared through the tunnel.

A sense of power thrilled through Hollyleaf from ears to tail-tip. ThunderClan had never felt so alive! Every cat was working together to face the threats that surrounded them. There was nothing they couldn't do! *And I could do anything too, if I could lead them!*

"Hollyleaf." The black she-cat started as Leafpool spoke behind her; dropping her prey on the fresh-kill pile, she spun around to see the medicine cat with Squirrelflight at her side.

"We need to talk," Squirrelflight mewed.

Hollyleaf stared at Leafpool, her heart suddenly thundering in her chest. *Is she going to tell the others what I did?*

Then Leafpool gave a tiny shake of her head, and Hollyleaf relaxed.

"What do you want to say to us?" Lionblaze asked; he had come up to deposit his prey in time to hear what Squirrelflight had said.

"Yes, what have we got to talk about?" Jayfeather added, his challenging tone muffled by his mouthful of yarrow stems.

"Not here," Leafpool murmured with a glance at the cats close by. "Come with us into the forest."

Hollyleaf hesitated, exchanging a glance with Lionblaze. He seemed to be waiting for her to decide. Then she nodded. "Okay. We'll talk to you."

When Jayfeather had deposited the yarrow in the medicine cats' den, Squirrelflight led the way into the forest as far as a huge oak tree with moss-covered roots.

"Well?" Jayfeather demanded, an edge to his tone. "What's this all about?"

Squirrelflight and Leafpool gave the three littermates a long look. Hollyleaf realized that although they were such different cats, the expression in their eyes was the same. She didn't want to recognize it; she didn't want to admit that it was love.

Finally Squirrelflight took a deep breath. "Leafpool is your mother," she began, "but I want to say that I couldn't have loved you more if I had given birth to you myself. We raised you together, and surely that's what matters."

"You raised us to believe in a *lie*!" Hollyleaf hissed, not giving her brothers a chance to respond. "We have nothing to say to either of you." Ignoring the shocked looks on Lionblaze's and Jayfeather's faces, she added, "Come on. There are no mothers here. A mother would love her kits enough to tell them the truth."

She stood for a moment longer, savoring the anguish her rejection had called up in the two she-cats, then whipped around and began stalking back to the camp.

"Hollyleaf, wait!" Lionblaze called.

Hollyleaf glanced over her shoulder; fury surged through her and she bared her teeth in a snarl. *"Come on!"*

Lionblaze bounded after her, followed a heartbeat later by Jayfeather. "This is mouse-brained," he protested. "We could at least talk. They might be prepared to tell us things we need to know."

"Like the name of our father?" Hollyleaf snapped, not breaking stride. "No, there's no point in asking them. We'd only get more lies." She lashed her tail, trying hard to dismiss Squirrelflight and Leafpool from her mind. "Sol will tell us," she declared.

"Bring the moss over here," Hollyleaf directed. "White-wing's kits will come soon, and she needs a really comfortable nest." Since the disastrous meeting with Sol the day before, she had struggled to put her sense of betrayal out of her mind and concentrate on her Clan duties, but she couldn't manage it. How could she make herself a good warrior when she knew she should never have been born at all? Every cat knew that medicine cats weren't allowed to have kits. She and her lit-termates were nothing more than a *mistake*. One that Leafpool had been too ashamed to own up to. Maybe their real father would feel differently. . . .

The nursery seemed full of queens and wriggling kits as Foxpaw and Icepaw staggered through the entrance with huge balls of moss. Whitewing was curled up nearby.

"Thanks, Hollyleaf," she mewed. "You'll make a great mentor when you have an apprentice of your own."

"I hope so," Hollyleaf replied. *How can I have an apprentice? How could I teach a young cat about the warrior code, knowing what I know?*

She was helping the two apprentices to spread out the moss

when she was startled by a sudden yowl of alarm from the clearing. Before she could do more than look up, Rosekit shot into the nursery with every hair on her pelt fluffed up. "It's ShadowClan!" she squealed. "ShadowClan cats are in the camp!"

While Daisy reached out to comfort the terrified kit, Hollyleaf thrust her way outside, her claws bared to fight off an attack. But once she was in the open, she relaxed. Only three cats were entering the camp, flanked by Spiderleg and Mousewhisker: Russetfur, Oakfur, and Ivytail. Firestar was already crossing the clearing to meet them, his flame-colored pelt gleaming in the scarlet light of the setting sun, while the rest of the Clan gathered behind him.

Hollyleaf padded over to join Lionblaze and Jayfeather. "What's all this about?" she whispered. "More trouble about Sol?"

Lionblaze shook his head. "I've no idea."

"Greetings." Firestar dipped his head to the patrol. "Sol has gone."

"We're not here about Sol," Russetfur informed him curtly. "Three of your cats were spotted near the ShadowClan border yesterday—well outside your territory. What were they doing?"

"Fox dung!" Jayfeather muttered, while Hollyleaf felt her pelt beginning to bristle. *If Firestar finds out what we were doing, we're crow-food!*

"Three ThunderClan cats?" Firestar asked. "Are you sure?"

"We know ThunderClan scent when we smell it," Russetfur

retorted. "And Ivytail got a good look at them. Ivytail, point them out."

The ShadowClan she-cat stepped forward and swept her tail around to point at Hollyleaf, Lionblaze, and Jayfeather. "Those three."

A gasp went up from the other ThunderClan cats. Hollyleaf faced them defiantly. *We weren't bothering ShadowClan! Why do they have to make trouble?*

Firestar gave the three littermates a thoughtful glance. Hollyleaf felt her fur grow uncomfortably hot, and she tried not to twitch. Then the ThunderClan leader turned back to the ShadowClan patrol.

"I'm sure my warriors had a very good reason to be there," he meowed. "You should know that a medicine cat is hardly likely to be part of an invading patrol. Have you considered that they might have been looking for herbs?"

All three cats nodded; Jayfeather added, "Yarrow," as if he was daring the ShadowClan cats to contradict him.

"Herbs . . ." Russetfur hissed the word just loud enough to be heard; clearly she didn't believe it, but she wasn't prepared to accuse the ThunderClan cats of lying.

"I apologize that they strayed so close to your border," Firestar continued. "It won't happen again."

"See that it doesn't," Russetfur retorted. Turning, she gathered her patrol together with a flick of her tail and headed toward the thorn tunnel. Spiderleg and Mousewhisker followed, to escort them out of the territory.

At the camp entrance, Russetfur glanced back. "Firestar, I

hope you get your Clan under control again soon," she mewed, and vanished into the tunnel before any cat could reply.

Hollyleaf knew her Clanmates were staring at her and her brothers as Firestar stalked across the clearing to confront them. She forced herself to meet his searing green gaze.

"Whatever you were doing, I don't want to know." His voice was tight with tension. "Just don't do it again. Do you think I haven't got enough to deal with right now?"

What about us? Hollyleaf thought resentfully. *You have no idea what we're going through.*

"Sorry, Firestar," Lionblaze mewed.

Firestar just let out a sigh before bounding off to join Sandstorm, Graystripe, and the other cats around the fresh-kill pile.

Once he was out of earshot, Hollyleaf turned to her brothers. "We'll have to—"

She broke off at a warning touch on her shoulder from Lionblaze's tail, and glanced around to see Brambleclaw padding up. *Oh, great.*

The deputy halted and raked the three cats with a cold yellow gaze. "Are you going to tell me what you were doing?"

Hollyleaf clamped her jaws shut and stared mutinously at the tabby warrior. Beside her, Lionblaze and Jayfeather were silent, too.

"I don't know what's gotten into you lately." Brambleclaw sighed. "You're all—"

"Hey, Brambleclaw!" Dustpelt interrupted from outside the warriors' den. "I'm leading the evening patrol. Which cats do you want to go with me?"

"I have to go," Brambleclaw meowed to Hollyleaf and her littermates. "Just try to keep out of trouble, okay?"

Hollyleaf watched him go, then drew her brothers into a tight huddle. "We'll go back to Sol tomorrow. I don't care what ShadowClan thinks. We have to know the truth!"

Lionblaze was gazing warily at her, as if he was wondering whether she would lose her temper with Sol again, but Jayfeather just looked thoughtful. At last he nodded. "I agree. This time, he's *got* to talk to us. And if he refuses, we'll *make* him. The prophecy belongs to us, remember. Not to him."

CHAPTER 25

❧

Sunhigh had come and gone by the time Hollyleaf and her brothers were able to slip away and head for the old Twoleg nest. Clouds had gathered during the night, and by the time they reached the border of their own territory, rain was hissing down steadily.

Once they had crossed the border, Lionblaze led them by a roundabout route through the spindly trees, keeping as far away as possible from the ShadowClan border. All three cats stayed alert for any sign of a ShadowClan patrol.

There'll be real trouble if we're caught this time, Hollyleaf thought.

When they reached the old Twoleg nest, Sol was sitting in the entrance as if he had been expecting them.

"Greetings," he meowed, rising to his paws as the three cats picked their way among the dripping brambles to reach the nest. "I thought you would come today."

"Let's get this straight." Hollyleaf drew ahead of the others. "We don't want any more arguments. We'll let you help us fulfill the prophecy, as long as you tell us the name of our father."

Sol's eyes glowed as he gazed at her, and Hollyleaf shivered. Once she had felt as if she could spend her whole life looking into this cat's eyes and hearing his voice. Even though she knew how dangerous he was, she still wasn't quite free from the snare of his charm.

"Shall we go inside?" Sol offered, as if this was nothing more than a friendly visit.

Hollyleaf and the others followed him into the damp interior and shook the raindrops from their pelts before finding a place to crouch on the cracked stones.

"You might need to find a new place to stay," Hollyleaf warned the loner. "ShadowClan sent a patrol to report us to Firestar for being outside our territory."

"What?" Sol's fur began to bristle. "Blackstar dared to do that? Is he allowed to dictate where cats go outside his own borders?"

"Well, he thinks he is," Jayfeather muttered.

"You were doing nothing wrong!" Sol declared, his fur fluffing up even more and his amber eyes burning. "Blackstar is using this as a way to humiliate ThunderClan."

"I'm not sure." Lionblaze was looking uneasy. "I think Blackstar is just being a bit overly keen to prove that he's keeping the warrior code again."

Sol gave a snort of contempt. "The warrior code! Belief in StarClan! I can't understand why you cats think all that is so important."

Hollyleaf's belly lurched. *No! The warrior code matters more than anything!* But she knew that she had to stay calm. If they quarreled with Sol, they would lose the chance of discovering who their father was.

"I know so much more than StarClan does," Sol continued. "Did they tell you that the sun would vanish? You know very well they didn't. Doesn't that make me more powerful than your warrior ancestors? And if I'm so powerful *without* a prophecy, then the powers you three share must be magnificent!"

Lionblaze's eyes glowed, and Jayfeather was unconsciously flexing his claws in and out. Hollyleaf had to make a huge effort not to be enthralled by Sol's voice. *So far he's given us nothing,* she reminded herself. *His words are nothing but mist and sunshine, impossible to hold down.*

"That's all very well," she snapped, "but what do we have to *do?*"

"ShadowClan cats are worthless!" Sol went on. "They have no right to their territory—and if they are left alone, they'll soon be invading yours. You need to fake evidence that ShadowClan is stealing ThunderClan prey, so that your Clan leader can launch an attack on them. Once you have Shadow-Clan's territory, you can invade RiverClan and WindClan." He glanced around, lowering his voice to a deep, vibrating purr as he continued, "That's what absolute power is. Controlling every cat in the territories by the lake!"

Hollyleaf stared at Sol, feeling her paws tingle. Was this really what they had to do to gain power—fight against every cat in the rival Clans? She tried to imagine Firestar allowing that to happen, and couldn't.

"I don't think—" she began uncertainly.

But Sol wasn't listening to her. He padded off into a far corner of the den and hauled a rabbit out of the shadows. As he dropped it in front of her, Hollyleaf picked up the scent of ShadowClan mingled with the smell of fresh-kill.

"I caught this in ShadowClan territory, and rubbed it on their scent markers," Sol explained. "You can take it back to the camp with you, and tell your Clan that you chased off a ShadowClan patrol." His eyes glinted with cold amusement. "What can ShadowClan do to deny it? Those stupid cats, they'd rather believe in nursery tales about dead ancestors than try figuring things out for themselves. All that nonsense about signs from StarClan!"

Hollyleaf glanced at Lionblaze; he was staring at Sol with narrowed eyes, and his neck fur was slowly rising.

"You're no different from Tigerstar," Lionblaze growled. "You don't want this for our sake. This is *your* ambition."

Bunching his muscles, he launched himself upward, his claws extended toward Sol. Hollyleaf flung herself at him, just managing to knock him away before he slashed into Sol's pelt.

"What are you doing?" she gasped, pinning her brother to the floor.

"This isn't part of the prophecy." Lionblaze shook Hollyleaf off and sat up, glaring at Sol. "He just wants to use us. The power is ours, not his!"

"You're right." Jayfeather rose to his paws and flicked his tail toward Sol, who had not flinched at Lionblaze's attack or tried to respond to his accusation. "Sol doesn't care about us. He's still fighting his private battle with ShadowClan because Blackstar made him leave their territory. That battle has nothing to do with us. The truth about our father exists somewhere, but this is not the way to find it."

Lionblaze rose to his paws. "We're leaving," he announced. "And we're not coming back."

Hollyleaf stared at him in disbelief. "We can't!" she protested. "We need to know—"

"We don't need anything that Sol can tell us," Lionblaze insisted. "We've been fools to trust him, when we *know* what he's done to other cats. Can't you see that he just wants war between all the Clans? The prophecy says nothing about that. It says we were *born* with power—we shouldn't have to fight for it! Come on."

He strode out of the den with Jayfeather hard on his paws. Hollyleaf took a pace after him, then glanced over her shoulder at Sol, but the loner simply stared back at her, giving her no help.

With a hiss of mingled fury and desperation, Hollyleaf sprang after her littermates. *We're the Three! I can't do this on my own!*

Lionblaze and Jayfeather stood a few fox-lengths away from the den, waiting for her in the pouring rain. As she joined them, Sol appeared in the entrance.

"Wait!" he called. "Don't you want to know who your father is?"

Lionblaze ignored him. "Come on," he meowed to Hollyleaf. "This isn't the only way to find the truth. We have to do this for ourselves, not for any other cat."

Hollyleaf bowed her head, giving in, but as she picked her way through the soaking grass beside Lionblaze she could still feel Sol's amber gaze burning into her pelt.

CHAPTER 26

By the time the three littermates stumbled back into the hollow, Jayfeather was so exhausted he could hardly feel his paws, and the rain had plastered his pelt to his sides. He felt as if he were struggling in a vast cobweb woven of lies and shadows, with an unseen spider waiting to pounce.

Back in the old Twoleg nest, he had been certain that they were right to abandon Sol, but now he wasn't so sure. What if the loner really was the only way to the truth?

And what are we going to say when Firestar asks us where we've been? He'll claw us to pieces and toss us on the fresh-kill pile!

But as he staggered into the clearing, he heard a buzz of excitement rising from his Clanmates, who were clustered together near the nursery. No cat was paying any attention to Jayfeather or his littermates.

"What's going on?" Lionblaze asked.

A sudden rush of paw steps answered him as Foxpaw raced up to them. "It's Whitewing!" he burst out. "She's having her kits."

At the same moment, Jayfeather heard Brightheart calling from the nursery. "Jayfeather! Come quick—Leafpool needs you!"

Jayfeather stifled a sigh. He would far rather have crept into his nest to dry off his pelt and sleep. Instead he headed for the nursery, brushing past Birchfall, who was tearing up grass in his anxiety.

Inside, Daisy and Millie had drawn their own kits into their nests to give Whitewing and Leafpool space. The young white she-cat was lying on one side, her breath coming fast and shallow.

"You're doing fine," Leafpool reassured her. "And so are your kits. They'll be born before you know it."

"I hope so," Whitewing panted.

Even though Leafpool sounded calm, Jayfeather could sense her fear. Leaning over, she whispered in his ear, "She's exhausted. I'm afraid she won't have enough strength left to deliver the kits."

Jayfeather rested one paw lightly on Whitewing's distended belly and concentrated. He could feel a double heartbeat inside her, frail but steady. "She's having two kits," he announced. "Come on, Whitewing! You can do it."

It's okay, little kits, he thought as he crouched over the laboring she-cat, murmuring encouragement. *You're nearly safe. Just a little farther.*

Suddenly his mind slid into Whitewing's. He heard a vicious snarling and saw a vision of gaping fangs and lolling tongues, as if the young white queen was imagining her kits savaged by dogs, just as her mother Brightheart had been. He heard the screech of battle with other Clans and saw blood welling in deep claw marks, scarlet against pale fur. He felt the grip of hunger in his belly as he looked out across a forest deep under the snow.

Jayfeather started back, his mind reeling. *Does a mother really imagine her kits' whole lives before they're born?* He sensed Whitewing's terror as she lay silently begging him for help.

Recovering, he bent close to the young she-cat. "Don't worry," he whispered. "Your daughters will be fine. They will be loved and protected by their Clanmates." He stroked one paw gently across Whitewing's belly. "It's time now."

"Yes," Whitewing gasped.

Jayfeather felt a strong ripple pass through her belly. She let out a screech, and a tiny wet bundle slithered out onto the moss.

"Is she all right?" Whitewing panted.

"She's fine," Jayfeather assured her. "Now the next one."

Whitewing lay still for a moment; then her back arched as another ripple passed across her belly, and a second tiny bundle slid into the nest.

"Well done!" Leafpool exclaimed. "Greetings, little kits. Welcome to ThunderClan."

The first kit squeaked loudly, and Leafpool uttered a soft *mrrow* of laughter. "This one's tiny, but she's strong. There, little ones, go to your mother."

"They're beautiful!" Whitewing purred. "Thank you, Jayfeather. And you, Leafpool." With one paw, she drew the tiny kits toward her and started to lick them vigorously.

A wave of triumph swept through Jayfeather as he headed for the entrance to the nursery. "Birchfall!" he called. "Come and meet your daughters."

Birchfall brushed past Jayfeather as he stumbled inside. Jayfeather almost staggered under the wave of his relief and joy. "Whitewing, are you okay?" he choked out. "Oh, thank StarClan! What beautiful kits!"

Crouching beside Leafpool as she tended to Whitewing, Jayfeather wondered whether she had felt the same when he and her other kits were born. *Did our father share that joy?*

More than anything, he wanted to talk to Leafpool, to hear her side of the story and learn the truth. In the closeness of working together, he felt for a few heartbeats that it might be possible. "Leafpool . . . ," he began.

Leafpool turned to him. "She'll be fine now," the medicine cat meowed, cutting off what Jayfeather meant to say. "Go and fetch me some strengthening herbs, and a few leaves of borage to help her milk come."

The moment was gone. "Sure," Jayfeather replied, and slipped out of the nursery.

By the time he had delivered the herbs, the rain was easing off. Jayfeather padded over to the fresh-kill pile for a bite to eat before he went back to his den. Several cats were clustered around it, sharing prey; their delight washed over Jayfeather as he crouched to gulp down his vole.

"It's hard to give birth to kits in leaf-bare," Ferncloud mewed. "Whitewing has done really well."

"She'll raise them well, too." That was Mousefur, sounding less crotchety than usual. "Whitewing is one of the best cats in this Clan. When she was an apprentice she always made sure we had fresh moss, and it was dry, too."

"We'll all have to watch our tails when these kits are old enough to leave the nursery." Dustpelt's voice held a hint of amusement. "They have your blood, Cloudtail, and we all know what a hard time you gave Firestar when you were a kit."

Cloudtail snorted. "They'll be fine warriors, Dustpelt, and I'll claw any cat who says different."

Jayfeather, who was eating his prey, paused for a heartbeat as Hollyleaf and Lionblaze padded up and sat down beside him, listening to the cheerful talk in silence. None of them wanted to join in, but Jayfeather sensed that all of them felt cut off from one another, too.

"I remember when you three were kits," Brackenfur meowed; paw steps approached and the golden brown tabby flicked Jayfeather on the ear with his tail. "Chasing foxes! It's a wonder any of you survived to be apprentices."

"Yeah, right," Jayfeather muttered. Suddenly the happiness of his Clanmates was more than he could bear. Without another word, even to his littermates, he swallowed the last mouthful of vole and headed for his den.

Curled up in his nest, Jayfeather woke to the sound of paw steps, and opened his eyes to see a skinny gray she-cat bending over him.

"Yellowfang!" he exclaimed, sitting up. He was still in the medicine cats' den, bathed in the pale glow of moonlight. Leafpool was curled up asleep a couple of tail-lengths away.

The former medicine cat dropped a long dark feather onto the moss of Jayfeather's nest. "The time for lies and secrets is over," she meowed. "The truth must come out. StarClan was wrong not to tell you who you were a long time ago."

"Then what—?" Jayfeather began, but already Yellowfang's shape was beginning to fade, melting into the moonlight until she was gone. The moonlight abruptly vanished, leaving Jayfeather in darkness as he woke from his dream.

"Mouse dung! Why can't any cat speak straight out?" he hissed. But an icy weight in his belly made him realize that Yellowfang had told him all he needed to know.

Feeling around his nest, he found the feather she had dropped, and drew his paw down the long, smooth length. He could picture how it had gleamed black in the silver moonlight.

"She brought me a crow's feather . . . ," he whispered.

Scrambling out of his nest, he padded softly out of the den, taking care not to wake Leafpool. Once he was in the clearing, he bounded over to the warriors' den. He crept around the outside of it, tasting the air until he located Lionblaze sleeping close to the outer branches.

Jayfeather scrabbled around to find a loose bit of branch and poked it through the thorns until he felt the other end prod Lionblaze.

"Uh? Get off!" Lionblaze swatted at the branch.

"Lionblaze!" Jayfeather hissed, pressing as close as he could to his brother inside the den. "I have to talk to you. Fetch Hollyleaf."

"It's the middle of the night!" Lionblaze protested.

"Keep your voice down! Do you want to wake every cat in

the camp? This is *important*! We have to go somewhere."

"Okay, okay, keep your fur on."

Jayfeather waited impatiently until his littermates pushed their way out through the branches.

"What do you mean, 'go somewhere'?" Lionblaze whispered. "Where?"

"Into the forest. Somewhere we can talk."

Hollyleaf yawned. "This had better be worth it."

"It will be," Jayfeather promised.

All three cats slid out of the camp through the dirtplace tunnel, clinging to the shadows so as not to alert Poppyfrost, who was on watch. Then Jayfeather led them through the trees in the direction of the WindClan border.

"It's freezing out here," Hollyleaf complained. "I'm not going another paw step until you explain."

"Okay." Jayfeather turned to face his littermates. "I know who our father is." He hesitated, almost knocked over by the sudden surge of feelings that came from his brother and sister. He took a deep breath and went on. "It's Crowfeather."

For a few heartbeats there was silence. The emotions that churned out of his littermates now were so complex that Jayfeather knew he could never unravel them.

"We're *half-Clan*?" Hollyleaf choked out at last.

"How do you know about this?" Lionblaze sounded baffled.

"Yellowfang came to me in a dream," Jayfeather explained. "She told me it was time we knew the truth, and she brought me a crow's feather."

"But that still might not mean . . ." Hollyleaf's protest died away. All three cats knew the meaning of the sign. There was no point trying to pretend it wasn't true.

"Does Crowfeather know about this?" Lionblaze demanded.

"Is that why Leafpool had to keep us a secret?" Hollyleaf put in.

Their questions battered at Jayfeather. "I don't know," he told them. "We have to talk to Crowfeather. Come on."

The three cats headed silently through the forest. Drops from the recent heavy rain spattered their pelts as they brushed through the undergrowth. A chill breeze sprang up, ruffling their fur. Above his head, Jayfeather could hear the first chirps of waking birds.

His mind was spinning. *How could this have happened?* Their mother was a medicine cat, their father a WindClan warrior. Both of them should have known they could never be together.

How can we be part of the prophecy when we should never have been born?

Padding along by Jayfeather's side, Lionblaze was sending out steady surges of rage, a burning fury toward those cats who had abandoned the warrior code and piled up a heap of lies for the kits who were born as a result. On his other side, Hollyleaf was dazed, her whirling thoughts still too difficult to read.

At last Jayfeather could hear the gurgling of the border stream and taste the scent of fresh water. "It's still early," he remarked, "but we might spot their dawn patrol."

They drew to a halt on the bank of the stream. Jayfeather's

legs were trembling with weariness; he would have liked to sink down into the long grass at the water's edge, but he knew he had to confront his father standing on his paws.

Birdsong grew louder around them, and the bitter cold of night gradually eased. At last Jayfeather caught a whiff of WindClan scent; at the same moment Hollyleaf exclaimed, "There they are!"

"Owlwhisker, Gorsetail, and Weaselfur," Lionblaze meowed. "Wait here. I'm going to talk to them."

"Wait—" Jayfeather protested as he heard Lionblaze leap across the stream, but his brother was gone, too angry to worry about crossing the border.

"What do you think you're doing?" Owlwhisker demanded.

All Lionblaze's suppressed rage came out in his voice. "Fetch Crowfeather. Now."

"What?" Weaselfur exclaimed indignantly. "Who do you think you are, telling us what to do?"

"Yeah," Gorsetail added. "Get back into your own territory, or we'll tear your fur off."

A low growl came from Lionblaze; Jayfeather pictured him looming over the three WindClan cats, his golden fur fluffed out until he was twice his size. "Just do it!" he ordered.

"Okay," Owlwhisker mewed, his voice shrill as he tried to conceal his fear. "But you can wait on your own side of the border."

Jayfeather heard the WindClan warriors bounding away, then a thud as Lionblaze jumped back across the stream and landed beside him. His claws tore up the grass as they waited, as if his fury had to find some kind of outlet.

Jayfeather's belly churned when he caught the scent of an approaching WindClan cat on the breeze. Just one: Crowfeather had come alone. He could feel Hollyleaf quivering beside him; her tail kept twitching, brushing against his pelt.

At last Crowfeather's voice came from the other side of the border. "What do you want?"

Words choked in Jayfeather's throat as the three littermates faced the WindClan warrior across the stream. He heard a sharp intake of breath from Hollyleaf.

But Lionblaze didn't hesitate. "Brambleclaw and Squirrelflight are not our parents," he declared. "Leafpool is our mother and you are our father."

There was a pause. Then, "Don't be mouse-brained," Crowfeather snapped. "That's impossible."

He sounded so certain that for a heartbeat Jayfeather wondered if they could possibly be mistaken. Taking a deep breath, he stepped into Crowfeather's mind. A tangle of undergrowth faced him, and he realized that he was standing at the top of the cliff above the stone hollow. Leafpool was clinging to the edge, her face upturned pleadingly as Crowfeather grabbed her by the scruff and hauled her back to safety.

Then he glimpsed them crouched together under a bush, and heard Crowfeather meow, "Come away with me, Leafpool. I'll take good care of you, I promise." Now the two of them were trekking side by side up a long slope of moorland, then in a hollow, talking to Midnight the badger. "I have to go back," Leafpool mewed.

Caterwauling ripped through Jayfeather's vision and he glimpsed the stone hollow full of warring badgers, while his Clanmates attacked them fiercely. Last of all, Leafpool faced Crowfeather in the clearing, among the debris of the battle. "Your heart lies here," Crowfeather murmured; Jayfeather could hardly believe the warrior could sound so gentle. "Not with me. It was never truly with me."

The vision had taken no more than a moment, but when Jayfeather let go of the WindClan warrior's mind, he was sure that Yellowfang's sign had not deceived him. Just as he was sure that Crowfeather had no idea he had fathered Leafpool's kits.

"It's true," he meowed. "You didn't know, did you?"

"No. . . ." For a heartbeat, Crowfeather sounded dazed. Then Jayfeather felt anger growing within him. "I have one mate," he snarled. "Her name is Nightcloud. We have one son, Breezepelt. I don't know why you've come to me with these lies. Go home, and don't come back. Why should I care about ThunderClan cats? You mean nothing to me. Nothing!"

Jayfeather heard a gasp from Hollyleaf, and the sound of Lionblaze's claws scraping against stone.

Calmly he faced his father. "The truth is out now," he warned. "None of us can hide from it again."

CHAPTER 27

The rest of the day passed in a haze of pain, and when Hollyleaf finally curled up in her nest, her dreams were full of darkness. Thick undergrowth surrounded her, leaving scarcely a glimpse of the sky. She heard cats yowling at a distance, but however fast she ran toward them, she never managed to catch up with them.

When she woke to see dawn light filtering through the branches of the den, she still felt exhausted, as though she had really been running through that dark forest. She staggered to her paws and prodded Lionblaze.

"What are we going to do?" she demanded in an urgent whisper as her brother blinked up at her. "I can't go on like this!"

"I don't know." Lionblaze gave a quick glance around the den, as if he was afraid that some cat would overhear. "We'll talk later." He pushed his way out through the branches; convinced that he was trying to avoid her, Hollyleaf followed hard on his paws.

"Hollyleaf! Lionblaze!" Brambleclaw spotted them as soon as they emerged from the warriors' den. "Sandstorm is taking out a hunting patrol. Can you go with her?"

"Sure," Lionblaze meowed, swerving across the clearing to where Sandstorm waited beside the deputy with Berrynose and Hazeltail.

Hollyleaf was still dazed as she followed, as if her paws belonged to some other cat. How could she fit into the Clan's everyday routine, now that she knew the terrible secret of her birth? She felt as if the sky should have cracked open or the moon fallen down into the hollow.

"Don't forget, it's the Gathering tonight," Brambleclaw reminded them. "The Clan needs to eat well before the journey."

"We will—don't worry," Sandstorm promised, her whiskers twitching as she signaled to her patrol with her tail and headed for the camp entrance.

Hollyleaf followed, but she couldn't concentrate on hunting. Pain dazzled her mind like lightning splitting the sky. She had built her life on the warrior code, and now it had failed her. It didn't matter anymore; it had been broken too many times. Squirrelflight had broken it by lying; Crowfeather, by falling in love with a medicine cat; but most of all, Leafpool had shattered the code and trampled it into dust. She had betrayed her Clan, her duty as a medicine cat, and her kits.

A mouse darted out in front of Hollyleaf's paws and instinctively she leaped on it, her claws sinking into the soft body. A picture of Leafpool flashed in front of her eyes in a pulsing red haze, and she tore at the prey, imagining that she was clawing the life out of the cat she hated so much.

"Hollyleaf, stop!" Hazeltail's voice was shocked. "What are you doing?"

Hollyleaf's vision cleared. She saw her paws dripping with scarlet: The prey she had caught was reduced to a red pulp. There was nothing left to take back to the fresh-kill pile.

Fury surging through her, she rounded on Hazeltail. "Stay out of my fur!"

Hazeltail backed away, her eyes wide and scared, then whipped around and plunged away into the bracken.

After the hunting patrol returned, Hollyleaf was too disturbed to stay in the camp. She didn't want to talk anymore, especially not to Lionblaze or Jayfeather. Instead she headed out alone, down to the lake and then along the WindClan border until she reached the ridge and could look out across the rolling moorland.

Somewhere out there was the WindClan camp and the cat who was her father. His WindClan blood ran in her veins. *But I don't feel half-WindClan!*

Hollyleaf knew her home was under the trees, hunting mice and squirrels. The WindClan rabbits looked scrawny and tasteless from running across the hills. She hated the open spaces and the unrelenting wind.

Gazing out across her father's territory, she yowled silently, *No! No! No!*

As shadows fell across the stone hollow, Firestar called together the cats who were going to the Gathering. Hollyleaf padded up to join Jayfeather and Lionblaze, deliberately not looking at Squirrelflight and Leafpool a few paces away. Graystripe, Brambleclaw, and Sandstorm bounded up, followed by

Cinderheart, Poppyfrost, and Berrynose.

"Let's go," Firestar meowed. "And the less we say about Sol, the better, okay?"

He led them down to the lake and along the edge of the water, splashing through the border stream. Hollyleaf felt every hair on her pelt prickle with disgust as she set paw on WindClan territory. *I don't belong here! I want nothing to do with WindClan!*

More rain had fallen earlier in the day, but now the clouds had cleared away, leaving the full moon to shine brightly. Hollyleaf stopped and stared up at it. *Do you approve of what I'm going to do, StarClan?*

With every paw step she was alert for the sight or scent of WindClan cats. She wondered if Crowfeather had been chosen to go to the Gathering. *Why should it matter?* she thought fiercely. *He's nothing to me. Nothing!*

Just ahead of her, Firestar was flanked by Graystripe and Sandstorm. "You know, I still miss Fourtrees," Sandstorm murmured. "The moon seemed brighter there, somehow."

Firestar gave her an affectionate nudge. "You sound like an elder!"

Sandstorm swatted at him with her tail. "You wait. I'll be the crankiest elder the Clans have ever seen. Mousefur will seem sweet and gentle next to me!"

"And hedgehogs will fly," Graystripe meowed. "But I miss the old forest, too," he added. "It's the place we were born. These younger cats will feel just the same about the lake. Isn't that right?" He glanced over his shoulder at Lionblaze and Hollyleaf.

Lionblaze managed a brief nod, but Hollyleaf couldn't reply at all. Sheer envy surged over her, jealousy of these cats who knew where they belonged, who had good memories of living by the warrior code, season after season.

They don't know it's all a lie!

The horseplace was dark and silent when the ThunderClan cats padded past. There was still no sign of WindClan; Hollyleaf assumed they had already made their way to the island.

When they reached the tree-bridge, they found River-Clan in the middle of crossing; Firestar held back his warriors with a polite nod to Leopardstar. While she waited, Hollyleaf flexed her claws in and out, her belly churning.

This will be a Gathering none of them will ever forget!

Leaping from the roots at the other end of the tree-bridge, she paused to taste the mingled scents of the other three Clans.

"We're the last," Cinderheart meowed, landing beside her. "We'd better be quick."

Hollyleaf followed her Clanmate across the strip of pebbles and into the undergrowth. There was no need to hurry. She had set her paws on the path she had chosen, and the time for her to act would come as surely as one season gave way to the next.

When she pushed through the bushes and into the clearing around the Great Oak, she hesitated, awed in spite of herself by the mass of cats in front of her. Clan mixed with Clan as the cats found themselves places around the tree. Then Hollyleaf's paws carried her forward, weaving a path through the crowd. She was scarcely aware of Tawnypelt greeting her, or of the

ShadowClan queen's affronted look as she brushed past. She ignored the snatches of gossip that she picked up as she padded past. *What has all that got to do with me now?*

She found a place to sit, close to the Great Oak, where she could look up and see the Clan leaders crouched among the branches: Onestar, comfortably settled in the fork of a branch; Blackstar, crouched on the lowest branch with his tail hanging down; Leopardstar, standing a tail-length higher, impatiently scratching at the bark. Firestar leaped up to join them, scattering a few late acorns as the branch he chose swayed under him.

Lionblaze had followed Hollyleaf across the clearing, and sat down next to her. "Crowfeather's here," he muttered.

"I know." Hollyleaf had already spotted the WindClan warrior, but he hadn't seemed to notice her. Now she glanced to where Lionblaze was pointing with his tail, and she saw her father sitting close to Nightcloud and Breezepelt. His head was turned away, but Hollyleaf guessed that he knew exactly where she and her brothers were. *All his kits together at once. How nice for him.*

A shrill yowl sounded from the branches of the tree, and Leopardstar stepped forward. The noise in the clearing stilled as the cats fell silent and turned to look up at her.

"The Gathering has begun," she announced. "RiverClan will report first. Prey is running well. Mistyfoot, Reedwhisker, and Rainstorm drove a fox out of our territory." She stepped back with a curt nod to Blackstar.

The ShadowClan leader rose, while below him Hollyleaf drove her claws into the ground, her whole body quivering with tension. Suddenly she wasn't sure she would know when her time to act had come. *StarClan, give me a sign! If you're even watching....*

"ShadowClan is thriving," Blackstar reported. "Littlecloud has taken Flamepaw as his apprentice, and introduced him to StarClan at the Moonpool."

A murmur of congratulation rose from the assembled cats, with a few yowls of "Flamepaw! Flamepaw!" Hollyleaf spotted the young cat sitting with Littlecloud and the other medicine cats, his eyes shining with pride. Claws tore at her heart. *I felt like that once.*

Onestar followed Blackstar, but he had nothing to tell them about except a dead sheep in the border stream, which his warriors had dragged out to keep the water clean.

Then it was Firestar's turn. Rising to his paws, he balanced on his branch and looked down into the clearing with his green eyes glowing in the moonlight. "Sol has left the forest," he began. "We—"

"About time, too," Blackstar growled.

Leopardstar dipped her head to Firestar with cold courtesy. "I'm glad you saw sense at last, Firestar."

Firestar returned the nod equally politely, though Hollyleaf could see his claws tighten on his branch. "Besides that—"

Now!

"Wait!" Hollyleaf leaped to her paws. "There's something that I have to say that all the Clans should hear."

"What?" Lionblaze reached up and dragged at her with one paw, trying to get her to sit down again. "Are you mouse-brained? Warriors don't speak here!"

"This one does," Hollyleaf hissed, shaking him off. She

spotted Jayfeather among the other medicine cats, his expression utterly horrified, but she ignored him.

"You think you—" she began.

"Hollyleaf!" Firestar's voice rang out from the branch where he stood looking down at her; his eyes smoldered with green fire. "If you have anything important to say here, it should have been discussed with me first. Be silent now, and whatever's troubling you, I'll talk to you about it tomorrow."

Moons spent following the warrior code almost forced Hollyleaf to clamp her jaws shut and sit down. *I have to obey my Clan leader!* Then she braced herself. *The warrior code is dead! There's no point in trying to follow it anymore.*

"No!" she meowed, ignoring the gasps of shock from the cats around her. "I *will* speak now!"

"Yes, let her speak." Leopardstar stepped forward again, looking down curiously at Hollyleaf. "I'd like to hear what she has to say."

"So would I," Onestar growled.

"Or has ThunderClan got secrets that they're too scared to reveal?" Blackstar taunted, flicking his tail contemptuously at Firestar.

Yowling broke out all around the clearing as the cats from the other three Clans challenged ThunderClan. Hollyleaf stood in the middle of the uproar, feeling strangely calm; she knew she needed to wait only a few heartbeats more.

At last Firestar raised his tail for silence. "Very well, Hollyleaf," he mewed when the noise had died down. "Say what you have to. And StarClan grant you don't regret it."

Now the clearing was so quiet that Hollyleaf could hear a

mouse scuttering among the dead leaves under the Great Oak. "You think you know me," she began again. "And my brothers, Lionblaze and Jayfeather of ThunderClan. You think you know us, but everything you have been told about us is a lie! We are not the kits of Brambleclaw and Squirrelflight."

"What?" Brambleclaw shot to his paws from where he sat with the other deputies among the roots of the Great Oak. His amber eyes flamed. "Squirrelflight, why is she talking such nonsense?"

Squirrelflight stood up. The flare of panic in her eyes faded and was replaced with—what? Regret? Guilt? Or the sorrow of a mother who was about to lose her kits forever . . . ?

"I'm sorry, Brambleclaw, but it's true. I'm not their mother, and you are not their father."

The Clan deputy stared at her. "Then who is?"

Squirrelflight turned her sad green gaze on the cat she had always claimed as her daughter. "Tell them, Hollyleaf. I kept the secret for seasons; I'm not going to reveal it now."

"Coward!" Hollyleaf flashed at her. Her gaze swept around the clearing, seeing the eyes of every single cat trained on her. "I'm not afraid of the truth! Leafpool is our mother, and Crowfeather—yes, Crowfeather of WindClan—is our father."

Yowls of shock greeted her words, but Hollyleaf shouted over them. "These cats were so ashamed of us that they gave us away and lied to every single one of you to hide the fact that they had broken the warrior code. It's all *her* fault." She whipped her tail around to point at Leafpool. "How can the Clans survive when there are cowards and liars at the very heart of them?"

The screeches and gasps of horror grew so loud that Holly-leaf couldn't make herself heard anymore. But there was no need. She had said what she had come to say. Her legs trembled as if she had run all the way across the territory, and she had to sit down. Inside she felt a curious peace, as if she had lanced a festering sore and was watching the poison drain away.

Crowfeather's voice rose above the rest in a furious yowl. "It's not true!" He had sprung to his paws, his dark gray fur bristling. Beside him, Nightcloud and Breezepelt looked bewildered and angry. "She's the one who's lying!"

Then Leafpool stood up. The crowd of cats fell silent, their eyes turned toward her.

"It's true, Crowfeather," she meowed. "I'm sorry. I wanted to tell you, but there was never a right time."

Her amber eyes were seared with grief. Pity stirred in Hollyleaf, but she choked it down. *I hate her! She lied and betrayed us all!*

"You mean nothing to me, Leafpool." Crowfeather's voice was cold. "That moon has passed. My loyalty is only to Wind-Clan, and I have no kits other than Breezepelt." He glanced to where Nightcloud and Breezepelt stood beside him; the black she-cat had her ears flattened to her head, while Breezepelt's teeth were bared in a snarl.

Leafpool dipped her head as if she wasn't going to argue; then she looked up at Firestar, who was crouched on his branch, as still as a cat made out of stone. "I know that I cannot be ThunderClan's medicine cat any longer," she meowed. "I'm so very sorry to you, Firestar, and to all my Clanmates.

Please know that I tried my best, and regretted what I had done with every single breath." Her voice cracked on the last word, and she paused, swallowing, before she continued. "But I couldn't regret having my kits. They are fine cats, and I will always be proud of them."

She gave Crowfeather one last glance, then padded across the clearing with her head bowed. Cats scrambled out of her way as she made for the bushes and pushed her way through, out of sight. Every cat stared after her, still shocked into silence.

Brambleclaw was the first to move, padding forward until he stood face to face with Squirrelflight. "Why?" he meowed.

Squirrelflight's voice was desperate. "I had to! She's my sister!"

"And you couldn't trust me?" Brambleclaw's voice was shaking, and Hollyleaf saw a deep shudder pass through his body. For a heartbeat, she was sorry for what she had done. This was a noble cat, and he had not been responsible for any of the lies. *I was so proud when I thought he was my father.*

Squirrelflight did not reply, just held his gaze without flinching.

"You couldn't trust me," he repeated. "Don't you think I would have helped you, if you'd told me the truth? But it's too late now."

He turned away, shouldering a path through the crowd.

"Brambleclaw—" Squirrelflight took a pace after him, then halted, her head hanging and her tail drooping in despair.

Hollyleaf turned her back. *Let her suffer. She deserves it!*

A cat nudged her from behind. It was Cinderheart. "What have you done?" she cried.

Hollyleaf blinked in surprise. "I did the right thing."

The gray she-cat shook her head. "There is no right thing. Everything to do with this leads to more pain." The wisdom in her voice seemed to come from a much older and more experienced cat. Hollyleaf waited for her to say something else, something to show how sorry she felt for Hollyleaf and her littermates. But Cinderheart just turned and padded away.

Hollyleaf stared after her. Why didn't she understand? Surely any cat could see that they couldn't have carried on living a lie? Besides, StarClan hadn't sent clouds to cover the moon. Her warrior ancestors must be pleased that the secrets were out and the deceit was at an end.

But none of the cats here seemed pleased. Not even her own Clanmates. Sandstorm was staring at her, bewilderment and sorrow in her green gaze. Graystripe's amber eyes were blank with disbelief. Poppyfrost and Berrynose had their heads close together, talking urgently and shooting hostile glances at her.

Suddenly Hollyleaf couldn't bear to be stared at for another heartbeat. Blundering through the crowd, she thrust through the bushes, ignoring the thorns that tore her pelt, and fled across the strip of pebbles and over the tree-bridge. Racing past the horseplace, she began to climb the ridge, skirting the WindClan border until she reached the very top and could look out over the lake.

A silver path of moonlight stretched across the surface of

the water. The reflections of countless warriors of StarClan glittered around it.

"Was it all worth it?" Hollyleaf wailed to them. "Being an apprentice, working hard to learn the warrior code? What could any of us have done to make things different?"

The flickering stars gave her no answer.

Hollyleaf padded along the ridge until she reached her own territory and could plunge back into the trees. When she arrived in the stone hollow, everything was quiet. The Gathering patrol had not yet returned, and the other cats were asleep, except for Brightheart, on watch beside the entrance. Hollyleaf brushed past her, ignoring the she-cat's greeting.

She stalked across the clearing in the bright wash of moonlight and entered the medicine cats' den. Her heartbeat quickened when she saw there was no sign of Leafpool. *I know what I'm going to do. All this is Leafpool's fault.*

Crawling right to the back of the storage cave, she found the leaf wrap with the deathberries and drew it out carefully. She placed it on the floor of the den and unfolded the leaf so the glossy red berries were exposed. They had begun to shrivel, but she knew they still held their deadly poison.

Hollyleaf sat beside the berries, wrapped her tail over her paws, and waited. Soon she heard a slow paw step outside, and Leafpool brushed past the bramble screen and stood in front of her.

"Hollyleaf." She didn't sound surprised to find her daughter there. Her eyes were full of weariness and sorrow. "It's all right," she mewed. "I forgive you."

"What!" Hollyleaf sprang to her paws. "*You* forgive *me*? You're the one who needs forgiveness! You abandoned your kits! You let us grow up in a web of lies, and now the warrior code might be broken forever because of your stupid, selfish actions."

"Do you think you need to tell me that?" Leafpool asked, still with the same exhausted calm. "I can only tell you how much I love you. I'm so sorry for what I did."

"And you expect me to forgive you?" Hollyleaf snarled. "Well, I don't. I never will." Fur bristling, she padded around Leafpool until she blocked the entrance to the den. "See those deathberries? You're going to eat them—or I'll make you!"

"What?" Leafpool sounded bewildered.

"Eat them! You deserve to die." Hollyleaf crouched, ready to spring, when the medicine cat made no move toward the deadly berries. "I've killed once," she snarled. "And I can do it again."

A gleam of some emotion that Hollyleaf couldn't read woke in her mother's eyes. "Hollyleaf," Leafpool meowed. "I have lost my kits, the one cat I loved, and my calling as a medicine cat. Which do you think would be easier for me, to die or to go on living?"

There was only one answer to that question. Silently Hollyleaf stood aside, and Leafpool padded past her and out of the den.

CHAPTER 28

Jayfeather slid through the thorn tunnel and stood panting in the middle of the clearing. He had raced back from the island as soon as the Gathering broke up, struggling through the mass of bewildered cats to get across the tree-bridge.

He scented Leafpool leaving their den; right now she was the last cat he wanted to talk to. Beyond her, fainter, he picked up Hollyleaf's scent.

What's she doing in our den? What did she say to Leafpool?

Darting across the clearing, he crashed through the brambles and confronted his littermate. "Hollyleaf! What are you doing here?" Sniffing, he detected another scent. "Why are those deathberries out here?"

"Leave me alone!" Hollyleaf screeched.

Before Jayfeather could dodge, she leaped at him, bowling him over and raking her claws across his shoulder. Jayfeather's legs flailed and his hind paws connected with Hollyleaf's belly. Her anger and despair flooded over him as she gave him a cuff over the ear and fled out of the den.

"Hollyleaf, wait!" Jayfeather scrambled to his paws and launched himself after her.

When he emerged into the clearing, Hollyleaf was already

plunging into the thorn tunnel. Jayfeather raced after her, his belly fur brushing the ground as he broke out into the forest. The scents of more cats greeted him as the rest of the Gathering patrol returned to the camp.

"Jayfeather, what's wrong?" Lionblaze called out. He turned and bounded along beside him. "What's happening?" he gasped.

"It's Hollyleaf," Jayfeather panted. "We've got to catch her."

Hollyleaf was heading deep into the forest, crashing through bracken and brambles as if she had suddenly lost her sight.

"Hollyleaf, come back!" Lionblaze yowled. "We need to talk!"

But Hollyleaf didn't slacken her pace. Briefly she burst out onto the old Twoleg path that led past the abandoned den, then veered into the undergrowth again.

"I know where she's going!" Jayfeather panted, feeling a chill run through him. "The old tunnels . . ."

"But she can't!" Lionblaze sounded terrified. "Hollyleaf, stop!"

Racing around a bramble thicket, Jayfeather and Lionblaze came face-to-face with their sister; she had halted just inside the mouth of a tunnel halfway up the ridge, above the abandoned Twoleg nest. It wasn't one Jayfeather had used before; there was a stale scent of fox, overlaid with the smell of water and stone drifting from the darkness behind her.

Jayfeather tried to speak calmly. "Hollyleaf, you've got to listen to us."

Hollyleaf didn't seem to hear. "I'm sorry," she meowed softly. "I was only trying to do what was best. I couldn't let Ashfur live! For all our sakes! You understand that, don't you?"

Jayfeather caught his breath. Beside him, he heard Lionblaze gasp, "*You* killed Ashfur?"

If Hollyleaf replied, Jayfeather didn't hear it. Hating his power more than he ever had before, he had reached out to his sister's memories. She was stalking Ashfur along the Wind-Clan border stream, treading lightly, avoiding boulders where her claws might scrape or ferns that would brush against her fur. Ashfur, intent on hunting, never noticed she was there. Hollyleaf followed him like a shadow until they came to a place where the bank was steep and slippery, and the stream was a foaming snake far below. She pounced on him from a rock, gripping his shoulders with her forepaws and twisting her head around to sink her teeth into his throat. Inside the red mist that clouded her senses, Ashfur was nothing but prey, something that had to be killed to protect the warrior code and the future of her Clan.

Ashfur clawed feebly at her, but blood was gushing from his throat. His body went limp and Hollyleaf leaped away, letting it crash into the stream. She stood watching it for a while, until the swift-flowing water had washed away the blood. Then she padded up to a pool of water on top of the bank and rinsed her paws, turning the water red. Behind her, Ashfur's body bobbed against the bank before floating away downstream.

"He should have been swept into the lake and never seen

again." Hollyleaf's voice wrenched Jayfeather out of her terrible memories. "But they found him, and now everything is ruined. I can't stay here."

Despair vibrated in her voice. "I *know* I did the right thing, but no cat will ever understand."

There was a patter of paws as she turned and fled down the tunnel. Running forward, Jayfeather could hear the roaring of the river underground, pounding hungrily against the stone.

"Hollyleaf, no!" he yowled. "We can figure this out together—" A deafening rumble interrupted him; it went on and on. He pictured wet soil and rock raining down as the tunnel collapsed, crashing onto his sister, knocking her to the floor, crushing her, burying her. . . .

He darted forward. *"Hollyleaf!"*

Lionblaze charged into him, knocking him off his paws and pinning him down; Jayfeather writhed furiously underneath him. "Let me up!" he screeched. "We have to get her out!"

"We can't help her," Lionblaze growled. "The tunnel has collapsed. There's no way we can follow her in."

Jayfeather lay still, panting, as the tumult of falling earth and stones died away. In the silence, Lionblaze stepped back and let him clamber to his paws. Hollyleaf had seen the tunnels as a way to escape her Clan and everything that had gone wrong. Except she hadn't escaped—not in the way she wanted.

"It's over," Lionblaze meowed, his voice shaking.

"I don't understand." Jayfeather was trembling with shock

and grief. "She killed Ashfur to keep the secret safe. But then *she* revealed it to every cat at the Gathering."

"It wasn't the same." Lionblaze pressed up against him until Jayfeather felt his brother's dismay mingling with his own. "Hollyleaf couldn't bear the thought of being a medicine cat's kit. She couldn't bear the idea that she was half-Clan. The warrior code meant everything to her, and our birth smashed it to pieces."

"We should have done something," Jayfeather insisted. "What are we going to tell the Clan?"

Lionblaze let out an exhausted sigh. "We *can't* tell them she killed Ashfur. How can we let that be the only thing she's remembered for?"

Jayfeather nodded. After all this, there was one more secret to keep, for Hollyleaf's sake. "Let's say that she chased a squirrel into the tunnel, and it collapsed on her. They can remember her for being a brave hunter, feeding her Clan. They don't need to know the truth—that she was trying to escape from them."

Slowly they began limping back to the camp. Jayfeather felt a fresh breeze ruffling his fur, and he drew in long, cold gulps of air. A new day was beginning, but all he wanted was to go back to his den, curl up, and try to escape into sleep. How could the sun rise today, after everything that had happened?

Suddenly he halted. "The prophecy!" he burst out.

Lionblaze, who had padded on a few paw steps, stopped. "How can you think about that now?"

"But don't you see?" Jayfeather clawed at the grass. "What happens to the prophecy if Hollyleaf is dead? It said there would be three cats, and now there are only two!"

Jayfeather stretched his cramped limbs and turned his face up to the first feeble rays of the sun. All night his Clanmates had kept vigil for Hollyleaf, even though there was no body to be buried. Cats were beginning to stir around him, and a few fox-lengths away he could hear Brambleclaw quietly calling together the dawn patrol.

A full day and night had passed since the Gathering and the death of Hollyleaf in the tunnels. The day before, Firestar had addressed the shattered ThunderClan from the Highledge.

"Last night Hollyleaf revealed secrets that shocked us all," he meowed. "But that prey is eaten. There can be no going back. Instead we must find the way forward, for all of us."

"What about the other Clans?" Dustpelt called out. "They all know what happened, thanks to Hollyleaf."

"Maybe Hollyleaf should not have spoken out," Firestar admitted. "But she has paid terribly. As for the other Clans—they think we are broken. It's up to us to show them that we are *not*. ThunderClan will survive!"

Yowls of agreement rose from the listening cats; Jayfeather could feel their shock and distress giving way to a new sense of purpose.

Now he rose, gave himself a long stretch, and sat down to groom his pelt, craning his neck to reach over to the fur on his back. After a few moments he became aware of movement outside the nursery as several of his Clanmates gathered there; he padded across to find out what was going on.

"It's Whitewing's kits," Lionblaze told him. "It's the first time they've left the nursery."

"Their eyes are open!" Whitewing was announcing delightedly as Jayfeather and his brother approached. "Aren't they beautiful?"

A loud squeaking and the patter of tiny paws drew closer and then stopped. Jayfeather felt a powerful curiosity trained on him.

"Hello, little kits," Lionblaze murmured. "Welcome to ThunderClan."

"This one has such fluffy gray fur," Sandstorm commented. "And the little one's tabby-and-white pelt is so pretty. Have you given them names yet?"

"Yes." It was Birchfall who replied, sounding ready to burst with pride. "We've called the gray one Dovekit, and the tabby-and-white one is Ivykit."

"Those are beautiful names," Brightheart purred.

The ginger-and-white she-cat was sitting close by, with Cloudtail beside her, watching their daughter's kits; Jayfeather could feel their happiness at seeing all their kin healthy and strong. It was brighter than the sun just breaking over the trees at the top of the hollow.

Another scent wafted past him as Firestar bounded up. "This is good to see," the Clan leader meowed. "They'll be apprentices before we know it."

Jayfeather suddenly felt a jolt in his belly like a blow from some cat's paw. He clawed at Lionblaze. "The prophecy . . ." he whispered.

"What? Get off!" Lionblaze sounded irritated.

"There will be three, kin of your kin. . . ." Jayfeather's voice shook as he wondered if he could possibly be right. "Cloudtail is Firestar's kin, Whitewing is Cloudtail's daughter, and now Dovekit and Ivykit. . . . Don't you see? The prophecy isn't over! We aren't the only kin of Firestar's kin. It doesn't matter which of Whitewing's kits is the one. *There are still three of us!*"

ERIN HUNTER

is inspired by a love of cats and a
fascination with the ferocity of the
natural world. As well as having great
respect for nature in all its forms,
Erin enjoys creating rich mythical
explanations for animal behavior. She
is also the author of the bestselling
Seekers and Survivors series.

Download the free Warriors app
and chat on the Warriors message
boards at www.warriorcats.com!

CHAPTER 1

A *full moon floated in a* cloudless sky, casting thick black shadows across the island. The leaves of the Great Oak rustled in a hot breeze. Crouched between Sorreltail and Graystripe, Lionblaze felt as though he couldn't get enough air.

"You'd think it would be cooler at night," he grumbled.

"I know," Graystripe sighed, shifting uncomfortably on the dry, powdery soil. "This season just gets hotter and hotter. I can't even remember when it last rained."

Lionblaze stretched up to peer over the heads of the other cats at his brother, Jayfeather, who was sitting with the medicine cats. Onestar had just reported the death of Barkface, and Kestrelflight, the remaining WindClan medicine cat, looked rather nervous to be representing his Clan alone for the first time.

"Jayfeather says StarClan hasn't told him anything about the drought," Lionblaze mewed to Graystripe. "I wonder if any of the other medicine cats—"

He broke off as Firestar, the leader of ThunderClan, rose to his paws on the branch where he had been sitting while he waited for his turn to speak. RiverClan's leader, Leopardstar,

3

glanced up from the branch just below, where she was crouching. Onestar, the leader of WindClan, was perched in the fork of a bough a few tail-lengths higher, while ShadowClan's leader, Blackstar, was visible just as a gleam of eyes among the clustering leaves above Onestar's branch.

"Like every other Clan, ThunderClan is troubled by the heat," Firestar began. "But we are coping well. Two of our apprentices have been made into warriors and received their warrior names: Toadstep and Rosepetal."

Lionblaze sprang to his paws. "Toadstep! Rosepetal!" he yowled. The rest of ThunderClan joined in, along with several cats from WindClan and ShadowClan, though Lionblaze noticed that the RiverClan warriors were silent, looking on with hostility in their eyes.

Who ruffled their fur? he wondered. It was mean-spirited for a whole Clan to refuse to greet a new warrior at a Gathering. He twitched his ears. He wouldn't forget this the next time Leopardstar announced a new RiverClan appointment.

The two new ThunderClan warriors ducked their heads in embarrassment, though their eyes shone as they were welcomed by the Clans. Cloudtail, Toadstep's former mentor, was puffed up with pride, while Squirrelflight, who had mentored Rosepetal, watched the young warriors with gleaming eyes.

"I'm still surprised Firestar picked Squirrelflight to be a mentor," Lionblaze muttered to himself. "After she told all those lies about us being her kits."

"Firestar knows what he's doing," Graystripe responded; Lionblaze winced as he realized the gray warrior had overheard every word of his criticism. "He trusts Squirrelflight, and he wants to show every cat that she's a good warrior and a valued member of ThunderClan."

"I suppose you're right." Lionblaze blinked miserably. He had loved and respected Squirrelflight so much when he thought she was his mother, but now he felt cold and empty when he looked at her. She had betrayed him, and his litter-mates, too deeply for forgiveness. Hadn't she?

"If you've quite finished . . ." Leopardstar spoke over the last of the yowls of welcome and rose to her paws, fixing Firestar with a glare. "RiverClan still has a report to make."

Firestar dipped his head courteously to the RiverClan leader and took a pace back, sitting down again with his tail wrapped around his paws. "Go ahead, Leopardstar."

The RiverClan leader was the last to speak at the Gathering; Lionblaze had seen her tail twitching impatiently while the other leaders made their reports. Now her piercing gaze traveled across the cats crowded together in the clearing, while her neck fur bristled in fury.

"Prey-stealers!" she hissed.

"What?" Lionblaze sprang to his paws; his startled yowl was lost in the clamor as more cats from ThunderClan, Wind-Clan, and ShadowClan leaped up to protest.

Leopardstar stared down at them, teeth bared, making no attempt to quell the tumult. Instinctively Lionblaze glanced upward, but there were no clouds to cover the moon; StarClan wasn't showing any anger at the outrageous accusation. *As if any of the other Clans would want to steal slimy, stinky fish!*

He noticed for the first time how thin the RiverClan leader looked, her bones sharp as flint beneath her dappled fur. The other RiverClan warriors were the same, Lionblaze realized, glancing around; even thinner than his own Clanmates and the ShadowClan warriors—and even thinner than the Wind-Clan cats, who looked skinny when they were full-fed.

"They're starving . . ." he murmured.

"We're all starving," Graystripe retorted.

Lionblaze let out a sigh. What the gray warrior said was true. In ThunderClan they had been forced to hunt and train at dawn and dusk in order to avoid the scorching heat of the day. In the hours surrounding sunhigh, the cats spent their time curled up sleeping in the precious shade at the foot of the walls of the stone hollow. For once the Clans were at peace, though Lionblaze suspected it was only because they were all too weak to fight, and no Clan had any prey worth fighting for.

Firestar rose to his paws again and raised his tail for silence. The caterwauling gradually died away and the cats sat down again, directing angry glares at the RiverClan leader.

"I'm sure you have good reason for accusing us all like that," Firestar meowed when he could make himself heard. "Would you like to explain?"

Leopardstar lashed her tail. "You have all been taking fish from the lake," she snarled. "And those fish belong to River-Clan."

"No, they don't," Blackstar objected, poking his head out from the foliage. "The lake borders all our territories. We're just as entitled to the fish as you are."

"Especially now," Onestar added. "We're all suffering from the drought. Prey is scarce in all our territories. If we can't eat fish, we'll starve."

Lionblaze stared at the two leaders in astonishment. Were ShadowClan and WindClan really so hungry that they'd been adding fish to their fresh-kill pile? Things must be *really* bad.

"But it's worse for us," Leopardstar insisted. "RiverClan doesn't eat any other kind of prey, so all the fish should belong to us."

"That's mouse-brained!" Squirrelflight sprang to her paws, her bushy tail lashing. "Are you saying that RiverClan can't eat any other prey? Are you admitting that your warriors are so incompetent they can't even catch a mouse?"

"Squirrelflight." Brambleclaw, the ThunderClan deputy, spoke commandingly as he rose from the oak root where he had been sitting with the other Clan deputies. His voice was coldly polite as he continued. "It's not your place to speak here. However," he added, looking up at Leopardstar, "she does have a point."

Lionblaze winced at Brambleclaw's tone, and he couldn't repress a twinge of sympathy for Squirrelflight as she sat down again, her head bent like an apprentice scolded in public by her mentor. Even after six moons, two whole seasons, Brambleclaw had not forgiven his former mate for claiming her sister Leafpool's kits as her own—and therefore his as well. Lionblaze still felt dazed whenever he reminded himself that Brambleclaw and Squirrelflight were not his real mother and father. He and his brother, Jayfeather, were the kits of the former ThunderClan medicine cat, Leafpool, and Crowfeather, a WindClan warrior. Since the truth came out, Brambleclaw and Squirrelflight had barely spoken to each other, and although Brambleclaw never punished Squirrelflight by giving her the hardest tasks or the most dangerous patrols, he made sure that their paths never crossed as they carried out their duties.

Squirrelflight's lie had been bad enough, but everything went wrong when she admitted what she had done. She had told the truth in a desperate attempt to save her kits from Ashfur's murderous fury at being passed over in favor of Brambleclaw, moons before Lionblaze and his littermates were born. Lionblaze's and Jayfeather's sister, Hollyleaf, had killed Ashfur to prevent him from revealing the secret at a Gathering. Then Hollyleaf vanished behind a fall of earth when she tried to escape through the tunnels to start a new life. Now the brothers had to accept that they were half-Clan, and that their father, Crowfeather, wanted nothing to do with them. And, on top of that, there were still suspicious looks from some of their own Clanmates, which made Lionblaze's pelt turn hot with rage.

As if we're suddenly going to turn disloyal because we've found out our father is a WindClan warrior! Who'd want to join those scrawny rabbit-munchers?

Lionblaze watched Jayfeather, wondering if he was thinking the same thing. His brother's sightless blue eyes were turned toward Brambleclaw, and his ears were alert, but it was hard to tell what was going through his mind. To Lionblaze's relief, the rest of the cats seemed too intent on what Leopardstar was saying to pay any attention to the rift between Brambleclaw and Squirrelflight.

"The fish in the lake belong to RiverClan," Leopardstar went on, her voice thin and high-pitched like wind through the reeds. "Any cat who tries to take them will feel our claws. From now on, I will instruct our border patrols to include the area around the water on every side."

"You can't do that!" Blackstar shouldered his way out of the leaves and leaped down to a lower branch, from where he could glare threateningly at Leopardstar. "Territories have never been extended into the lake."

Lionblaze pictured the lake as it had been, its waves lapping gently against grassy banks with only narrow strips of sand and pebbles here and there on the shore. Now the water had shrunk away into the middle, leaving wide stretches of mud that dried and cracked in the merciless greenleaf sun. Surely Leopardstar didn't want to claim those barren spaces as RiverClan territory?

"If any RiverClan patrols set paw on *our* territory," Onestar growled, baring his teeth, "they'll wish they hadn't."

"Leopardstar, listen." Lionblaze could tell that Firestar was trying hard to stay calm, even though the fur on his neck and shoulders was beginning to fluff up. "If you carry on like this, you're going to cause a war between the Clans. Cats will be injured. Haven't we got troubles enough without going to look for more?"

"Firestar's right," Sorreltail murmured into Lionblaze's ear.

"We should be trying to help one another, not fluffing up our fur ready for a fight."

Leopardstar crouched down as if she wanted to leap at the other leaders, letting out a wordless snarl and sliding out her claws.

This is a time of truce! Lionblaze thought, his eyes stretching wide in dismay. *A Clan leader attacking another cat at a Gathering? It can't happen!*

Firestar had tensed, bracing himself in case Leopardstar hurled herself at him. Instead she jumped down to the ground with a furious hiss, waving her tail for her warriors to gather around her.

"Stay away from our fish!" she spat as she led the way through the bushes that surrounded the clearing, toward the tree-bridge that led off the island. Her Clanmates followed her, shooting hostile looks at the other three Clans as they passed them. Murmurs of speculation and comment broke out as they left, but then Firestar's voice rang with authority above the noise.

"The Gathering is at an end! We must return to our territories until the next full moon. May StarClan light our paths!"

Lionblaze padded just behind his leader as the ThunderClan cats trekked around the edge of the lake toward their own territory. The water was barely visible, just a silver glimmer in the distance; pale moonlight reflected from the surface of the drying mud. Lionblaze wrinkled his nose at the smell of rotting fish.

If their prey stinks like that, RiverClan can have it!

Ahead of him, Brambleclaw trudged along next to Firestar, with Dustpelt and Ferncloud on the Clan leader's other side.

"What are we going to do?" the deputy asked. "Leopardstar *will* send out her patrols. What happens when we find them on our territory?"

Firestar twitched his ears. "We need to deal with this carefully," he meowed. "*Is* the bottom of the lake our territory? We would never have thought of claiming it when it was covered with water."

Dustpelt snorted. "If the dry land borders our territory, it's ours now. RiverClan has no rights to hunt or patrol there."

"But they look so hungry," Ferncloud mewed gently. "And ThunderClan never took fish from the lake anyway. Can't we let them have it?"

Dustpelt touched his nose briefly to his mate's ear. "Prey is scarce for us, too," he reminded her.

"We will not attack RiverClan warriors," Firestar decided. "Not unless they set paw on the ThunderClan territory within our scent marks—three tail-lengths from the shore, as we agreed when we came here. Brambleclaw, make sure that the patrols understand that when you send them out tomorrow."

"Of course, Firestar," the deputy replied, with a wave of his tail.

Lionblaze's pelt prickled. Even though he respected Firestar's conclusion because he was the Clan leader, Lionblaze wasn't sure that he had made the right decision this time.

Won't RiverClan think we're weak if we let them come around our side of the lake?

He jumped at the flick of a tail on his haunches and glanced around to see that Jayfeather had caught up to him.

"Leopardstar's got bees in her brain," his brother announced. "She'll never get away with this. Sooner or later, cats will get clawed."

"I know." Curiously, Lionblaze added, "I heard some ShadowClan cats at the Gathering saying that Leopardstar lost two lives recently. Is it true?"

Jayfeather gave him a curt nod. "Yes."

"She never announced it," Lionblaze commented.

Jayfeather halted, giving his brother a look of such sharp intelligence that Lionblaze found it hard to believe that his brilliant blue eyes couldn't see anything. "Come on, Lionblaze. When does a Clan leader ever announce they've lost a life? It would make them sound weak. Cats don't necessarily know how many lives their *own* leader has left."

"I suppose so," Lionblaze admitted, padding on.

"Leopardstar lost a life from a thorn scratch that got infected," Jayfeather continued. "And then straight after that she caught some kind of illness that made her terribly thirsty and weak, too. She couldn't even walk as far as the stream to get a drink."

"Mothwing and Willowshine told you all that?" Lionblaze asked, aware that medicine cats would confide in one another without thinking of the Clan rivalries that made warriors wary of saying too much.

"It doesn't matter how I found out," Jayfeather retorted. "I know, that's all."

Lionblaze suppressed a shiver. Even though he knew that Jayfeather's powers came from the prophecy, it still bothered him that his brother padded down paths that no cat, not even another medicine cat, had ever trodden before. Jayfeather *knew* things without being told—not even by StarClan. He could walk in other cats' dreams and learn their deepest secrets.

"I guess that's why Leopardstar is making such a nuisance of herself about the fish," Lionblaze murmured, pushing his uneasiness away. "She wants to prove to her Clan that she's still strong."

"She's going about it the wrong way," Jayfeather stated flatly. "She should know that she can't make the other Clans follow her orders. RiverClan will be worse off in the end than if they'd just struggled through the drought on their own territory, like the rest of us."

They were approaching the stream that marked the border between WindClan and ThunderClan. The water that had spilled into the lake with a rush and a gurgle just last newleaf had dwindled to a narrow stream of green slime, easily leaped over. Lionblaze drew a breath of relief as he plunged into the undergrowth beyond, under the familiar trees of his own territory.

"Maybe it'll all blow over," he meowed hopefully. "Leopardstar might see sense when she thinks about what the other leaders told her at the Gathering."

Jayfeather let out a contemptuous snort. "Hedgehogs will

fly before Leopardstar backs down. No, Lionblaze, the only thing that will solve our problem is for the lake to fill up again."

Lionblaze was padding through long, lush grass, his paws sinking into water at every step. A cool breeze ruffled his fur. Any moment now, he could put down his head and drink as much as he wanted, relieving the thirst that burned inside him like a thorn. A vole popped out of the reed bed in front of him, but before Lionblaze could leap on it, something hard poked him in the side. He woke up to find himself in his nest in the warriors' den, with Cloudtail standing over him. His fur felt sticky, and the air smelled of dust.

"Wake up," the white warrior meowed, giving Lionblaze another prod. "What are you, a dormouse?"

"Did you have to do that?" Lionblaze complained. "I was having this really great dream. . . ."

"And now you can go on a really great water patrol." Cloudtail's tone was unsympathetic. Since the streams that fed the lake had dried up, the only source of water was the shallow, brackish pool in the middle of the lake bed. Patrols went down several times a day to collect water for the Clan, in addition to hunting and patrolling as usual. The greenleaf nights seemed shorter than ever when every cat was tired out from extra duties.

Lionblaze's jaws gaped in an enormous yawn. "Okay, I'm coming."

He followed Cloudtail out of the den, shaking scraps of

moss from his pelt. The sky was pale with the first light of dawn, and although the sun had not yet risen the air was hot and heavy. Lionblaze groaned inwardly at the thought of yet another dry, scorching day.

Hazeltail, her apprentice, Blossompaw, Berrynose, and Icecloud were sitting outside the den; they rose to their paws as Cloudtail appeared with Lionblaze. None of them had been to the Gathering the night before, but Lionblaze could tell from their tense expressions that they knew about Leopardstar's threats.

"Let's go." Cloudtail waved his tail toward the thorn tunnel.

As Lionblaze padded through the forest behind the white warrior, he overheard Berrynose boasting to Icecloud: "River-Clan had better not mess with us when we get to the lake. I'll teach any cat not to get in my fur."

Icecloud murmured something in reply that Lionblaze didn't catch. *Berrynose thinks he's so great,* he thought. *But it's mouse-brained to go looking for trouble when none of us is strong enough for a battle.*

To his relief, Cloudtail took his patrol to the foot of a huge oak tree and instructed them to collect bundles of moss to soak in the lake. Berrynose couldn't go on telling Icecloud what a fantastic warrior he was when his jaws were stuffed with fluffy green stalks.

When they reached the lake, Cloudtail paused briefly at the edge, gazing out across the lake bottom. It looked dry and powdery near the bank, with jagged cracks stretching across it; farther out it glistened in the pale light of dawn. As he tried to work out where the mud ended and the water began, Lionblaze spotted the tiny figures of four cats, far out across the mud. He set down his bundle of moss and tasted the air; the faint scent of RiverClan wafted toward him, mingled with the familiar stink of dead fish.

"Now listen," Cloudtail began, setting down his own bundle. "RiverClan can't object to us taking water, and Firestar has already said that he doesn't want any fighting. Have you got that, Berrynose?" He gave the younger warrior a hard stare.

Reluctantly Berrynose nodded. "'Kay," he mumbled around his mouthful of moss.

"Make sure you don't forget." With a final glare Cloudtail led his patrol out across the mud toward the distant lake.

The surface of the mud was hard at first, but as the patrol drew closer to the water Lionblaze found his paws sinking in at every step. "This is disgusting," he muttered, his words muffled by the moss as he tried to shake off the sticky, pale brown blobs. "I'll never get clean again."

As they approached the water's edge, he saw that the River-Clan cats had clustered together and were waiting for them, blocking their way: Reedwhisker and Graymist, with Otter-heart and her apprentice, Sneezepaw. They all looked thin and exhausted, but their eyes glittered with hostility and their fur was bristling as if they would leap into battle for a couple of mousetails.

THE TIME HAS COME
FOR DOGS TO RULE THE WILD

SURVIVORS

BOOK ONE:
THE EMPTY CITY

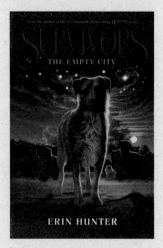

Lucky is a golden-haired mutt with a nose for survival. Other dogs have Packs, but Lucky stands on his own . . . until the Big Growl strikes. Suddenly the ground splits wide open. The longpaws disappear. And enemies threaten Lucky at every turn. For the first time in his life, Lucky needs to rely on other dogs to survive. But can he ever be a true Pack dog?

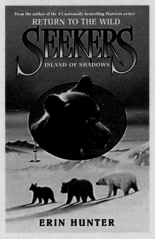

WARRIORS: THE NEW PROPHECY

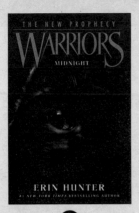

1

2

3

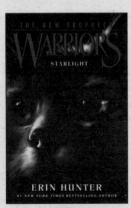

4

5

6

In the second series, follow the next generation of heroic cats as they set off on a quest to save the Clans from destruction.

HARPER
An Imprint of HarperCollinsPublishers

www.warriorcats.com

WARRIORS: POWER OF THREE

THE SIGHT

ERIN HUNTER

#1 NEW YORK TIMES BESTSELLING AUTHOR

1

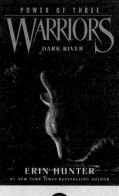

DARK RIVER

ERIN HUNTER

#1 NEW YORK TIMES BESTSELLING AUTHOR

2

OUTCAST

ERIN HUNTER

#1 NEW YORK TIMES BESTSELLING AUTHOR

3

ECLIPSE

ERIN HUNTER

#1 NEW YORK TIMES BESTSELLING AUTHOR

4

LONG SHADOWS

ERIN HUNTER

#1 NEW YORK TIMES BESTSELLING AUTHOR

5

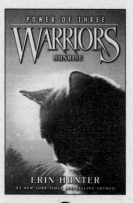

POWER OF THREE

SUNRISE

ERIN HUNTER

#1 NEW YORK TIMES BESTSELLING AUTHOR

6

In the third series, Firestar's grandchildren begin their
training as warrior cats. Prophecy foretells that they will
hold more power than any cats before them.

HARPER
An Imprint of HarperCollinsPublishers

www.warriorcats.com

WARRIORS: OMEN OF THE STARS

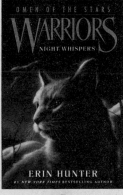

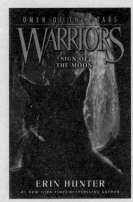

In the fourth series, find out which ThunderClan apprentice will complete the prophecy.

HARPER
An Imprint of HarperCollins*Publishers*

WARRIORS: DAWN OF THE CLANS

1

2

3

4

5

In this prequel series,
discover how the warrior Clans came to be.

HARPER
An Imprint of HarperCollinsPublishers

www.warriorcats.com

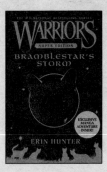

WARRIORS: BONUS STORIES

Discover the untold stories of the warrior cats and Clans when you download the separate ebook novellas—or read them in two paperback bind-ups!

WARRIORS: FIELD GUIDES

Delve deeper into the Clans with these Warriors field guides.

HARPER
An Imprint of HarperCollins Publishers

ALSO BY ERIN HUNTER:
SEEKERS

SEEKERS: THE ORIGINAL SERIES

Three young bears . . . one destiny.
Discover the fate that awaits them on their adventure.

SEEKERS: RETURN TO THE WILD

The stakes are higher than ever as the bears search for a way home.

SEEKERS: MANGA

The bears come to life in manga!

HARPER
An Imprint of HarperCollinsPublishers

www.seekerbears.com